Aliens Among Us
Edited by Jack Dann & Gardner Dozois

Edited by Jack Dann & Gardner Dozois

Edited by Terri Windling

ALIENS AMONG US

EDITED BY
JACK DANN & GARDNER DOZOIS

ACE BOOKS, NEW YORK

This is a work of fiction. Names, characters, places, and incidents are either the product of the author's imagination or are used fictitiously, and any resemblance to actual persons, living or dead, business establishments, events, or locales is entirely coincidental.

ALIENS AMONG US

An Ace Book / published by arrangement with the editors

PRINTING HISTORY
Ace mass-market edition / June 2000

All rights reserved.
Copyright © 2000 by Jack Dann & Gardner Dozois.
Cover art by Walter Velez.
This book may not be reproduced in whole or in part,
by mimeograph or any other means, without permission.
For information address: The Berkley Publishing Group,
a division of Penguin Putnam, Inc.
375 Hudson Street, New York, New York 10014.

The Penguin Putnam Inc. World Wide Web site address is
http://www.penguinputnam.com

Check out the ACE Science Fiction & Fantasy newsletter
and much more on the Internet at Club PPI!

ISBN: 0-441-00704-X

ACE®
Ace Books are published
by The Berkley Publishing Group,
a division of Penguin Putnam Inc.,
375 Hudson Street, New York, New York 10014.
ACE and the "A" design are trademarks
belonging to Penguin Putnam Inc.

PRINTED IN THE UNITED STATES OF AMERICA

10 9 8 7 6 5 4 3 2 1

"The Autopsy," by Michael Shea. Copyright © 1984 by Michael Shea. First published in *The Magazine of Fantasy and Science Fiction*, December 1980. Reprinted by permission of the author and the author's agent.

"Or All the Seas with Oysters," by Avram Davidson. Copyright © 1957 by Galaxy Publishing Corp. First published in *Galaxy*, May 1958. Reprinted by permission of the author's estate and the executor of that estate, Grania Davis.

"Angel," by Pat Cadigan. Copyright © 1987 by Davis Publications, Inc. First published in *Isaac Asimov's Science Fiction Magazine*, May 1987. Reprinted by permission of the author.

"Among the Hairy Earthmen," by R. A. Lafferty. Copyright © 1966 by U.P.D. Publishing Corporation. First published in *Galaxy*, August 1966. Reprinted by permission of the author and the author's agent, the Virginia Kidd Literary Agency.

"I'm Too Big But I Love to Play," by James Tiptree Jr. Copyright © 1970 by Ultimate Publishing Co., Inc. First published in *Amazing Stories*, March 1970. Reprinted by permission of the author's estate and the agent for that estate, the Virginia Kidd Literary Agency.

"The Hero as Werwolf," by Gene Wolfe. Copyright © 1975 by Thomas Disch. From *The New Improved Sun* (Harper & Row, 1975). Reprinted by permission of the author and the author's agent, the Virginia Kidd Literary Agency.

"Motherhood, Etc.," by L. Timmel Duchamp. Copyright © 1993 by L. Timmel Duchamp. First published in *Full Spectrum 4* (Bantam Spectra, 1993). Reprinted by permission of the author.

CONTENTS

PREFACE

The idea that aliens are in hiding among us—watching, observing, maybe drawing up nefarious plans against us, plotting in secret to conquer us, manipulating society in subtle ways, perhaps even secretly *ruling* us already, directing world events to further their own ends, alien eyes gleaming from behind their human masks—is one that probably goes way back into history, and probably even into prehistory—back to a time when people from outside your immediate tribal group were regarded with automatic suspicion, and not considered to be *really* human, not like the People, not like you and me. Even the Romans, at the height of an Empire that anticipated most of the tropes of sophisticated urban society thousands of years before we reinvented them, had this same attitude toward outsiders, toward "barbarians" (so named because they didn't *really* speak in a *human* tongue, just made inarticulate animal noises that sounded to the Romans like "bar-bar-bar")—they weren't *really* human at all.

This attitude is convenient in some ways because, since outsiders aren't human, it allows you to treat them with a total lack of compassion or moral or ethical scruples, and you can slaughter them or rape them or buy them and sell them as you like and still consider yourself to be a good upright honest citizen, operating completely within the Law (since the laws that are designed to keep you from doing these things to *other* humans don't apply to Them, the non-human Outsiders), a mindset common ever since in everybody from players in the African slave-trade to Hitler and the Nazis.

It's an attitude that has traditionally lead to paranoia, though. *Some* of the outsiders are easy enough to spot, being obliging enough to have different-colored skin, for instance—but *some* of the outsiders *look just like us*. Why, if they dress in human clothes and learn to speak in the human tongue, you might not be able to *tell* that they were an outsider at all! There might be one living *right next door to you*, and

you wouldn't even know it! You wouldn't even know it—
until it was *too late*! For certainly these outsiders are hiding
among us for no good purpose—certainly they must be plotting against us, planning our overthrow, sabotaging the public works, poisoning the wells, setting fire to the cities, stealing
our women and children, introducing fluoride into the water
supply to pollute our precious bodily fluids . . .

Throughout history, the identity of these Outsiders in
hiding among us has changed; at one time or another in
European history, they were Christians, pagans, witches,
Jews, heretics, Communists.

Today, they are aliens.

The idea that aliens, creatures from outer space, are in
hiding among us is very wide-spread today, almost ubiq-
uitous, certainly as widely accepted as many more formally
organized faiths, and can be seen in everything from the
supermarket tabloids to television documentaries about
Roswell to *The X-Files*.

Print science fiction is where this idea got its start, though,
decades before *The X-Files* was even a gleam in some pro-
ducer's eye, and is still where the theme is handled with the
most imagination and ingenuity (including stuff far weirder
and more bizarre than anything you'll see on television), and
where it's explored in the most variety and depth (because
not all of those aliens are in hiding among us for *sinister*
reasons, you know, nor are all of them interested in admin-
istering anal probes or mutilating cattle <does it ever strike
you that it must be *really dull* in outer space, if this is all
you can think of to do on a slow weekend?>), with the most
sophistication and profundity and power.

And the most entertainment value as well—because, of
course, the colorful, fast-paced, and wildly imaginative stories that follow were written to *entertain*, not to warn hu-
mankind of some sinister alien menace . . . although many
of them will scare the pants off you nevertheless.

So sit back, relax, make sure the lights are on and the
doors are locked, and enjoy. And when your spouse gets
home, examine them with a suspicious eye. Are you *sure*
you know where they come from . . . ?

THE OTHER CELIA

Theodore Sturgeon

The late Theodore Sturgeon was one of the true giants of the field, a man who produced stylish, innovative, and poetically intense fiction for more than forty years; a writer who was as important to H. L. Gold's Galaxy*-era revolution in the '50s as he'd been to John W. Campbell's Golden Age revolution at* Astounding *in the '40s. Sturgeon's stories such as "It," "Microcosmic God," "Killdozer," "Bianca's Hands," "Maturity," "The Other Man," and the brilliant "Baby Is Three"—which was eventually expanded into Sturgeon's most famous novel,* More Than Human*—helped to expand the boundaries of the SF story, and push it in the direction of artistic maturity. In Sturgeon's hands, the SF story would be made to do things that no one had ever believed it capable of doing before, and several generations of SF writers to come would cite him as a major—in some cases,* the *major—influence on their work.*

The sly little story that follows, a classic tale of aliens among us, gives us a vivid glimpse of the strangeness that underlies the everyday world. It's Sturgeon at the very top of his form . . . which places it among the best work ever done in the genre.

Theodore Sturgeon's other books include the novels Some of Your Blood, Venus Plus X, *and* The Dreaming Jewels, *and the collections* A Touch of Strange, Caviar, The Worlds of Theodore Sturgeon, Not Without Sorcery, The Stars Are the Styx, *and the posthumously published* Godsbody. *His most recent books are a series of massive posthumous retrospective collections, part of an ambitious and admirable scheme to return every short story Sturgeon ever wrote to print. The first five volumes of this sequence have been published:* The Ultimate Egoist, Microcosmic God, Killdozer!, Thunder and Roses, *and* The Perfect Host. *You may be unable to find these books other than through mailorder, so for information contact: North Atlantic Books, P.O. Box 12327, Berkeley, CA, 94701.*

I*f you live* in a cheap enough rooming house and the doors are made of cheap enough pine, and the locks are old-fashioned single-action jobs and the hinges are loose, and if you have a hundred and ninety lean pounds to operate with, you can grasp the knob, press the door sidewise against its hinges, and slip the latch. Further, you can lock the door the same way when you come out.

Slim Walsh lived in, and was, and had, and did these things partly because he was bored. The company doctors had laid him up—not off, up —for three weeks (after his helper had hit him just over the temple with a fourteen-inch crescent wrench) pending some more X-rays. If he was going to get just sick-leave pay, he wanted to make it stretch. If he was going to get a big fat settlement—all to the good; what he saved by living in this firetrap would make the money look even better. Meanwhile, he felt fine and had nothing to do all day.

"Slim isn't dishonest," his mother used to tell Children's Court some years back. "He's just curious."

She was perfectly right.

Slim was constitutionally incapable of borrowing your bathroom without looking into your medicine chest. Send him into your kitchen for a saucer and when he came out a minute later, he'd have inventoried your refrigerator, your vegetable bin, and (since he was six feet three inches tall) he would know about a moldering jar of maraschino cherries in the back of the top shelf that you'd forgotten about.

Perhaps Slim, who was not impressed by his impressive size and build, felt that a knowledge that you secretly use hair-restorer, or are one of those strange people who keeps a little mound of unmated socks in your second drawer, gave him a kind of superiority. Or maybe security is a better word. Or maybe it was an odd compensation for one of the most advanced cases of gawking, gasping shyness ever recorded.

Whatever it was, Slim liked you better if, while talking to you, he knew how many jackets hung in your closet, how old that unpaid phone bill was, and just where you'd hidden those photographs. On the other hand, Slim didn't insist on knowing bad or even embarrassing things about you. He just wanted to know things about you, period.

His current situation was therefore a near-paradise. Flimsy doors stood in rows, barely sustaining vacuum on aching vacuum of knowledge; and one by one they imploded at the nudge of his curiosity. He touched nothing (or if he did, he replaced it carefully) and removed nothing, and within a week he knew Mrs Koyper's roomers far better than she could, or cared to. Each secret visit to the rooms gave him a starting point; subsequent ones taught him more. He knew not only what these people had, but what they did, where, how much, for how much, and how often. In almost every case, he knew why as well.

Almost every case. Celia Sarton came.

Now, at various times, in various places, Slim had found strange things in other people's rooms. There was an old lady in one shabby place who had an electric train under her bed; used it, too. There was an old spinster in this very building who collected bottles, large and small, of any value or capacity, providing they were round and squat and with long necks. A man on the second floor secretly guarded his desirables with the unloaded .25 automatic in his top bureau drawer, for which he had a half-box of .38 cartridges.

There was a (to be chivalrous) girl in one of the rooms who kept fresh cut flowers before a photograph on her night-table—or, rather, before a frame in which were stacked eight photographs, one of which held the stage each day. Seven days, eight photographs: Slim admired the system. A new love every day and, predictably, a different love on successive Wednesdays. And all of them movie stars.

Dozens of rooms, dozens of imprints, marks, impres-

sions, overlays, atmospheres of people. And they needn't
be odd ones. A woman moves into a room, however stan-
dardized; the instant she puts down her dusting powder on
top of the flush tank, the room is *hers*. Something stuck
in the ill-fitting frame of a mirror, something draped over
the long-dead gas jet, and the samest of rooms begins to
shrink toward its occupant as if it wished, one day, to be
a close-knit, formfitting, individual integument as intimate
as a skin.

But not Celia Sarton's room.

Slim Walsh got a glimpse of her as she followed Mrs
Koyper up the stairs to the third floor. Mrs Koyper, who
hobbled, slowed any follower sufficiently to afford the most
disinterested witness a good look, and Slim was anything
but disinterested. Yet for days he could not recall her clearly.
It was as if Celia Sarton had been—not invisible, for that
would have been memorable in itself—but translucent or,
chameleonlike, drably re-radiating the drab wall color, carpet color, woodwork color.

She was—how old? Old enough to pay taxes. How tall?
Tall enough. Dressed in . . . whatever women cover themselves with in their statistical thousands. Shoes, hose, skirt,
jacket, hat.

She carried a bag. When you go to the baggage window at a big terminal, you notice a suitcase here, a steamer-
trunk there; and all around, high up, far back, there are
rows and ranks and racks of luggage not individually noticed but just *there*. This bag, Celia Sarton's bag, was one
of them.

And to Mrs Koyper, she said—she said—She said whatever is necessary when one takes a cheap room; and to
find her voice, divide the sound of a crowd by the number of people in it.

So anonymous, so unnoticeable was she that, aside from
being aware that she left in the morning and returned in
the evening, Slim let two days go by before he entered her
room; he simply could not remind himself about her. And
when he did, and had inspected it to his satisfaction, he
had his hand on the knob, about to leave, before he re-

called that the room was, after all, occupied. Until that second, he had thought he was giving one of the vacancies the once-over. (He did this regularly; it gave him a reference-point.)

He grunted and turned back, flicking his gaze over the room. First he had to assure himself that he was in the right room, which, for a man of his instinctive orientations, was extraordinary. Then he had to spend a moment of disbelief in his own eyes, which was all but unthinkable. When that passed, he stood in astonishment, staring at the refutation of everything his—hobby—had taught him about people and the places they live in.

The bureau drawers were empty. The ashtray was clean. No toothbrush, toothpaste, soap. In the closet, two wire hangers and one wooden one covered with dirty quilted silk, and nothing else. Under the grime-gray dresser scarf, nothing. In the shower stall, the medicine chest, nothing and nothing again, except what Mrs Koyper had grudgingly installed.

Slim went to the bed and carefully turned back the faded coverlet. Maybe she had slept in it, but very possibly not; Mrs Koyper specialized in unironed sheets of such a ground-in gray that it wasn't easy to tell. Frowning, Slim put up the coverlet again and smoothed it.

Suddenly he struck his forehead, which yielded him a flash of pain from his injury. He ignored it. "The bag!"

It was under the bed, shoved there, not hidden there. He looked at it without touching it for a moment, so that it could be returned exactly. Then he hauled it out.

It was a black gladstone, neither new nor expensive, of that nondescript rusty color acquired by untended leatherette. It had a worn zipper closure and was not locked. Slim opened it. It contained a cardboard box, crisp and new, for a thousand virgin sheets of cheap white typewriter paper surrounded by a glossy bright blue band bearing a white diamond with the legend: *Nonpareil the writers friend 15% cotton fiber trade mark registered.*

Slim lifted the paper out of the box, looked under it, riffled a thumbful of the sheets at the top and the same from the bottom, shook his head, replaced the paper, closed the box, put it back into the bag and restored everything precisely as he had found it. He paused again in the middle of the room, turning slowly once, but there was simply nothing else to look at. He let himself out, locked the door, and went silently back to his room.

He sat down on the edge of his bed and at last protested, "Nobody *lives* like that!"

His room was on the fourth and topmost floor of the old house. Anyone else would have called it the worst room in the place. It was small, dark, shabby and remote and it suited him beautifully.

Its door had a transom, the glass of which had many times been painted over. By standing on the foot of his bed, Slim could apply one eye to the peephole he had scratched in the paint and look straight down the stairs to the third-floor landing. On this landing, hanging to the stub of one of the ancient gas jets, was a cloudy mirror surmounted by a dust-mantled gilt eagle and surrounded by a great many rococo carved flowers. By careful propping with folded cigarette wrappers, innumerable tests and a great deal of silent mileage up and down the stairs, Slim had arranged the exact tilt necessary in the mirror so that it covered the second floor landing as well. And just as a radar operator learns to translate glowing pips and masses into aircraft and weather, so Slim became expert at the interpretation of the fogged and distant image it afforded him. Thus he had the comings and goings of half the tenants under surveillance without having to leave his room.

It was in this mirror, at twelve minutes past six, that he saw Celia Sarton next, and as he watched her climb the stairs, his eyes glowed.

The anonymity was gone. She came up the stairs two at a time, with a gait like bounding. She reached the landing and whirled into her corridor and was gone, and while a part of Slim's mind listened for the way she opened her door (hurriedly, rattling the key against the lock-plate, banging the door open, slamming it shut), another part studied a mental photograph of her face.

What raised its veil of the statistical ordinary was its set purpose. Here were eyes only superficially interested in cars, curbs, stairs, doors. It was as if she had projected every important part of herself into that empty room of hers and waited there impatiently for her body to catch up. There was something in the room, or something she had to do there, which she could not, would not, wait for. One goes this way to a beloved after a long parting, or to a deathbed in the last, precipitous moments. This was not the arrival of one who wants, but of one who needs.

Slim buttoned his shirt, eased his door open and sidled through it. He poised a moment on his landing like a great moose sensing the air before descending to a waterhole, and then moved downstairs.

Celia Sarton's only neighbor in the north corridor—the spinster with the bottles—was settled for the evening; she was of very regular habits and Slim knew them well.

Completely confident that he would not be seen, he drifted to the girl's door and paused.

She was there, all right. He could see the light around the edge of the ill-fitting door, could sense that difference between an occupied room and an empty one, which exists however silent the occupant might be. And this one *was* silent. Whatever it was that had driven her into the room with such headlong urgency, whatever it was she was doing (*had* to do) was being done with no sound or motion that he could detect.

For a long time—six minutes, seven—Slim hung there, open-throated to conceal the sound of his breath. At last, shaking his head, he withdrew, climbed the stairs, let himself into his own room and lay down on the bed, frowning.

He could only wait. Yet he *could* wait. No one does any single thing for very long. Especially a thing not involving movement. In an hour, in two—

It was five. At half-past eleven, some faint sound from the floor below brought Slim, half-dozing, twisting up from the bed and to his high peephole in the transom. He saw the Sarton girl come out of the corridor slowly, and stop, and look around at nothing in particular, like someone confined too long in a ship's cabin who has emerged on deck, not so much for the lungs' sake, but for the eyes'. And when she went down the stairs, it was easily and without hurry, as if (again) the important part of her was in the room. But the something was finished with for now and what was ahead of her wasn't important and could wait.

Standing with his hand on his own doorknob, Slim decided that he, too, could wait. The temptation to go straight to her room was, of course, large, but caution also loomed. What he had tentatively established as her habit patterns did not include midnight exits. He could not know when she might come back and it would be foolish indeed to jeopardize his hobby—not only where it included her, but all of it—by being caught. He sighed, mixing resignation with anticipatory pleasure, and went to bed.

Less than fifteen minutes later, he congratulated himself with a sleepy smile as he heard her slow footsteps mount the stairs below. He slept.

There was nothing in the closet, there was nothing in the ashtray, there was nothing in the medicine chest nor under the dresser scarf. The bed was made, the dresser drawers were empty, and under the bed was the cheap gladstone. In it was a box containing a thousand sheets of typing paper surrounded by a glossy blue band. Without disturbing this, Slim riffled the sheets, once at the top, once at the bottom. He grunted, shook his head and then proceeded, automatically but meticulously, to put everything back as he had found it.

"Whatever it is this girl does at night," he said glumly, "it leaves tracks like it makes noise."

He left.

The rest of the day was unusually busy for Slim. In the morning he had a doctor's appointment, and in the afternoon he spent hours with a company lawyer who seemed determined to (a) deny the existence of any head injury and (b) prove to Slim and the world that the injury must have occurred years ago. He got absolutely nowhere. If Slim had another characteristic as consuming and compulsive as his curiosity, it was his shyness; these two could stand on one another's shoulders, though, and still look upward at Slim's stubbornness. It served its purpose. It took hours, however, and it was after seven when he got home.

He paused at the third-floor landing and glanced down the corridor. Celia Sarton's room was occupied and silent. If she emerged around midnight, exhausted and relieved, then he would know she had again raced up the stairs to her urgent, motionless task, whatever it was . . . and here he checked himself. He had long ago learned the uselessness of cluttering up his busy head with conjectures. A thousand things might happen; in each case, only one would. He would wait, then, and could.

And again, some hours later, he saw her come out of her corridor. She looked about, but he knew she saw very little; her face was withdrawn and her eyes wide and unguarded. Then, instead of going out, she went back into her room.

He slipped downstairs half an hour later and listened at her door, and smiled. She was washing her lingerie at the handbasin. It was a small thing to learn, but he felt he was making progress. It did not explain why she lived as she did, but indicated how she could manage without so much as a spare handkerchief.

Oh, well, maybe in the morning.

In the morning, there was no maybe. He found it, he found it, though he could not know what it was he'd found. He laughed at first, not in triumph but wryly, calling himself a clown. Then he squatted on his heels in the middle of the floor (he would not sit on the bed, for fear of leaving wrinkles of his own on those Mrs. Koyper supplied) and carefully lifted the box of paper out of the suitcase and put it on the floor in front of him.

Up to now, he had contented himself with a quick riffle of the blank paper, a little at the top, a little at the bottom. He had done just this again, without removing the box from the suitcase, but only taking the top off and tilting up the banded ream of *Non-pareil-the-writers-friend*. And almost in spite of itself, his quick eye had caught the briefest flash of pale blue.

Gently, he removed the band, sliding it off the pack of paper, being careful not to slit the glossy finish. Now he could freely riffle the pages, and when he did, he discovered that all of them except a hundred or so, top and bottom, had the same rectangular cut-out, leaving only a narrow margin all the way around. In the hollow space thus formed, something was packed.

He could not tell what the something was, except that it was pale tan, with a tinge of pink, and felt like smooth untextured leather. There was a lot of it, neatly folded so that it exactly fitted the hole in the ream of paper.

He puzzled over it for some minutes without touching it again, and then, scrubbing his fingertips against his shirt until he felt that they were quite free of moisture and grease, he gently worked loose the top corner of the substance and unfolded a layer. All he found was more of the same.

He folded it down flat again to be sure he could, and then brought more of it out. He soon realized that the material was of an irregular shape and almost certainly of one piece, so that folding it into a tight rectangle required care and great skill. Therefore he proceeded very slowly, stopping every now and then to fold it up again, and it took him more than an hour to get enough of it out so that he could identify it.

Identify? It was completely unlike anything he had ever seen before.

It was a human skin, done in some substance very like the real thing. The first fold, the one which had been revealed at first, was an area of the back, which was why it showed no features. One might liken it to a balloon, except that a deflated balloon is smaller in every dimension than an inflated one. As far as Slim could judge, this was life-sized—a little over five feet long and proportioned accordingly. The hair was peculiar, looking exactly like the real thing until flexed, and then revealing itself to be one piece.

It had Celia Sarton's face.

Slim closed his eyes and opened them, and found that it was still true. He held his breath and put forth a careful, steady forefinger and gently pressed the left eyelid upward. There was an eye under it, all right, light blue and seemingly moist, but flat.

Slim released the breath, closed the eye and sat back on his heels. His feet were beginning to tingle from his having knelt on the floor for so long.

He looked all around the room once, to clear his head of strangeness, and then began to fold the thing up again. It took a while, but when he was finished, he knew he had it right. He replaced the typewriter paper in the box and the box in the bag, put the bag away and at last stood in the middle of the room in the suspension which overcame him when he was deep in thought.

After a moment of this, he began to inspect the ceiling. It was made of stamped tin, like those of many old-fashioned houses. It was grimy and flaked and stained; here and there, rust showed through, and in one or two places, edges of the tin sheets had sagged. Slim nodded to himself in profound satisfaction, listened for a while at the door, let himself out, locked it and went upstairs.

He stood in his own corridor for a minute, checking the position of doors, the hall window, and his accurate orientation of the same things on the floor below. Then he went into his own room.

His room, though smaller than most, was one of the few in the house which was blessed with a real closet instead of a rickety off-the-floor wardrobe. He went into it and knelt, and grunted in satisfaction when he found how loose the ancient, unpainted floorboards were. By removing the side baseboard, he found it possible to get to the air-space between the fourth floor and the third-floor ceiling.

He took out boards until he had an opening perhaps fourteen inches wide, and then, working in almost total silence, he began cleaning away dirt and old plaster. He did this meticulously, because when he finally pierced the tin sheeting, he wanted not one grain of dirt to fall into the room below. He took his time and it was late in the afternoon when he was satisfied with his preparations and began, with his knife, on the tin.

It was thinner and softer than he had dared to hope; he almost overcut on the first try. Carefully he squeezed the sharp steel into the little slot he had cut, lengthening it. When it was somewhat less than an inch long, he withdrew all but the point of the knife and twisted it slightly, moved it a sixteenth of an inch and twisted again, repeating this all down the cut until he had widened it enough for his purpose.

He checked the time, then returned to Celia Sarton's room for just long enough to check the appearance of his work from that side. He was very pleased with it. The little cut had come through a foot away from the wall over the bed and was a mere pencil line lost in the baroque design with which the tin was stamped and the dirt and rust that marred it. He returned to his room and sat down to wait.

He heard the old house coming to its evening surge of life, a voice here, a door there, footsteps on the stairs. He ignored them all as he sat on the edge of his bed, hands folded between his knees, eyes half closed, immobile like a machine fueled, oiled, tuned and ready, lacking only the right touch on the right control. And like that touch, the faint sound of Celia Sarton's footsteps moved him.

To use his new peephole, he had to lie on the floor half in and half out of the closet, with his head in the hole, actually below floor level. With this, he was perfectly content, any amount of discomfort being well worth his trouble—an attitude he shared with many another ardent hobbyist, mountain-climber or speleologist, duck-hunter or bird-watcher.

When she turned on the light, he could see her splendidly, as well as most of the floor, the lower third of the door and part of the washbasin in the bathroom.

She had come in hurriedly, with that same agonized haste he had observed before. At the same second she turned on the light, she had apparently flung her handbag toward the bed; it was in mid-air as the light appeared. She did not even glance its way, but hastily fumbled the old gladstone from under the bed, opened it, removed the box, opened it, took out the paper, slipped off the blue band and removed the blank sheets of paper which covered the hollowed-out ream.

She scooped out the thing hidden there, shaking it once like a grocery clerk with a folded paper sack, so that the long limp thing straightened itself out. She arranged it carefully on the worn linoleum of the floor, arms down at the side, legs slightly apart, face up, neck straight. Then she lay down on the floor, too, head-to-head with the deflated thing. She reached up over her head, took hold of the collapsed image of herself about the region of the ears, and for a moment did some sort of manipulation of it against the top of her own head.

Slim heard faintly a sharp, chitinous click, like the sound one makes by snapping the edge of a thumbnail against the edge of a fingernail.

Her hands slipped to the cheeks of the figure and she pulled at the empty head as if testing a connection. The head seemed now to have adhered to hers.

Then she assumed the same pose she had arranged for this other, letting her hands fall wearily to her sides on the floor, closing her eyes.

For a long while, nothing seemed to be happening, except for the odd way she was breathing, very deeply but very slowly, like the slow-motion picture of someone panting, gasping for breath after a long hard run. After perhaps ten minutes of this, the breathing became shallower and even slower, until, at the end of a half-hour, he could detect none at all.

Slim lay there immobile for more than an hour, until his body shrieked protest and his head ached from eyestrain. He hated to move, but move he must. Silently he backed out of the closet, stood up and stretched. It was a great luxury and he deeply enjoyed it. He felt moved to think over what he had just seen, but clearly and consciously decided not to—not yet, anyway.

When he was unkinked, again, he crept back into the closet, put his head in the hole and his eye to the slot.

Nothing had changed. She still lay quiet, utterly relaxed, so much so that her hands had turned palm upward.

Slim watched and he watched. Just as he was about to conclude that this was the way the girl spent her entire nights and that there would be nothing more to see, he saw a slight and sudden contraction about the region of her solar plexus, and then another. For a time, there was nothing more, and then the empty thing attached to the top of her head began to fill.

And Celia Sarton began to empty.

Slim stopped breathing until it hurt and watched in total astonishment.

Once it had started, the process progressed swiftly. It was as if something passed from the clothed body of the girl to this naked empty thing. The something, whatever it might be, had to be fluid, for nothing but a fluid would fill a flexible container in just this way, or make a flexible container slowly and evenly flatten out like this. Slim could see the fingers, which had been folded flat against the palms, inflate and move until they took on the normal relaxed curl of a normal hand. The elbows shifted a little to lie more normally against the body. And yes, it was a body now.

The other one was not a body any more. It lay foolishly limp in its garment, its sleeping face slightly distorted by its flattening. The fingers fell against the palms by their own limp weight. The shoes thumped quietly on their sides, heels together, toes pointing in opposite directions.

The exchange was done in less than ten minutes and then the newly filled body moved.

It flexed its hands tentatively, drew up its knees and stretched its legs out again, arched its back against the floor. Its eyes flickered open. It put up its arms and made some deft manipulation at the top of its head. Slim heard another version of the soft-hard click and the now-empty head fell flat to the floor.

The new Celia Sarton sat up and sighed and rubbed her hands lightly over her body, as if restoring circulation and sensation to a chilled skin. She stretched as comfortably and luxuriously as Slim had a few minutes earlier. She looked rested and refreshed.

At the top of her head, Slim caught a glimpse of a slit through which a wet whiteness showed, but it seemed to be closing. In a brief time, nothing showed there but a small valley in the hair, like a normal parting.

She sighed again and got up. She took the clothed thing on the floor by the neck, raised it and shook it twice to make the clothes fall away. She tossed it to the bed and carefully picked up the clothes and deployed them about the room, the undergarments in the washbasin, the dress and slip on a hanger in the wardrobe.

Moving leisurely but with purpose, she went into the bathroom and, except from her shins down, out of Slim's range of vision. There he heard the same faint domestic sounds he had once detected outside her door, as she washed her underclothes. She emerged in due course, went to the wardrobe for some wire hangers and took them into the bathroom. Back she came with the underwear folded on the hangers. which she hooked to the top of the open wardrobe door. Then she took the deflated integument which lay crumpled on the bed, shook it again, rolled it up into a ball and took it into the bathroom.

Slim heard more water-running and sudsing noises, and, by ear, followed the operation through a soaping and two rinses. Then she came out again, shaking out the object, which had apparently just been wrung, pulled it through a wooden clothes-hanger, arranged it creaselessly suspending from the crossbar of the hanger with the bar about at its waistline, and hung it with the others on the wardrobe door.

Then she lay down on the bed, not to sleep or to read or even to rest—she seemed very rested—but merely to wait until it was time to do something else.

• • •

By now, Slim's bones were complaining again, so he wormed noiselessly backward out of his lookout point, got into his shoes and a jacket, and went out to get something to eat. When he came home an hour later and looked, her light was out and he could see nothing. He spread his overcoat carefully over the hole in the closet so no stray light from his room would appear in the little slot in the ceiling, closed the door, read a comic book for a while, and went to bed.

The next day, he followed her. What strange occupation she might have, what weird vampiric duties she might disclose, he did not speculate on. He was doggedly determined to gather information first and think later.

What he found out about her daytime activities was, if anything, more surprising than any wild surmise. She was a clerk in a small five-and-ten on the East Side. She ate in the store's lunch bar at lunchtime—a green salad and a surprising amount of milk—and in the evening she stopped at a hot-dog stand and drank a small container of milk, though she ate nothing.

Her steps were slowed by then and she moved wearily, speeding up only when she was close to the rooming house, and then apparently all but overcome with eagerness to get home and . . . into something more comfortable. She was watched in this process, and Slim, had he disbelieved his own eyes the first time, must believe them now.

So it went for a week, three days of which Slim spent in shadowing her, every evening in watching her make her strange toilet. Every twenty-four hours, she changed bodies, carefully washing, drying, folding and putting away the one she was not using.

Twice during the week, she went out for what was apparently a constitutional and nothing more—a half-hour around midnight, when she would stand on the walk in front of the rooming house, or wander around the block.

At work, she was silent but not unnaturally so; she spoke, when spoken to, in a small, unmusical voice. She seemed to have no friends; she maintained her aloofness by being uninteresting and by seeking no one out and by needing no one. She evinced no outside interests, never going to the movies or to the park. She had no dates, not even with girls Slim thought she did not sleep, but lay quietly in the dark waiting for it to be time to get up and go to work.

And when he came to think about it, as ultimately he did, it occurred to Slim that within the anthill in which we all live and have our being, enough privacy can be exacted to allow for all sorts of strangeness in the members of society, providing the strangeness is not permitted to show. If it is a man's pleasure to sleep upside-down like a bat, and if he so arranges his life that no one ever sees him sleeping, or his sleeping-place, why, batlike he may sleep all the days of his life.

One need not, by these rules, even *be* a human being. Not if the mimicry is good enough. It is a measure of Slim's odd personality to report that Celia Sarton's ways did not frighten him. He was, if anything, less disturbed by her now than he'd been before he had begun to spy on her. He knew what she did in her room and how she lived. Before, he had not known. Now he did. This made him much happier.

He was, however, still curious.

His curiosity would never drive him to do what another man might—to speak to her on the stairs or on the street, get to know her and more about her. He was too shy for that. Nor was he moved to report to anyone the odd practice he watched each evening. It wasn't his business to report. She was doing no harm as far as he could see. In his cosmos, everybody had a right to live and make a buck if they could.

Yet his curiosity, its immediacy taken care of, did undergo a change. It was not in him to wonder what sort of being this was and whether its ancestors had grown up among human beings, living with them in caves and in tents, developing and evolving along with *homo sap* until it could assume the uniform of the smallest and most invisible of wage-workers. He would never reach the conclusion that in the fight for survival, a species might discover that a most excellent characteristic for survival

among human beings might be not to fight them but to join
them.

No, Slim's curiosity was far simpler, more basic and
less informed than any of these conjectures. He simply
changed the field of his wonderment from *what* to *what
if?*

So it was that on the eighth day of his survey, a Tues-
day, he went again to her room, got the bag, opened it, removed the box, opened it, removed the ream of paper, slid
the blue band off, removed the covering sheets, took out
the second Celia Sarton, put her on the bed and then replaced paper, blue band, box-cover, box, and bag as he had
found them. He put the folded thing under his shirt and
went out, carefully locking the door behind him in his special way, and went upstairs to his room. He put his prize
under the four clean shirts in his bottom drawer and sat
down to await Celia Sarton's homecoming.

She was a little late that night—twenty minutes, perhaps. The delay seemed to have increased both her fatigue
and her eagerness; she burst in feverishly, moved with the
rapidity of near-panic. She looked drawn and pale and her
hands shook. She fumbled the bag from under the bed,
snatched out the box and opened it, contrary to her usual
measured movements, by inverting it over the bed and
dumping out its contents.

When she saw nothing there but sheets of paper, some
with a wide rectangle cut from them and some without,
she froze. She crouched over that bed without moving for
an interminable two minutes. Then she straightened up
slowly and glanced about the room. Once she fumbled
through the paper, but resignedly, without hope. She made
one sound, a high, sad whimper, and, from that moment
on, was silent.

She went to the window slowly, her feet dragging, her
shoulders slumped. For a long time, she stood looking out
at the city, its growing darkness, its growing colonies of
lights, each a symbol of life and life's usages. Then she
drew down the blind and went back to the bed.

She stacked the papers there with loose uncaring fingers and put the heap of them on the dresser. She took off her shoes and placed them neatly side by side on the floor by the bed. She lay down in the same utterly relaxed pose she affected when she made her change, hands down and open, legs a little apart.

Her face looked like a death-mask, its tissues sunken and sagging. It was flushed and sick-looking. There was a little of the deep regular breathing, but only a little. There was a bit of the fluttering contractions at the midriff, but only a bit. Then—nothing.

Slim backed away from the peephole and sat up. He felt very bad about this. He had been only curious; he hadn't wanted her to get sick, to die. For he was sure she had died. How could he know what sort of sleep-surrogate an organism like this might require, or what might be the results of a delay in changing? What could he know of the chemistry of such a being? He had thought vaguely of slipping down the next day while she was out and returning her property. Just to see. Just to know *what if*. Just out of curiosity.

Should he call a doctor?

She hadn't. She hadn't even tried, though she must have known much better than he did how serious her predicament was. (Yet if a species depended for its existence on secrecy, it would be species-survival to let an individual die undetected.) Well, maybe not calling a doctor meant that she'd be all right, after all. Doctors would have a lot of silly questions to ask. She might even tell the doctor about her other skin, and if Slim was the one who had fetched the doctor, Slim might be questioned about that.

Slim didn't want to get involved with anything. He just wanted to know things.

He thought, "I'll take another look."

He crawled back into the closet and put his head in the hole. Celia Sarton, he knew instantly, would not survive this. Her face was swollen, her eyes protruded, and her purpled tongue lolled far— too far—from the corner of her mouth. Even as he watched, her face darkened still more and the skin of it crinkled until it looked like carbon paper which has been balled up tight and then smoothed out.

The very beginnings of an impulse to snatch the thing she needed out of his shirt drawer and rush it down to her died within him, for he saw a wisp of smoke emerge from her nostrils and then—

Slim cried out, snatched his head from the hole, bumping it cruelly, and clapped his hands over his eyes. Put the biggest size flash-bulb an inch from your nose, and fire it, and you might get a flare approaching the one he got through his little slot in the tin ceiling.

He sat grunting in pain and watching, on the insides of his eyelids, migrations of flaming worms. At last they faded and he tentatively opened his eyes. They hurt and the after-image of the slot hung before him, but at least he could see.

Feet pounded on the stairs. He smelled smoke and a burned, oily unpleasant something which he could not identify. Someone shouted. Someone hammered on the door. Then someone screamed and screamed.

It was in the papers next day. Mysterious, the story said. Charles Fort, in *Lo!*, had reported many such cases and there had been others since—people burned to a crisp by a fierce heat which had nevertheless not destroyed clothes or bedding, while leaving nothing for autopsy. This was, said the paper, either an unknown kind of heat or heat of such intensity and such brevity that it would do such a thing. No known relatives, it said. Police mystified—no clues or suspects.

Slim didn't say anything to anybody. He wasn't curious about the matter any more. He closed up the hole in the closet that same night, and next day, after he read the story, he used the newspaper to wrap up the thing in his shirt drawer. It smelled pretty bad and, even that early, was too far gone to be unfolded. He dropped it into a garbage can on the way to the lawyer's office on Wednesday.

They settled his lawsuit that afternoon and he moved.

RESIDUALS

Paul J. McAuley & Kim Newman

*Born in Oxford, England, in 1955, Paul J. McAuley now
makes his home in London. He is considered to be one of
the best of the new breed of British writers (although a few
Australian writers could be fit in under this heading as well)
who are producing that sort of revamped, updated,
widescreen Space Opera sometimes referred to as "radical
hard science fiction," and is a frequent contributor to* Interzone, *as well as to markets such as* Amazing, The Magazine of Fantasy and Science Fiction, Asimov's Science
Fiction, When the Music's Over, *and elsewhere. His first
novel,* Four Hundred Billion Stars, *won the Philip K. Dick
Award. His other books include the novels* Of The Fall, Eternal Light, *and* Pasquale's Angel, *two collections of his short
work,* The King of the Hill and Other Stories *and* The Invisible Country, *and an original anthology coedited with Kim
Newman,* In Dreams. *His acclaimed novel,* Fairyland *won
both the Arthur C. Clarke Award and the John W. Campbell
Award in 1996. His most recent books are* Child of the River
and Ancient of Days, *the first two volumes of a major new
trilogy of ambitious scope and scale,* Confluence, *set ten million years in the future.*

*Kim Newman made his original reputation as a film critic,
is a commentator on films on British television, and has published several books of film criticism, including* Nightmare
Movies *and* Wild West Movies. *Of late, though, his career
as a fiction writer has also shifted into high gear—and he
has published a number of novels in the '90s, many of them
gaming novels published under his pseudonym of "Jack
Yeovil." Novels published under his own name include* The
Night Mayor, Bad Dreams, Jago, *and* Anno Dracula. *He has
also published a critical study,* Horror: 100 Best Books, *written in collaboration with Stephen Jones, and an original anthology, coedited with Paul J. McAuley, called* In Dreams.
He won the British Science Fiction Award for his story "The

Original Dr. Shade," and has been a frequent contributor to Interzone, *and to various British anthology series. His most recent books include the critically acclaimed* The Bloody Red Baron. *He lives in London, England.*

In the wry but suspenseful story that follows, they join forces to spin a thrilling tale of secret alien invasion, warn us to keep watching the skies, and examine some of the un-expected consequences of world-shaking events, some of which may not even arise until years down the road . . .

O_n his way out, the motel guy switches on the TV and the AC without bothering to ask if I want either. The unit over the door rattles and starts to drip on the purple shag carpet. On a dusty screen, a cowboy hunkers down over the Sci-Fi Channel station ident, squinting from under a Stetson. It ought to be like looking at myself because the cowboy is supposed to be me. But it's not.

The Omega Encounter is always playing somewhere on a rerun channel, I guess, but here and now it's like an omen.

I'm still living off the *Omega* residuals because it's *my* version of what went down, officially adapted from the "as told to" book Jay Anson did for me. Nyquist sold *Starlight*, the book Tom Fuckin' Wolfe wrote with him, for twenty times as much to Universal

There's a little skip where there used to be a shot of a fly-blown, bloodied rubber cow carcass. It could be a censor cut or a snip to reduce the running time. When E.W. Swackhamer directed *Omega*, there were thirteen minutes of commercials in an hour of TV; now there are eighteen, so five minutes of each hour have to be lost from everything made before the nineties.

I don't unpack, except for the bottles of Cuervo Gold Tequila I bought at the airport, and sit up on the bed, watching two days of my life processed and packaged as a sixteen-year-old movie-of-the-week.

It's gotten to the part where I find the first of the mutilated cattle. I'm showing one to Mr. Nyquist, played by Dennis Weaver the way he plays McCloud, shrewd and upright. To tell the truth, Nyquist was always half bombed even before it all started, and had a mean streak in him that was nothing to do with drink. The bastard would hit Susan when he was loaded, going off like a firecracker over the slightest thing and stomping out, banging the screen door hard, leaving her holding her cheek and me looking down at my dinner. He was crazy even then, I guess, but still able to hold it down.

The movie makes me a lot more talkative than I ever was around Nyquist. Susan is Cybill Shepherd in her post-*Last Picture Show*, pre-*Moonlighting* career slump. I am Jan-Michael Vincent in his post-birth, pre-death career trough.

I watch until I follow the slime trails in the grass and see the lights of the mothership off in the distance hovering above the slough, and then I flip channels because I can't stand to watch anymore.

They didn't have the budget to do the aliens properly on TV and only used long shots, but I still don't want to watch. I can take the expensive computer-controlled models in the movie because they're too real in the way Main Street in Disneyland is too real. So perfect a reproduction it doesn't fool anyone for a second. But show me a couple of out-of-focus midgets jumping around inside silvered plastic bags in slow motion with the setting sun behind them, and my imagination fills in the blanks. The sour reek. And the noise the things made as they hopped around, like they were filled with Jell-O and broken bones.

QVC is less of a blow to the heart. I drink tequila out of the bathroom glass and consider calling a toll-free number to order a zircon chandelier. Then I drink some more and decide against it.

Despite Steven Spielberg, Harrison Ford (as Nyquist), and five million preinflation bucks of ILM, *Starlight: The Motion Picture* was a box-office disappointment. By the time the effects were developed, *Omega* had spun off a mid-season replacement series with Sam Groom (as me) and Gretchen Corbett that got canceled after three episodes. The aliens were old news, and everybody knew how the story came out. In *Starlight*, I'm rewritten as a codger farmhand who sacrifices himself for Boss Man Ford, stealing the film with a dignified death scene. Richard Farnsworth got an Oscar nomination for Best Supporting Actor, but lost out to the gook in *The Killing Fields*.

I give up TV and call my agent, using the room phone because my mobile doesn't want to work out here in the desert, all that radar, or the microwave signals they send to the secret Moon colony (ha ha), and I tell him where I am. He says to watch my ass, and that when I get back he thinks he might have another hardware store commercial lined up ("fix your Starship, lady?"). It's just for New York cable, but it'll pay the rent a while. He doesn't think I can pull off this reunion, is what it is, and I tell him that, and then I hang up and I watch an old *Saturday Night Live* for a while.

I was on one show for about five minutes, in a Conehead episode with Dan Ackroyd and Jane Curtin. Can't hardly remember that night—I was drunk at the time—but now I guess those five minutes are always showing somewhere, just like everything else that ever went through a transmitter. If aliens out there have been monitoring our broadcasts like they did in old movies to explain why they speak perfect English, just about the first question we'd ask them was if they taped those lost episodes of *The Honeymooners*. I watch Chevy Chase do Jerry Ford falling over just about everything in the studio set, and drink some more tequila, and fall asleep a while.

It's been a long day, the flight out from New York delayed two hours, then a long drive through Los Angeles, where I've never driven because I was chauffeured around when all the deals were in the air, and which is ten times more packed with traffic than I remember, and out into the high desert along Pearblossom Highway with all the big trucks driving in bright sunlight and blowing dust with their headlights on.

The phone wakes me up. I use the remote to turn down Dave Letterman, and pick up. A voice I haven't heard for twenty years says, "Hello, Ray."

At first, only the *Enquirer* and the *Weekly World News* were interested. But when the reports came back and the FBI slapped a security classification on them, and Elliot Mitchell started making a fuss because he was transferred to the Texas panhandle and his field notes and his twenty rolls of film and six hours of cassette recordings were "lost," *Newsweek* and *Rolling Stone* showed up. Tom Wicker's piece in *Rolling Stone* said it was all part of a government plot stretching back to Roswell, and that the U.S. Army was covering up tests with hallucinogenic weapons.

Then the artifacts went on view, and ten types of expert testified they were "non-terrestrial." It wasn't a government conspiracy any more, it was a goddamn alien *invasion*, just like Nyquist and me had been saying. Mitchell had rewritten his field notes from memory, and sent photocopies to *Science* and *Nature*. He even got his name as discoverer on the new hyperstable transuranic element, which along with the bodies was one of the few tangible residues of the whole thing. I wonder how he felt when Mitchellite was used in the Gulf War to add penetrative power to artillery shells?

Then the Washington *Post* got behind the story, and all the foreign press, and the shit hit the fan. For a while, it was all anybody talked about. We got to meet President Carter, who made a statement supporting our side of things, and declared he would see that no information was withheld from the public.

I was on the *Tonight Show* with Johnny Carson, back when that meant something. I did Dick Cavett, *CBS News* with Walter Cronkite, *60 Minutes* with Mike Wallace, *NBC Weekend News* with Jessica Savitch. Me and Nyquist were scurrying to get our book deals sorted out, then our screen rights. People were crawling all over, desperate to steal our lives, and we went right along with the feeding frenzy.

We wrapped each other up with restraints and gag or-

ders, and shot off our mouths all the time. Mitchell was
out of the loop: instead of deals with Hollywood produc-
ers and long lunches with New York publishers, he got tied
up in a civil liberties suit because he tried to resign from
the U.S. geological survey and the government wouldn't
let him.

Then the Ayatollah took the hostages, and everyone had
something else to worry about. Carter became a hostage in
his own White House and most of the artifacts disappeared
in the C-130 air crash the conspiracy theorists said was
staged. Reagan never said anything on record, but the official line changed invisibly when he became President.
The reports on the reports questioned the old findings, and
deposits of Mitchellite showed up on Guam and somewhere in Alaska.

I did *Geraldo* with Whitley Strieber and Carl Sagan,
and came off like a hick caught between a rock and a hard
place. I had started drinking by then, and tried to punch
out one or the other of them after the show, and spent the
night in a downtown holding tank. I faced a jury of skep-
tics on *Oprah* and was cut to pieces, not by reasoned scientific arguments and rationalizations but by cheap-shot
jokes from a studio audience of stand-up wannabes.

I told my side of it so many times that I caught myself
using exactly the same words each time, and I noticed that
on prerecorded shows, the presenter's nods and winks—always shot from a reverse angle after the main interview—
were always cut in at exactly the same points. An
encouraging dip of the head laced with a concerned look
in the eyes, made in reaction to a cameraman's thumb, not
an already-forgotten line from me.

Besides *The Omega Encounter* and *Starlight*, there were
dozens of books, movies, TV specials, magazine articles,
a Broadway play, even a music album. Creedence Clear-
water Revival's "It Came Out of the Sky" was reissued
and charted strongly. Some English band did a concept
album. John Sladek and Tom Disch collaborated on a novel-
length debunking, *The Sentients: A Tragi-Comedy*. That's
in development as a movie, maybe with Fred Ward.

Sam Shepard's *Alienation*, which Ed Harris did on Broadway and Shepard starred in and directed for HBO, looked at it all from the dirt farmer's point of view, suggesting that Nyquist and me were looking for fresh ways of being heroes since we'd lost touch with the land. The main character was a combination of the two of us, and talked in paragraphs, and the scientist—Dean Stockwell on TV—was a black-hatted villain, which displeased Mitchell no end. He sued and lost, I recall.

By then I was looking at things through the blurry dimple at the bottom of the bottle, living off the residuals from commercials and guest appearances in rock videos and schlock direct-to-video horror movies shot by postmodernist *auteurs* just out of UCLA film school, though I recall that Sam Raimi's *The Color Out of Time* was kind of not bad.

Then I read in *Variety* that Oliver Stone has a treatment in development raking the whole thing up, blaming it all on J. Edgar Hoover, Armand Hammer and Henry Kissinger. There was an article in the New York *Times* that Norman Mailer had delivered his thousand-page summation of the phenomenon, *The Visitation*. And that's where I got the idea to get in touch with Mitchell and make some cash on the back of Stone and Mailer's publicity, and maybe Mitchell had been reading the same articles, because before I can begin to think how to try and track him down, he calls me.

I drive past the place I'm to meet Mitchell and have to double back, squinting in the glare of the big rigs that roar out of the darkness, all strung up with fairylights like the spaceship in *Closer Encounters*. I do what sounds like serious damage to the underside of the rental when I finally pull off.

The ruins are close to the highway, but there's a spooky feeling that makes me leave the car's headlights on. Out across the dark desert basin, where the runways of Edwards Air Force Base are outlined in patterns of red and green lights a dozen miles long, some big engine makes a long drawn-out rumble that rises to a howl before cutting off.

I sit in the car and take a few pulls on my bottle to get some courage, or at least burn away the fluttering in my gut, looking at the arthritic shapes that Joshua trees make in the car headlights. Then I make myself get out and look around. There's not much to the ruins, just a chimney stack and a line of pillars where maybe a porch stood. People camping out have left circles of ash in the sand and dented cans scattered around; when I stumble over a can and it rattles off a stone, I realize how quiet the desert is, beyond the noise of the trucks on the highway. I get a feeling like the one I had when the three of us were waiting that last night, before we blew up the mothership, and have to take another inch off the level of the tequila to calm down.

That's when my rental car headlights go out and I almost lose it, because that's what happened when they tried to kidnap me, the lights and then the dashboard on my pickup going out and then a bright light all around, coming from above. That time, I had a pump-action shotgun on the rack in the cab, which is what saved me. Now, I have a tequila bottle with a couple of inches sloshing in it, and a rock I pick up.

A voice behind me says my name, and I spin and lose my balance and fall on my ass, the tequila bottle emptying over my pants leg. A flashlight beam pins me, and behind it, Elliot Mitchell says, "This was the last socialist republic in the USA, did you know that? They called the place Llano del Rio. This was their meeting hall. They built houses, a school, planted orchards. But the government gave their water rights to the local farmers and they had to move out. All that's left are the orchards, and those will go because they're subdividing the desert for housing tracts to take LA's overspill."

I squint into the light, but can't see anything of the man holding it.

"Never put your faith in government, Ray. Its first instinct is not to protect the people it's supposed to serve but to protect its own self. People elect politicians, not governments. Don't get up. I'm happier to see you sitting down. Do you think you were followed here?"

"Why would I be followed? No one cares about it anymore. That's why I'm here."

"You want to make another movie, Ray? Who is it with? Oliver Stone? He came out to see me. Or sent one of his researchers anyway. You know his father was in the Navy, don't you, and he's funded by the UN counterpropaganda unit, the same one that tried to assassinate Reagan. The question is, who's paying you?"

"Crazy Sam's Hardware back in Brooklyn, if I do the ad."

I have a bad feeling. Mitchell appears to have joined the right-wing nuts who believe that little black helicopters follow them everywhere, and that there are secret codes on the back of traffic signs to direct the UN invasion force when it comes.

I say, "I don't have any interest except the same one that made you want to call me. We saved the world, Elliot, and they're ripping off our story . . ."

"You let them. You and Nyquist. How *is* old Nyquist?"

"Sitting in a room with mattresses on the walls, wearing a backward jacket and eating cold creamed corn. They made him the hero, when it was *us* who blew up the mothership, it was *us* who captured that stinking silver beachball, it was *us* who worked out how to poison most of them."

I put the bottle to my lips, but there's hardly a swallow left. I toss it away. This isn't going the way I planned, but I'm caught up in my anger. It's come right back, dull and heavy. "We're the ones that saved Susan, not her lousy husband!"

"We didn't save her, Ray. That was in your TV movie, *The Omega Encounter*. We got her back, but the things they'd put inside her killed her anyway."

"Well, we got her back, and if fuckin' Doc Jensen had listened, we *would* have saved her, too!"

I sit there, looking into the flashlight beam with drunken tears running down my face.

"How much do you remember, Ray? Not the movies, but the *real thing*? Do you remember how we got Susan out of the mothership?"

"I stay away from shopping malls, because they give me flashbacks. Maybe I'm as crazy as Nyquist. Sometimes, I dream I'm in one of those old-fashioned hedge mazes, like in *The Shining*. Sometimes, I'm trying to get out of the hospital they put us in afterward. But it's always the same, you know."

Mitchell switches off the flashlight. I squint into the darkness, but all I see is swimming afterimages.

"Come tomorrow," Mitchell says, and something thumps beside me.

It is a rock, with a piece of torn paper tied to it. Under the dome light of the rental car, I smooth out the paper and try to make sense of the map Mitchell has drawn.

Two days. That's how long it took. Now, my life is split into Before and After. What no one gets is that the thing itself—the event, the encounter, the invasion, the incursion, the whatever—was over inside two days. I've had head colds and belly-aches that lasted a whole lot longer. That's what marks me out. When I die, my obits will consist of three paragraphs about those two days and two sentences about everything else. Like I said about Jan-Michael, I have a post-birth, pre-death rut for a life. Except for those two days.

After about a decade, it got real old. It was as if everyone was quizzing me about some backyard baseball game I pitched in when I was a kid, blotting out all of the rest of my life—parents, job, marriages, kid, love, despair—with a couple of hours on the mound. I even tried clamming up, refusing to go through it all again for the anniversary features. I turned my back on those two days and tried to fix on something else worth talking about. I'd come close to making it with Adrienne Barbeau, didn't I? Or was it Heather Locklear? Maybe it was just in one of the scripts and some actor played me. I was doing harder stuff than alcohol just then.

That phase lasted maybe three months. I was worn down in the end. I realized that I *needed* to tell it again. For me, as much as for everyone else. I was like those talking books in that Bradbury novel—yeah, I admit it, I read science fiction when I was a kid, and doesn't *that* blow my whole story to bits, proving that I made it all up out of half-remembered bits of pulp magazine stories—my whole life was validated by my story, and telling it was as necessary to me as breathing. Over the years, it got polished and shiny. More than a few folks told me it sounded like Bradbury.

"A million years ago, Nyquist's farm was the bottom of the ocean," I would always begin, paraphrasing the opening of my book. "Susan Nyquist collected sea-shells in the desert. Just before I looked up and saw the spinning shape in the sky, I was sifting through the soft white sand, dredging up a clam-shaped rock that might once have been alive . . ."

No, I'm not going to tell it all again here. That's not what this is about at all.

Do you know what a palimpsest is? It's old parchment that has been written on once, had the writing rubbed out, and been written on again. Sometimes several times. Only, with modern techniques, scientists can read the original writing, looking underneath the layers.

That's my story. Each time I've told it, I've whited out the version underneath. It's built up, like lime on a dripping faucet. In telling it so many times, I've buried the actual thing.

Maybe that's why I've done it.

Regardless of the movies, it wasn't a B picture, with simple characters and actions. Okay, there were aliens (everyone else calls them that except Strieber, so I guess I can too), a woman was taken, and we poisoned most of them and dug out dynamite and blew up their spaceship (I've never liked calling it that—it was more like one of Susan's shells blown up like a balloon, only with light instead of helium or air). We saved the world, right?

Or maybe we just killed a bunch of unknowable Gandhis from the Beyond. That's what some woman accused me of at a book-signing. She thought they'd come to save us, and that we'd doomed the world by scaring them off.

That gave me a shock. I tried to see the story the way she might.

It didn't play in Peoria. The woman—pink bib overalls, bird's-nest hair, Velma-from-*Scooby-Doo* glasses, a "Frodo Lives!" badge—hadn't seen the visitors, the aliens.

She hadn't seen what they'd done to Susan.

But I was up close.

The little fuckers were evil. No, make that Evil. I don't know if they were from outer space, the third circle of Hell, or the Land of Nod, but they weren't here to help anyone but themselves.

What they did to the cattle, what they did to Susan, wasn't science, wasn't curiosity. They *liked* taking things apart, the way Mikey Bignell in third grade liked setting fire to cats, and Mikey grew up to get shot dead while pistol-whipping a fifty-two-year-old married lady during a filling station hold-up. If the visitors ever grow up beyond the cat-burning phase, I figure they could do some serious damage.

I am not just trying to justify what we did to them.

Now, without trying to tell the story yet again, I'm tapping into what I really felt at the time: half-scared, half-enraged. No Spielberg sense of wonder. No TV movie courage. No Ray Bradbury wistfulness.

"Inside the Ship was all corridors and no rooms, criss-crossing tunnels through what seemed like a rocky rubber solid stuff. Mitchell went ahead, and I followed. We blundered any which way, down passages that made us bend double and kink our knees, and trusted to luck that we'd find where they'd taken Susan. I don't know whether or not we were lucky to find her or whether they intended it. I don't know if we were brave and lucky, or dumb rats in a maze.

"Mitchell claims the thing told us where to go, flashed a floor-plan into our minds, like the escape lights in an airliner. I guess that's his scientific mind talking. For me, it was different. I had a sense of being myself and being above myself, looking down. We didn't take a direct route to Susan, but spiraled around her, describing a mandala with an uneven number of planes of symmetry. It was like the New Math: finding the answer wasn't as important as knowing how to get there, and I think Mitchell and I, in our different ways, both flunked."

I didn't say so in the book, but I think that's why what happened to Susan afterward went down. When we dragged Susan, alive but unconscious, out of the hot red-black half-dark at the heart of the ship we were too exhausted to feel any sense of triumph. We went in, we found her, we got her out. But we didn't get the trick quite right.

Here's how I usually end it:

"Nyquist was shaking too bad to aim the rifle. I don't amount to much, but while I can't shoot good enough to take the eye out of the eagle if you toss a silver dollar in the air, nine times out of ten I'll at least clip the coin. Mitchell was shouting as he ran toward us with two of the things hopping after him. The reel of wire was spinning in his hands as he ran. Nyquist snapped out of it and tossed me the gun"—in his version, he gets both of the critters with two shots, bing-bang—"and I drew a bead, worried that Mitchell would zigzag into the line of fire, then put a bullet into the first alien. Pink stuff burst out of the back of it in midleap, and it tumbled over, deflating like a pricked party balloon.

"Even from where I was, I could smell the stink, and Nyquist started to throw up. The second critter was almost on Mitchell when I fired again, the hot casing stinging my cheek as I worked the bolt, and fired, and fired, and kept shooting as Mitchell threw himself down in a tangle of wire while the thing went scooting off back toward the ship. My hands shaking so bad I sliced my hand bad when I trimmed the wires back to bare copper. Mitchell snatched them from me and touched them to the terminals of the truck's battery.

"We didn't have more than a dozen sticks of low-grade dynamite for getting out tree stumps, and Mitchell hadn't had time to place them carefully when those things came scooting out like hornets out of a bottle. And Mitchell hadn't even wanted to do it, saying that the ship must be fireproofed, like the Apollo module, or it wouldn't have survived atmospheric entry. But it was our last best hope, and when the sticks blew, the ship went up like a huge magnesium flare. I put my hands over my eyes, and saw the bones of my hands against the light. The burst was etched into my eyeballs for months. It hardly left any debris, just evaporated into burning light, blasting the rock beneath to black crystal. You can still see the glassy splash where it stood if you can get the security clearance. There was a scream like a dying beast, but it was all over quickly. When we stopped blinking and the echo was dead, there was almost nothing where the ship had been. They were gone."

Is that an ending? If it is, what has the *rest* of my life been? An epilogue, like on some Quinn Martin series episode, with William Conrad reporting that I am still at large, still running off my mouth, still living it down?

Or has it just been an interlude before the sequel?

I wake up the next morning with the shakes. There's not even fumes in the tequila bottle I clutched to my chest all night, and nothing but warm cans of Dr Pepper in the motel vending machine, so I drive the mile into town and buy a twelve pack of Bud, giving thanks to California's liberal liquor-license laws. I'm coming out of the 7 Eleven when two men in sunglasses fall in step with me on either side, and I don't need to see their badges to know what they are.

They make me leave my beer in the car and take me across the dusty highway to the town's diner, an Airstream trailer with a tattered awning shading one side. The older guy orders coffee and pancakes, and grins across the table while his partner crowds me on the bench. I can't help looking through the greasy window at my car, where the beer is heating up on the front seat, and the older guy's grin gets wider. He gets out a hip flask and pours a shot into my coffee, and I can't help myself and guzzle it down, scalding coffee running down my chin.

"Jesus," the young guy, Duane Bissette, says, disgusted.

He's the local field agent, blond hair slicked back from his rawboned face. He hasn't taken off his mirrorshades, and a shoulder harness makes a bulge under his tailored suit jacket.

"Judge not," the other guy says, and pours me another shot, twinkling affably. He has curly white hair and a comfortable gut, like Santa Claus's younger brother. He's hung his seersucker jacket on the back of his chair. There are half-moon sweat stains under his arms, and sweat beads under his hairline. "Ray's living out his past, and he's having a hard time with it. Am I right, or am I right?"

I ignore the rye whiskey in the coffee mug. I say, "If you want to talk to me, talk to my agent first. Murray Weiss, he's in the Manhattan Directory."

"But you're one of us," the older guy says, widening his eyes in mock innocence. "You got your badge, when? '77? '78?"

It was 1976 and I'm sure he damn well knows it, done right out on the White House lawn, with a silver band playing and the Stars and Stripes snapping in the breeze under a hot white sky. The Congressional Medal of Honor for me and Nyquist, and honorary membership in the FBI. I'd asked for that because if it was good enough for Elvis, it was good enough for me. It was the last time I saw Nyquist, and even then he was ignoring me with the same intensity with which I'm right now ignoring that rye.

I say, "Your young friend here was polite enough to show me his badge. I don't believe I know you."

"Oh, we met, very briefly. I was part of the team that helped clean up." He smiles and holds out his hand over the coffee mugs and plates of pancakes, then shrugs. "Guerdon Winter. I'll never forget that first sight of the crater, and the carcass you had."

"You were all wearing those spacesuits and helmets. 'Scuse me for not recognizing you."

The FBI agents looked more like space aliens than the things we killed. They cleared out everything, from the scanty remains of the mothership to my collection of tattered paperbacks. I still have the receipts. They took me and Nyquist and Mitchell and put us in isolation chambers somewhere in New Mexico and put us through thirty days of interrogation and medical tests. They took Susan's body and we never saw it again. I think of the C-130 crash, and I say, "You should have taken more care of what you appropriated, Agent Winter."

Guerdon Winter takes a bite of pancake.

"We could have had that alien carcass stuffed and mounted and put on display in the Smithsonian, and in five years it would have become one more exhibit worth maybe ten seconds' gawping. The public doesn't need any help in getting distracted, and everything gets old fast. You know better than me how quickly they forget. You're the one in showbiz. But *we* haven't forgotten, Ray."

"You want me to find out what Mitchell is doing."

"Mitchell phoned you from a pay phone right here in town ten days ago, and you wrote him at the box number he gave you, and then you came down here. You saw him last night."

Duane Bissette stirs and says, "He's been holed up for two years now. He's been carrying out illegal experiments."

"If you were following me you could have arrested him last night."

Guerdon Winter looks at Duane Bissette, then looks at me. He says, "We could arrest him each time he comes into town for supplies, but that wouldn't help us get into his place, and we know enough about his interrogation profile to know he wouldn't give it up to us. But he wants to talk to *you,* Ray. We just want to know what it is he's doing out there."

"He believes you have the map," Duane Bissette says.

I remember the scrap of paper Mitchell gave me last night and say, "You want the map?"

"It isn't important," Guerdon Winter says quickly. "What's important is that you're here, Ray."

I look out at my rental car again, still thinking about the beer getting warm. Just beyond it, a couple of Mexicans in wide-brimmed straw hats are offloading watermelons from a dusty Toyota pickup. One is wearing a very white T-shirt with the Green Lantern symbol. They could be agents, too; so could the old galoot at the motel.

I know Duane Bissette was in my motel room last night; I know he took Mitchell's map and photocopied it and put it back. The thing is, it doesn't seem like betrayal. It stirs something inside me, not like the old excitement of those two crystal-clear days when everything we did was a heroic gesture, nothing like so strong or vivid, but alive all the same. Like waking up to a perfect summer's day after a long uneasy sleep full of nightmares.

I push the coffee away from me and say, "What kind of illegal experiments?"

If Mitchell hadn't been a government employee, if they hadn't ridiculed and debunked his theories, and spirited him off to the ass end of nowhere—no Congressional Medal ceremony for him, he got his by registered mail—if they hadn't stolen the discovery of Mitchellite from him, then maybe he wouldn't have ended up madder than a dancing chicken on a hot plate at the state fair. Maybe he wouldn't have taken it into his head to try what he did. Or maybe he would have done it anyway. Like me, he was living in After, with those two bright days receding like a train. Like me, he wanted them back. Unlike me, he thought he had a way to do it.

Those two agents don't tell me as much as I need to know, but I suspect that they don't know what it is Mitchell is doing. I have an idea that he's building something out in the desert that'll bring those old times back again.

Driving out to Mitchell's place takes a couple of hours. The route on the map he gave me is easy enough: south along Pearblossom's two-lane blacktop, then over the concrete channel of the aqueduct that carries water taken from Washington State—did you see *Chinatown*? yeah, there—and up an unmade track that zigzags along the contours of the Piñon Hills and into a wide draw that runs back a couple of miles. The light in the draw is odd. Cold and purple, like expensive sunglasses. Either side of the road is nothing but rocks, sand, dry scrub, and scattered Joshua trees.

I start to feel a grudging sympathy for Agent Bissette. No matter how he hangs back, it's impossible to tail a car out here without your mark knowing. I have the urge to wait for a dip that puts me momentarily out of his sight and swerve off into a patch of soft sand, sinking the rental like a boat in shallows, creating another unexplained mystery.

Mitchell's place is right at the top of the draw, near the beginning of the tree line. In the high desert, trees grow only on the tops of the mountains. The FBI parks under a clump of stunted pines and lets me go on alone. I'm lucky they didn't want me to wear a wire. They'll just wait, and see if I can cope with Crazy Elliot. For them, it'll be a boring afternoon, with maybe an exciting apprehension about nightfall.

Me. I'm going back to the Days of Sharp Focus.

The rye in the coffee has burned out and I've not touched the soup-warm beer on the passenger seat. I can feel the heat steaming the booze out of my brain. I'm going into this alone.

I get out of the rental, aware of Winter and Bissette watching me through the tinted windshield of their Lincoln Continental. Of Mitchell, there's not a trace. Not even footprints or tire marks in the sandy track. I crouch down, and run a handful of warm sand through my fingers, making like an Indian tracker in some old Western while I ponder my next move.

There are tine-trails in the sand. The whole area has been raked, like a Japanese garden. I can imagine Mitchell working by night, raking a fan-shaped wake as he backs toward the paved area I see a dozen yards away.

I walk across the sand, and reach the flagstones. This was the floor of a house that's long gone. I can see the fieldstone hearth, and the ruts where wooden walls had been.

Beyond the stone is a gentle incline, sloping down maybe twenty feet, then leveling off. Down there, protected from

sight, Mitchell has been building. I look at his paper, and
see what he means. The FBI think it's a circuit diagram,
but it really *is* a map. Mitchell has made himself a maze,
but there's nothing on his map that shows me how to get
through it.

I know now where the old timbers of the house have
gone. Mitchell has cannibalized everything carriable within
a mile, and some things I would have sworn you'd need a
bulldozer at least to shift, but he must have had a few truck-
loads of chickenwire, wood, and just plain junk hauled out
here. The archway entrance is a Stonehenge arrangement of
two 1950s junkers buried hood-first like standing stones,
with their tailfins and clusters of egg-shaped rear lights pro-
jecting into the air. A crosspiece made of three supermarket shopping carts completes the arch.

There are other old cars parked and piled in a curving
outer wall, built on with wire and wood. And all over the
place, sticking up through the sand, are sharp spars and
spines that sparkle in the sun.

I know that glittery look, a glinting like the facets of an
insect's eye or 1970s eye makeup under fluorescent disco
lights. It's Mitchellite.

I walk up to the gateway and stop, careful not to touch
the spars. They dot everything—stone, wood, metal—like
some sort of mineral mold. Crusty little alien points that
seem to be growing out of the ordinary Earth stuff. About
ten years ago, a couple of crazy English physicists claimed
you could use Mitchellite to get unlimited energy by cold
fusion and end up with more Mitchellite than you started
with, but they were debunked, defrocked, and for all I know
defenestrated, and that was the end of it. But maybe they
were right. It looks like the Mitchellite is transmuting ordinary stuff into itself.

There's an iron crowbar, untouched by Mitchellite,
propped against a stone. I pick it up, heft it in my hands.
It has a good weight. I always felt better with a simple tool,
something you could trust.

Planks are set between the half-buried cars, a path into
the interior of the maze. They are pocked with Mitchellite

spars that splinter the rotten wood from the inside. I smash down with the poker and split a plank, scraping away bone-dry wood fragments from the Mitchellite nerve-tangles that have been growing inside, sucking strength from the material.

It looks fragile, but it doesn't crumple under my boots.

On the other side of the arch hangs a shower curtain that leaves a three-foot gap beneath it. I push it aside with the crowbar and step into the maze.

The structure is open to the sky, mostly. The walls are of every kind of junk, wood, lines of rocks or unmortared concrete blocks, even barbed wire, grown through or studded with Mitchellite. A few yuccas rise up from the maze's low walls, their fleshy leaves sparkling as if dusted with purplish snow. The floor is made of Mitchellite-eaten planks. There are stretches of clean, unmarked sand. But by each of them is propped a rake, for obscuring footprints. By the first rake is a pane of glass in the sand, and in the hollow under the glass is a handgun wrapped in a plastic baggie, and a handwritten note. *In case of F(B)IRE smash glass.* So that's what the crowbar is for. I leave the gun where it is and turn and stare at the maze again.

After a while I fish out the map and look at it. It takes me a while even to work out where I am, but with a creepy chill I realize I'm standing on the spot where Mitchell has drawn a stick figure. In the center of the map is a white space, where there's another, bigger stick figure. Dotted throughout are smaller figures, drawn in red. I know what they're supposed to be. Some are drawn over black lines that represent walls.

I call out Mitchell's name.

The maze funnels my own voice back to me, distorted and empty.

"Ray, come on, what are you waiting for?"

It was obviously a doorway. Mitchell bent down low—the round opening was the creatures' size—and squeezed into the ship.

I hesitated, but thought of Susan, and the things that had taken her.

"I'm coming, Mitchell."

I followed the geologist. Inside, was another world.

"I'm coming, Mitchell."

I know at once what he's done. This isn't really a maze. It's a model, twice as big again as the real thing, of the aliens' ship.

My knees are weak and I'm shaking. I'm back on the mandala path. I'm above myself and in myself, and I know where to go. I know the route, just as I know the ache that sets into my knees after a minute, an ache that grows to a crippling pain. Just as I remember finding Susan. And finding out later what they'd done to her.

Mitchell took the lead, that time. I followed, forgetting Nyquist chicken-heartedly frozen at the entrance, not daring to go further.

Remembering, I follow Mitchell's lead again. Around and inward, spiral across a DNA coil or a wiring diagram, a bee-dance through catacombs. The route is a part of me.

The deeper inside the maze I get, the more Mitchellite there is. The original wood and stone and wire and concrete has been almost completely eaten away. Purple light glitters everywhere, dazzling even through my sunglasses. Without them, I'd be snow-blind in a minute.

When the process is finished, when there's nothing more of Earth in the maze, will this thing be able to fly? Will Mitchell carry the war to the enemy?

"Ray," someone—not Mitchell—shouts, from behind me.

It's the FBI. I thought I was supposed to haul Mitchell out on my own. Now the pros are here, I wonder why I've bothered.

I feel like a sheep driven across a minefield. A Judas goat.

I got into the maze and I'm still alive, so Guerdon Winter and Bissette know it's safe.

I turn, shading my eyes against the tinted glare that shines up from everything around me. The agents are following my footprints. Bissette doesn't duck under the crossbar of an arch nailed up of silvery grey scraps of wood, and scrapes his forehead against a Mitchellite-spackled plank.

I know what will happen.

It's like sandpaper stuck with a million tiny fishhooks and razor blades. The gentlest touch opens deep gashes. Bissette swears, not realizing how badly he's hurt, and a curtain of blood bursts from the side of his head. A flap of scalp hangs down. Red rain spatters his shades.

Bissette falls to his knees. Guerdon Winter plucks out a handkerchief from the breast pocket of his sweat-stained seersucker jacket. A bedsheet won't staunch the flow.

"You can't go on," Guerdon Winter tells the junior agent, who can't protest for the pain. "We'll come back for you."

Naturally, Guerdon Winter has his gun out. When Mitchell and I went into the mothership, we didn't even think of guns. I left my shotgun in the pickup, and Nyquist held on to his rifle like it was a comforter blanket and wouldn't give it up to us. Some heroes, huh? Every single version of the story rectifies the omission, and we go in tooled up fit to face Bonnie and Clyde.

The FBI has made a bad mistake.

They've changed the story again. By adding the guns, and maybe themselves, they've made me lose my place.

I don't know which way to go from here.

My feet and my spine and my aching knees were remembering. But the memory's been wiped.

Bissette is groaning. His wound is tearing worse—there are tiny particles of alien matter in it, ripping his skin apart as they grow—and the whole right side of his head and his suit-shoulder are deep crimson.

"Ray," prompts Guerdon Winter. There's a note of pleading in his voice.

I look at the fork ahead of us, marked with a cow's skull nodding on a pole, and suddenly have no idea which path to take. I look up at the sky. There's a canopy of polythene up there, scummy with sand-drifts in the folds. I look at the aisles of junk. They mean nothing to me. I'm as blank as the middle of the map Mitchell gave me.

Then Winter does something incredibly stupid. He offers me a hip flask and smiles and says, "Loosen up, Ray. You'll do fine."

I knock the flask away, and it hits a concrete pillar laced with Mitchellite and sticks there, leaking amber booze from a dozen puncture points. The smell does something to my hindbrain and I start to run, filled with blind panic just the way I was when I followed behind Mitchell, convinced alien blimps would start nibbling at my feet.

I run and run, turning left, turning right, deeper and deeper into the maze. The body remembers, if it's allowed. Someone shouts behind me, and then there's a shot and a bullet spangs off an engine block and whoops away into the air; another turns the windshield of a wheelless truck to lace which holds its shape for a moment before falling away. I leap over a spar of Mitchellite like an antelope and run on, feeling the years fall away. I've dropped the map, but it doesn't matter. The body remembers. Going in, and coming out. Coming out with Susan. That's the name I yell, but ahead, through a kind of hedge of twisted wire coated with a sheen of Mitchellite, through the purple glare and a singing in my ears, I see Mitchell himself, standing in the doorway of a kind of bunker.

He's older than I remember or imagined, the Boy Scout look transmuted into a scrawny geezer wearing only ragged oil-stained shorts, desert boots, and wraparound shades, his skin tanned a mahogany brown. I lean on the crowbar, taking great gulps of air as I try and get my breath back, and he looks at me calmly. There's a pump-action Mossbauer shotgun leaning on the wall beside him.

At last, I can say, "This is some place you got here, Elliot. Where did you get all the stuff?"

"It's a garden," Mitchell says, and picks up the shotgun and walks off around the bunker. He has half-healed scars on his back. Maybe he brushed a little too close to something in his maze.

I follow. The bunker is a poured concrete shell, a low round dome like a turtle shell half-buried in the dry desert dirt. There's a battered Blazer parked at the back, and a little Honda generator and a TV satellite dish. A ramp of earth leads up to the top of the bunker, and we climb up there and stand side by side, looking out over the maze. It extends all around the bunker. The sun is burning over our shoulders, and the concentric spirals of encrusted junk shimmer and glitter, taking the light and making it into something else, a purple haze that glistens in the air, obscuring more than it reveals.

"How long have you been doing this, Elliot? It looks like you've been here years."

Elliot Mitchell says, "You ever been to South America, Ray? You should have. They're very big on flying saucers in South America. Out in Peru, there are patterns of stones in the deserts that only make sense from the air. Like landing strips, parking aprons."

A chill grips me. "You're building a spaceport?"

"We never had any evidence that they came from outer space," Mitchell says.

"What are you saying, they're from *Peru*? There's some bad shit on Earth, but nothing like those things. What are you doing here, Elliot? Trying to turn yourself into one of them? Listen, if you've found anything out, it'll mean a shitload of attention. That's what I . . ."

"More talk shows, Ray? More ten-line fillers in *Time*? I had some guy from the *National Enquirer* come by a month or so ago. He tried to get in. Maybe he's still in here, somewhere."

I remember the red marks on Mitchell's map, in the otherwise blank space of the maze.

I say, "You let me in, Elliot."

"You understand, Ray. You were *there*, with me. You know what it was like. Only you and me really know what it was like."

I see why he wants me here. Mitchell has built this for a purpose, and I'm supposed to tell the world what that is. I say, "What are you planning. Elliot? What are you going to do with all this?"

Mitchell giggles. "I don't control it, Ray. Not anymore.

It's more and more difficult to get out each time. When we went to get Susan, where did we go?"

He's setting me up for something. I say dumbly, "Into the ship. That's how I knew to get to you here. This is like the ship."

"It's how I started it out. But it's been *growing*. Started with a bare ounce of Mitchellite, grew this garden over the template I made. Now it grows itself. Like the ship. We went in, and we went somewhere else. Not all the way, because it hadn't finished growing, but a good way. Back toward where they came from. Wherever it was."

"You're saying the ship didn't come from Outer Space?"

"It *grew* here. Like this." Mitchell makes a sweeping gesture with the shotgun, including everything around him. He's King of the Hill. "Once a critical density had been reached, the gateway would have opened, and they would have come through."

"They *did* come through. We poisoned them, we shot them, we blew up their fucking ship—"

"Mitchellite is strange stuff, Ray. Strange matter. It shouldn't exist, not in our universe, at least. It's a mixture of elements all with atomic weights more than ten times that of uranium. It shouldn't even get together in the first place without tremendous energies forcing the quarks together, and it should fly apart in a picosecond after its creation. But it doesn't. It's metastable. It makes holes in reality, increases quantum tunneling so that things can leak through from one universe to another. That's how they probed us. Sent a probe through on the atomic scale and let it grow. Maybe they sent millions of probes, and only one hit the right configuration. Before we sent up astronauts, we sent up chimps and dogs. That's what they did. They sent through seeds of the things we saw, and they lodged and grew."

"In the cows."

Great chunks had been ripped out of the cows I found. Nyquist thought it was chainsaw butchers, until I dug around and found the blisters inside the meat. Like tapeworm cysts. And Susan, Susan, when we got her out . . .

"In the cows," Mitchell says. "That was the first stage. And then they took Susan. That was the second stage, Ray. First chimps, then the astronauts. But we stopped it."

"Yeah. We stopped it."

Mitchell doesn't hear me. He's caught up in his own story.

He says, "They gave the first *astronauts* ticker-tape parades down Wall Street, but what happened to the chimps? First time around they picked us up and husked us of our stories and forgot us. *Second* time is the ticker-tape parade."

Susan never came around. That was a blessing at least. Doc Jensen wouldn't believe me when I told him that I figured what had happened to the cattle was happening to her. Not until that night, when the things started moving under her skin. He tried to cut them out then, but they were all *through* her. So I did the right thing. Doc Jensen couldn't, even though he saw what was inside her. He'd still stuck with his oath, even though he had a bottle of whiskey inside him. So I did what had to be done, and then we went out and blew up the ship.

Mitchell tells me, "You have to believe it, Ray. *This* time they won't forget us. This time we'll control it. They tried to discredit me. They stole my records, they said I was as crazy as Nyquist and tried to section me, they made up stories about finding terrestrial deposits of Mitchellite. Well, maybe those were real. Maybe those were from previous attempts. It's a matter of configuration."

He gestures with the shotgun again, and that's when I cold-cock him.

He thought I'd be on his side. He thought I wanted nothing more than fame, than to get back the feeling we had in those two days. He was right. I did. His mistake was that he thought I'd pay *any* price. And forgetting to put on a shirt.

The crowbar bounces off his skull, and he falls like an

unstrung puppet. I kick the shotgun off the domed roof and then he looks up at me and I see what he's done to himself. The sunglasses have come off, and his left eye is a purple mandala.

When I finish, there isn't much left of the top of his head. In amongst the blood and brains: glittering purple-sheened strands, like cords of fungus through rotten wood. A couple of the things inside him try to get out through the scars on his back, but I squash them back into Mitchell's flesh.

After I kill Mitchell, I take the gasoline from his generator and burn the dome without looking to see what's inside it, and smash as much of the whole center of the maze as I can. I work in a kind of cold fury, choking in the black smoke pouring out of the dome, until I can hardly stand. Then I toss the crowbar into the flames and walk out of there.

There's no sign of the FBI agents, although their car is still there when I get out. Winter and Bissette are still back there, incorporated. I hope to God they're dead, although it isn't likely. But the maze has stopped growing, I know that. The light's gone from it. There's a cell phone in the glove compartment, and I use the redial button and tell the guy on the other end that Winter and Bissette are lost, that the whole place has to be destroyed.

"Don't go in there to look for them. Burn it from the air, it would give them a kindlier death. Burn it down and blow it up. Do the right thing. I made a start. They won't come back."

When I say it, for the first time, it sounds finished.

EIGHT O'CLOCK IN THE MORNING

Ray Nelson

Here's one of the classic SF paranoia stories, a tale of aliens hiding among us with nefarious schemes. One day the world may wake up to their plans ... but it would probably be a bad idea if you did. All by yourself. Alone. Very alone ...

Born in 1931, Ray Nelson made his first sale in 1963, and has since worked in both the science fiction and the mystery genres. Not a prolific writer by genre standards, he has produced a small but distinguished body of work, with sales to The Magazine of Fantasy and Science Fiction, Again, Dangerous Visions *(almost certainly the only story in genre history to suggest masturbation as a method for time-travel!), and elsewhere. His novels include* The Ganymede Takeover, *written in collaboration with the late Philip K. Dick,* Blake's Progress, Then Beggars Could Ride, Revolt of the Unemployables, *and* The Prometheus Man.

At the end of the show the hypnotist told his subjects, "Awake."

Something unusual happened.

One of the subjects awoke all the way. This had never happened before. His name was George Nada and he blinked out at the sea of faces in the theatre, at first unaware of anything out of the ordinary. Then he noticed, human faces, the faces of the Fascinators. They had been there all along, of course, but only George was really awake, so only George recognized them for what they were. He understood everything in a flash, including the fact that if he were to give any outward sign, the Fascinators would instantly command him to return to his former state, and he would obey.

He left the theatre, pushing out into the neon night, carefully avoiding giving any indication that he saw the green, reptilian flesh or the multiple yellow eyes of the rulers of earth. One of them asked him, "Got a light, buddy?" George gave him a light, then moved on.

At intervals along the street George saw the posters hanging with photographs of the Fascinators' multiple eyes and various commands printed under them, such as, "Work eight hours, play eight hours, sleep eight hours," and "Marry and Reproduce." A TV set in the window of a store caught George's eye, but he looked away in the nick of time. When he didn't look at the Fascinator in the screen, he could resist the command, "Stay tuned to this station."

George lived alone in a little sleeping room, and as soon as he got home, the first thing he did was to disconnect the TV set. In other rooms he could hear the TV sets of his neighbors, though. Most of the time the voices were human, but now and then he heard the arrogant, strangely bird-like croaks of the aliens. "Obey the government," said one croak. "We are the government," said another. "We are your friends, you'd do anything for a friend, wouldn't you?"

"Obey!"

"Work!"

Suddenly the phone rang.

George picked it up. It was one of the Fascinators.

"Hello," it squawked. "This is your control, Chief of Police Robinson. You are an old man, George Nada. Tomorrow morning at eight o'clock, your heart will stop. Please repeat."

"I am an old man," said George. "Tomorrow morning at eight o'clock, my heart will stop."

The control hung up.

"No, it won't," whispered George. He wondered why they wanted him dead. Did they suspect that he was awake? Probably. Someone might have spotted him, noticed that he didn't respond the way the others did. If George were

alive at one minute after eight tomorrow morning, then
they would be sure.

"No use waiting here for the end," he thought.

He went out again. The posters, the TV, the occasional
commands from passing aliens did not seem to have absolute power over him, though he still felt strongly tempted
to obey, to see these things the way his master wanted him
to see them. He passed an alley and stopped. One of the
aliens was alone there, pissing against the wall. George
walked up to him.

"Move on," grunted the thing, focusing his deadly eyes
on George.

George felt his grasp on awareness waver. For a moment the reptilian head dissolved into the face of a lovable old drunk. Of course the drunk would be lovable.
George picked up a brick and smashed it down on the old
drunk's head with all his strength. For a moment the image
blurred, then the bluegreen blood oozed out of the face and
the lizard fell, twitching and writhing. After a moment it
was dead.

George dragged the body into the shadows and searched
it. There was a tiny radio in its pocket and a curiously
shaped knife and fork in another. The tiny radio said something in an incomprehensible language. George put it down
beside the body, but kept the eating utensils.

"I can't possibly escape," thought George. "Why fight
them?"

But maybe he could.

What if he could awaken others? That might he worth
a try.

He walked twelve blocks to the apartment of his girlfriend, Lil, and knocked on her door. She came to the door
in her bathrobe.

"I want you to wake up," he said.

"I'm awake," she said. "Come on in."

He went in. The TV was playing. He turned it off.

"No," he said. "I mean really wake up." She looked at
him without comprehension, so he snapped his fingers and

shouted, "*Wake up!* The masters command that you wake up!"

"Are you off your rocker, George?" she asked suspiciously. "You sure are acting funny." He slapped her face. "Cut that out!" she cried. "What the hell are you up to anyway?"

"Nothing," said George, defeated. "I was just kidding around."

"Slapping my face wasn't just kidding around!" she cried.

There was a knock at the door.

George opened it.

It was one of the aliens.

"Can't you keep the noise down to a dull roar?" it said.

The eyes and reptilian flesh faded a little and George saw the flickering image of a fat middle-aged man in shirt-sleeves. It was still a man when George slashed its throat with the eating knife, but it was an alien before it hit the floor. He dragged it into the apartment and kicked the door shut.

"What do you see there?" he asked Lil, pointing to the many-eyed snake thing on the floor.

"Mister . . . Mister Coney," she whispered, her eyes wide with horror. "You . . . just killed him, like it was nothing at all."

"Don't scream," warned George, advancing on her.

"I won't, George. I swear I won't, only please, for the love of God, put down that knife." She backed away until she had her shoulder blades pressed to the wall.

George saw that it was no use.

"I'm going to tie you up," said George. "First tell me which room Mister Coney lived in."

"The first door on your left as you go toward the stairs," she said. "Georgie . . . Georgie. Don't torture me. If you're going to kill me, do it clean. Please, Georgie, please."

He tied her up with bedsheets and gagged her, then searched the body of the Fascinator. There was another one of the little radios that talked a foreign language, another set of eating utensils, and nothing else.

George went next door.

When he knocked, one of the snake-things answered, "Who is it?"

"Friend of Mister Coney. I wanna see him," said George.

"He went out for a second, but he'll be right back." The door opened a crack, and four yellow eyes peeped out. "You wanna come in and wait?"

"Okay," said George, not looking at the eyes.

"You alone here?" he asked, as it closed the door, its back to George.

"Yeah, why?"

He slit its throat from behind, then searched the apartment.

He found human bones and skulls, a half-eaten hand.

He found tanks with huge fat slugs floating in them.

"The children," he thought, and killed them all.

There were guns too, of a sort he had never seen before. He discharged one by accident, but fortunately it was noiseless. It seemed to fire little poisoned darts.

He pocketed the gun and as many boxes of darts as he could and went back to Lil's place. When she saw him she writhed in helpless terror.

"Relax, honey," he said, opening her purse. "I just want to borrow your car keys."

He took the keys and went downstairs to the street.

Her car was still parked in the same general area in which she always parked it. He recognized it by the dent in the right fender. He got in, started it, and began driving aimlessly. He drove for hours, thinking—desperately searching for some way out. He turned on the car radio to see if he could get some music, but there was nothing but news and it was all about him, George Nada, the homicidal maniac. The announcer was one of the masters, but he sounded a little scared. Why should he be? What could one man do?

George wasn't surprised when he saw the road block, and he turned off on a side street before he reached it. No little trip to the country for you, Georgie boy, he thought to himself.

They had just discovered what he had done back at Lil's place, so they would probably be looking for Lil's car. He parked it in an alley and took the subway. There were no aliens on the subway, for some reason. Maybe they were too good for such things, or maybe it was just because it was so late at night.

When one finally did get on, George got off.

He went up to the street and went into a bar. One of the Fascinators was on the TV, saying over and over again, "We are your friends. We are your friends. We are your friends." The stupid lizard sounded scared. Why? What could one man do against all of them?

George ordered a beer, then it suddenly struck him that the Fascinator on the TV no longer seemed to have any power over him. He looked at it again and thought, "It has to believe it can master me to do it. The slightest hint of fear on its part and the power to hypnotize is lost." They flashed George's picture on the TV screen and George retreated to the phone booth. He called his control, the Chief of Police.

"Hello, Robinson?" he asked.

"Speaking."

"This is George Nada. I've figured out how to wake people up."

"What? George, hang on. Where are you?" Robinson sounded almost hysterical.

He hung up and paid and left the bar. They would probably trace his call.

He caught another subway and went downtown.

It was dawn when he entered the building housing the biggest of the city's TV studios. He consulted the building directory and then went up in the elevator. The cop in front of the studio entrance recognized him. "Why, you're Nada!" he gasped.

George didn't like to shoot him with the poison dart gun, but he had to.

He had to kill several more before he got into the studio itself, including all the engineers on duty. There were a lot of police sirens outside, excited shouts, and running footsteps on the stairs. The alien was sitting before the TV camera saying, "We are your friends. We are your friends," and didn't see George come in. When George shot him with the needle gun he simply stopped in mid-sentence and sat there, dead. George stood near him and said, imitating the alien croak, "Wake up. Wake up. See us as we are and kill us!"

It was George's voice the city heard that morning, but it was the Fascinator's image, and the city did awake for the very first time and the war began.

George did not live to see the victory that finally came. He died of a heart attack at exactly eight o'clock.

EXPENDABLE

Philip K. Dick

*Here's a wry little story—but one with a sting in its tail—
that demonstrates that sometimes our worst enemies, as well
as some unexpected allies, can literally be right under our
feet...*

*A dedicated investigator of the elusive nature of reality,
an intrepid explorer of alternate states of consciousness, a
wickedly effective and acidulous satirist, the late Philip K.
Dick wrote some of the most brilliant novels and short stories in the history of the SF genre, and is now being widely
recognized as one of the major authors of the late 20th cen-
tury, in any genre. He won a Hugo Award for his novel* The
Man in the High Castle, *and his many other novels include*
Ubik, Martian Time Slip, The Three Stigmata of Palmer El-
drich, Time Out of Joint, *and* Do Androids Dream of Electric Sheep, *which was somewhat disappointingly filmed as*
Bladerunner. *His most recent books, published posthumously,
include* The Transmigration of Timothy Archer, Radio Free
Albemuth, Puttering About in a Small Land, The Man Whose
Teeth Were all Exactly Alike, *and the massive three-volume
set* The Collected Stories of Philip K. Dick.

The man came out on the front porch and examined the
day. Bright and cold—with dew on the lawns. He buttoned
his coat and put his hands in his pockets.

As the man started down the steps the two caterpillars
waiting by the mailbox twitched with interest.

"There he goes," the first one said. "Send in your report."

As the other began to rotate his vanes the man stopped,
turning quickly.

"I heard that," he said. He brought his foot down against the wall, scraping the caterpillars off, onto the concrete. He crushed them.

Then he hurried down the path to the sidewalk. As he walked he looked around him. In the cherry tree a bird was hopping, pecking bright-eyed at the cherries. The man studied him. All right? Or— The bird flew off. Birds all right. No harm from them.

He went on. At the corner he brushed against a spider web, crossed from the bushes to the telephone pole. His heart pounded. He tore away, batting in the air. As he went on he glanced over his shoulder. The spider was coming slowly down the bush, feeling out the damage to his web.

Hard to tell about spiders. Difficult to figure out. More facts needed—No contact, yet.

He waited at the bus stop, stomping his feet to keep them warm.

The bus came and he boarded it, feeling a sudden pleasure as he took his seat with all the warm, silent people, staring indifferently ahead. A vague flow of security poured through him.

He grinned, and relaxed, the first time in days.

The bus went down the street.

Tirmus waved his antennae excitedly.

"Vote, then, if you want." He hurried past them, up onto the mound. "But let me say what I said yesterday, before you start."

"We already know it all," Lala said impatiently. "Let's get moving. We have the plans worked out. What's holding us up?"

"More reason for me to speak." Tirmus gazed around at the assembled gods. "The entire Hill is ready to march against the giant in question. Why? We know he can't communicate to his fellows— It's out of the question. The type of vibration, the language they use makes it impossible to convey such ideas as he holds about us, about our—"

"Nonsense," Lala stepped up. "Giants communicate well enough."

"There is no record of a giant having made known information about us!"

The army moved restlessly.

"Go ahead," Tirmus said. "But it's a waste of effort. He's harmless—cut off. Why take all the time and—"

"Harmless?" Lala stared at him. "Don't you understand? He knows!"

Tirmus walked away from the mound. "I'm against unnecessary violence. We should save our strength. Someday we'll need it."

The vote was taken. As expected, the army was in favor of moving against the giant. Tirmus sighed and began stroking out the plans on the ground.

"This is the location that he takes. He can be expected to appear there at period-end. Now, as I see the situation—"

He went on, laying out the plans in the soft soil.

One of the gods leaned toward another, antennae touching. "This giant. He doesn't stand a chance. In a way, I feel sorry for him. How'd he happen to butt in?"

"Accident." The other grinned. "You know, the way they do, barging around."

"It's too bad for him, though."

It was nightfall. The street was dark and deserted. Along the sidewalk the man came, a newspaper under his arm. He walked quickly, glancing around him. He skirted around the big tree growing by the curb and leaped agilely into the street. He crossed the street and gained the opposite side. As he turned the corner he entered the web, sewn from bush to telephone pole. Automatically he fought it, brushing it off him. As the strands broke a thin humming came to him, metallic and wiry.

". . . wait!"

He paused.

". . . careful . . . inside . . . wait . . ."

His jaw set. The last strands broke in his hands and he walked on. Behind him the spider moved in the fragment of his web, watching. The man looked back.

"Nuts to you," he said. "I'm not taking any chances, standing there all tied up."

He went on, along the sidewalk, to his path. He skipped up the path, avoiding the darkening bushes. On the porch he found his key, fitting it into the lock.

He paused. Inside? Better than outside, especially at night. Night a bad time. Too much movement under the bushes. Not good. He opened the door and stepped inside. The rug lay ahead of him, a pool of blackness. Across on the other side he made out the form of the lamp.

Four steps to the lamp. His foot came up. He stopped.

What did the spider say? Wait? He waited, listening. Silence.

He took his cigarette lighter and flicked it on.

The carpet of ants swelled toward him, rising up in a flood. He leaped aside, out onto the porch. The ants came rushing, hurrying, scratching across the floor in the half light.

The man jumped down to the ground and around the side of the house. When the first ants came flowing over the porch he was already spinning the faucet handle rapidly, gathering up the hose.

The burst of water lifted the ants up and scattered them, flinging them away. The man adjusted the nozzle, squinting through the mist. He advanced, turning the hard stream from side to side.

"God damn you," he said, his teeth locked. "Waiting inside—"

He was frightened. Inside—never before! In the night cold sweat came out on his face. Inside. They had never got inside before. Maybe a moth or two, and flies, of course. But they were harmless, fluttery, noisy—

A carpet of ants!

Savagely, he sprayed them until they broke rank and fled into the lawn, into the bushes, under the house.

He sat down on the walk, holding the hose, trembling from head to foot.

They really meant it. Not an anger raid, annoyed, spasmodic; but planned, at attack, worked out. They had waited for him. One more step—

Thank God for the spider.

Presently he shut the hose off and stood up. No sound; silence everywhere. The bushes rustled suddenly. Beetle? Something black scurried—he put his foot on it. A messenger, probably. Fast runner. He went gingerly inside the dark house, feeling his way by the cigarette lighter.

Later, he sat at his desk, the spray gun beside him, heavy-duty steel and copper. He touched its damp surface with his fingers.

Seven o'clock. Behind him the radio played softly. He reached over and moved the desk lamp so that it shone on the floor beside the desk.

He lit a cigarette and took some writing paper and his fountain pen. He paused, thinking.

So they really wanted him, badly enough to plan it out. Bleak despair descended over him like a torrent. What could he do? Whom could he go to? Or tell? He clenched his fists, sitting bolt upright in the chair.

The spider slid down beside him onto the desk top. "Sorry. Hope you aren't frightened, as in the poem."

The man stared. "Are you the same one? The one at the corner? The one who warned me?"

"No. That's somebody else. A Spinner. I'm strictly a Cruncher. Look at my jaws." He opened and shut his mouth. "I bite them up."

The man smiled. "Good for you."

"Sure. Do you know how many there are of us in— say—an acre of land? Guess."

"A thousand."

"No. Two and a half million. Of all kinds. Crunchers, like me, or Spinners, or Stingers."

"Stingers?"

"The best. Let's see." The spider thought. "For instance, the black widow, as you call her. Very valuable." He paused. "Just one thing."

"What's that?"

"We have our problems. The gods—"

"Gods!"

"Ants, as you call them. The leaders. They're beyond us. Very unfortunate. They have an awful taste—makes one sick. We have to leave them for the birds."

The man stood up. "Birds? Are they—"

"Well, we have an arrangement. This has been going on for ages. I'll give you the story. We have some time left."

The man's heart contracted. "Time left? What do you mean?"

"Nothing. A little trouble later on, I understand. Let me give you the background. I don't think you know it."

"Go ahead. I'm listening." He stood up and began to walk back and forth.

"*They* were running the Earth pretty well, about a billion years ago. You see, men came from some other planet. Which one? I don't know. They landed and found the Earth quite well cultivated by them. There was a war."

"So we're the invaders," the man murmured.

"Sure. The war reduced both sides to barbarism, them and yourselves. You forgot how to attack, and they degenerated into closed social factions, ants, termites—"

"I see."

"The last group of you that knew the full story started us going. We were bred"—the spider chuckled in its own fashion—"bred some place for this worthwhile purpose. We keep them down very well. You know what they call us? The Eaters. Unpleasant, isn't it?"

Two more spiders came drifting down on their web-strands, alighting on the desk. The three spiders went into a huddle.

"More serious than I thought," the Cruncher said easily. "Didn't know the whole dope. This Stinger here—"

The black widow came to the edge of the desk. "Giant," she piped, metallically. "I'd like to talk with you."

"Go ahead," the man said.

"There's going to be some trouble here. They're moving, coming here, a lot of them. We thought we'd stay with you awhile. Get in on it."

"I see." The man nodded. He licked his lips, running his fingers shakily through his hair. "Do you think—that is, what are the chances—"

"Chances?" The Stinger undulated thoughtfully. "Well, we've been in this work a long time. Almost a million years. I think that we have the edge over them, in spite of drawbacks. Our arrangements with the birds, and of course, with the toads—"

"I think we can save you," the Cruncher put in cheerfully. "As a matter of fact, we look forward to events like this."

From under the floorboards came a distant scratching sound, the noise of a multitude of tiny claws and wings, vibrating faintly, remotely. The man heard. His body sagged all over.

"You're really certain? You think you can do it?" He wiped the perspiration from his lips and picked up the spray gun, still listening.

The sound was growing, swelling beneath them, under the floor, under their feet. Outside the house bushes rustled and a few moths flew up against the window. Louder and louder the sound grew, beyond and below, everywhere, a rising hum of anger and determination. The man looked from side to side.

"You're sure you can do it?" he murmured. "You can really save me?"

"Oh," the Stinger said, embarrassed. "I didn't mean *that*. I meant the species, the race . . . not you as an individual."

The man gaped at him and the three Eaters shifted uneasily. More moths burst against the window. Under them the floor stirred and heaved.

"I see," the man said. "I'm sorry I misunderstood you."

THE REALITY TRIP

Robert Silverberg

If you're a scholar observing primitive cultures, it's best to resist the temptation to go native—because if you don't, *as the wry and funny story that follows proves, you may suffer all kinds of consequences!*

Robert Silverberg is one of the most famous SF writers of modern times, with dozens of novels, anthologies, and collections to his credit. Silverberg has won five Nebula Awards and four Hugo Awards. His novels include Dying Inside, Lord Valentine's Castle, The Book of Skulls, Downward to the Earth, Tower of Glass, Son of Man, Nightwings, The World Inside, Born With The Dead, Shadrack In The Furnace, Thorns, Up the Line, The Man in the Maze, Tom O' Bedlam, Star of Gypsies, At Winter's End, The Face of the Waters, Kingdoms of the Wall, Hot Sky at Morning, *and two novel-length expansions of famous Isaac Asimov stories,* Nightfall *and* The Ugly Little Boy. *His collections include* Unfamiliar Territory, Capricorn Games, Majipoor Chronicles, The Best of Robert Silverberg, At The Conglomeroid Cocktail Party, Beyond the Safe Zone, *and a massive retrospective collection* The Collected Stories of Robert Silverberg, Volume One: Secret Sharers. *His reprint anthologies are far too numerous to list here, but include* The Science Fiction Hall of Fame, Volume One *and the distinguished* Alpha *series, among dozens of others. His most recent books are the novels* The Alien Years *and* Mountains of Majipoor. *He lives with his wife, writer Karen Haber, in Oakland, California.*

I am a reclamation project for her. She lives on my floor of the hotel, a dozen rooms down the hall: a lady poet, private income. No, that makes her sound too old, a middle-aged eccentric. Actually she is no more than thirty. Taller than I am, with long kinky brown hair and a sharp, bony nose that has a bump on the bridge. Eyes are very glossy. A studied raggedness about her dress; carefully chosen shabby clothes. I am in no position really to judge the sexual attractiveness of Earthfolk but I gather from remarks made by men living here that she is not considered good-looking. I pass her often on my way to my room. She smiles fiercely at me. Saying to herself, no doubt, You poor lonely man. Let me help you bear the burden of your unhappy life. Let me show you the meaning of love, for I too know what it is like to be alone.

Or words to that effect. She's never actually said any such thing. But her intentions are transparent. When she sees me, a kind of hunger comes into her eyes, part maternal, part (I guess) sexual, and her face takes on a wild crazy intensity. Burning with emotion. Her name is Elizabeth Cooke. "Are you fond of poetry, Mr. Knecht?" she asked me this morning, as we creaked upward together in the ancient elevator. And an hour later she knocked at my door. "Something for you to read," she said. "I wrote them." A sheaf of large yellow sheets, stapled at the top; poems printed in smeary blue mimeography. *The Reality Trip*, the collection was headed. *Limited Edition: 125 Copies.* "You can keep it if you like," she explained. "I've got lots more." She was wearing bright corduroy slacks and a flimsy pink shawl through which her breasts plainly showed. Small tapering breasts, not very functional-looking. When she saw me studying them her nostrils flared momentarily and she blinked her eyes three times swiftly. Tokens of lust?

I read the poems. Is it fair for me to offer judgment on them? Even though I've lived on this planet eleven of its years, even though my command of colloquial English is quite good, do I really comprehend the inner life of poetry? I thought they were all quite bad. Earnest, plodding poems, capturing what they call slices of life. The world around her, the cruel, brutal, unloving city. Lamenting the failure of people to open to one another. The title poem began this way:

He was on the reality trip. Big black man,
bloodshot eyes, bad teeth. Eisenhower jacket,
frayed. Smell of cheap wine. I guess a knife
in his pocket. Looked at me mean. Criminal
record. Rape, child-beating, possession of drugs.
In his head saying, slavemistress bitch, and me in
my head saying, black brother, let's freak in to-
gether, let's trip on love—

And so forth. Warm, direct emotion; but is the urge to
love all wounded things a sufficient center for poetry? I
don't know. I did put her poems through the scanner and
transmit them to Homeworld, although I doubt they'll learn
much from them about Earth. It would flatter Elizabeth to
know that while she has few readers here, she has acquired
some ninety light-years away. But of course I can't tell her
that.

She came back a short while ago. "Did you like them?"
she asked.

"Very much. You have such sympathy for those who
suffer."

I think she expected me to invite her in. I was careful
not to look at her breasts this time.

The hotel is on West Twenty-third Street. It must be over
a hundred years old; the façade is practically baroque and
the interior shows a kind of genteel decay. The place has
a bohemian tradition. Most of its guests are permanent residents and many of them are artists, novelists, playwrights,
and such. I have lived here nine years. I know a number
of the residents by name, and they me, but I have dis-
couraged any real intimacy, naturally, and everyone has re-
spected that choice. I do not invite others into my room.
Sometimes I let myself be invited to visit theirs, since one
of my responsibilities on this world is to get to know something of the way Earthfolk live and think. Elizabeth is the
first to attempt to cross the invisible barrier of privacy I
surround myself with. I'm not sure how I'll handle that.
She moved in about three years ago; her attentions became

noticeable perhaps ten months back, and for the last five or six weeks she's been a great nuisance. Some kind of confrontation is inevitable: either I must tell her to leave me alone, or I will find myself drawn into a situation impossible to tolerate. Perhaps she'll find someone else to feel even sorrier for, before it comes to that.

My daily routine rarely varies. I rise at seven. First Feeding. Then I clean my skin (my outer one, the Earthskin, I mean) and dress. From eight to ten I transmit data to Homeworld. Then I go out for the morning field trip: talking to people, buying newspapers, often some library research. At one I return to my room. Second Feeding. I transmit data from two to five. Out again, perhaps to the theater, to a motion picture, to a political meeting. I must soak up the flavor of this planet. Often to saloons; I am equipped for ingesting alcohol, though of course I must get rid of it before it has been in my body very long, and I drink and listen and sometimes argue. At midnight back to my room. Third Feeding. Transmit data from one to four in the morning. Then three hours of sleep, and at seven the cycle begins anew. It is a comforting schedule. I don't know how many agents Homeworld has on Earth, but I like to think that I'm one of the most diligent and useful. I miss very little. I've done good service, and, as they say here, hard work is its own reward. I won't deny that I hate the physical discomfort of it and frequently give way to real despair over my isolation from my own kind. Sometimes I even think of asking for a transfer to Homeworld. But what would become of me there? What services could I perform? I have shaped my life to one end: that of dwelling among the Earthfolk and reporting on their ways. If I give that up, I am nothing.

Of course there is the physical pain. Which is considerable.

The gravitational pull of Earth is almost twice that of Homeworld. It makes for a leaden life for me. My inner organs always sagging against the lower rim of my carapace. My muscles cracking with strain. Every movement a willed effort. My heart in constant protest. In my eleven years I have as one might expect adapted somewhat to the conditions; I have toughened, I have thickened. I suspect that if I were transported instantly to Homeworld now I would be quite giddy, baffled by the lightness of everything. I would leap and soar and stumble, and might even miss this crushing pull of Earth. Yet I doubt that. I suffer here; at all times the weight oppresses me. Not to sound too self-pitying about it. I knew the conditions in advance. I was placed in simulated Earth gravity when I volunteered, and was given a chance to withdraw, and I decided to go anyway. Not realizing that a week under double gravity is not the same thing as a lifetime. I could always have stepped out of the simulation chamber. Not here. The eternal drag on every molecule of me. The pressure. My flesh is always in mourning.

And the outer body I must wear. This cunning disguise. Forever to be swaddled in thick masses of synthetic flesh, smothering me, engulfing me. The soft slippery slap of it against the self within. The elaborate framework that holds it erect, by which I make it move: a forest of struts and braces and servoactuators and cables, in the midst of which I must unendingly huddle, atop my little platform in the gut. Adopting one or another of various uncomfortable positions, constantly shifting and squirming, now jabbing myself on some awkwardly placed projection, now trying to make my inflexible body flexibly to bend. Seeing the world by periscope through mechanical eyes. Enwombed in this mountain of meat. It is a clever thing; it must look convincingly human, since no one has ever doubted me, and it ages ever so slightly from year to year, graying a bit at the temples, thickening a bit at the paunch. It walks. It talks. It takes in food and drink, when it has to. (And deposits them in a removable pouch near my leftmost arm.) And I within it. The hidden chess player; the invisible rider. If I dared, I would periodically strip myself of this cloak of flesh and crawl around my room in my own guise. But it is forbidden. Eleven years now and I have not been outside my protoplasmic housing. I feel sometimes that it has come to adhere to me, that it is no longer merely around me but by now a part of me.

In order to eat I must unseal it at the middle, a process that takes many minutes. Three times a day I unbutton myself so that I can stuff the food concentrates into my true gullet. Faulty design, I call that. They could just as easily have arranged it so I could pop the food into my Earth-mouth and have it land in my own digestive tract. I suppose the newer models have that. Excretion is just as troublesome for me; I unseal, reach in, remove the cubes of waste, seal my skin again. Down the toilet with them. A nuisance.

And the loneliness! To look at the stars and know Home-world is out there somewhere! To think of all the others, mating, chanting, dividing, abstracting, while I live out my days in this crumbling hotel on an alien planet, tugged down by gravity and locked within a cramped counterfeit body—always alone, always pretending that I am not what I am and that I am what I am not, spying, questioning, recording, reporting, coping with the misery of solitude, hunting for the comforts of philosophy—

In all of this there is only one real consolation, aside, that is, from the pleasure of knowing that I am of service to Homeworld. The atmosphere of New York City grows grimier every year. The streets are full of crude vehicles belching undigested hydrocarbons. To the Earthfolk, this stuff is pollution, and they mutter worriedly about it. To me it is joy. It is the only touch of Homeworld here: that sweet soup of organic compounds adrift in the air. It intoxicates me. I walk down the street breathing deeply, suck-ing the good molecules through my false nostrils to my authentic lungs. The natives must think I'm insane. Trip-ping on auto exhaust! Can I get arrested for overenthusi-astic public breathing? Will they pull me in for a mental checkup?

Elizabeth Cooke continues to waft wistful attentions at me. Smiles in the hallway. Hopeful gleam of the eyes. "Per-haps we can have dinner together some night soon, Mr.

Knecht. I know we'd have so much to talk about. And
maybe you'd like to see the new poems I've been doing."
She is trembling. Eyelids flickering tensely; head held rigid
on long neck. I know she sometimes has men in her room,
so it can't be out of loneliness or frustration that she's cul-
tivating me. And I doubt that she's sexually attracted to
my outer self. I believe I'm being accurate when I say that
women don't consider me sexually magnetic. No, she loves
me because she pities me. The sad shy bachelor at the end
of the hall, dear unhappy Mr. Knecht; can I bring some
brightness into his dreary life? And so forth. I think that's
how it is. Will I be able to go on avoiding her? Perhaps I
should move to another part of the city. But I've lived here
so long; I've grown accustomed to this hotel. Its easy ways
do much to compensate for the hardships of my post. And
my familiar room. The huge many-paned window; the
cracked green floor tiles in the bathroom; the lumpy patterns of replastering on the wall above my bed. The high
ceiling; the funny chandelier. Things that I love. But of
course I can't let her try to start an affair with me. We are
supposed to observe Earthfolk, not to get involved with
them. Our disguise is not that difficult to penetrate at close
range. I must keep her away somehow. Or flee.

Incredible! There is another of us in this very hotel!
   As I learned through accident. At one this afternoon, returning from my morning travels: Elizabeth in the lobby,
as though lying in wait for me, chatting with the manager.
Rides up with me in the elevator. Her eyes looking into
mine. "Sometimes I think you're afraid of me," she begins. "You mustn't be. That's the great tragedy of human
life, that people shut themselves up behind walls of fear
and never let anyone through, anyone who might care about
them and be warm to them. You've got no reason to be
afraid of me." I do, but how to explain that to her? To
sidestep prolonged conversation and possible entanglement
I get off the elevator one floor below the right one. Let
her think I'm visiting a friend. Or a mistress. I walk slowly
down the hall to the stairs, using up time, waiting so she

will be in her room before I go up. A maid bustles by me. She thrusts her key into a door on the left: a rare *faux pas* for the usually competent help here, she forgets to knock before going in to make up the room. The door opens and the occupant, inside, stands revealed. A stocky, muscular man, naked to the waist. "Oh, excuse me," the maid gasps, and backs out, shutting the door. But I have seen. My eyes are quick. The hairy chest is split, a dark gash three inches wide and some eleven inches long, beginning between the nipples and going past the navel. Visible within is the black shiny surface of a Homeworld carapace. My countryman, opening up for Second Feeding. Dazed, numbed, I stagger to the stairs and pull myself step by leaden step to my floor. No sign of Elizabeth. I stumble into my room and throw the bolt. Another of us here? Well, why not? I'm not the only one. There may be hundreds in New York alone. But in the same hotel? I remember, now, I've seen him occasionally: a silent, dour man, tense, hunted-looking, unsociable. No doubt I appear the same way to others. Keep the world at a distance. I don't know his name or what he is supposed to do for a living.

We are forbidden to make contact with fellow Homeworlders except in case of extreme emergency. Isolation is a necessary condition of our employment. I may not introduce myself to him; I may not seek his friendship. It is worse now for me, knowing that he is here, than when I was entirely alone. The things we could reminisce about! The friends we might have in common! We could reinforce one another's endurance of the gravity, the discomfort of our disguises, the vile climate. But no. I must pretend I know nothing. The rules. The harsh, unbending rules. I to go about my business, he his; if we meet, no hint of my knowledge must pass.

So be it. I will honor my vows. But it may be difficult.

He goes by the name of Swanson. Been living in the hotel eighteen months; a musician of some sort, according to the manager. "A very peculiar man. Keeps to himself; no small talk, never smiles. Defends his privacy. The other day a

maid barged into his room without knocking and I thought
he'd sue. Well, we get all sorts here." The manager thinks
he may actually be a member of one of the old European
royal families, living in exile, or something romantic. The
manager would be surprised.

I defend my privacy too. From Elizabeth, another assault
on it.

In the hall outside my room. "My new poems," she said.
"In case you're interested." And then: "Can I come in? I'd
read them to you. I love reading out loud." And: "Please
don't always seem so terribly afraid of me. I don't bite,
David. Really I don't. I'm quite gentle."

"I'm sorry."

"so am I." Anger, now, lurking in her shiny eyes, her
thin taut lips. "If you want me to leave you alone, say so,
I will. But I want you to know how cruel you're being. I
don't *demand* anything from you. I'm just offering some
friendship. And you're refusing. Do I have a bad smell?
Am I so ugly? Is it my poems you hate and you're afraid
to tell me?"

"Elizabeth—"

"We're only on this world such a short time. Why can't
we be kinder to each other while we are? To love, to share,
to open up. The reality trip. Communication, soul to soul."
Her tone changed. An artful shading. "For all I know,
women turn you off. I wouldn't put anybody down for that.
We've all got our ways. But it doesn't have to be a sexual thing, you and me. Just talk. Like, opening the channels. Please? Say no and I'll never bother you again, but
don't say no, please. That's like shutting a door on life,
David. And when you do that, you start to die a little."

Persistent. I should tell her to go to hell. But there is
the loneliness. There is her obvious sincerity. Her warmth,
her eagerness to pull me from my lunar isolation. Can there
be harm in it? Knowing that Swanson is nearby, so close
yet sealed from me by iron commandments, has intensified my sense of being alone. I can risk letting Elizabeth
get closer to me. It will make her happy; it may make me

happy; it could even yield information valuable to Homeworld. Of course I must still maintain certain barriers.

"I don't mean to be unfriendly. I think you've misunderstood, Elizabeth. I haven't really been rejecting you. Come in. Do come in." Stunned, she enters my room. The first guest ever. My few books; my modest furnishings; the ultrawave transmitter, impenetrably disguised as a piece of sculpture. She sits. Skirt far above the knees. Good legs, if I understand the criteria of quality correctly. I am determined to allow no sexual overtures. If she tries anything, I'll resort to—I don't know—hysteria. "Read me your new poems," I say. She opens her portfolio. Reads.

> In the midst of the hipster night of doubt and
> Emptiness, when the bad-trip god came to me with
> Cold hands, I looked up and shouted yes at the
> Stars. And yes and yes again. I groove on yes;
> The devil grooves on no. And I waited for you to
> Say yes, and at last you did. And the world said
> The stars said the trees said the grass said the
> Sky said the streets said yes and yes and yes—

She is ecstatic. Her face is flushed; her eyes are joyous. She has broken through to me. After two hours, when it becomes obvious that I am not going to ask her to go to bed with me, she leaves. Not to wear out her welcome. "I'm so glad I was wrong about you, David," she whispers. "I couldn't believe you were really a life-denier. And you're not." Ecstatic.

I am getting into very deep water.

We spend an hour or two together every night. Sometimes in my room, sometimes in hers. Usually she comes to me, but now and then, to be polite, I seek her out after Third Feeding. By now I've read all her poetry; we talk instead of the arts in general, politics, racial problems. She has a lively, well-stocked, disorderly mind. Though she probes constantly for information about me, she realizes how sensitive I am, and quickly withdraws when I parry her. Asking about my work; I reply vaguely that I'm doing research for a book, and when I don't amplify she drops it, though she tries again, gently, a few nights later. She drinks a lot of wine, and offers it to me. I nurse one glass through a whole visit. Often she suggests we go out together for dinner; I explain that I have digestive problems and prefer to eat alone, and she takes this in good grace but immediately resolves to help me overcome those problems, for soon she is asking me to eat with her again. There is an excellent Spanish restaurant right in the hotel, she says. She drops troublesome questions. Where was I born? Did I go to college? Do I have family somewhere? Have I ever been married? Have I published any of my writings? I improvise evasions. Nothing difficult about that, except that never before have I allowed anyone on Earth such sustained contact with me, so prolonged an opportunity to find inconsistencies in my pretended identity. What if she sees through?

And sex. Her invitations grow less subtle. She seems to think that we ought to be having a sexual relationship, simply because we've become such good friends. Not a matter of passion so much as one of communication: we talk, sometimes we take walks together, we should do *that* together too. But of course it's impossible. I have the external organs but not the capacity to use them. Wouldn't want her touching my false skin in any case. How to deflect her? If I declare myself impotent she'll demand a chance to try to cure me. If I pretend homosexuality she'll start some kind of straightening therapy. If I simply say she doesn't turn me on physically she'll be hurt. The sexual thing is a challenge to her, the way merely getting me to talk with her once was. She often wears the transparent pink shawl that reveals her breasts. Her skirts are hip high. She does herself with aphrodisiac perfumes. She grazes my body with hers whenever opportunity arises. The tension mounts; she is determined to have me.

I have said nothing about her in my reports to Homeworld. Though I do transmit some of the psychological data I have gathered by observing her.

"Could you ever admit you were in love with me?" she asked tonight.

And she asked, "Doesn't it hurt you to repress your feelings all the time? To sit there locked up inside yourself like a prisoner?"

And, "There's a physical side of life too, David. I don't mind so much the damage you're doing to me by ignoring it. But I worry about the damage you're doing to you."

Crossing her legs. Hiking her skirt even higher.

We are heading toward a crisis. I should never have let this begin. A torrid summer has descended on the city, and in hot weather my nervous system is always at the edge of eruption. She may push me too far. I might ruin everything. I should apply for transfer to Homeworld before I cause trouble. Maybe I should confer with Swanson. I think what is happening now qualifies as an emergency.

Elizabeth stayed past midnight tonight. I had to ask her finally to leave: work to do. An hour later she pushed an envelope under my door. Newest poems. Love poems. In a shaky hand: *"David you mean so much to me. You mean the stars and nebulas. Can't you let me show my love? Can't you accept happiness? Think about it. I adore you."*

What have I started?

103°F. today. The fourth successive day of intolerable heat. Met Swanson in the elevator at lunch time; nearly blurted the truth about myself to him. I must be more careful. But my control is slipping. Last night, in the worst of the heat, I was tempted to strip off my disguise. I could no longer stand being locked in here, pivoting and ducking to avoid all the machinery festooned about me. Resisted the temptation; just barely. Somehow I am more sensitive to the gravity too. I have the illusion that my carapace is developing cracks. Almost collapsed in the street this afternoon. All I need: heat exhaustion, whisked off to the hospital, routine fluoroscope exam. "You have a very odd skeletal structure, Mr. Knecht." Indeed. Dissecting me, next, with three thousand medical students looking on. And then the United Nations called in. Menace from outer space. Yes. I

must be more careful. I must be more careful. I must be
more—

Now I've done it. Eleven years of faithful service destroyed
in a single wild moment. Violation of the Fundamental
Rule. I hardly believe it. How was it possible that I—that
I—with my respect for my responsibilities—that I could
have—even considered, let alone actually done—

But the weather was terribly hot. The third week of the
heat wave. I was stifling inside my false body. And the
gravity: was New York having a gravity wave too? That
terrible pull, worse than ever. Bending my internal organs
out of shape. Elizabeth a tremendous annoyance: passionate, emotional, teary, poetic, giving me no rest, pleading
for me to burn with a brighter flame. Declaring her love
in sonnets, in rambling hip epics, in haiku. Spending two
hours in my room, crouched at my feet, murmuring about
the hidden beauty of my soul. "Open yourself and let love
come in," she whispered. "It's like giving yourself to God.
Making a commitment; breaking down all walls. Why not?
For love's sake, David, why not?" I couldn't tell her why
not, and she went away, but about midnight she was back
knocking at my door. I let her in. She wore an ankle-length
silk housecoat, gleaming, threadbare. "I'm stoned," she said
hoarsely, voice an octave too deep. "I had to bust three
joints to get up the nerve. But here I am. David, I'm sick
of making the turnoff trip. We've been so wonderfully
close, and then you won't go the last stretch of the way."
A cascade of giggles. "Tonight you will. Don't fail me.
Darling." Drops the housecoat. Naked underneath it: narrow waist, bony hips, long legs, thin thighs, blue veins
crossing her breasts. Her hair wild and kinky. A sorceress.
A seeress. Berserk. Approaching me, eyes slit-wide, mouth
open, tongue flickering snakily. How fleshless she is! Beads
of sweat glistening on her flat chest. Seizes my wrists; tugs
me roughly toward the bed. We tussle a little. Within my
false body I throw switches, nudge levers. I am stronger
than she is. I pull free, breaking her hold with an effort.
She stands flat-footed in front of me, glaring, eyes fiery.

So vulnerable, so sad in her nudity. And yet so fierce. "David! David! David!" Sobbing. Breathless. Pleading with her eyes and the tips of her breasts. Gathering her strength; now she makes the next lunge, but I see it coming and let her topple past me. She lands on the bed, burying her face in the pillow, clawing at the sheet. "Why? Why why why WHY?" she screams.

In a minute we will have the manager in here. With the police.

"Am I so hideous? I love you, David, do you know what that word means? Love. Love." Sits up. Turns to me. Imploring. "Don't reject me," she whispers. "I couldn't take that. You know, I just wanted to make you happy, I figured I could be the one, only I didn't realize how unhappy you'd make me. And you just stand there. And you don't say anything. What are you, some kind of machine?"

"I'll tell you what I am," I said.

That was when I went sliding into the abyss. All control lost; all prudence gone. My mind so slathered with raw emotion that survival itself means nothing. I must make things clear to her, is all. I must show her. At whatever expense. I strip off my shirt. She glows, no doubt thinking I will let myself be seduced. My hands slide up and down my bare chest, seeking the catches and snaps. I go through the intricate, cumbersome process of opening my body. Deep within myself something is shouting NO NO NO NO NO, but I pay no attention. The heart has its reasons.

Hoarsely: "Look, Elizabeth. Look at me. This is what I am. Look at me and freak out. The reality trip."

My chest opens wide.

I push myself forward, stepping between the levers and struts, emerging halfway from the human shell I wear. I have not been this far out of it since the day they sealed me in, on Homeworld. I let her see my gleaming carapace. I wave my eyestalks around. I allow some of my claws to show. "See? See? Big black crab from outer space. That's what you love, Elizabeth. That's what I am. David Knecht's just a costume, and this is what's inside it." I have gone insane. "You want reality? Here's reality, Elizabeth. What good is the Knecht body to you? It's a fraud. It's a machine. Come on, come closer. Do you want to kiss me? Should I get on you and make love?"

During this episode her face has displayed an amazing range of reactions. Open-mouthed disbelief at first, of course. And frozen horror: gagging sounds in throat, jaws agape, eyes wide and rigid. Hands fanned across breasts. Sudden modesty in front of the alien monster? But then, as the familiar Knecht-voice, now bitter and impassioned, continues to flow from the black thing within the sundered chest, a softening of her response. Curiosity. The poetic sensibility taking over. Nothing human is alien to me: Terence, quoted by Cicero. Nothing alien is alien to me. Eh? She will accept the evidence of her eyes. "What are you? Where did you come from?" And I say, "I've violated the Fundamental Rule. I deserve to be plucked and thinned. We're not supposed to reveal ourselves. If we get into some kind of accident that might lead to exposure, we're supposed to blow ourselves up. The switch is right here." She comes close and peers around me, into the cavern of David Knecht's chest. "From some other planet? Living here in disguise?" She understands the picture. Her shock is fading. She even laughs. "I've seen worse than you on acid," she says. "You don't frighten me now, David. David? Shall I go on calling you David?"

This is unreal and dreamlike to me. I have revealed myself, thinking to drive her away in terror; she is no longer aghast, and smiles at my strangeness. She kneels to get a better look. I move back a short way. Eyestalks fluttering: I am uneasy, I have somehow lost the upper hand in this encounter.

She says, "I knew you were unusual, but not like this. But it's all right. I can cope. I mean, the essential personality, that's what I fell in love with. Who cares that you're a crab-man from the Green Galaxy? Who cares that we can't be real lovers? I can make that sacrifice. It's your soul I dig, David. Go on. Close yourself up again. You don't look comfortable this way." The triumph of love. She will not abandon me, even now. Disaster. I crawl back into

Knecht and lift his arms to his chest to seal it. Shock is glazing my consciousness: the enormity, the audacity. What have I done? Elizabeth watches, awed, even delighted. At last I am together again. She nods. "Listen," she tells me, "you can trust me. I mean, if you're some kind of spy, checking out the Earth, I don't care. *I don't care.* I won't tell anybody. Pour it all out, David. Tell me about yourself. Don't you see, this is the biggest thing that ever happened to me. A chance to show that love isn't just physical, isn't just chemistry, that it's a soul trip, that it crosses not just racial lines but the lines of the whole damned species, the planet itself—"

It took several hours to get rid of her. A soaring, intense conversation, Elizabeth doing most of the talking. She putting forth theories of why I had come to Earth, me nodding, denying, amplifying, mostly lost in horror at my own perfidy and barely listening to her monologue. And the humidity turning me into rotting rags. Finally: "I'm down from the pot, David. And all wound up. I'm going out for a walk. Then back to my room to write for a while. To put this night into a poem before I lose the power of it. But I'll come to you again by dawn, all right? That's maybe five hours from now. You'll be here? You won't do anything foolish? Oh, I love you so much, David! Do you believe me? Do you?"

When she was gone I stood a long while by the window, trying to reassemble myself. Shattered. Drained. Remembering her kisses, her lips running along the ridge marking the place where my chest opens. The fascination of the abomination. She will love me even if I am crustaceous beneath.

I have to have help.

I went to Swanson's room. He was slow to respond to my knock; busy transmitting, no doubt. I could hear him within, but he didn't answer. "Swanson?" I called. "Swanson?" Then I added the distress signal in the Homeworld tongue. He rushed to the door. Blinking, suspicious. "It's

all right," I said. "Look, let me in. I'm in big trouble."
Speaking English, but I gave him the distress signal again.

"How did you know about me?" he asked.

"The day the maid blundered into your room while you
were eating, I was going by. I saw."

"But you aren't supposed to—"

"Except in emergencies. This is an emergency." He shut
off his ultrawave and listened intently to my story. Scowl-
ing. He didn't approve. But he wouldn't spurn me. I had
been criminally foolish, but I was of his kind, prey to the
same pains, the same loneliness, and he would help me.

"What do you plan to do now?" he asked. "You can't
harm her. It isn't allowed."

"I don't want to harm her. Just to get free of her. To
make her fall out of love with me."

"How? If showing yourself to her didn't—"

"Infidelity," I said. "Making her see that I love someone else. No room in my life for her. That'll drive her
away. Afterwards it won't matter that she knows: who'd
believe her story? The FBI would laugh and tell her to lay
off the LSD. But if I don't break her attachment to me
I'm finished."

"Love someone else? Who?"

"When she comes back to my room at dawn," I said,
"she'll find the two of us together, dividing and abstracting. I think that'll do it, don't you?"

So I deceived Elizabeth with Swanson.

The fact that we both wore male human identities was
irrelevant, of course. We went to the room and stepped out
of our disguises—a bold, dizzying sensation!—and suddenly we were just two Homeworlders again, receptive to
one another's needs. I left the door unlocked. Swanson and
I crawled up on my bed and began the chanting. How
strange it was, after these years of solitude, to feel those
vibrations again! And how beautiful. Swanson's vibrissae
touching mine. The interplay of harmonies. An underlying
sternness to his technique—he was contemptuous of me
for my idiocy, and rightly so—but once we passed from

the chanting to the dividing all was forgiven, and as we moved into the abstracting it was truly sublime. We climbed through an infinity of climactic emptyings. Dawn crept upon us and found us unwilling to halt even for rest.

A knock at the door. Elizabeth.

"Come in," I said.

A dreamy, ecstatic look on her face. Fading instantly when she saw the two of us entangled on the bed. A questioning frown. "We've been mating," I explained. "Did you think I was a complete hermit?" She looked from Swanson to me, from me to Swanson. Hand over her mouth. Eyes anguished. I turned the screw a little tighter. "I couldn't stop you from falling in love with me, Elizabeth. But I really do prefer my own kind. As should have been obvious."

"To have her here now, though—when you knew I was coming back—"

"Not *her*, exactly. Not *him* exactly either, though."

"—so cruel, David! To ruin such a beautiful experience." Holding forth sheets of paper with shaking hands. "A whole sonnet cycle," she said. "About tonight. How beautiful it was, and all. And now—and now—" Crumpling the pages. Hurling them across the room. Turning. Running out, sobbing furiously. Hell hath no fury like. "*David!*" A smothered cry. And slamming the door.

She was back in ten minutes. Swanson and I hadn't quite finished donning our bodies yet; we were both still unsealed. As we worked, we discussed further steps to take: he felt honor demanded that I request a transfer back to Homeworld, having terminated my usefulness here through tonight's indiscreet revelation. I agreed with him to some degree but was reluctant to leave. Despite the bodily torment of life on Earth I had come to feel I belonged here. Then Elizabeth entered, radiant.

"I mustn't be so possessive," she announced. "So bourgeois. So conventional. I'm willing to share my love." Embracing Swanson. Embracing me. "A *ménage à trois*," she said. "I won't mind that you two are having a physical relationship. As long as you don't shut me out of your lives completely. I mean, David, we could never have been physical anyway, right, but we can have the other aspects of love, and we'll open ourselves to your friend also. Yes? Yes? Yes?"

Swanson and I both put in applications for transfer, he to Africa, me to Homeworld. It would be some time before we received a reply. Until then we were at her mercy. He was blazingly angry with me for involving him in this, but what choice had I had? Nor could either of us avoid Elizabeth. We were at her mercy. She bathed both of us in shimmering waves of tender emotion; wherever we turned, there she was, incandescent with love. Lighting up the darkness of our lives. You poor lonely creatures. Do you suffer much in our gravity? What about the heat? And the winters. Is there a custom of marriage on your planet? Do you have poetry?

A happy threesome. We went to the theater together. To concerts. Even to parties in Greenwich Village. "My friends," Elizabeth said, leaving no doubt in anyone's mind that she was living with both of us. Faintly scandalous doings; she loved to seem daring. Swanson was sullenly obliging, putting up with her antics but privately haranguing me for subjecting him to all this. Elizabeth got out another mimeographed booklet of poems, dedicated to both of us. *Triple Tripping*, she called it. Flagrantly erotic. I quoted a few of the poems in one of my reports to Homeworld, then lost heart and hid the booklet in the closet. "Have you heard about your transfer yet?" I asked Swanson at least twice a week. He hadn't. Neither had I.

Autumn came. Elizabeth, burning her candle at both ends, looked gaunt and feverish. "I have never known such happiness," she announced frequently, one hand clasping Swanson, the other me. "I never think about the strangeness of you anymore. I think of you only as people. Sweet, wonderful, lonely people. Here in the darkness of this horrid city." And she once said, "What if everybody here is like you, and I'm the only one who's really human? But

that's silly. You must be the only ones of your kind here.
The advance scouts. Will your planet invade ours? I do
hope so! Set everything to rights. The reign of love and
reason at last!"

"How long will this go on?" Swanson muttered.

At the end of October his transfer came through. He left
without saying good-bye to either of us and without leaving a forwarding address. Nairobi? Addis Ababa? Kin-
shasa?"

I had grown accustomed to having him around to share the
burden of Elizabeth. Now the full brunt of her affection
fell on me. My work was suffering; I had no time to file
my reports properly. And I lived in fear of her gossiping.
What was she telling her Village friends? ("You know
David? He's not really a man, you know. Actually inside
him there's a kind of crab-thing from another solar system. But what does that matter? Love's a universal phenomenon. The truly loving person doesn't draw limits
around the planet.") I longed for my release. To go home;
to accept my punishment; to shed my false skin. To empty
my mind of Elizabeth.

My reply came through the ultrawave on November 13.
Application denied. I was to remain on Earth and continue
my work as before. Transfers to Homeworld were granted
only for reasons of health.

I debated sending a full account of my treason to Homeworld and thus bringing about my certain recall. But I hesitated, overwhelmed with despair. Dark brooding seized me.
"Why so sad?" Elizabeth asked. What could I say? That
my attempt at escaping from her had failed? "I love you,"
she said. "I've never felt so *real* before." Nuzzling against
my cheek. Fingers knotted in my hair. A seductive whisper. "David, open yourself up again. Your chest, I mean.
I want to see the inner you. To make sure I'm not frightened of it. Please? You've only let me see you once." And
then, when I had: "May I kiss you, David?" I was appalled.

But I let her. She was unafraid. Transfigured by happiness. She is a cosmic nuisance, but I fear I'm getting to like her.

Can I leave her? I wish Swanson had not vanished. I need advice.

Either I break with Elizabeth or I break with Homeworld. This is absurd. I find new chasms of despondency every day. I am unable to do my work. I have requested a transfer once again, without giving details. The first snow of the winter today.

Application denied.

"When I found you with Swanson," she said, "it was a terrible shock. An even bigger blow than when you first came out of your chest. I mean it was startling to find out you weren't human, but it didn't hit me in any emotional way, it didn't threaten me. But then, to come back a few hours later and find you with one of your own kind, to know that you wanted to shut me out, that I had no place in your life—Only we worked it out, didn't we?" Kissing me. Tears of joy in her eyes. How did this happen? Where did it all begin? Existence was once so simple. I have tried to trace the chain of events that brought me from there to here, and I cannot. I was outside of my false body for eight hours today. The longest spell so far. Elizabeth is talking of going to the islands with me for the winter. A secluded cottage that her friends will make available. Of course, I must not leave my post without permission. And it takes months simply to get a reply.

Let me admit the truth: I love her.

January 1. The new year begins. I have sent my resignation to Homeworld and have destroyed my ultrawave equipment. The links are broken. Tomorrow, when the city offices are open, Elizabeth and I will go to get the marriage license.

DECENCY

Robert Reed

*Robert Reed sold his first story in 1986, and quickly estab-
lished himself as a frequent contributor to* The Magazine of
Fantasy and Science Fiction *and* Asimov's Science Fiction,
as well as selling many stories to Science Fiction Age, Universe, New Destinies, Tomorrow, Synergy, Starlight, *and
elsewhere. Reed is almost as prolific as a novelist as he is
as a short story writer, having produced eight novels to date,
including* The Leeshore, The Hormone Jungle, Black Milk,
The Remarkables, Down the Bright Way, Beyond the Veil
of Stars, An Exaltation of Larks, *and* Beneath the Gated
Sky. *His most recent book is his long-overdue first collection,* The Dragons of Springplace. *He lives in Lincoln, Nebraska, where he's at work on a novel-length version of his
1997 novella, "Marrow."*

*In the ingenious story that follows, he explores the pos-
sibility that when star-travelling aliens do finally contact us,
it may not be our leader they want to be taken to, nor our
best and brightest that they're interested in . . .*

The venerable old Hubble telescope saw it first.

A silvery splash moving against the stars, the object
proved enormous—larger than some worlds—and it was
faster than anything human-built, still out among the comets
but coming, the first touch of cold light just beginning to
brake its terrific fall.

"It's a light sail," astronomers announced, giddy as children, drunk by many means. "Definitely artificial. Probably automated. No crew, minimal mass. Photons move the
thing, and even accounting for deceleration, it's going to
make a quick flyby of the Earth."

By the time the sail crossed Saturn's orbit, a three-inch reflector cost its weight in platinum. Amateur astronomers were quitting their day jobs in order to spend nights plotting trajectories. Novice astronomers, some armed with nothing but binoculars or rifle sights, risked frostbite for the privilege of a glimpse. But it was the professionals who remained the most excited: every topflight facility in the northern hemisphere studied the object, measuring its mass, its albedo, its vibrations, and its damage—ragged mile-wide punctures scattered across its vast surface, probably stemming from collisions with interstellar comets. The sail's likely point of origin was a distant G-class sun; its voyage must have taken a thousand years, perhaps more. Astronomers tried to contact the automated pilot. Portions of the radio spectrum were cleared voluntarily for better listening. Yet nothing was heard, ever. The only sign of a pilot was a subtle, perhaps accidental, twisting of the sail, the pressure of sunlight altering its course, the anticipated flyby of the Earth becoming an impact event.

Insubstantial as a soap bubble, the sail offered little risk to people or property. Astronomers said so. Military and political people agreed with them. And despite Hollywood conventions, there was no great panic among the public. No riots. No religious upheavals. A few timid souls took vacations to New Zealand and Australia, but just as many southerners came north to watch the spectacle. There were a few ugly moments involving the susceptible and the emotionally troubled; but generally people responded with curiosity, a useful fatalism, and the gentle nervousness that comes with a storm front or a much-anticipated football game.

The world watched the impact. Some people used television, others bundled up and stepped outdoors. In the end, the entire northern sky was shrouded with the brilliant sail. In the end, as the Earth's gravity embraced it, scientists began to find structures within its thin, thin fabric. Like a spiderweb, but infinitely more complex, there were fibers and veins that led to a central region—a square mile of indecipherable machinery—and the very last images showed damaged machines, the sail's tiny heart wounded by a series of swift murderous collisions.

The impact itself was beautiful. Ghostly fires marked where the leading edge bit into the stratosphere. Without sound or fuss, the sail evaporated into a gentle rain of atomized metals. But the spiderweb structures were more durable, weathering the impact, tens of thousands of miles of material falling over three continents and as many oceans, folding and fracturing on their way down, the most massive portions able to kill sparrows and crack a few windows and roof tiles.

No planes were flying at the time, as a precaution. Few people were driving. Subsequent figures showed that human death rates had dropped for that critical hour, a worldly caution in effect; then they lifted afterward, parties and carelessness taking their inevitable toll.

The sail's central region detached itself at the end, then broke into still smaller portions. One portion crashed along the shore of Lake Superior. The Fox affiliate in Duluth sent a crew, beating the military by twenty minutes. The only witness to the historic event was a temperamental bull moose. Only when it was driven off did the crew realize that the sail wasn't an automated probe. A solitary crew member lay within a fractured diamond shell, assorted life-support equipment heaped on all sides. Despite wounds and the fiery crash, it was alive—an organism built for gravity, air, and liquid water. A trembling camera showed the world its first genuine alien sprawled out on the forest floor, a dozen jointed limbs reaching for its severed web, and some kind of mouth generating a clear, strong, and pitiful wail that was heard in a billion homes.

A horrible piercing wail.

The scream of a soul in perfect agony.

Caleb was one of the guards supplied by the U.S. Marines.

Large in a buttery way, with close-cropped hair and tiny suspicious eyes, Caleb was the kind of fellow who would resemble a guard even without his uniform or bulky side arm. His service record was flawless. Of average intellect and little creativity, nonetheless he possessed a double dose of what, for lack of a better word, could be called shrewdness.

Working the security perimeter, he helped control access to the alien. *The bug*, as he dubbed it, without a shred of originality. Twice in the first two days he caught unauthorized civilians attempting to slip inside—one using a false ID, the other hiding inside bales of computer paper. Late on the third day he found a fellow guard trying to smuggle out a piece of the bug's shell. "It's a chunk of diamond," was the man's pitiful defense. "Think what it's worth, Caleb. And I'll give you half . . . what do you say . . . ?"

Nothing. He saw no reason to respond, handcuffing the man—a sometime acquaintance—then walking him back toward the abrupt little city that had sprung up on the lakeshore. Double-walled tents were kept erect with pressurized air and webs of rope, each tent lit and heated, the rumble of generators and compressors making the scene appear busier than it was. Most people were asleep; it was three in the morning. A quarter moon hung overhead, the January stars like gemstones, brighter and more perfect than the battered diamond shard that rode against Caleb's hip. But the sky barely earned a glance, and despite the monumental events of the last weeks and days, the guard felt no great fortune for being where he was. His job was to deliver the criminal to his superiors, which he did, and he did it without distraction, acting with a rigorous professionalism.

The duty officer, overworked and in lousy spirits, didn't want the shard. "You take it back to the science people," he ordered. "I'll call ahead. They'll be watching for you."

Mistrust came with the job; Caleb expected nothing less from his superior.

The bug was at the center of the city, under a converted circus tent. Adjacent tents and trailers housed the scientists and their machinery. One facility was reserved for the press, but it was almost empty, what with the hour and the lack of fresh events. Overflow equipment was stored at the back of the tent, half-unpacked and waiting to be claimed by experts still coming from the ends of the world. Despite the constant drone of moving air, Caleb could hear the bug now and again. A wail, a whimper. Then another, deeper wail. Just for a moment, the sound caused him to turn his head, listening now, feeling something that he couldn't name, something without a clear source. An emotion, liquid and intense, made him pay close attention. But then the bug fell silent, or at least it was quieter than the manmade wind, and the guard was left feeling empty, a little cold, confused and secretly embarrassed.

He was supposed to meet a Dr. Lee in the press tent; those were his orders, but nobody was waiting for him.

Caleb stood under a swaying fluorescent light, removing the diamond shard from his pocket and examining it for the first time. Cosmic dust and brutal radiations had worn at it; he'd seen prettier diamonds dangling from men's ears. What made it valuable? Why care half this much about the bug? The Earth had never been in danger. The sail's lone passenger was dying. Everyone who visited it said it was just a matter of time. To the limits of his vision, Caleb could see nothing that would significantly change people's lives. Scientists would build and destroy reputations. Maybe some fancy new machines would come from their work. Maybe. But the young man from central Missouri understood that life would go on as it always had, and so why get all worked up in the first place?

"You've got something for me?"

Caleb looked up, finding a middle-aged woman walking toward him. A very tired, red-eyed woman. She was one of the nation's top surgeons, although he didn't know or particularly care.

"I'll take that for you—"

"Sorry, ma'am." He had read her ID tag, adding, "I'm expecting Marvin Lee. Material studies."

"I know. But Marvin's busy, and I like the press tent's coffee. Since I was coming this way, I volunteered."

"But I can't give it to you. Ma'am." Caleb could see how the shard had been stolen in the first place.

Red eyes rolled, amused with his paranoia.

Not for the first time, he felt frustration. No sense of protocol here; no respect for sensible rules. The name on the ID was Hilton. Showing none of his feeling, Caleb said, "Perhaps you could take me to him, Dr. Hilton. If it's no trouble."

"I guess." She poured black coffee into a Styrofoam cup, a knowing little smile appearing. "Now I get it. You're after a trip to the big tent, aren't you?"

Hadn't he just said that?

A sly wink and she said, "Come on then. I'll take you."

They left the press tent, the doctor without a coat and the guard not bothering to zip his up. A twenty-yard walk, then they entered the bug's enormous tent, three sets of sealed doors opening for them. The last pair of guards waved them on without a look. Caleb smelled liquor, for just a moment, and as he stepped through the door he was wondering whom to warn about this serious breach of the rules—

—and there was a horrible, horrible wail.

Caleb stopped in midstride, his breath coming up short, a bolt of electricity making his spine straighten up and his face reflexively twist as if in agony.

Turning, showing the oddest half-grin, Dr. Hilton inquired, "Is something wrong?"

It took him a moment to say, "No, I'm fine."

"But it's your first time here, isn't it?"

What was her point?

"You've heard stories about it, haven't you?"

"Some."

"And you're curious. You want to see it for yourself."

"Not particularly," he answered, with conviction.

Yet she didn't believe him. She seemed to enjoy herself. "Marvin's on the other side. Stay with me."

Caleb obeyed. Walking between banks of instruments, he noticed that the technicians wore bulky, heavily padded headphones to blunt the screams. Now and again, at unpredictable moments, the bug would roar, and again Caleb would pause, feeling a little ill for that terrible moment when the air itself seemed to rip apart. Then just as suddenly there was silence, save for the clicking machines and hushed, respectful voices. In silence, Caleb found himself wondering if the guards drank because of the sounds. Not that he could condone it, but he could anticipate their excuse. Then he stepped off a floor of particle boards, onto rocky earth punctuated with tree stumps, and in the middle of that cleared patch of forest, stretched out on its apparent back, was the very famous bug. Not close enough to touch, but nearly so. Not quite dead, but not quite alive, either.

There was some kind of face on a wounded appendage, a silent mouth left open, and what seemed to be eyes that were huge and strange and haunted. Dark liquid centers stared helplessly at the tent's high ceiling. It was no bug, Caleb realized. It didn't resemble an insect, or any mammal, for that matter. Were those legs? Or arms? Did it eat with that flexible mouth? And how did it breathe? Practical questions kept offering themselves, but he didn't ask any of them. Instead, he turned to the surgeon, dumbfounded. "Why bring me here?" he inquired.

She was puzzled. "I'm sorry, isn't that what you wanted? I assumed seeing Marvin was an excuse."

Not at all.

"You know," she informed him, "anyone else would give up a gland to be here. To stand with us."

True. He didn't quite see why, but he knew it was true.

Another pair of guards watched them from nearby. They knew the doctor. They had seen her come and go dozens of times, struggling to help her patient. In the course of three days, they had watched her face darken, her humor growing cynical, and her confidence languishing as every effort failed. They felt sorry for her. Maybe that was why they allowed Caleb to stand too close to government property. The soldier lacked clearance, but he was with Hilton, and he was safe looking, and how could this tiny indiscretion hurt? It made no sense to be hard-asses. Glancing at their watches, they measured the minutes before their shift ended . . . and once more that gruesome critter gave a big roar . . . !

"It's in pain," Caleb muttered afterward.

The doctor looked at him, then away. "Are you sure?"

What a strange response. Of course it was in pain. He searched for the usual trappings of hospitals and illness. Where were the dangling bags of medicine and food? "Are you giving it morphine?" he asked, fully expecting to be told "Of course."

But instead Hilton said, "Why? Why morphine?"

As if speaking to an idiot, Caleb said each word with care. "In order to stop the pain, naturally."

"Except morphine is an intricate, highly specific compound. It kills the hurt in Marines, but probably not in aliens." She waited a moment, then gestured. "You've got more in common—biochemically speaking—with these birch trees. Or a flu virus, for that matter."

He didn't understand, and he said so.

"This creature has DNA," she explained, "but its genetic codes are all different. It makes different kinds of amino acids, and very unusual proteins. Enzymes nothing like ours. And who knows what kinds of neurotransmitters."

The alien's mouth opened, and Caleb braced himself.

It closed, and he sighed.

"We've found organs," said Hilton, sipping her coffee. "Some we know, some we don't. Three hearts, but two are punctured. Dead. The scar tissue shows radiation tracks. Count them, and we get an estimate of the tissue's age. A thousand years, maybe. Which means it was injured when it flew through a dust storm, probably on its way out of the last solar system."

The alien was about the size of a good riding horse. It seemed larger only because of its peculiar flattened shape. The wounds were surgically precise holes, wisps of dust having pierced diamond as well as flesh. Knowing what ballistic wounds meant, he asked, "How is it even alive?"

"Implanted machinery, in part. Most of the machinery isn't working, but what does is repairing some tissues, some

organs." She took a big swallow of coffee. "But its wounds
may not have been the worst news. Marvin and my other
esteemed colleagues think that the cosmic buckshot crippled most of the sail's subsystems. The reactors, for instance. There were three of them, a city block square each,
thick as a playing card. Without power, the creature had
no choice but to turn *everything* off, including itself. A des-
peration cryogenic freeze, probably for most of the voyage. And it didn't wake until it was over our heads, almost.
Its one maneuver might have been a doomed skydiver's attempt to strike a mound of soft hay."

Caleb turned and asked, "Will it live?"

Hilton was tiring of the game. "Eventually, no. There's
talk about another freeze, but we can't even freeze humans
yet."

"I said it was in pain, and you said, 'Are you sure?' "

"It's not us. We can't measure its moods, or how it feels.
Empirical evidence is lacking—"

As if to debate the point, the alien screamed again. The
eyes kept shaking afterward, the closing mouth making a
low wet sound. Watching the eyes, Caleb asked, "Do you
think it means, 'Hi, how are you?' "

Hilton didn't respond. She didn't have time.

Again the alien's mouth opened, black eyes rippling as
the air was torn apart; and Caleb, hands to his ears and
undistracted by nasty gray abstractions, knew exactly what
that horrible noise meant.

Not a doubt in him, his decision already made.

For three days and several hours, a worldwide controversy
had been brewing, sweeping aside almost every other
human concern.

What should be done with the alien?

Everyone who would care knew about the wounds and
screams. Almost everyone had seen those first horrid tapes
of the creature, and they'd watched the twice-daily news
conferences, including Dr. Hilton's extended briefings. No
more network cameras were being allowed inside the central tent, on the dubious ground of cleanliness. (How did

you infect such an odd creature with ordinary human pathogens?) But the suffering continued, without pause, and it was obvious that the people in charge were overmatched. At least according to those on the outside.

The United Nations should take over, or some trustworthy civilian agency. Said many.

But which organization would be best?

And assuming another caretaker, what kinds of goals would it try to accomplish?

Some observers wanted billions spent in a crash program, nothing more important now than the alien's total recovery. Others argued for a kind death, then a quick disposal of the body, all evidence of the tragedy erased in case a second sail-creature came searching for its friend. But the Earth was littered with wreckage; people couldn't hope to salvage every incriminating fiber. That led others to argue that nothing should be done, allowing Nature and God their relentless course. And should death come, the body could be preserved in some honorable way, studied or not, and should more aliens arrive in some distant age—unlikely as that seemed—they could see that people were decent, had done their best, and no blame could possibly be fixed to them.

Anne Hilton despised all those options. She wanted to heal her patient, but crash programs were clumsy and expensive, and she was a pragmatic doctor who realized that human patients would suffer as a result, no money left for their mortal ills. Besides, she doubted if there was time. The fiery crash had plainly damaged the tissue-repairing systems. And worse, there was no easy way to give the creature its simplest needs. Its oxygen use was falling. Nitrogen levels were building in the slow, clear blood. Teams of biochemists had synthesized a few simple sugars, amino acids, and other possible metabolites; yet the creature's success with each was uneven, the intravenous feedings canceled for now.

The truth told, Hilton's patient was collapsing at every level, and all that remained for the doctor was some of the oldest, most venerable skills.

Patience.

Prayer.

And whatever happened: "Do no harm."

For the next days, months, and years, Dr. Anne Hilton would wrestle with her memories, trying to decide why she had acted as she did that morning. Why get coffee at that particular moment? Why offer to retrieve the diamond shard? And why invite Caleb on that impromptu tour?

The last question had many answers. She had assumed that he wanted a tour, that he was being stubborn about the shard for no other reason. And because he was a Marine, he represented authority, order, and ignorance. She'd already had several collisions with his sort, politicians and other outsiders without enough mental activity to form a worthy thought. Maybe she'd hoped that shocking him would help her mood. She'd assumed that he was a big thoughtless lump of a man, the very worst kind . . . ! Imagine. Stationed here for three days, guarding something wondrous, and precious, yet he didn't have the feeblest grasp of what was happening . . . !

The last scream done, Caleb asked, "Where's its brain?"

She glanced at him, noticing a change in his eyes.

"Doctor?" he asked. "Do you know where it does its thinking?"

She was suddenly tired of dispensing free knowledge, yet something in his voice made her answer. A sip of coffee, an abbreviated gesture. Then she said, "Below the face. Inside what you'd call its chest," and with that she turned away.

She should have watched him.

She could have been more alert, like any good doctor, reading symptoms and predicting the worst.

But an associate was approaching, some nonvital problem needing her best guess. She didn't guess that anything was wrong until she saw her associate's face change. One moment he was smiling. Then he became suddenly confused. Then, horrified. And only after that did she bother to ask herself why that Marine would want to know where to find the brain.

Too late, she wheeled around.

Too late and too slow, she couldn't hope to stop him, or even slow him. Caleb had removed his side arm from its holster, one hand holding the other's wrist, the first shot delivered to the chest's exact center, missing the brain by an inch. Security cameras on all sides recorded the event, in aching detail. The alien managed to lift one limb, two slender fingers reaching for the gun. Perhaps it was defending itself. Or perhaps, as others have argued, it simply was trying to adjust its killer's aim. Either way, the gesture was useless. And Hilton was superfluous. Caleb emptied his clip in short order, achieving a perfectly spaced set of holes. Two bullets managed to do what bits of relativistic dust couldn't, devastating a mind older than civilization. And the eyes, never human yet obviously full of intelligence, stared up at the tent's high ceiling, in thanks, perhaps, seeing whatever it is that only the doomed can see.

There was a trial.

The charge, after all the outcry and legal tap dancing, was reduced to felony destruction of federal property. Caleb offered no coordinated defense. His attorneys tried to argue for some kind of alien mind control, probably wishing for the benefit of the doubt. But Caleb fired them for trying it, then went on the stand to testify on his own behalf. In a quiet, firm voice, he described his upbringing in the Ozarks and the beloved uncle who had helped raised him, taking him hunting and fishing, instructing him in the moral codes of the decent man.

" 'Aim to kill,' he taught me. 'Don't be cruel to any creature, no matter how lowborn.' " Caleb stared at the camera, not a dab of doubt entering his steady voice. "When I see suffering, and when there's no hope, I put an end to it. Because that's what's right." He gave examples of his work: Small game. A lame horse. And dogs, including an arthritic Labrador that he'd raised from a pup. Yet that wasn't nearly enough reason, and he knew it. He paused for a long moment, wiping his forehead with his right palm. Then with a different voice, he said, "I was a senior, in high school, and my uncle got the cancer. In his lungs, his bones. Every-where." He was quieter, if anything. Firmer. More in con-trol, if that was possible. "It wasn't the cancer that killed him. His best shotgun did. His doctor and the sheriff talked it over, deciding that he must have held the twelve gauge up like this, then tripped the trigger like this." An imagi-nary gun lay in his outstretched arms, the geometry diffi-cult even for a healthy oversized man. For the first time, the voice broke. But not badly and not for long. "People didn't ask questions," Caleb explained, arms dropping. "They knew what my uncle was feeling. What he wanted. They knew how we were, the two of us. And where I come from, decent people treat people just as good as they'd treat a sick farm cat. Dying stinks, but it might as well be done fast. And that's all I've got to say about that."

He was sentenced to five years of hard labor, serving every month without incident, without complaint, obeying the strict rules well enough that the prison guards voted him to be a model citizen of their intense little community.

Released, Caleb returned to Missouri, taking over the daily operations of the impoverished family farm.

Networks and new services pleaded for interviews; none were granted.

Some idiots tried sneaking onto his property. They were met by dogs and a silent ex-Marine—lean as a fence post now—and the famous shotgun always cradled in his wiry long arms.

He never spoke to trespassers.

His dogs made his views known.

Eventually, people tired of running in the woods. Pub-lic opinions began to soften. The alien had been dying, it was decided. Nothing good could have been done for it. And if the Marine wasn't right in what he did, at least he'd acted according to his conscience.

Caleb won his privacy.

There were years when no one came uninvited.

Then it was a bright spring day twenty-some years after the killing, and a small convoy drove in past the warning signs, through the tall barbed-wire gates, and right up to the simple farmhouse. As it happened, a Marine colonel had been selected to oversee the operation. Flanked by government people, he met with the middle-aged farmer, and with a crisp no-nonsense voice said, "Pack your bags, soldier. But I'll warn you, you don't need to bring much."

"Where am I going?"

"I'll give you one guess."

Something had happened; that much was obvious. With a tight, irritated voice, Caleb told the colonel, "I want you all off my land. Now."

"Goddamn! You really don't know, do you?" The colonel gave a big laugh, saying, "Nothing else is on the news anymore."

"I don't have a television," said Caleb.

"Or a family anymore. And precious few friends." He spoke as if he'd just read the man's file. Then he pointed skyward, adding, "I just assumed you'd have seen it. After dusk is a good time—"

"I get to bed early," was Caleb's excuse. Then a sudden hard chill struck him. He leaned against his doorjamb, thinking that he understood, the fight suddenly starting to leave him. "There's another sail, isn't there? That's what this is all about."

"One sail? Oh, that's wonderful!" All the government men were giggling. "Make it three hundred and eighteen sails, and that's just *today's* count!"

"An armada of them," said someone.

"Gorgeous, gorgeous," said another, with feeling.

Caleb tried to gather himself. Then with a calm, almost inaudible voice, he asked, "But what do you want with me?"

"We don't want you," said the quick reply.

No?

"*They* do." The colonel kept smiling. "*They* asked specifically for *you*, soldier."

He knew why. Not a doubt in him.

Caleb muttered, "Just a minute," and dropped back into the house, as if to get ready.

The colonel waited for a couple seconds, then knew better. He burst through the door and tried to guess where Caleb would have gone. Upstairs? No, there was an ominous *click* from somewhere on his right. Caleb was in a utility room, his shotgun loaded and cocked, the double barrels struggling to reach his long forehead; and the colonel grabbed the gun's butt and trigger, shouting, "No! Wait!" Then half a dozen government men were helping him, dark suits left rumpled and torn. But they wrestled the shotgun away from their charge, and the colonel stood over him, asking, "What were you thinking? Why in hell would you—?"

"I killed one of theirs," Caleb said. "Now they want their revenge. Isn't that it?"

"Not close." The colonel was too breathless to put much into his laugh. "In fact, I don't think you could be more wrong, soldier. The last thing they want to kill is you . . . !"

Caleb was packed into a new shuttle and taken to orbit, an ungainly lunar tug carrying him the rest of the way. There was a new moon in a high, safe orbit. One of the sail creatures had captured a modest nickel-iron asteroid and brought it there. Healthy and whole, the creature scarcely resembled its dead brother. Its vast sail was self-repairing, and it possessed an astonishing grace, superseding the most delicate butterfly. Partially folded, riding the captive asteroid, it swallowed the tug, guiding it into a docking facility built recently from the native ores. Other tugs had brought up dignitaries, scientists, and a complete medical team. Everyone had gathered in the central room. As the onetime guard drifted into view, there was applause—polite but not quite enthusiastic—and from some of the faces, envy. Incandescent green envy.

Anne Hilton was among that number.

Old and long retired, she was present at the request of the sail creatures. Caleb didn't recognize her at first glance. She shook his hand, tried smiling, then introduced him to each member of her team. "We're just advisers," she informed him. "Most of the work will be done by our host."

Caleb flinched, just for a moment.

Their "host" didn't resemble the first alien, save for the artificial trappings. Sail creatures were an assemblage of sentient species. Perhaps dozens of them. Caleb had seen photographs of this particular species: fishlike; human-sized; blackish gills flanking an unreadable carpish mouth. It had disgusted him at first glance, and the memory of it disgusted him now.

Dr. Hilton asked, "Would you like to meet her?"

He spoke honestly, saying, "Not particularly."

"But she wants to meet you." A cutting smile, then she promised, "I'll take you to her. Come on."

They had done this before, more than two decades ago. She had taken him to meet an alien, and for at least this moment she could feel superior in the same way. In charge.

There was a narrow tunnel with handholds, toeholds.

Suddenly they were alone, and with a soft, careful voice, Caleb confessed, "I don't understand. Why *me*?"

"Why not you?" Hilton growled.

"I'm not smart. Or clever. Not compared to everyone else up here, I'm not."

She lifted her eyebrows, watching him.

"These aliens should pick a scientist. Someone who cares about stars and planets. . . ."

"You're going to be young again." Hilton said the words as if delivering a curse. "It'll take her some time to learn our genetics, but she's promised me that she can reverse the aging process. A twenty-year-old body again."

"I know."

"As for being smart," she said, "don't worry. She's going to tease your neurons into dividing, like inside a baby's head. By the time you leave us, you'll be in the top ninety-nine percentile among humans. And as creative as can be."

He nodded, already aware of the general plan.

Then they were near the entrance to *her* chamber. Hilton stopped, one hand resting on Caleb's nearer arm, a firm and level voice telling him, "I would do anything—almost—for the chance to go where you're going. To live for aeons, to see all those wondrous places!"

In a quiet, almost conspiratorial tone, he said, "I'll tell
her to take you instead of me."

Hilton knew that he meant it, and she grew even an-
grier.

Then again, Caleb asked, "Why *me*?"

"They think they know you, I guess. They've been studying our telecommunications noise for years, and you certainly earned their attention." Her withered face puckered,
tasting something sour. "You acted out of a kind of moral-
ity. You didn't hesitate, and you didn't make excuses. Then
you accepted the hardships of prison, and the hardships
that came afterward. Being able to live alone like you
did . . . well, that's a rare talent for our species, and it's in-
valuable. . . ."

He gave a little nod, a sigh.

"These creatures don't treasure intelligence," she exclaimed. "That's something they can grow, in vats. The
same with imagination. But there's some quality in you
that makes you worth taking. . . ."

A dull ocher button would open the hatch.

Hilton reached for it, and her hand was intercepted, frail
bones restrained by an unconscious strength.

Caleb put his face close to hers, and whispered.

"What I did for that alien," he confessed, "I would have
done for a dog." She opened her mouth, but said nothing.
After a moment, he continued: "Or a bug, or *anything*."

She stared at him, pulling at her hand until he abruptly
let go.

"Time to get this business started," Caleb announced.

With an elbow, he smacked the button. There was a hiss,
a little wind blowing as the hatch pulled open, carrying
with it the smell of warm water and things unnamed.

He turned and left her.

And she hugged herself as if cold, and she watched him,
her mouth open and nothing to say, the ex-Marine growing small with the distance as her bewilderment grew vast
and bitter and black.

THE MINDWORM

C. M. Kornbluth

*Here's a classic SF horror story, and one of the classic tales
of aliens in hiding among us—except that this is an alien
you'd better not try to find. You'd better hope he doesn't find
you, either.*

*The late C. M. Kornbluth first started selling stories as
a teenage prodigy in 1940, making his first sale to* Super
Science Stories, *and writing vast amounts of pulp fiction
under many different pseudonyms in the years before World
War II, most of it unknown today. Only after the war, in the
booming SF scene of the early '50s, did Kornbluth begin to
attract some serious attention. As a writer, C. M. Kornbluth
first came to widespread prominence with a series of novels
written in collaboration with Frederik Pohl, including* The
Space Merchants *(one of the most famous SF novels of the
'50s),* Gladiator-at-Law, Search the Sky, *and* Wolfbane; *he
also produced two fairly routine novels in collaboration with
Judith Merill as "Cyril Judd,"* Outpost Mars *and* Gunner
Cade, *that were moderately well-received at the time but are
largely forgotten today, as well as several long-forgotten
mainstream novels in collaboration with Pohl. As a solo
writer—in addition to several mainstream novels under different pseudonyms—he produced three interesting but largely
unsuccessful novels (*Not This August, The Syndic, *and* Take-
off) *that had little impact on the SF world of the day.*

*What did have a powerful impact on the SF world, though,
was Kornbluth's short fiction. Kornbluth was a master of the
short story, working with a sophistication, maturity, elegance,
and grace rarely seen in the genre, then or now. He was one
of those key authors—one also thinks of Damon Knight,
Theodore Sturgeon, Alfred Bester, Algis Budrys, and a few
others—who were busy in the '50s redefining what you could
do with the instrument known as the science fiction short
story, and greatly expanding its range. In the years before
his tragically early death in 1958, Kornbluth created some*

of the best short work of the '50s, including the classic "The Little Black Bag," "The Marching Morons," "Shark Ship," "Two Dooms," "Gomez," "The Last Man Left in the Bar," "The Advent on Channel Twelve," "Ms. Found in a Chinese Fortune Cookie," "With These Hands," and dozens of others.

Kornbluth won no major awards during his lifetime, but one story of his, completed from a partial draft by Pohl years after his death, "The Meeting," won a Hugo Award in 1972. Kornbluth's solo short work was collected in The Explorers, A Mile Beyond the Moon, The Marching Morons, Thirteen O'Clock and Other Zero Hours, *and* The Best of C. M. Kornbluth. *Pohl and Kornbluth's collaborative short work has been collected in* The Wonder Effect, Critical Mass, Before the Universe, *and* Our Best. *Until recently, I would have said that everything by Kornbluth was long out of print, but, fortunately, NESFA Press published a massive retrospective Kornbluth collection in 1996,* His Share of the Glory: The Complete Short Fiction of C. M. Kornbluth *(NESFA Press, P.O. Box 809, Framingham, MA 07101-0203), a collection which, true to its name, assembles almost everything Kornbluth ever wrote under his own name, and one which belongs in every serious SF reader's library.*

The handsome J. G. and the pretty nurse held out against it as long as they reasonably could, but blue Pacific water, languid tropical nights, the low atoll dreaming on the horizon—and the complete absence of any other nice young people for company on the small, uncomfortable parts boat—did their work. On June 30th they watched through dark glasses as the dazzling thing burst over the fleet and the atoll. Her manicured hand gripped his arm in excitement and terror. Unfelt radiation sleeted through their loins.

A storekeeper-third-class named Bielaski watched the young couple with more interest than he showed in Test Able. After all, he had twenty-five dollars riding on the nurse. That night he lost it to a chief bosun's mate who had backed the j.g.

In the course of time, the careless nurse was discharged under conditions other than honorable. The j.g., who didn't like to put things in writing, phoned her all the way from Manila to say it was a damned shame. When her gratitude gave way to specific inquiry, their overseas connection went bad and he had to hang up.

She had a child, a boy, turned it over to a foundling home, and vanished from his life into a series of good jobs and finally marriage.

The boy grew up stupid, puny and stubborn, greedy and miserable. To the home's hilarious young athletics director he suddenly said: "You hate me. You think I make the rest of the boys look bad."

The athletics director blustered and laughed, and later told the doctor over coffee: "I watch myself around the kids. They're sharp—they catch a look or a gesture and it's like a blow in the face to them, I know that, so I watch myself. So how did he know?"

The doctor told the boy: "Three pounds more this month isn't bad, but how about you pitch in and clean up your plate *every* day? Can't live on meat and water; those vegetables make you big and strong."

The boy said: "What's 'neurasthenic' mean?"

The doctor later said to the director: "It made my flesh creep. I was looking at his little spindling body and dishing out the old pep talk about growing big and strong, and inside my head I was thinking 'we'd call him neurasthenic in the old days' and then out he popped with it. What should we do? Should we do anything? Maybe it'll go away. I don't know anything about these things. I don't know whether anybody does."

"Reads minds, does he?" asked the director. *Be damned if he's going to read my mind about Schultz Meat Market's ten percent.* "Doctor, I think I'm going to take my vacation a little early this year. Has anybody shown any interest in adopting the child?"

"Not him. He wasn't a baby doll when we got him, and at present he's an exceptionally unattractive-looking kid. You know how people don't give a damn about anything but their looks."

"*Some* couples would take anything, or so they tell me."

"Unapproved for foster-parenthood, you mean?"

"Red tape and arbitrary classification sometimes limit us too severely in our adoptions."

"If you're going to wish him on some screwball couple that the courts turned down as unfit, I want no part of it."

"You don't have to have any part of it, doctor. By the way, which dorm does he sleep in?"

"West," grunted the doctor, leaving the office.

The director called a few friends—a judge, a couple the judge referred him to, a court clerk. Then he left by way of the east wing of the building.

The boy survived three months with the Berrymans. Hard-drinking Mimi alternately caressed and shrieked at him; Edward W. tried to be a good scout and just gradually lost interest, looking clean through him. He hit the road in June and got by with it for a while. He wore a Boy Scout uniform, and Boy Scouts can turn up anywhere, any time. The money he had taken with him lasted a month. When the last penny of the last dollar was three days spent, he was adrift on a Nebraska prairie. He had walked out of the last small town because the constable was beginning to wonder what on earth he was hanging around for and who he belonged to. The town was miles behind on the two-lane highway; the infrequent cars did not stop.

One of Nebraska's "rivers", a dry bed at this time of year, lay ahead, spanned by a railroad culvert. There were some men in its shade, and he was hungry.

They were ugly, dirty men, and their thoughts were muddled and stupid. They called him "Shorty" and gave him a little dirty bread and some stinking sardines from a can. The thoughts of one of them became less muddled and uglier. He talked to the rest out of the boy's hearing, and they whooped with laughter. The boy got ready to run, but his legs wouldn't hold him up.

He could read the thoughts of the men quite clearly as they headed for him. Outrage, fear, and disgust blended in him and somehow turned inside-out and one of the men was dead on the dry ground, grasshoppers vaulting onto his flannel shirt, the others backing away, frightened now, not frightening.

He wasn't hungry any more; he felt quite comfortable and satisfied. He got up and headed for the other men, who ran. The rearmost of them was thinking *Jeez he folded up the evil eye we was only gonna—*

Again the boy let the thoughts flow into his head and again he slipped his own thoughts around them; it was quite easy to do. It was different—this man's terror from the other's lustful anticipation. But both had their points . . .

At his leisure, he robbed the bodies of three dollars and twenty-four cents.

Thereafter his fame preceded him like a death wind. Two years on the road and he had his growth and his fill of the dull and stupid minds he met there. He moved to northern cities, a year here, a year there, quiet, unobtrusive, prudent, an epicure.

Sebastian Long woke suddenly, with something on his mind. As night fog cleared away he remembered, happily. Today he started the Demeter Bowl! At last there was time, at last there was money—six hundred and twenty-three dollars in the bank. He had packed and shipped the three dozen cocktail glasses last night, engraved with Mrs. Klausman's initials—his last commercial order for as many months as the Bowl would take.

He shifted from nightshirt to denims, gulped coffee, boiled an egg but was too excited to eat it. He went to the front of his shop-workroom-apartment, checked the lock, waved at neighbors' children on their way to school, and ceremoniously set a sign in the cluttered window.

It said: "NO COMMERCIAL ORDERS TAKEN UNTIL FURTHER NOTICE."

From a closet he tenderly carried a shrouded object that made a double armful and laid it on his workbench. Unshrouded, it was a glass bowl—*what* a glass bowl! The clearest Swedish lead glass, the purest lines he had ever seen, his secret treasure since the crazy day he had bought it, long ago, for six months' earnings. His wife had given him hell for that until the day she died. From the closet he brought a portfolio filled with sketches and designs dating back to the day he had bought the bowl. He smiled over the first, excitedly scrawled—a florid, rococo conception, unsuited to the classicism of the lines and the serenity of the perfect glass.

Through many years and hundreds of sketches he had refined his conception to the point where it was, he humbly felt, not unsuited to the medium. A strongly-molded Demeter was to dominate the piece, a matron as serene as the glass, and all the fruits of the earth would flow from her gravely outstretched arms.

Suddenly and surely, he began to work. With a candle he thinly smoked an oval area on the outside of the bowl. Two steady fingers clipped the Demeter drawing against the carbon black; a hair-fine needle in his other hand traced her lines. When the transfer of the design was done, Sebastian Long readied his lathe. He fitted a small copper wheel, slightly worn as he liked them, into the chuck and with his fingers charged it with the finest rouge from Rouen. He took an ashtray cracked in delivery and held it against the spinning disk. It bit in smoothly, with the *wiping* feel to it that was exactly right.

Holding out his hands, seeing that the fingers did not tremble with excitement, he eased the great bowl to the lathe and was about to make the first tiny cut of the millions that would go into the masterpiece.

Somebody knocked on his door and rattled the doorknob.

Sebastian Long did not move or look toward the door. Soon the busybody would read the sign and go away. But the pounding and rattling of the knob went on. He eased down the bowl and angrily went to the window, picked up the sign, and shook it at whoever it was—he couldn't make out the face very well. But the idiot wouldn't go away.

The engraver unlocked the door, opened it a bit, and snapped: "The shop is closed. I shall not be taking any orders for several months. Please don't bother me now."

"It's about the Demeter Bowl," said the intruder.

Sebastian Long stared at him. "What the devil do you know about my Demeter Bowl?" He saw the man was a stranger, undersized by a little, middle-aged . . .

"Just let me in please," urged the man. "It's important. Please!"

"I don't know what you're talking about," said the engraver. "But what do you know about my Demeter Bowl?" He hooked his thumbs pugnaciously over the waistband of his denims and glowered at the stranger. The stranger promptly took advantage of his hand being removed from the door and glided in.

Sebastian Long thought briefly that it might be a nightmare as the man darted quickly about his shop, picking up a graver and throwing it down, picking up a wire scratch-wheel and throwing it down. "Here, you!" he roared, as the stranger picked up a crescent wrench which he did not throw down.

As Long started for him, the stranger darted to the workbench and brought the crescent wrench down shatteringly on the bowl.

Sebastian Long's heart was bursting with sorrow and rage; such a storm of emotions as he never had known thundered through him. Paralyzed, he saw the stranger smile with anticipation.

The engraver's legs folded under him and he fell to the floor, drained and dead.

The Mindworm, locked in the bedroom of his brownstone front, smiled again, reminiscently.

Smiling, he checked the day on a wall calendar.

• • •

"Dolores!" yelled her mother in Spanish. "Are you going to pass the whole day in there?"

She had been practicing low-lidded, sexy half-smiles like Lauren Bacall in the bathroom mirror. She stormed out and yelled in English: "I don't know how many times I tell you not to call me that Spick name no more!"

"Dolly!" sneered her mother. "Dah-lee! When was there a Saint Dah-lee that you call yourself after, eh?"

The girl snarled a Spanish obscenity at her mother and ran down the tenement stairs. Jeez, she was gonna be late for sure!

Held up by a stream of traffic between her and her streetcar, she danced with impatience. Then the miracle happened. Just like in the movies, a big convertible pulled up before her and its lounging driver said, opening the door: "You seem to be in a hurry. Could I drop you somewhere?"

Dazed at the sudden realization of a hundred daydreams, she did not fail to give the driver a low-lidded, sexy smile as she said: "Why, *thanks!*" and climbed in. He wasn't no Cary Grant, but he had all his hair . . . kind of small, but so was she . . . and jeez, the convertible had *leopard-skin seat covers!*

The car was in the stream of traffic, purring down the avenue. "It's a lovely day," she said. "Really too nice to work."

The driver smiled shyly, kind of like Jimmy Stewart but of course not so tall, and said: "I feel like playing hooky myself. How would you like a spin down Long Island?"

"Be wonderful!" The convertible cut left on an odd-numbered street.

"Play hooky, you said. What do you do?"

"Advertising."

"*Advertising!*" Dolly wanted to kick herself for ever having doubted, for ever having thought in low, self-loathing moments that it wouldn't work out, that she'd marry a grocer or a mechanic and live forever after in a smelly tenement and grow old and sick and stooped. She felt vaguely in her happy daze that it might have been cuter, she might have accidentally pushed him into a pond or something, but this was cute enough. An advertising man, leopard-skin seat covers . . . what more could a girl with a sexy smile and a nice little figure want?

Speeding down the South Shore she learned what his name was Michael Brent, exactly as it ought to be. She wished she could tell him she was Jennifer Brown or one of those real cute names they had nowadays, but was reassured when he told her he thought Dolly Gonzalez was a beautiful name. He didn't, and she noticed the omission, add: "It's the most beautiful name I ever heard!" That, she comfortably thought as she settled herself against the cushions, would come later.

They stopped at Medford for lunch, a wonderful lunch in a little restaurant where you went down some steps and there were candles on the table. She called him "Michael" and he called her "Dolly." She learned that he liked dark girls and thought the stories in *True Story* really were true, and that he thought she was just tall enough, and that Greer Garson was wonderful, but not the way she was, and that he thought her dress was just wonderful.

They drove slowly after Medford, and Michael Brent did most of the talking. He had traveled all over the world. He had been in the war and wounded—just a flesh wound. He was thirty-eight, and had been married once, but she died. There were no children. He was alone in the world. He had nobody to share his town house in the 50's, his country place in Westchester, his lodge in the Maine woods. Every word sent the girl floating higher and higher on a tide of happiness; the signs were unmistakable.

When they reached Montauk Point, the last sandy bit of the continent before blue water and Europe, it was sunset, with a great wrinkled sheet of purple and rose stretching half across the sky and the first stars appearing above the dark horizon of the water.

The two of them walked from the parked car out onto the sand, alone, bathed in glorious Technicolor. Her heart was nearly bursting with joy as she heard Michael Brent say, his arms tightening around her: "Darling, will you marry me?"

"Oh, *yes*, Michael!" she breathed, dying.

The Mindworm, drowsing, suddenly felt the sharp sting of danger. He cast out through the great city, dragging tentacles of thought:

". . . die if she don't let me . . ."

". . . six an' six is twelve an' carry one an' three is four . . ."

". . . gobblegobble madre de dios pero soy gobblegobble . . ."

". . . parlay Domino an' Missab and shoot the roll on Duchess Peg in the feature . . ."

". . . melt resin add the silver chloride and dissolve in oil of lavender stand and decant and fire to cone zero twelve give you shimmering streaks of luster down the walls . . ."

". . . moiderin' square-headed gobblebobble tried ta poke his eye out wassamatta witta ref . . ."

". . . O God I am most heartily sorry I have offended thee in . . ."

". . . talk like a commie . . ."

". . . gobblegobblegobble two dolla twenny-fi' sense gobble . . ."

". . . just a nip and fill it up with water and brush my teeth . . ."

". . . really know I'm God but fear to confess their sins . . ."

". . . dirty lousy rock-headed claw-handed paddle-footed goggle-eyed snot-nosed hunch-backed feeble-minded pot-bellied son of . . ."

". . . write on the wall alfie is a stunkur and then . . ."

". . . thinks I believe it's a television set but I know he's got a bomb in there but who can I tell who can help so alone . . ."

". . . gabble was ich weiss nicht gabble geh bei Broadvay gabble . . ."

". . . habt mein daughter Rosie such a fella gobblegobble . . ."

". . . wonder if that's one didn't look back . . ."

". . . seen with her in the Medford restaurant . . ."

The Mindworm struck into that thought.

". . . not a mark on her but the M. E.'s have been wrong before and heart failure don't mean a thing anyway try to talk to her old lady authorize an autopsy get Pancho little guy talks Spanish be best . . ."

The Mindworm knew he would have to be moving again—soon. He was sorry; some of the thoughts he had tapped indicated good . . . hunting?

Regretfully, he again dragged his net:

". . . with chartreuse drinks I mean drapes could use a drink come to think of it . . ."

". . . reep-beep-reep-beep reepiddy-beepiddy-beep bop man wadda beat . . ."

$$\sum_{k=m+1}^{n} \varphi\left(a_x, \ a_k\right) - \sum_{i=1}^{m} \varphi\left(a_x, \ a_i\right) \geqslant 0. \ \textit{What the Hell was that?}"$$

The Mindworm withdrew, in frantic haste. The intelligence was massive, its overtones those of a vigorous adult. He had learned form certain dangerous children that there was peril of a leveling flow. Shaken and scared, he contemplated traveling. He would need more than that wretched girl had supplied, and it would not be epicurean. There would be no time to find individuals at a ripe emotional crisis, or goad them to one. It would be plain—munching. The Mindworm drank a glass of water, also necessary to his metabolism.

EIGHT FOUND DEAD
IN UPTOWN MOVIE;
"MOLESTER" SOUGHT

Eight persons, including three women, were found dead Wednesday night of unknown causes in widely separated seats in the balcony of the Odeon Theater at 117th St. and Broadway. Police are seeking a man described by the balcony usher, Michael Fenelly, 18, as "acting like a woman-molester."

Fenelly discovered the first of the fatalities after seeing the man "moving from one empty seat to another several times." He went to ask a woman in a seat next to one the man had just vacated whether he had annoyed her. She was dead.

Almost at once, a scream rang out. In another part of the balcony Mrs. Sadie Rabinowitz, 40, uttered the cry when another victim toppled from his seat next to her.

Theater manager I. J. Marcusohn stopped the show and turned on the house lights. He tried to instruct his staff to keep the audience from leaving before the police arrived. He failed to get word to them in time, however, and most of the audience was gone when a detail from the 24th Pct. and an ambulance from Harlem hospital took over at the scene of the tragedy.

The Medical Examiner's office has not yet made a report as to the causes of death. A spokesman said the victims showed no signs of poisoning or violence. He added that it "was inconceivable that it could be a coincidence."

Lt. John Braidwood of the 24th Pct. said of the alleged molester: "We got a fair description of him and naturally we will try to bring him in for questioning."

Clickety-click, clickety-click, clickety-click sang the rails as the Mindworm drowsed in his coach seat.

Some people were walking forward from the diner. One was thinking: "Different-looking fellow. (a) he's aberrant. (b) he's nonaberrant and ill. Cancel (b)—respiration normal, skin smooth and healthy, no tremor of limbs, well-groomed. Is aberrant (1) trivially. (2) significantly. Cancel (1)—displayed no involuntary interest when . . . odd! *Running* for the washroom! Unexpected because (a) neat grooming indicates amour propre inconsistent with amusing others; (b) evident health inconsistent with . . ." It had taken one second, was fully detailed.

The Mindworm, locked in the toilet of the coach, wondered what the next stop was. He was getting off at it—

not frightened, just careful. Dodge them, keep dodging them
and everything would be all right. Send out no mental taps
until the train was far away and everything would be all
right.

He got off at a West Virginia coal and iron town surrounded
by ruined mountains and filled with the off-scourings of
Eastern Europe. Serbs, Albanians, Croats, Hungarians,
Slovenes, Bulgarians, and all possible combinations and
permutations thereof. He walked slowly from the smoke-
stained, brownstone passenger station. The train had roared
on its way.

". . . ain' no gemmum that's fo sho', fi-cen' tip fo' a
good shine lak ah give um . . ."

". . . dumb bassar don't know how to make out a billa
lading yet he ain't never gonna know so fire him get it
over with . . ."

". . . gabblegabblegabble . . ." Not a word he recognized
in it.

". . . gobblegobble dat tam vooman I brek she nack . . ."

". . . gobble trink visky chin glassabeer gobblegobblegobble . . ."

". . . gabblegabblegabble . . ."

". . . makes me so gobblegobble mad little no-good tramp
no she ain' but I don' like no standup from no dame . . ."

A blond, square-headed boy fuming under a street light.

". . . out wit' Casey Oswiak I could kill that dumb bohunk alla time trine ta paw her . . ."

It was a possibility. The Mindworm drew near.

". . . stand me up for that gobblegobble bohunk I oughta
slap her inna mush like my ole man says . . ."

"Hello," said the Mindworm.

"Waddaya wan'?"

"Casey Oswiak told me to tell you not to wait up for
your girl. He's taking her out tonight."

The blond boy's rage boiled into his face and shot from
his eyes. He was about to swing when the Mindworm began
to feed. It was like pheasant after chicken, venison after
beef. The coarseness of the environment, or the ancient

strain? The Mindworm wondered as he strolled down the street. A girl passed him:

". . . oh but he's gonna be mad like last time wish I came right away so jealous kinda nice but he might bust me one some day be nice to him tonight there he is lam'post leaning on it looks kinda funny gawd I hope he ain't drunk looks kinda funny sleeping sick or bozhe moi gabblegabblegabble . . ."

Her thoughts trailed into a foreign language of which the Mindworm knew not a word. After hysteria had gone she recalled, in the foreign language, that she had passed him.

The Mindworm, stimulated by the unfamiliar quality of the last feeding, determined to stay for some days. He checked in at a Main Street hotel.

Musing, he dragged his net:

". . . gobblegobblewhompyeargobblecheskygobblegabblechyesh . . ."

". . . take him down cellar beat the can off the damn chesky thief put the fear of god into him teach him can't bust into no boxcars in *mah* parta the caounty . . ."

". . . gabblegabble . . ."

". . . phone ole Mister Ryan in She-cawgo and he'll tell them three-card monte grifters who got the horseroom rights in this necka the woods by damn don't pay protection money for no protection . . ."

The Mindworm followed that one further; it sounded as though it could lead to some money if he wanted to stay in the town long enough.

The Eastern Europeans of the town, he mistakenly thought, were like the tramps and bums he had known and fed on during his years on the road—stupid and safe, safe and stupid, quite the same thing.

In the morning he found no mention of the squareheaded boy's death in the town's paper and thought it had gone practically unnoticed. It had—by the paper, which was of, by, and for the coal and iron company and its native-American bosses and straw bosses. The other town, the one without a charter or police force, with only an imported weekly newspaper or two from the nearest city, noticed it. The other town had roots more than two thousand years deep, which are hard to pull up. But the Mindworm didn't know it was there.

He fed again that night, on a giddy young streetwalker in her room. He had astounded and delighted her with a fistful of ten-dollar bills before he began to gorge. Again the delightful difference from city-bred folk was there. . . .

Again in the morning he had been unnoticed, he thought. The chartered town, unwilling to admit that there were streetwalkers or that they were found dead, wiped the slate clean; its only member who really cared was the native-American cop on the beat who had collected weekly from the dead girl.

The other town, unknown to the Mindworm, buzzed with it. A delegation went to the other town's only public officer. Unfortunately he was young, American-trained, perhaps even ignorant about some important things. For what he told them was: "My children, that is foolish superstition. Go home."

The Mindworm, through the day, roiled the surface of the town proper by allowing himself to be roped into a poker game in a parlor of the hotel. He wasn't good at it, he didn't like it, and he quit with relief when he had cleaned six shifty-eyed, hard-drinking loafers out of about three hundred dollars. One of them went straight to the police station and accused the unknown of being a sharper. A humorous sergeant, the Mindworm was pleased to note, joshed the loafer out of his temper.

Nightfall again, hunger again . . .

He walked the streets of the town and found them empty. It was strange. The native-American citizens were out, tending bar, walking their beats, locking up their newspaper on the stones, collecting their rents, managing their movies—but where were the others? He cast his net:

". . . gobblegobblegobble whomp year gobble . . ."

". . . crazy old pollack mama of mine try to lock me in with Errol Flynn at the Majestic never know the difference if I sneak out the back . . ."

That was near. He crossed the street and it was nearer. He homed on the thought:

". . . jeez he's a hunka man like Stanley but he never looks at me that Vera Kowalik I'd like to kick her just once in the gobblegobblegobble crazy old mama won't be American so ashamed . . ."

It was half a block, no more, down a side street. Brick houses, two stories, with back yards on an alley. She was going out the back way.

How strangely quiet it was in the alley.

". . . ea-sy down them steps fix that damn board that's how she caught me last time what the hell are they all so scared of went to see Father Drugas won't talk bet somebody got it again that Vera Kowalik and her big . . ."

". . . gobble bozhe gobble whomp year gobble . . ."

She was closer; she was closer.

"All think I'm a kid show them who's a kid bet if Stanley caught me all alone out here in the alley dark and all he wouldn't think I was a kid that damn Vera Kowalik her folks don't think she's a kid . . ."

For all her bravado she was stark terrified when he said: "Hello."

"Who—who—who?" she stammered.

Quick, before she screamed. Her terror was delightful. Not too replete to be alert, he cast about, questing.

". . . gobblegobblegobble whomp year."

The countless eyes of the other town, with more than two thousand years of experience in such things, had been following him. What he had sensed as a meaningless hash of noise was actually an impassioned outburst in a nearby darkened house.

"Fools! fools! Now he has taken a virgin! I said not to wait. What will we say to her mother?"

An old man with handlebar mustache and, in spite of the hat, his shirt sleeves decently rolled down and buttoned at the cuffs, evenly replied: "My heart in me died with hers, Casimir, but one must be sure. It would be a terrible thing to make a mistake in such an affair."

The weight of conservative elder opinion was with him.

Other old men with mustaches, some perhaps remembering mistakes long ago, nodded and said: "A terrible thing. A terrible thing."

The Mindworm strolled back to his hotel and napped on the made bed briefly. A tingle of danger awakened him. Instantly he cast out:

". . . gobblegobble whompyear."

". . . whampyir."

"WAMPYIR!"

Close! Close and deadly!

The door of his room burst open, and mustached old men with their shirt sleeves rolled down, and decently buttoned at the cuffs unhesitatingly marched in, their thoughts a turmoil of alien noises, foreign gibberish that he could not wrap his mind around, disconcerting, from every direction.

The sharpened stake was through his heart and the scythe blade through his throat before he could realize that he had not been the first of his kind; and that what clever people have not yet learned, some quite ordinary people have not yet entirely forgotten.

POPEYE AND POPS WATCH THE EVENING WORLD REPORT

Eliot Fintushel

Having aliens in hiding next door can be a trial even in day-to-day matters, as the bizarre and very funny story that follows demonstrates. A quiet evening in front of the TV turns into an intergalactic incident of immense significance...

New writer Eliot Fintushel made his first sale in 1993, to Tomorrow *magazine. Since then, he has appeared several more times in* Tomorrow, *has become a regular in* Asimov's Science Fiction, *with a large number of sales there, has appeared in* Amazing, Crank!, *and other markets. He is beginning to attract attention from* cognoscenti *as one of the most original and inventive writers to enter the genre in many years, worthy to be ranked among other practitioners of the fast-paced, wild and crazy, gonzo modern tall-tale such as R. A. Lafferty, Howard Waldrop, and Neal Barrett, Jr. Fintushel, a baker's son from Rochester, New York, is a performer and teacher of mask theater and mime, has won the National Endowment for the Arts' Solo Performer Award twice, and now lives in Santa Rosa, California.*

P*opeye and Pops* kept a dead raccoon in a busted fridge outside the tin hut they called home. When I asked where the bathroom was, Pops said, "You wanna take a bath?" He laughed beer smell right in my face. Popeye was kinder. He explained that I must mean the toilet, and he showed me outside to the ditch by the windbreak.

They called them, "staygrants" in Orleans County, mi-

grants who had come up from the South in buses and car
pools to harvest the apples, peaches, plums, and pears, and
then stayed on through the winter, working at the cannery
or doing odd jobs. They settled in, somehow. They got
hired for pruning in the spring. They drank. People began
to take their presence for granted in Holley, in Albion and
even in Brockport, and the staygrants were careful to stay
predictable. Popeye and Pops were like court jesters, for
example. People in town thought they were crazy and harmless, and so they let them be. They let them work and drink
and jabber about their magic *poojum*.

Myself, I never thought they were crazy or harmless.
From the beginning, I believed that Popeye and Pops knew
something that I desperately needed to find out. One day
when my girlfriend was at a dance class, I invited Pops
into my rented farmhouse on North Main Street Road. He
was timid at first, but once inside, he acted like he owned
the place, and me.

"Why you let someone plant those flowers around you?"
he said, taking another pull of his Budweiser. "Don't you
know they making a grave for you?" It gave me a shiver.
I always felt a little funny about those tulips. "Sure," said
Pops. "You can't let a body plant flowers around you. Hey,
some folks put flowers around me, my man, and I still here
a thousand million year later." Pops said crazy things. He
liked my house, he said. He could see how it might come
in handy one day. He wanted to know whether I had a TV,
not for now but for later, he said. Then we sat outside on
the front porch to have some coffee.

A hundred yards away down Main Street Road, my middle class neighbor was talking to a friend. Pops cocked his
ear and started talking to them the way a baby talks to angels, bobbing his head and staring into space. "Yes, yes,"
he said, "Those pool chemicals got to be changed! That's
right! Keep that water clean, clean! You better, hear? That's
right! What for lunch, honey? Honey that lunch up, Mister! You gonna have flowers round you just like my man
here. Mm-hmm!"

He was just like a voodoo man. Near and far meant

nothing to Pops—that's how I saw it. The night after I met them, I dreamed of Popeye and Pops in that tin hut that Leland Bower let them use while they worked his orchards. I dreamed that Pops lay awake nights like a huge satellite dish, picking up gossip from seven counties and sending more gossip back, while Popeye guarded the door and chanted magic words to keep me and the townies away.

One night I was lost in the snow with Corinne in the wide marshy field that separated our place from Leland Bower's house. Our electricity had gone out and we were sure it must be a blown fuse, but we didn't know where to look for it, and we didn't have a phone. Leland would know what to do, and he liked to talk to college students like me. But in half an hour Corinne and I managed to get ourselves lost, soaked to the bone, and howling mad at each other for not remembering the way.

That's when we bumped into Popeye and Pops. I thought I heard a voice coming from the windbreak—"They here!"—and then we saw them. They were doing something awful in the middle of the frozen stream. Pops was holding something dead. Popeye had his face in it. They were doing something that people used to do long ago, before we forgot how or got taught not to. Corinne pretended not to see; in fact, I never got her to admit that she'd seen anything out of the ordinary that whole night.

Pops looked up at me and grinned. He knew that I recognized something. "This could be for you," he said.

"Don't mystify him," Popeye told his friend. "Don't mystify that boy." He was cleaning the thing's blood off his face with a handful of snow and wiping it on his sleeve. Pops shoved the dead thing under his torn cloth coat. "I'll fix your electricity," Popeye told me.

"How did you know it needed fixing?" Corinne asked him.

There was a still moment. I could hear branches scraping and creaking in the chill wind. I could hear the moon rising. Then Popeye said, "Look! Your lights is all out." Pops started laughing so hard, he had to slap a hand over his mouth and nose to hold the laughter in.

"You follow me," Popeye said. "You don't need no Leland Bower. I'll fix you." He started walking, and we followed behind.

"What makes you think we were headed for Bower's?" Corinne asked.

"I just guessed, Miss," Popeye said uneasily.

There was another peal of wild laughter at our backs. Pops was rolling in the snow, snorting and howling.

"Is he drunk?" Corinne asked me.

"Don't worry about Pops," I said. "He's just like that."

"That's the truth," Pops said, suddenly very solemn, "Pops is just like that, Miss." Then he laughed again.

"I think we should still go to Mr. Bower's," Corinne said. "These guys are nuts."

"Shush," I said. "Pops hears everything."

"I don't give a damn what Pops hears. I'm telling you I want to go to Mr. Bower. What does Popeye know about electricity?"

I shrugged. I said, "I think he knows something."

"You're not going to Bower's with me, then?" She was fuming. She looked at me with disgust. She knew she couldn't find her way across the field alone. Corinne stomped away toward Popeye, who hadn't noticed that we'd dropped behind, and after that she made a point of keeping twenty yards between us.

Pops tagged behind, poking me and giggling every now and then. "We gonna fix your lights," he said.

It was slow going. The ground was not completely frozen yet; we kept sliding down into trenches of mud, and scrambling up, wet and shivering, into another snowdrift. When we reached the road, Pops grabbed my coat and held me at the edge of the field while Popeye and Corinne crossed over to our dark house.

"Let me go. I'm freezing," I said. He held me. Pops looked almost sad as he reached into his coat and took out the dead thing to show me.

"We not from here," Pops said. His face was troubled. He wanted something from me, but I couldn't understand what it was. "Looky," he said. He let go of me so he could

cradle the thing in both hands. He lifted it tenderly right
up to my face. It smelled a little like ether, a smell that
seemed to slice through my nostrils and the side of my
head and speak directly to my nerves and brain. It was a
smell deep in memory, cellular memory, electrical memory, before the womb, before the egg, before the chromosome.

I don't know what the thing looked like. I was overwhelmed by that odor. I just kept staring in amazement
right into Pops's bloodshot eyes. Pops stared back and nodded. I wanted to bury my face in that thing.

Then Corinne called out. Pops pushed the dead thing
back in his coat and laughed hard. "Let's git." The lights
had gone on. I crossed the road with Pops, and we entered
the cold house. Popeye was splitting wood with the hatchet
I kept by the wood stove. He had already gotten a small
fire going. Corinne had started some water boiling on the
hotplate for coffee.

"Let me take a hot shower here," Pops said.

Corinne looked at him like it was the craziest thing she
had ever heard a human being say. I said, "We don't have
a shower, Pops."

"You got a wash tub and a pail?"

"I'm going to bed." Corinne turned away. "You men do
whatever the hell you want to do. Thanks for fixing the
fuse. Don't let the water boil over, okay?"

"Don't go to bed, Miss," Popeye said.

"What?"

Pops said, "The man said, don't you go to bed, Miss."

"She's tired," I said. "I'll make the coffee."

"She's not tired," Pops said.

"Don't put words in her mouth," Popeye told Pops. Then
to Corinne: "Are you tired, Miss?"

"No," she said, "as a matter of fact I'm not. I just don't
want to be in here with you because I think your friend is
out of his mind, and my boyfriend isn't man enough to
kick him the hell out of here. You've been very nice, Popeye, but I'll be grateful if you finish rubbing your sticks

together and go home." Corinne stormed into the bedroom and shut the door.

"This is bad," Popeye said. "She's can't go to sleep."

"Don't fret about it," said Pops. "No way she gonna sleep now."

"What are you guys talking about?" I said.

"Did you show him?" Popeye asked Pops.

"Just started," said Pops. "Where's the tub?"

"In the little room off the kitchen," I said, "but why do you need Corinne?"

"We don't need her," Popeye explained. "We just need that she don't sleep."

Pops was dragging the tub in close to the woodstove. "I needs a bucket and hot water."

I started drawing hot water for him from the kitchen sink. The pipes had frozen and burst a few days earlier but were working well enough now.

"I'm glad you like Corinne's company," I said. "So do I."

"We don't like no Corinne's company," Pops scowled. "Ask him if he still gots the TV," he said to Popeye.

Popeye said, "Pops wants to know do you got a TV?"

"Sure." I went into the bedroom, where Corinne was curled up under four blankets. "I'm taking the television in to Pops," I whispered.

"Close the door, Alex." I turned around and closed the door. It was dark in the bedroom. "Come here." I sat down on the bed and leaned close. "Alex, I want you to get rid of them. I want you to get rid of them *now*."

"He's taking a shower. You know they haven't got anything over there in that shack."

"We haven't got anything over here in *this* shack. Get rid of them, Alex."

"I'm taking the TV." I unplugged it and carried it out of the room. When I closed the door again, I heard something thud against it from the other side. Probably her pillow. We had lately begun to break things and to throw things at each other when we were angry, which was often.

Pops was standing naked in the tub. His clothes, except

for the coat, were piled up on the floor next to the tub. He would not let go of the coat; something precious was rolled up in it. The bucket was flowing over into the steel sink. I put down the TV and shut off the water, then carried the bucket over to Pops.

Pops was a big man, barrel-chested and muscular, though he sagged around the middle. Popeye, on the other hand, was skeletal.

"Here," I said, offering Pops the bucket.

"No," said Pops. "You give the bucket to Popeye to pour on me. You go plug in the TV. We wanna see the Evening World Report."

I set up the TV so Pops could see it as he showered. From inside the bedroom, Corinne shouted, "Is that man naked in the living room?" No one paid her any attention. Synthesized strains of Beethoven's Fifth, the theme music for the Evening World Report, were just beginning. The anchor man, a substitute, someone I didn't recognize, was shuffling papers at his desk.

"Hold the water ready," Pops told Popeye. To me, he said, "we come from far away, you hear me, boy? Far, far away! That's the truth."

"That's the truth," Popeye echoed. "All Pops says is gospel true."

Something heavy slammed against the door. "Are they gone yet?" Corinne shouted.

"All Pops says is gospel truth," said Popeye. "It's true in this place. It was true in the other. If we stuck here another million years, it be true. If we be back home this night, it still be true."

"Tune that in better," Pops told me. I fiddled with the rabbit ears till the ghosts went away. Behind the anchor, numbers flashed with percent signs and dollar signs. There was a pie graph, followed by a bar graph and then pictures of long lines of grey people bundled up against the cold.

Pops started to unwrap the thing in his coat. "Pour a little," he told Popeye. "Ouch! That's hot, hot, hot!"

"Is it too hot?" I said.

"Quiet now," Pops warned me.

I looked at Pops head, and I couldn't stop looking. The flesh had melted away where the hot water had hit him. Pops's scalp was gone. The skin was folded down over his forehead and ears, hanging over the nape of his neck like damp rubber from a burst balloon. Nor was there a cranium to speak of. The bone had scattered like ash, powdering what was left of Pops's face with a fine white dust.

Something else hit the door. Corinne shouted, "I hate you, Alex!"

Popeye asked, "Can we lock that door?"

"Not from this side," I said.

"Never mind that," Pops commanded. "Turn up the juice on the Evening World Report, you. And you, Popeye, pour me some more hot."

I made it louder. "But it's just a commercial," I said.

"It's just a commercial!" Pops laughed as hot water erased his eyeballs, nose, ears, and the upper part of his jaw, burning streaks down to his ankles as if it were nitric acid. His brain slipped down like liver into a grinder, settling into his mouth and then his throat. Pops continued to stand erect. Pops continued to speak, although there seemed no place left for a voice to come from. "Just a commercial!" he howled.

Popeye said, "We don't know no commercial from no nothin' else. You see sun and you see sex, but it all just hot to Pops. If you please, now pinch the *poojum* before it fall away." He pointed to the thing cradled in Pops's melting hands. I pinched the end of it between the thumb and forefinger of my right hand. There was that smell again, acrid and cutting, reminding me of things no human being has a right to remember.

"Damn you, are you burning something in there?" Corinne shouted. We could hear her start to get up out of the bed.

"More hot!" cried Pops. And to me: "You, pull, man! Pull it to the tube, man! Give it to the big bow tie."

"To the what?" I said.

"Quick now!" Popeye said, pouring. "Are you deaf? To the big bow tie! Give it to the big bow tie!"

I was still pinching the thing. I had stretched it away
like bubble gum. The scent made my head spin. "What are
you talking about?" I said. "I see the bow tie, but how am
I supposed to . . ."

"Give, man! Give it!" Pops sang out. There was little
left of him besides a vertebral column balanced on the coc-
cyx, dripping slime, which smoked and ran in rivulets into
the old wash tub. I could not see which part of it held his
end of the poojum, but he held it still. "This my moment,
man! Give it quick, before the sports news!"

"If it go to the sports news, we gots to wait another
thousand million years," old Popeye said.

The door pushed open. Corinne came out in her bathrobe,
brandishing an iron lampstand.

"Do it now!" Pops commanded.

I pressed the gummy end of *poojum* onto the TV screen
where the image of the anchor man's bow tie floated.

"Pour!" screamed Pops. Popeye poured. The house filled
with steam, carrying that strange, ancient smell into every
room, into every crevice. The string of *poojum* connecting
the TV screen with the sliver of Pops sizzled and vibrated
in widening arcs. The TV man droned on. Corinne was
gasping, falling toward the vibrating string. Popeye leapt
toward her, deflecting her from it, so that she fell backward into the bedroom. The lampstand clattered to the floor.

"She out!" shrieked Pops. There was no more of him
now than a peak of whipped cream, with the *poojum* on
top, gradually sinking in, just as Pops's brain had sunk
down through his old body before.

"She out cold!" said Popeye. There was fear in his voice.
"She out, Pops! How'm I gonna leave this place? How'm
I gonna go with my Majesty now?"

"The sports news isn't on yet," I said. It was as if it
were an evening in someone else's life, a dream on the operating table, vivid but remote.

"He right," Pops declared. "Slap that Corinne. Wake that
Corinne. She your ticket to ride, Popeye."

"Corinne!" I shouted, trying to be helpful. "Get up,
honey! Get up! Wake up!"

"She out cold," Popeye whimpered. "Goodbye, Pops! Goodbye, my lord!"

"That's it, Popeye, my dear! You a loyal servant. Take the *poojum*. I gonna scoop you back to me, Popeye. Hold the *poojum* and wait."

On the TV, a woman in a blue blazer was reading football scores. The string of *poojum* hummed, then snapped. The steam, the smell, and the dark, viscous remains of Pops all whirled, roaring, into the insignia on the sportscaster's blazer.

"Goodbye, lord!" moaned Popeye, staring at the TV.

Then there was only the wind rattling the window panes and the dit-dit-dit-dah of the closing music for the Evening World Report. Popeye was scuttling around, picking up Pops's clothes and putting things away. He had already secreted the *poojum* somewhere on his person.

The top of the woodstove was glowing red. I grabbed Corinne's coffeepot off the hotplate. All the water in it had boiled away, and the metal was burning and stinking. I opened the door and laid the pot down in the snow. It sizzled. I left it there and went back into the house.

I felt drugged. Popeye stood before me as if he were waiting for permission to leave. "She gonna be all right," he said. "Just a bump on the head." His face was streaked with tears.

The TV was babbling behind us. "How did you get stuck here in the first place?" I said. "Who was it that planted flowers around Pops?"

"You don't wanna hear about *them*, son. They big. They old. They got more names than your earth and moon. We don't wanna talk about pyramids now, and big lizards and volcanos and holes in the sky."

"Is Pops back home now?"

"He got through."

"What happens to you?"

"I'll get by."

"What did you need from Corinne?"

"Her anger, son, just her powerful anger. I don't think you would understand."

"You probably don't want me to talk about any of this."

"It don't matter. Everybody knows I gots my *poojum*."

We caught each other's eye. Popeye laughed, and I tried to.

"I best be going now," he said.

I let him out the door and watched him disappear into the snowy field.

Corinne was moaning and pulling herself to her feet. "What happened?" she said.

"You fell," I said. "Are you okay?"

"I think so. My head hurts. Where did everybody go?"

"Pops went home after the Evening World Report. Popeye just left."

"Did Pops take his shower?"

"Yes."

"Alex, please don't let those men in here again."

"Okay, Corinne," I said.

Corinne shook her head and lumbered back into our small, dark bedroom. "Come on," she said.

"Corinne . . ."

"Yes, Alex?"

I looked at Corinne, sleepyhead, in her long, cotton nighty, wisps of brown hair half-covering her face, sweetly drowsy. There were no big lizards or volcanos in those eyes. She only wanted me, and a good night's sleep.

"It's a big world, Corinne," I sighed.

"I know it," she said. She came back out of the bedroom and kissed me. "You look lost, Alex."

"Your coffeepot's a goner, Corinne. I burned it."

"Don't worry,"—leaning her forehead against my cheek. "Do you think our bulbs will make it through the winter?"

"Always have," she yawned.

Tired as I was, I lifted Corinne into my arms—she smiled—and I carried her to bed.

THE AUTOPSY

Michael Shea

*Here's one of the scariest science fiction stories ever writ-
ten, showing that aliens may be hiding anywhere among us—
including some places no one would ever think to look . . .*

*Michael Shea has established a substantial reputation
working on the borderline between horror, fantasy, and science fiction. His collection of linked stories,* Nifft the Lean,
*won him a World Fantasy Award. His other books include
the novels* A Quest for Simbilis *(set, with the permission of
the author, in the universe of Jack Vance's Cugel the Clever
stories),* In Yana, the Touch of Undying, *and* The Color out
of Time *(a sequel to H. P. Lovecraft's story "The Colour
out of Space"), the chapbook* Fat Face, *and the acclaimed
collection* Polyphemus.

D*r. Winters stepped* out of the tiny Greyhound station and
into the midnight street that smelt of pines and the river,
though the street was in the heart of the town. But then it
was a town of only five main streets in breadth, and these
extended scarcely a mile and a half along the rim of the
gorge. Deep in that gorge though the river ran, its blurred
roar flowed, perfectly distinct, between the banks of dark
shop windows. The station's window showed the only light,
save for a luminous clock face several doors down and a
little neon beer logo two blocks farther on. When he had
walked a short distance, Dr. Winters set his suitcase down,
pocketed his hands, and looked at the stars—thick as cob-
blestones in the black gulf.

"A mountain hamlet—a mining town," he said. "Stars.
No moon. We are in Bailey."

He was talking to his cancer. It was in his stomach.

Since learning of it, he had developed this habit of wry communion with it. He meant to show courtesy to this uninvited guest. Death. It would not find him churlish, for that would make its victory absolute. Except, of course, that its victory would *be* absolute, with or without his ironies.

He picked up his suitcase and walked on. The starlight made faint mirrors of the windows' blackness and showed him the man who passed: lizard-lean, white-haired (at fifty-seven), a man traveling on death's business, carrying his own death in him, and even bearing death's wardrobe in his suitcase. For this was filled—aside from his medical kit and some scant necessities—with mortuary bags. The sheriff had told him on the phone of the improvisations that presently enveloped the corpses, and so the doctor had packed these, laying them in his case with bitter amusement, checking the last one's breadth against his chest before the mirror, as a woman will gauge a dress before donning it, and telling his cancer:

"Oh, yes, that's plenty roomy enough for both of us!"

The case was heavy and he stopped frequently to rest and scan the sky. What a night's work to do, probing soulless filth, eyes earthward, beneath such a ceiling of stars! It had taken five days to dig them out. The autumnal equinox had passed, but the weather here had been uniformly hot. And warmer still, no doubt, so deep in the earth.

He entered the courthouse by a side door. His heels knocked on the linoleum corridor. A door at the end of it, on which was lettered NATE CRAVEN, COUNTY SHERIFF, opened well before he reached it, and his friend stepped out to meet him.

"Damnit, Carl, you're *still* so thin they could use you for a whip. Gimme that. You're in too good a shape already. You don't need the exercise."

The case hung weightless from his hand, imparting no tilt at all to his bull shoulders. Despite his implied self-derogation, he was only moderately paunched for a man his age and size. He had a rough-hewn face and the bulk of brow, nose, and jaw made his greenish eyes look small until one engaged them and felt the snap and penetration of their intelligence. He half-filled two cups from a coffee urn and topped both off with bourbon from a bottle in his desk. When they had finished these, they had finished trading news of mutual friends. The sheriff mixed another round, and sipped from his, in a silence clearly prefatory to the work at hand.

"They talk about rough justice," he said. "I've sure seen it now. One of those . . . patients of yours that you'll be working on? He was a killer. 'Killer' don't even half say it, really. You could say that *he* got justly executed in that blast. That much was justice for damn sure. But rough as hell on those other nine. And the rough don't just stop with their being dead either. That kiss-ass boss of yours! He's breaking his god-damned back touching his toes for Fordham Mutual. How much of the picture did he give you?"

"You refer, I take it, to the estimable Coroner Waddleton of Fordham County." Dr. Winters paused to sip his drink. With a delicate flaring of his nostrils he communicated all the disgust, contempt and amusement he had felt in his four years as Pathologist in Waddleton's office. The sheriff laughed.

"Clear pictures seldom emerge from anything the coroner says," the doctor continued. "He took your name in vain. Vigorously and repeatedly. These expressions formed his opening remarks. He then developed the theme of our office's strict responsibility to the letter of the law, and of the workmen's compensation law in particular. Death benefits accrue only to the dependents of decedents whose deaths arise *out of the course* of their employment, not merely *in* the course of it. Victims of a maniacal assault, though they die on the job, are by no means necessarily compensable under the law. We then contemplated the tragic injustice of an insurance company—*any* insurance company—having to pay benefits to unentitled persons, solely through the laxity and incompetence of investigating officers. Your name came up again."

Craven uttered a bark of mirth and fury. "The impartial

public servant! Ha! The impartial brown-nose, flim-flam and bullshit man is what he *is*. Ten to one, Fordham Mutual will slip out of it *without* his help, and those men's families won't see a goddamn nickel." Words were an insufficient vent; the sheriff turned and spat into his wastebasket. He drained his cup, and sighed. "I beg your pardon, Carl. We've been five days digging those men out and the last two days sifting half that mountain for explosive traces, with those insurance investigators hanging on our elbows, and the most they could say was that there was 'strong presumptive evidence' of a bomb. Well, I don't budge for that because I don't have to. Waddleton can shove his 'extraordinary circumstances.' If you don't find anything in those bodies, then that's all the autopsy there is to it, and they get buried right here where their families want 'em."

The doctor was smiling at his friend. He finished his cup and spoke with his previous wry detachment, as if the sheriff had not interrupted.

"The honorable coroner then spoke with remarkable volubility on the subject of Autopsy Consent forms and the malicious subversion of private citizens by vested officers of the law. He had, as it happened, a sheaf of such forms on his desk, all signed, all with a rider clause typed in above the signatures. A cogent paragraph. It had, among its other qualities, the property of turning the coroner's face purple when he read it aloud. He read it aloud to me three times. It appeared that the survivors' consent was contingent on two conditions: that the autopsy be performed *in locem mortis*, that is to say in Bailey, and that only if the coroner's pathologist found concrete evidence of homicide should the decedents be subject either to removal from Bailey or to further necropsy. It was well written. I remember wondering who wrote it."

The sheriff nodded musingly. He took Dr. Winters' empty cup, set it by his own, filled both two-thirds with bourbon, and added a splash of coffee to the doctor's. The two friends exchanged a level stare, rather like poker players in the clinch. The sheriff regarded his cup, sipped from it,

"*In locem mortis*. What-all does that mean exactly?"

" 'In the place of death.' "

"Oh. Freshen that up for you?"

"I've just started it, thank you."

Both men laughed, paused, and laughed again, some might have said immoderately.

"He all but told me that I *had* to find something to compel a second autopsy," the doctor said at length. "He would have sold his soul—or taken out a second mortgage on it—for a mobile x-ray unit. He's right of course. If those bodies have trapped any bomb fragments, that would be the surest and quickest way of finding them. It still amazes me your Dr. Parsons could let his x-ray go unfixed for so long."

"He sets bones, stitches wounds, writes prescriptions, and sends anything tricky down the mountain. Just barely manages that. Drunks don't get much done."

"He's gotten that bad?"

"He hangs on and no more. Waddleton was right there, not deputizing him pathologist. I doubt he could find a cannonball in a dead rat. I wouldn't say it where it could hurt him, as long as he's still managing, but everyone here knows it. His patients sort of look after *him* half the time. But Waddleton would have sent you, so matter who was here. Nothing but his best for party contributors like Fordham Mutual."

The doctor looked at his hands and shrugged. "So. There's a killer in the batch. *Was* there a bomb?"

Slowly, the sheriff planted his elbows on the desk and pressed his hands against his temples, as if the question had raised a turbulence of memories. For the first time the doctor—half harkening throughout to the never-quite-muted stirrings of the death within him—saw his friend's exhaustion: the tremor of hand, the bruised look under the eyes.

"I'm going to give you what I have, Carl. I told you I don't think you'll find a damn thing in those bodies. You're probably going to end up assuming what I do about it, but assuming is as far as anyone's going to get with this one. It is truly one of those Nightmare Specials that the good

Lord tortures lawmen with and then hides the answers to forever.

"All right then. About two months ago, we had a man disappear—Ronald Hanley. Mine worker, rock-steady, family man. He didn't come home one night, and we never found a trace of him. OK, that happens sometimes. About a week later, the lady that ran the laundromat, Sharon Starker, *she* disappeared, no trace. We got edgy then. I made an announcement on the local radio about a possible weirdo at large, spelled out special precautions everybody should take. We put both our squadcars on the night beat, and by day we set to work knocking on every door in town collecting alibis for the two times of disappearance.

"No good. Maybe you're fooled by this uniform and think I'm a law officer, protector of the people, and all that? A natural mistake. A lot of people were fooled. In less than seven weeks, six people vanished, just like that. Me and my deputies might as well have stayed in bed round the clock, for all the good we did." The sheriff drained his cup.

"Anyway, at last we got lucky. Don't get me wrong now. We didn't go all hog-wild and actually prevent a crime or anything. But we *did* find a body—except it wasn't the body of any of the seven people that had disappeared. We'd took to combing the woods nearest town, with temporary deputies from the miners to help. Well, one of those boys was out there with us last week. It was hot—like it's been for a while now—and it was real quiet. He head this buzzing noise and looked around for it, and he saw a bee-swarm up in the crotch of a tree. Except he was smart enough to know that that's not usual around here—bee hives. So it wasn't bees. It was bluebottle flies, a god-damned big cloud of them, all over a bundle that was wrapped in a tarp."

The sheriff studied his knuckles. He had, in his eventful life, occasionally met men literate enough to understand his last name and rash enough to be openly amused by it, and the knuckles—scared knobs—were eloquent of his reactions. He looked back into his old friend's eyes.

"We got that thing down and unwrapped it. Billy Lee Davis, one of my deputies, he was in Viet Nam, been near some bad, bad things and held on. Billy Lee blew his lunch all over the ground when we unwrapped that thing. It was a man. Some of a man. We knew he'd stood six-two because all the bones were there, and he'd probably weighed between two fifteen and two twenty-five, but he folded up no bigger than a big-size laundry package. Still had his face, both shoulders, and the left arm, but all the rest was clean. It wasn't animal work. It was knife work, all the edges neat as butcher cuts. Except butchered meat, even when you drain it all you can, will bleed a good deal afterwards, and there wasn't one god-damned drop of blood on the tarp, nor in that meat. It was just as pale as fish meat."

Deep in his body's center, the doctor's cancer touched him. Not a ravening attack—it sank one fang of pain, questioningly, into new, untasted flesh, probing the scope for its appetite there. He disguised his tremor with a shake of the head.

"A cache, then."

The sheriff nodded. "Like you might keep a potroast in the icebox for making lunches. I took some pictures of his face, then we put him back and erased our traces. Two of the miners I'd deputized did a lot of hunting, were woodssmart. So I left them on the first watch. We worked out positions and cover for them, and drove back.

"We got right on tracing him, sent out descriptions to every town within a hundred miles. He was no one I'd ever seen in Bailey, nor anyone else either, it began to look like, after we'd combed the town all day with the photos. Then, out of the blue, Billy Lee Davis smacks himself on the forehead and says, 'Sheriff, *I* seen this man somewhere in town, and not long ago!'

"He'd been shook all day since throwing up, and then all of a sudden he just snapped to. Was dead sure. Except he couldn't remember where or when. We went over and over it and he tried and tried. It got to where I wanted to grab him by the ankles and hang him upside down and shake him till it dropped out of him. But it was no damn use. Just after dark we went back to that tree—we'd worked out a place to hide the cars and a route to it through the woods. When we were close we walkie-talkied the men we'd left for an all-clear to come up. No answer at all. And when we got there, all that was left of our trap was the tree. No body, no tarp, no Special Assistant Deputies. Nothing."

This time Dr. Winters poured the coffee and bourbon. "Too much coffee," the sheriff muttered, but drank anyway. "Part of me wanted to chew nails and break necks. And part of me was scared shitless. When we got back I got on the radio station again and made an emergency broadcast and then had the man at the station rebroadcast it every hour. Told everyone to do everything in groups of three, to stay together at night in threes at least, to go out little as possible, keep armed and keep checking up on each other. It had such a damn-fool sound to it, but just pairing-up was no protection if half of one of those pairs was the killer. I deputized more men and put them on the streets to beef up the night patrol.

"It was next morning that things broke. The sheriff of Rakehell called—he's over in the next county. He said our corpse sounded a lot like a man named Abel Dougherty, a millhand with Con Wood over there. I left Billy Lee in charge and drove right out.

"This Dougherty had a cripple older sister he always checked back to by phone whenever he left town for long, a habit no one knew about, probably embarrassed him. Sheriff Peck there only found out about it when the woman called him, said her brother'd been four days gone for vacation and not rung her once. Without that Peck might not've thought of Dougherty just from our description, though the photo I showed him clinched it, and one would've reached him by mail soon enough. Well, he'd hardly set it down again when a call came through for me. It was Billy Lee. He'd remembered.

"When he'd seen Dougherty was the Sunday night three days before we found him. Where he'd seen him was the

Trucker's Tavern outside the north end of town. The man had made a stir by being jolly drunk and latching onto a miner who was drinking there, man named Joe Allen, who'd started at the mine about two months back. Dougherty kept telling him that he wasn't Joe Allen, but Dougherty's old buddy named Sykes that had worked with him at Con Wood for a coon's age, and what the hell kind of joke was this, come have a beer old buddy and tell me why you took off so sudden and what the hell you been doing with yourself.

"Allen took it laughing. Dougherty'd clap him on the shoulder, Allen'd clap him right back and make every kind of joke about it, say 'Give this man another beer, I'm standing in for a long-lost friend of his.' Dougherty was so big and loud and stubborn, Billy Lee was worried about a fight starting, and he wasn't the only one worried. But this Joe Allen was a natural good ol' boy, handled it perfect. We'd checked him out weeks back along with everyone else, and he was real popular with the other miners. Finally Dougherty swore he was going to take him on to another bar to help celebrate the vacation Dougherty was starting out on. Joe Allen got up grinning, said god damn it, he couldn't accommodate Dougherty by being this fellow Sykes, but he could sure as hell have a glass with any serious drinking man that was treating. He went out with him, and gave everyone a wink as he left, to the general satisfaction of the audience."

Craven paused. Dr. Winters met his eyes and knew his thought, two images: the jolly wink that roused the room to laughter, and the thing in the tarp aboil with bright blue flies.

"It was plain enough for me," the sheriff said. "I told Billy Lee to search Allen's room at the Skettles' boarding house and then go straight to the mine and take him. We could fine-polish things once we had him. Since I was already in Rakehell, I saw to some of the loose ends before I started back. I went with Sheriff Peck down to Con Wood and we found a picture of Eddie Sykes in the personnel files. I'd seen Joe Allen often enough, and it was his picture in that file.

"We found out Sykes lived alone, was an on-again, off-again worker, private in his comings and goings, and hadn't been around for a while. But one of the sawyers there could be pretty sure of when Sykes left Rakehell because he'd gone to Sykes' cabin the morning after a big meteor shower they had out there about nine weeks back, since some thought the shower might have reached the ground, and not far from Sykes' side of the mountain. He wasn't in that morning, and the sawyer hadn't seen him since.

"It looked sewed up. It *was* sewed up. After all those weeks. I was less than a mile out of Bailey, had the pedal floored. Full of rage and revenge. I felt . . . like a *bullet*, like I was one big thirty-caliber slug that was going to go right through that blood-sucking cannibal, tear the whole truth right out of his heart, enough to hang him a hundred times. That was the closest I got. So close that I *heard* it when it all blew to shit.

"I sound squirrelly. I know I do. Maybe all this gave me something I'll never shake off. We had to put together what happened. Billy Lee didn't have my other deputy with him. Travis was out with some men on the mountain dragnetting around that tree for clues. By luck, he was back at the car when Billy Lee was trying to raise him. He said he'd just been through Allen's room and had got something we could maybe hold him on. It was a sphere, half again big as a basketball, heavy, made of something that wasn't metal or glass but was a little like both. He could half-see into it and it looked to be full of some kind of circuitry and components. If someone tried to spring Allen, we could make a theft rap out of this thing, or say we suspected it was a bomb. Jesus! Anyway, he said it was the only strange thing he found, but it was plenty strange. He told Travis to get up to the mine for back-up. He'd be there first and should already have Allen by the time Travis arrived.

"Tierney, the shift boss up there, had an assistant that told us the rest. Billy Lee parked behind the offices where the men in the yard wouldn't see the car. He went upstairs to arrange the arrest with Tierney. They got half a dozen men together. Just as they came out of the building, they saw Allen take off running from the squadcar with the sphere under his arm.

"The whole compound's fenced in and Tierney'd already phoned to have all the gates shut. Allen zigged and zagged some but caught on quick to the trap. The sphere slowed him, but he still had a good lead. He hesitated a minute and then ran straight for the main shaft. A cage was just going down with a crew, and he risked every bone in him jumping down after it, but he got safe on top. By the time they got to the switches, the cage was done to the second level, and Allen and the crew had got out. Tierney got it back up. Billy Lee ordered the rest back to get weapons and follow, and him and Tierney rode the cage right back down. And about two minutes later half the god-damned mine blew up."

The sheriff stopped as if cut off, his lips parted to say more, his eyes registering for perhaps the hundredth time his amazement that there was no more, that the weeks of death and mystification ended here, with this split-second recapitulation: more death, more answerless dark, sealing all.

"Nate."

"What."

"Wrap it up and go to bed. I don't need your help. You're dead on your feet."

"I'm not on my feet. And I'm coming along."

"Give me a picture of the victims' position relative to the blast. I'm going to work and you're going to bed."

The sheriff shook his head absently. "They're mining in shrinkage stopes. The adits—levels—branch off lateral from the vertical shaft. From one level they hollow out overhand up to the one above. Scoop out big chambers and let most of the broken rock stay inside so they can stand on the heaps to cut the ceilings higher. They leave sections of support wall between stopes, and those men were buried several stopes in from the shaft. The cave-in killed *them*. The mountain just folded them up in their own hill of tailings. No kind of fragments reached them. I'm dead sure.

The only ones they *found* were of some standard charges that the main blast set off, and those didn't even get close. The big one blew out where the adit joined the shaft, right where, and right when Billy Lee and Tierney got out of the cage. And there is *nothing* left there, Carl. No sphere, no cage, no Tierney, no Billy Lee Davis. Just rock blown fine as flour."

Dr. Winters nodded and, after a moment, stood up.

"Come on, Nate. I've got to get started. I'll be lucky to have even a few of them done before morning. Drop me off and go to sleep, till then at least. You'll still be there to witness most of the work."

The sheriff rose, took up the doctor's suitcase, and led him out of the office without a word, concession in his silence.

The patrol car was behind the building. The doctor saw a crueller beauty in the stars than he had an hour before. They got in, and Craven swung them out onto the empty street. The doctor opened the window and harkened, but the motor's surge drowned out the river sound. Before the thrust of their headlights, ranks of old-fashioned parking meters sprouted shadows tall across the sidewalks, shadows which shrank and were cut down by the lights' passage. The sheriff said:

"All those extra dead. For nothing! Not even to . . . *feed* him! If it *was* a bomb, and he made it, he'd know how powerful it was. He wouldn't try some stupid escape stunt with it. And how did he even know the thing was there? We worked it out that Allen was just ending a shift, but he wasn't even up out of the ground before Billy Lee'd parked out of sight."

"Let it rest, Nate. I want to hear more, but after you've slept. I know you. All the photos will be there, and the report complete, all the evidence neatly boxed and carefully described. When I've looked things over I'll know exactly how to proceed by myself."

Bailey had neither hospital nor morgue, and the bodies were in a defunct ice-plant on the edge of town. A generator had been brought down from the mine, lighting improvised, and the refrigeration system reactivated. Dr. Parsons' office, and the tiny examining room that served the sheriff's station in place of a morgue, had furnished this makeshift with all the equipment that Dr. Winters would need beyond what he carried with him. A quarter-mile outside the main body of the town, they drew up to it. Tree-flanked, unneighbored by any other structure, it was a double building; the smaller half—the office—was illuminated. The bodies would be in the big, windowless refrigerator segment. Craven pulled up beside a second squadcar parked near the office door. A short, rake-thin man wearing a large white stetson got out of the car and came over. Craven rolled down his window.

"Trav. This here's Dr. Winters."

"Lo, Nate. Dr. Winters. Everything's shipshape inside. Felt more comfortable out here. Last of those newshounds left two hours ago."

"They sure do hang on. You take off now, Trav. Get some sleep and be back at sunup. What temperature we getting?"

The pale stetson, far clearer in the starlight than the shadow-face beneath it, wagged dubiously. "Thirty-six. She won't get lower—some kind of leak."

"That should be cold enough," the doctor said.

Travis drove off and the sheriff unlocked the padlock on the office door. Waiting behind him, Dr. Winters heard the river again—a cold balm, a whisper of freedom—and overlying this, the stutter and soft snarl of the generator behind the building, a gnawing, remorseless sound that somehow fed the obscure anguish which the other soothed. They went in.

The preparations had been thoughtful and complete. "You can wheel 'em out of the fridge on this and do the examining in here," the sheriff said, indicating a table and a gurney. "You should find all the gear you need on this big table here, and you can write up your reports on that desk. The phone's not hooked up—there's a pay phone at that last gas station if you have to call me."

The doctor nodded, checking over the material on the larger table: scalpels, post-mortem and cartilage knives, intestine scissors, rib shears, forceps, probes, mallet and chisels, a blade saw and electric bone saw, scale, jars for specimens, needles and suture, sterilizer, gloves.... Beside this array were a few boxes and envelopes with descriptive sheets attached, containing the photographs and such evidentiary objects as had been found associated with the bodies.

"Excellent," he muttered.

"The overhead light's fluorescent, full spectrum or whatever they call it. Better for colors. There's a pint of decent bourbon in that top desk drawer. Ready to look at 'em?"

"Yes."

The sheriff unbarred and slid back the big metal door to the refrigeration chamber. Icy, tainted air boiled out of the doorway. The light within was dimmer than that provided in the office—a yellow gloom wherein ten oblong heaps lay on trestles.

The two stood silent for a time, their stillness a kind of unpremeditated homage paid the eternal mystery at its threshold. As if the cold room were in fact a shrine, the doctor found a peculiar awe in the row of veiled forms. The awful unison of their dying, the titan's grave that had been made for them, conferred on them a stern authority, Death's chosen Ones. His stomach hurt, and he found he had his hand pressed to his abdomen. He glanced at Craven and was relieved to see that his friend, staring wearily at the bodies, had missed the gesture.

"Nate. Help me uncover them."

Starting at opposite ends of the row, they stripped the tarps off and piled them in a corner. Both were brusque now, not pausing over the revelation of the swelled, pulpy faces—most three-lipped with the gaseous burgeoning of their tongues—and the fat, livid hands sprouting from the filthy sleeves. But at one of the bodies Craven stopped. The doctor saw him look, and his mouth twist. Then he flung the tarp on the heap and moved to the next trestle.

When they came out Dr. Winters took out the bottle and

glasses Craven had put in the desk, and they had a drink together. The sheriff made as if he would speak, but shook his head and sighed.

"I *will* get some sleep, Carl. I'm getting crazy thoughts with this thing." The doctor wanted to ask those thoughts. Instead he laid a hand on his friend's shoulder.

"Go home, Sheriff Craven. Take off the badge and lie down. The dead won't run off on you. We'll all still be here in the morning."

When the sound of the patrol car faded, the doctor stood listening to the generator's growl and the silence of the dead, resurgent now. Both the sound and the silence seemed to mock him. The after-echo of his last words made him uneasy. He said to his cancer:

"What about it, dear colleague? We *will* still be here tomorrow? All of us?"

He smiled, but felt an odd discomfort, as if he had ventured a jest in company and roused a hostile silence. He went to the refrigerator door, rolled it back, and viewed the corpses in their ordered rank, with their strange tribunal air. "What, sirs?" he murmured. "Do you judge me? Just who is to examine whom tonight, if I may ask?"

He went back into the office, where his first step was to examine the photographs made by the sheriff, in order to see how the dead had lain at their uncovering. The earth had seized them with terrible suddenness. Some crouched, some partly stood, others sprawled in crazy, free-fall postures. Each successive photo showed more of the jumble as the shovels continued their work between shots. The doctor studied them closely, noting the identifications inked on the bodies as they came completely into view.

One man, Robert Willet, had died some yards from the main cluster. It appeared he had just straggled into the stope from the adit at the moment of the explosion. He should thus have received, more directly than any of the others, the shockwaves of the blast. If bomb fragments were to be found in any of the corpses, Mr. Willet's seemed likeliest to contain them. Dr. Winters pulled on a pair of surgical gloves.

He lay at one end of the line of trestles. He wore a thermal shirt and overalls that were strikingly new beneath the filth of burial. Their tough fabrics jarred with that of his flesh—blue, swollen, seeming easily torn or burst, like ripe fruit. In life Willet had grease-combed his hair. Now it was a sculpture of dust, spikes and whorls shaped by the head's last grindings against the mountain that clenched it.

Rigor had come and gone—Willet rolled laxly onto the gurney. As the doctor wheeled him past the others, he felt a slight self-consciousness. The sense of some judgment flowing from the dead assembly—unlike most such vagrant emotional embellishments of experience—had an odd tenacity in him. This stubborn unease began to irritate him with himself, and he moved more briskly.

He put Willet on the examining table and cut the clothes off him with shears, storing the pieces in an evidence box. The overalls were soiled with agonal waste expulsions. The doctor stared a moment with unwilling pity at his naked subject.

"You won't ride down to Fordham in any case," he said to the corpse. "Not unless I find something pretty damned obvious." He pulled his gloves tighter and arranged his implements.

Waddleton had said more to him than he had reported to the sheriff. The doctor was to find, and forcefully to record that he had found, strong "indications" absolutely requiring the decedents' removal to Fordham for x-ray and an exhaustive second post-mortem. The doctor's continued employment with the Coroner's Office depended entirely on his compliance in this. He had received this stipulation with a silence Waddleton had not thought it necessary to break. His present resolution was all but made at that moment. Let the obvious be taken as such. If the others showed as plainly as Willet did the external signs of death by asphyxiation, they would receive no more than a thorough external exam. Willet he would examine internally as well, merely to establish in depth for this one what should ap-

pear obvious in all. Otherwise, only when the external exam
revealed a clearly anomalous feature—and clear and sug-
gestive it must be—would he look deeper.

He rinsed the caked hair in a basin, poured the sedi-
ment into a flask and labeled it. Starting with the scalp, he
began a minute scrutiny of the body's surfaces, recording
his observations as he went.

The characteristic signs of asphyxial death were evident,
despite the complicating effects of autolysis and putrefac-
tion. The eyeballs' bulge and the tongue's protrusion were
by now at least partly due to gas pressure as well as the
mode of death, but the latter organ was clamped between
locked teeth, leaving little doubt as to that mode. The coloration of degenerative change—a greenish-yellow tint, a
darkening and mapping-out of superficial veins—was
marked, but not sufficient to obscure the blue of cyanosis
on the face and neck, nor the pinpoint hemorrhages freck-
ling neck, chest, and shoulders. From the mouth and nose
the doctor scraped matter he was confident was the blood-
tinged mucus typically ejected in the airless agony.

He began to find a kind of comedy in his work. What
a buffoon death made of a man! A blue, pop-eyed, three-
lipped thing. And there was himself, his curious, solicitous
intimacy with this clownish carrion. Excuse me, Mr. Willet, while I probe this laceration. How does it feel when I
do this? Nothing? Nothing at all? Fine, now what about
these nails. Split them clawing at the earth, did you? Yes.
A nice bloodblister under this thumbnail I see—got it on
the job a few days before your accident no doubt? Remarkable calluses here, still quite tough. . . .

The doctor looked for an unanalytic moment at the
hands—puffed, dark paws, gestureless, having renounced
all touch and grasp. He felt the wastage of the man concentrated in the hands. The painful futility of the body's
fine articulation when it is seen in death—this poignancy
he had long learned not to acknowledge when he worked.
But now he let it move him a little. This Roger Willet,
plodding to his work one afternoon, had suddenly been
scrapped, crushed to a nonfunctional heap of perishable

materials. It simply happened that his life had chanced to move too close to the passage of a more powerful life, one of those inexorable and hungry lives that leave human wreckage—known or undiscovered—in their wakes. Bad luck, Mr. Willet. Naturally, we feel very sorry about this. But this Joe Allen, your co-worker. Apparently he was some sort of . . . cannibal. It's complicated. We don't understand it all. But the fact is we have to dismantle you now to a certain extent. There's really no hope of your using these parts of yourself again, I'm afraid. Ready now?

The doctor proceeded to the internal exam with a vague eagerness for Willet's fragmentation, for the disarticulation of that sadness in his natural form. He grasped Willet by the jaw and took up the post-mortem knife. He sank its point beneath the chin and began the long, gently sawing incision that opened Willet from throat to groin.

In the painstaking separation of the body's laminae Dr. Winters found absorption and pleasure. And yet throughout he felt, marginal but insistent, the movement of a stream of irrelevant images. These were of the building that contained him, and of the night containing it. As from outside, he saw the plant—bleached planks, iron roofing—and the trees crowding it, all in starlight, a ghost-town image. And he saw the refrigerator vault beyond the wall as from within, feeling the stillness of murdered men in a cold, yellow light. And at length a question formed itself, darting in and out of the weave of his concentration as the images did: Why did he still feel, like some stir of the air, that sense of mute vigilance surrounding his action, furtively touching his nerves with its inquiry as he worked? He shrugged, overtly angry now. Who else was attending but Death? Wasn't he Death's hireling, and this Death's place? Then let the master look on.

Peeling back Willet's cover of hemorrhage-stippled skin, Dr. Winters read the corpse with an increasing dispassion, a mortuary text. He confined his inspection to the lungs and mediastinum and found there unequivocal testimony to Willet's asphyxial death. The pleurae of the lungs exhibited the expected ecchymoses—bruised spots in the glassy, enveloping membrane. Beneath, the polyhedral surface lobules of the lungs themselves were bubbled and blistered—the expected interstitial emphysema. The lungs, on section, were intensely and bloodily congested. The left half of the heart he found contracted and empty, while the right was over-distended and engorged with dark blood, as were the large veins of the upper mediastinum. It was a classic picture of death by suffocation, and at length the doctor, with needle and suture, closed up the text again.

He returned the corpse to the gurney and draped one of his mortuary bags over it in the manner of a shroud. When he had help in the morning, he would weigh the bodies on a platform scale the office contained and afterwards bag them properly. He came to the refrigerator door, and hesitated. He stared at the door, not moving, not understanding why.

Run. Get out, now.

The thought was his own, but it came to him so urgently he turned around as if someone behind him had spoken. Across the room a thin man in smock and gloves, his eyes shadows, glared at the doctor from the black windows. Behind the man was a shrouded cart; behind that, a wide metal door.

Quietly, wonderingly, the doctor asked, "Run from what?" The eyeless man in the glass was still half-crouched, afraid.

Then, a moment later, the man straightened, threw back his head, and laughed. The doctor walked to the desk and sat down shoulder to shoulder with him. He pulled out the bottle and they had a drink together, regarding each other with identical bemused smiles. Then the doctor said, "Let me pour you another. You need it, old fellow. It makes a man himself again."

Nevertheless his re-entry of the vault was difficult, toilsome, each step seeming to require a new summoning of the will to move. In the freezing half-light all movement felt like defiance. His body lagged behind his craving to be quick, to be done with this molestation of the gathered dead. He returned Willet to his pallet and took his neigh-

bor. The name on the tag wired to his boot was Ed Moses.
Dr. Winters wheeled him back to the office and closed the
big door behind him.

With Moses his work gained momentum. He expected
to perform no further internal necropsies. He thought of
his employer, rejoicing now in his seeming-submission to
Waddleton's ultimatum. The impact would be dire. He pic-
tured the coroner in shock, a sheaf of Pathologist's Reports in one hand, and smiled.

Waddleton could probably make a plausible case for in-
complete examination. Still, a pathologist's discretionary
powers were not well-defined. Many good ones would approve the adequacy of the doctor's method, given his working conditions. The inevitable litigation with a coalition of
compensation claimants would be strenuous and protracted.
Win or lose, Waddleton's venal devotion to the insurance
company's interest would be abundantly displayed. Further,
immediately on his dismissal the doctor would formally
disclose its occult cause to the press. A libel action would
ensue which he would have as little cause to fear as he
had to fear his firing. Both his savings and the lawsuit
would long outlast his life.

Externally, Ed Moses exhibited a condition as typically
asphyxial as Willet's had been, with no slightest mark of
fragment entry. The doctor finished his report and returned
Moses to the vault, his movements brisk and precise. His
unease was all but gone. That queasy stirring of the air—
had he really felt it? It had been, perhaps, some new re-
verberation of the death at work in him, a psychic shudder
of response to the cancer's stealthy probing for his life. He
brought out the body next to Moses in the line.

Walter Lou Jackson was big, 6' 2" from heel to crown,
and would surely weigh out at more than two hundred
pounds. He had writhed mightily against his million-ton
coffin with an agonal strength that had torn his face and
hands. Death had mauled him like a lion. The doctor set
to work.

His hands were fully themselves now—fleet, exact, intricately testing the corpse's character as other fingers might

explore a keyboard for its latent melodies. And the doctor
watched them with an old pleasure, one of the few that
had never failed him, his mind at one remove from their
busy intelligence. All the hard deaths! A worldful of them,
time without end. Lives wrenched kicking from their snug
meat-frames. Walter Lou Jackson had died very hard. Joe
Allen brought this on you, Mr. Jackson. We think it was
part of his attempt to escape the law.

But what a botched flight! The unreason of it—more
than baffling—was eerie in its colossal futility. Beyond
question, Allen had been cunning. A ghoul with a psy-
chopath's social finesse. A good old boy who could make
a tavernful of men laugh with delight while he cut his victim from their midst, make them applaud his exit with the
prey, who stepped jovially into the darkness with murder
at his side clapping him on the shoulder. Intelligent, certainly, with a strange technical sophistication as well, suggested by the sphere. Then what of the lunacy yet more
strongly suggested by the same object? In the sphere was
concentrated all the lethal mystery of Bailey's long nightmare.

Why the explosion? Its location implied an ambush for
Allen's pursuers, a purposeful detonation. Had he aimed at
a limited cave-in from which he schemed some inconceivable escape? Folly enough in this—far more if, as
seemed sure, Allen had made the bomb himself, for then
he would have to know its power was grossly inordinate
to the need.

But if it was not a bomb, had a different function and
only incidentally an explosive potential, Allen might un-
derestimate the blast. It appeared the object was somehow
remotely monitored by him, for the timing of events showed
he had gone straight for it the instant he emerged from the
shaft—shunned the bus waiting to take his shift back to
town and make a beeline across the compound for a patrol car that was hidden from his view by the office building. This suggested something more complex than a mere
explosive device, something, perhaps, whose destruction

was itself more Allen's aim than the explosion produced thereby.

The fact that he risked the sphere's retrieval at all pointed to this interpretation. For the moment he sensed its presence at the mine, he must have guessed that the murder investigation had led to its discovery and removal from his room. But then, knowing himself already liable to the extreme penalty, why should Allen go to such lengths to recapture evidence incriminatory of a lesser offense, possession of an explosive device?

Then grant that the sphere was something more, something instrumental to his murders that could guarantee a conviction he might otherwise evade. Still, his gambit made no sense. Since the sphere—and thus the lawmen he could assume to have taken it—were already at the mine office, he must expect the compound to be sealed at any moment. Meanwhile, the gate was open, escape into the mountains a strong possibility for a man capable of stalking and destroying two experienced and well-armed woodsmen lying in ambush for him. Why had he all but insured his capture to weaken a case against himself that his escape would have rendered irrelevant? Dr. Winters saw his fingers, like a hunting pack round a covert, converge on a small puncture wound below Walter Lou Jackson's xiphoid process, between the eighth ribs.

His left hand touched its borders, the fingers' inquiry quick and tender. The right hand introduced a probe, and both together eased it into the wound. It inched unobstructed deep into the body, curving upwards through the diaphragm towards the heart. The doctor's own heart accelerated. He watched his hands move to record the observation, watched them pause, watched them return to their survey of the corpse, leaving pen and page untouched.

Inspection revealed no further anomaly. All else he observed the doctor recorded faithfully, wondering throughout at the distress he felt. When he had finished, he understood it. Its cause was not the discovery of an entry wound that might bolster Waddleton's case. For the find had, within moments, revealed to him that, should he encounter anything he thought to be a mark of fragment penetration, he was going to ignore it. The damage Joe Allen had done was going to end here, with this last grand slaughter, and would not extend to the impoverishment of his victims' survivors. No more internals. The externals will-they nill-they, would from now on explicitly contraindicate the need for them.

The problem was that he did not believe the puncture in Jackson's thorax *was* a mark of fragment entry. Why? And, finding no answer to this question, why was he, once again, afraid? Slowly, he signed the report on Jackson, set it aside, and took up the post-mortem knife.

First the long, sawing slice, unzipping the mortal overcoat. Next, two great, square flaps of flesh reflected, scrolled laterally to the armpits' line, disrobing the chest: one hand grasping the flap's skirt, the other sweeping beneath it with the knife, flensing through the glassy tissue that joined it to the chest-wall, and shaving all muscles from their anchorages to bone and cartilage beneath. Then the dismantling of the strong-box within. Rib-shears—so frank and forward a tool, like a gardener's. The steel beak bit through each rib's gristle anchor to the sternum's centerplate. At the sternum's crownpiece the collarbones' ends were knifed, pried, and sprung free from their sockets. The coffer unhasped, unhinged, a knife teased beneath the lid and levered it off.

Some minutes later the doctor straightened up and stepped back from his subject. He moved almost drunkenly, and his age seemed scored more deeply in his face. With loathing haste he stripped his gloves off. He went to the desk, sat down, and poured another drink. If there was something like horror in his face, there was also a hardening in his mouth's line, and the muscles of his jaw. He spoke to his glass: "So be it, your Excellency. Something new for your humble servant. Testing my nerve?"

Jackson's pericardium, the shapely capsule containing his heart, should have been all but hidden between the big, blood-fat loaves of his lungs. The doctor had found it fully exposed, the lungs flanking it wrinkled lumps less than a third their natural bulk. Not only they, but the left heart and the superior mediastinal veins—all the regions that should have been grossly engorged with blood—were utterly drained of it.

The doctor swallowed his drink and got out the photographs again. He found that Jackson had died on his stomach across the body of another worker, with the upper part of a third trapped between them. Neither these two subjacent corpses nor the surrounding earth showed any stain of a blood loss that must have amounted to two liters.

Possibly the pictures, by some trick of shadow, had failed to pick it up. He turned to the Investigator's Report, where Craven would surely have mentioned any significant amounts of bloody earth uncovered during the disinterment. The sheriff recorded nothing of the kind. Dr. Winters returned to the pictures.

Ronald Pollock, Jackson's intimate associate in the grave, had died on his back, beneath and slightly askew of Jackson, placing most of their torsos in contact, save where the head and shoulder of the third interposed. It seemed inconceivable Pollock's clothing should lack any trace of such massive drainage from a death mate thus embraced.

The doctor rose abruptly, pulled on fresh gloves, and returned to Jackson. His hands showed a more brutal speed now, closing the great incision temporarily with a few widely spaced sutures. He replaced him in the vault and brought out Pollock, striding, heaving hard at the dead shapes in the shifting of them, thrusting always—so it seemed to him—just a step ahead of urgent thoughts he did not want to have, deformities that whispered at his back, emitting faint, chill gusts of putrid breath. He shook his head—denying, delaying—and pushed the new corpse onto the worktable. The scissors undressed Pollock in greedy bites.

But at length, when he had scanned each scrap of fabric and found nothing like the stain of blood, he came to rest again, relinquishing that simplest, desired resolution he had made such haste to reach. He stood at the instrument table, not seeing it, submitting to the approach of the half-formed things at his mind's periphery.

The revelation of Jackson's shriveled lungs had been more than a shock. He felt a stab of panic too, in fact that same curiously explicit terror of this place that had urged him to flee earlier. He acknowledged now that the germ of that quickly suppressed terror had been a premonition of this failure to find any trace of the missing blood. Whence the premonition? It had to do with a problem he had steadfastly refused to consider: the mechanics of so complete a drainage of the lungs' densely reticulated vascular structure. Could the earth's crude pressure by itself work so thoroughly, given only a single vent both slender and strangely curved? And then the photograph he had studied. It frightened him now to recall the image—some covert meaning stirred within it, struggling to be seen. Dr. Winters picked the probe up from the table and turned again to the corpse. As surely and exactly as if he had already ascertained the wound's presence, he leaned forward and touched it: a small, neat puncture, just beneath the xiphoid process. He introduced the probe. The wound received it deeply, in a familiar direction.

The doctor went to the desk, and took up the photograph again. Pollock's and Jackson's wounded areas were not in contact. The third man's head was sandwiched between their bodies at just that point. He searched out another picture, in which this third man was more central, and found his name inked in below his image: Joe Allen.

Dreamingly, Dr. Winters went to the wide metal door, shoved it aside, entered the vault. He did not search, but went straight to the trestle where his friend had paused some hours before, and found the same name on its tag.

The body, beneath decay's spurious obesity, was trim and well-muscled. The face was square-cut, shelf-browed, with a vulpine nose skewed by an old fracture. The swollen tongue lay behind the teeth, and the bulge of decomposition did not obscure what the man's initial impact must have been—handsome and open, his now-waxen black eyes sly and convivial. Say, good buddy, got a minute? I see

you comin' on the swing shift every day, don't I? Yeah,
Joe Allen. Look, I know it's late, you want to get home,
tell the wife you ain't been in there drinkin' since you got
off, right? Oh, yeah, I heard that. But this damn disappearance thing's got me so edgy, and I'd swear to God just
as I was coming here I seen someone moving around back
of that frame house up the street. See how the trees thin
out a little down back of the yard, where the moonlight
gets in? That's right. Well, I got me this little popper here.
Oh, yeah, that's a beauty, we'll have it covered between
us. I knew I could spot a man ready for some trouble—
couldn't find a patrol car anywhere on the street. Yeah, just
down in here now, to that clump of pine. Step careful, you
can barely see. That's right. . . .

The doctor's face ran with sweat. He turned on his heel
and walked out of the vault, heaving the door shut behind
him. In the office's greater warmth he felt the perspiration
soaking his shirt under the smock. His stomach rasped with
steady oscillations of pain, but he scarcely attended it. He
went to Pollock and seized up the post-mortem knife.

The work was done with surreal speed, the laminae of
flesh and bone recoiling smoothly beneath his desperate
but unerring hands, until the thoracic cavity lay exposed,
and in it, the vampire-stricken lungs, two gnarled lumps of
grey tissue.

He searched no deeper, knowing what the heart and
veins would show. He returned to sit at the desk, weakly
drooping, the knife, forgotten, still in his left hand. He
looked at the window, and it seemed his thoughts origi-
nated with that fainter, more tenuous Dr. Winters hanging
like a ghost outside.

What was this world he lived in? Surely, in a lifetime,
he had not begun to guess. To feed in such a way! There
was horror enough in this alone. But to feed thus *in his
own grave*. How had he accomplished it—leaving aside
how he had fought suffocation long enough to do anything
at all? How was it to be comprehended, a greed that raged
so hotly it would glut itself at the very threshold of its

own destruction? That last feast was surely in his stomach
still.

Dr. Winters looked at the photograph, at Allen's head
snugged into the others' middles like a hungry suckling
nuzzling to the sow. Then he looked at the knife in his
hand. The hand felt empty of all technique. Its one impulse was to slash, cleave, obliterate the remains of this
gluttonous thing, this Joe Allen. He must do this, or flee
it utterly. There was no course between. He did not move.

"I *will* examine him," said the ghost in the glass, and
did not move. Inside the refrigerator vault, there was a
slight noise.

No. It had been some hitch in the generator's murmur.
Nothing in there could move. There was another noise, a
brief friction against the vault's inner wall. The two old
men shook their heads at one another. A catch clicked and
the metal door slid open. Behind the staring image of his
own amazement, the doctor saw that a filthy shape stood
in the doorway and raised his arms towards him in a gesture of supplication. The doctor turned in his chair. From
the shape came a whistling groan, the decayed fragment of
a human voice.

Pleadingly, Joe Allen worked his jaw and spread his purple hands. As if speech were a maggot struggling to emerge
from his mouth, the blue, tumescent face toiled, the huge
tongue wallowed helplessly between the viscid lips.

The doctor reached for the telephone, lifted the receiver.
Its deadness to his ear meant nothing—he could not have
spoken. The thing confronting him, with each least movement that it made, destroyed the very frame of sanity in
which words might have meaning, reduced the world itself
around him to a waste of dark and silence, a starlit ruin
where already, everywhere, the alien and unimaginable was
awakening to its new dominion. The corpse raised and
reached out one hand as if to stay him—turned, and walked
towards the instrument table. Its legs were leaden, it rocked
its shoulders like a swimmer, fighting to make its passage
through gravity's dense medium. It reached the table and
grasped it exhaustedly. The doctor found himself on his

feet, crouched slightly, weightlessly still. The knife in his
hand was the only part of himself he clearly felt, and it
was like a tongue of fire, a crematory flame. Joe Allen's
corpse thrust one hand among the instruments. The thick
fingers, with a queer, simian ineptitude, brought up a
scalpel. Both hands clasped the little handle and plunged
the blade between the lips, as a thirsty child might a pop-
sicle, then jerked it out again, slashing the tongue. Turbid
fluid splashed down to the floor. The jaw worked stiffly,
the mouth brought out words in a wet, ragged hiss:

"Please. Help me. Trapped in *this*." One dead hand struck
the dead chest. "Starving."

"What are you?"

"Traveler. Not of earth."

"An eater of human flesh. A drinker of human blood."

"No. No. Hiding only. Am small. Shape hideous to you.
Feared death."

"You brought death." The doctor spoke with the calm
of perfect disbelief, himself as incredible to him as the
thing he spoke with. It shook its head, the dull, popped
eyes glaring with an agony of thwarted expression.

"Killed none. Hid in this. Hid in this not to be killed.
Five days now. Drowning in decay. Free me. Please."

"No. You have come to feed on us, you are not hiding
in fear. We are your food, your meat and drink. You fed
on those two men within your grave. *Their* grave. For you,
a delay. In fact, a diversion that has ended the hunt for
you."

"No! No! Used men already dead. For me, five days,
starvation. Even less. Fed only from necessity. Horrible necessity!"

The spoiled vocal instrument made a mangled gasp of
the last word—an inhuman, snakepit noise the doctor felt
as a cold flicker of ophidian tongues within his ears—while
the dead arms moved in a sodden approximation of the
body language that swears truth.

"No," the doctor said. "You killed them all. Including
your . . . tool—this man. *What are you?*" Panic erupted in
the question which he tried to bury by answering himself

instantly. "Resolute, yes. That surely. You used death for an escape route. You need no oxygen perhaps."

"Extracted more than my need from gasses of decay. A lesser component of our metabolism."

The voice was gaining distinctness, developing makeshifts for tones lost in the agonal rupturing of the valves and stops of speech, more effectively wrestling vowel and consonant from the putrid tongue and lips. At the same time the body's crudity of movement did not quite obscure a subtle, incessant experimentation. Fingers flexed and stirred, testing the give of tendons, groping the palm for the old points of purchase and counterpressure there. The knees, with cautious repetitions, assessed the new limits of their articulation.

"What was the sphere?"

"My ship. Its destruction our first duty facing discovery." (Fear touched the doctor, like a slug climbing his neck; he had seen, as it spoke, a sharp, spastic activity of the tongue, a pleating and shrinkage of its bulk as at the tug of some inward adjustment.) "No chance to re-enter. Leaving this take far too long. Not even time to set for destruct—must extrude a cilium, chemical key to broach hull shield. In shaft my only chance to halt host."

The right arm tested the wrist, and the scalpel the hand still held cut white sparks from the air, while the word "host" seemed itself a little knife-prick, a teasing abandonment of fiction—though the dead mask showed no irony—preliminary to attack.

But he found that fear had gone from him. The impossibility with which he conversed, and was about to struggle, was working in him an overwhelming amplification of his life's long helpless rage at death. He found his parochial pity for earth alone stretched to the trans-stellar scope this traveler commanded, to the whole cosmic trashyard with its bulldozed multitudes of corpses; galactic wheels of carnage—stars, planets with their most majestic generations—all trash, cracked bones and foul rags that pooled, settled, reconcatenated in the futile symmetries gravid with new multitudes of briefly animate trash.

And this, standing before him now, was the death it was given him particularly to deal—his mite was being called in by the universal Treasury of death, and Dr. Winters found himself, an old healer, on fire to pay. His own, more lethal, blade tugged at his hand with its own sharp appetite. He felt entirely the Examiner once more, knew the precise cuts he would make, swiftly and without error. *Very soon now*, he thought and cooly probed for some further insight before its onslaught:

"Why must your ship be destroyed, even at the cost of your hosts's life?"

"We must not be understood."

"The livestock must not understand what is devouring them."

"Yes, doctor. Not all at once. But one by one. You will understand what is devouring you. That is essential to my feast."

The doctor shook his head. "You are in your grave already, Traveler. That body will be your coffin. You will be buried in it a second time, for all time."

The thing came one step nearer and opened its mouth. The flabby throat wrestled as with speech, but what sprang out was a slender white filament, more than whip-fast. Dr. Winters saw only the first flicker of its eruption, and then his brain nova-ed, thinning out at light-speed to a white nullity.

When the doctor came to himself, it was in fact to a part of himself only. Before he had opened his eyes he found that his wakened mind had repossessed proprioceptively only a bizarre truncation of his body. His head, neck, left shoulder, arm and hand declared themselves—the rest was silence.

When he opened his eyes, he found that he lay supine on the gurney, and naked. Something propped his head. A strap bound his left elbow to the gurney's edge, a strap he could feel. His chest was also anchored by a strap, and this he could not feel. Indeed, save for its active remnant, his entire body might have been bound in a block of ice, so numb was it, and so powerless was he to compel the slightest movement from the least part of it.

The room was empty, but from the open door of the vault there came slight sounds: the creak and soft frictions of heavy tarpaulin shifted to accommodate some business involving small clicking and kissing noises.

Tears of fury filled the doctor's eyes. Clenching his one fist at the starry engine of creation that he could not see, he ground his teeth and whispered in the hot breath of strangled weeping:

"Take it back, this dirty little shred of life! I throw it off gladly like the filth it is." The slow knock of bootsoles loudened from within the vault, and he turned his head. From the vault door Joe Allen's corpse approached him.

It moved with new energy, though its gait was grotesque, a ducking, hitching progress, jerky with circumventions of decayed muscle, while above this galvanized, struggling frame, the bruise-colored face hung inanimate, an image of detachment. With terrible clarity it revealed the thing for what it was—a damaged hand-puppet vigorously worked from within. And when that frozen face was brought to hang above the doctor, the reeking hands, with the light, solicitous touch of friends at sickbeds, rested on his naked thigh.

The absence of sensation made the touch more dreadful than if felt. It showed him that the nightmare he still desperately denied at heart had annexed his body while he—holding head and arm free—had already more than half-drowned in its mortal paralysis. There lay his nightmare part, a nothingness freely possessed by an unspeakability. The corpse said:

"Rotten blood. Thin nourishment. Only one hour alone before you came. Fed from neighbor to my left—barely had strength to extend siphon. Fed from the right while you worked. Tricky going—you are alert. Expected Dr. Parsons. Energy needs of animating this"—one hand left the doctor's thigh and smote the dusty overalls—"and of host-transfer, very high. Once I have you synapsed, will be near starvation again."

A sequence of unbearable images unfolded in the doctor's mind, even as the robot carrion turned from the gurney and walked to the instrument table: the sheriff's arrival just after dawn, alone of course, since Craven always took thought for his deputies' rest and because on this errand he would want privacy to consider any indiscretion on behalf of the miners' survivors that the situation might call for; his finding his old friend, supine and alarmingly weak; his hurrying over, his leaning near. Then, somewhat later, a police car containing a rack of still wet bones might plunge off the highway above some deep spot in the gorge.

The corpse took an evidence box from the table and put the scalpel in it. Then it turned and retrieved the mortuary knife from the floor and put that in as well, saying as it did so, without turning, "The sheriff will come in the morning. You spoke like close friends. He will probably come alone."

The coincidence with his thoughts had to be accident, but the intent to terrify and appall him was clear. The tone and timing of that patched-up voice were unmistakably deliberate—sly probes that sought his anguish specifically, sought his mind's personal center. He watched the corpse—back at the table—dipping an apish but accurate hand and plucking up rib shears, scissors, clamps, adding all to the box. He stared, momentarily emptied by shock of all but the will to know finally the full extent of the horror that had appropriated his life. Joe Allen's body carried the box to the worktable beside the gurney, and the expressionless eyes met the doctor's.

"I have gambled. A grave gamble. But now I have won. At risk of personal discovery we are obliged to disconnect, contract, hide as well as possible in host body. Suicide in effect. I disregarded situational imperatives, despite starvation before disinterment and subsequent autopsy all but certain. I caught up with crew, tackled Pollock and Jackson microseconds before blast. Computed five days' survival from this cache, could disconnect at limit of strength to do so, but otherwise would chance autopsy, knowing doctor was alcoholic incompetent. And now see my gain.

You are a prize host, can feed with near impunity even
when killing too dangerous. Safe meals delivered to you
still warm."

The corpse had painstakingly aligned the gurney parallel to the worktable but offset, the table's foot extending
past the gurney's, and separated from it by a distance somewhat less than the reach of Joe Allen's right arm. Now the
dead hands distributed the implements along the right edge
of the table, save for the scissors and the box. These the
corpse took to the table's foot, where it set down the box
and slid the scissors' jaws round one strap of its overalls.
It began to speak again, and as it did, the scissors dis-
membered its cerements in unhesitating strokes.

"The cut must be medical, forensically right, though a
smaller one easier. Must be careful of the pectoral muscles or arms will not convey me. I am no larva anymore—
over fifteen hundred grams."

To ease the nightmare's suffocating pressure, to thrust
out some flicker of his own will against its engulfment,
the doctor flung a question, his voice more cracked than
the other's now was:

"Why is my arm free?"

"The last, fine neural splicing needs a sensory-motor
standard, to perfect my brain's fit to yours. Lacking this
eye-hand coordinating check, much coarser motor control
of host. This done, I flush out the paralytic, unbind us, and
we are free together."

The grave-clothes had fallen in a puzzle of fragments,
and the cadaver stood naked, its dark, gas-rounded contours making it seem some sleek marine creature, ruddered
with the black-veined, gas-distended sex. Again the voice
had teased for his fear, had uttered the last word with a
savoring protraction, and now the doctor's cup of anguish
brimmed over; horror and outrage wrenched his spirit in
brutal alternation as if trying to tear it naked from its captive frame. He rolled his head in this deadlock, his mouth
beginning to split with the slow birth of a mind-emptying
outcry.

The corpse watched this, giving a single nod that might

have been approbation. Then it mounted the worktable and, with the concentrated caution of some practiced convalescent reentering his bed, lay on its back. The dead eyes again sought the living and found the doctor staring back, grinning insanely.

"Clever corpse!" the doctor cried. "Clever, carnivorous corpse! Able alien! Please don't think I'm criticizing. Who am I to criticize? A mere arm and shoulder, a talking head, just a small piece of a pathologist. But I'm confused." He paused, savoring the monster's attentive silence and his own buoyancy in the hysterical levity that had unexpectedly liberated him. "You're going to use your puppet there to pluck you out of itself and put you on me. But once he's pulled you from your driver's seat, won't he go dead, so to speak, and drop you? You could get a nasty knock. Why not set a plank between the tables—the puppet opens the door, and you scuttle, ooze, lurch, flop, slither, as the case may be, across the bridge. No messy spills. And in any case, isn't this an odd, rather clumsy way to get around among your cattle? Shouldn't you at least carry your own scalpels when you travel? There's always the risk you'll run across that one host in a million that isn't carrying one with him.

He knew his gibes would be answered to his own despair. He exulted, but solely in the momentary bafflement of the predator—in having, for just a moment, mocked its gloating assurance to silence and marred its feast.

Its right hand picked up the post-mortem knife beside it, and the left wedged a roll of gauze beneath Allen's neck, lifting the throat to a more prominent arch. The mouth told the ceiling:

"We retain larval form till entry of the host. As larvae we have locomotor structures, and sense-buds usable outside our ships' sensory amplifiers. I waited coiled round Ed Sykes' bed leg till night, entered by his mouth as he slept." Allen's hand lifted the knife, held it high above the dull, quick eyes, turning it in the light. "Once lodged, we have three instars to adult form," the voice continued absently—the knife might have been a mirror from which the corpse read its features. "Larvally we have only a sketch of our full neural tap. Our metamorphosis is cued and determined by the host's endosomatic ecology. I matured in three days." Allen's wrist flexed, tipping the knife's point downmost. "Most supreme adaptations are purchased at the cost of inessential capacities." The elbow pronated and slowly flexed, hooking the knife body-wards. "Our hosts are all sentients, eco-dominants, are already carrying the baggage of coping structures for the planetary environment. Limbs, sensory portals"—the fist planted the fang of its tool under the chin, tilted it and rode it smoothly down the throat, the voice proceeding unmarred from under the furrow that the steel ploughed—"somatic envelopes, instrumentalities"—down the sternum, diaphragm, abdomen the stainless blade painted its stripe of gaping, muddy tissue— "with a host's brain we inherit all these, the mastery of any planet, netted in its dominant's cerebral nexus. Thus our genetic codings are now all but disencumbered of such provisions."

So swiftly the doctor flinched, Joe Allen's hand slashed four lateral cuts from the great wound's axis. The seeming butchery left two flawlessly drawn thoracic flaps cleanly outlined. The left hand raised the left flap's hem, and the right coaxed the knife into the aperture, deepening it with small stabs and slices. The posture was a man's who searches a breast pocket, with the dead eyes studying the slow recoil of flesh. The voice, when it resumed, had geared up to an intenser pitch:

"Galactically, the chordate nerve/brain paradigm abounds, and the neural labyrinth is our dominion. Are we to make plank bridges and worm across them to our food? Are cockroaches greater than we for having legs to run up walls and antennae to grope their way! All the quaint, hinged crutches that life sports! The stilts, fins, fans, springs, stalks, flippers and feathers, all in turn so variously terminating in hooks, clamps, suckers, scissors, forks or little cages of digits! And besides all the gadgets it concocts for wrestling through its worlds, it is all knobbed, whiskered, crested, plumed, vented, spiked or measeled over with perceptual gear for combing pittances of noise or color from the environing plentitude."

Invincibly calm and sure, the hands traded tool and tasks. The right flap eased back, revealing ropes of ingeniously spared muscle while promising a genuine appearance once sutured back in place. Helplessly the doctor felt his delirious defiance bleed away and a bleak fascination rebind him.

"We are the taps and relays that share the host's aggregate of afferent nerve-impulse precisely at its nodes of integration. We are the brains that peruse these integrations, integrate them with our existing banks of host-specific data, and, lastly, let their consequences flow down the motor pathway—either the consequences they seek spontaneously, or those we wish to graft upon them. We are besides a streamlined alimentary/circulatory system and a reproductive apparatus. And more than this we need not be."

The corpse had spread its bloody vest, and the feculent hands now took up the rib shears. The voice's sinister coloration of pitch and stress grew yet more marked—the phrases slid from the tongue with a cobra's seeking sway, winding their liquid rhythms round the doctor till a gap in his resistance should let them pour through to slaughter the little courage left him.

"For in this form we have inhabited the densest brain-web of three hundred races, lain intricately snug within them like thriving vine on trelliswork. We've looked out from too many variously windowed masks to regret our own vestigial senses. None read their worlds definitely. Far better then, our nomad's range and choice, than an unvarying tenancy of one poor set of structures. Far better to slip on as we do whole living beings and wear at once all of their limbs and organs, memories and powers—wear all as tightly congruent to our wills as a glove is to the hand that fills it."

The shears clipped through the gristle, stolid, bloody jaws monotonously feeding, stopping short of the sternoclavicular joint in the manubrium where the muscles of the pectoral girdle have an important anchorage.

"No consciousness of the chordate type that we have found has been impermeable to our finesse—no dendritic pattern so elaborate we could not read its stitchwork and thread ourselves to match, precisely map its each synaptic seam till we could loosen it and re-tailor all to suit ourselves. We have strutted costumed in the bodies of planetary autarchs, venerable manikins of moral fashion, but cut of the universal cloth: the weave of fleet electric filaments of experience which we easily re-shuttled to the warp of our wishes. Whereafter—newly hemmed and gathered— their living fabric hung obedient to our bias, investing us with honor and influence unlimited."

The tricky verbal melody, through the corpse's deft, unfaltering self-dismemberment—the sheer neuromuscular orchestration of the compound activity—struck Dr. Winters with the detached enthrallment great keyboard performers could bring him. He glimpsed the alien's perspective—a Gulliver waiting in a brobdingnagian grave, then marshaling a dead giant against a living, like a dwarf in a huge mechanical crane, feverishly programming combat on a battery of levers and pedals, waiting for the robot arms' enactments, the remote, titanic impact of the foes—and he marveled, filled with a bleak wonder at life's infinite strategy and plasticity. Joe Allen's hands reached into his half-opened abdominal cavity, reached deep below the uncut anterior muscle that was exposed by the shallow, spurious incision of the epidermis, till by external measure they were extended far enough to be touching his thighs. The voice was still as the forearms advertised a delicate rummaging with the buried fingers. The shoulders drew back. As the steady withdrawal brought the wrists into view, the dead legs tremored and quaked with diffuse spasms.

"You called your kind our food and drink, doctor. If you were merely that, an elementary usurpation of your motor tracts alone would satisfy us, give us perfect cattle-control—for what rarest word or subtlest behavior is more than a flurry of varied muscles? That trifling skill was ours long ago. It is not mere blood that feeds this lust I feel now to tenant you, this craving for an intimacy that years will not stale. My truest feast lies in compelling you to feed in that way and in the utter deformation of your will this will involve. Had gross nourishment been my prime need, then my gravemates—Pollock and Jackson—could have eked out two weeks of life for me or more. But I scorned a cowardly parsimony in the face of death. I reinvested more than half the energy that their blood gave me in fabricating chemicals to keep their brains alive, and fluid-bathed with oxygenated nutriment."

Out of the chasmed midriff the smeared hands dragged two long tresses of silvery filament that writhed and sparkled with a million simultaneous coilings and contractions. The legs jittered with faint, chaotic pulses throughout their musculature, until the bright, vermiculate tresses had gathered into two spheric masses which the hands laid carefully within the incision. Then the legs lay still as death.

"I had accessory neural taps only to spare, but I could access much memory, and all of their cognitive responses, and having in my banks all the organ of Corti's electro-chemical conversions of English words, I could whisper anything to them directly into the eighth cranial nerve. Those are our true feast, doctor, such bodiless electric storms of impotent cognition as I tickled up in those two little bone globes. I was forced to drain them yesterday, just before disinterment. They lived till then and understood everything—*everything* I did to them."

When the voice paused, the dead and living eyes were locked together. They remained so a moment, and then the dead face smiled.

It recapitulated all the horror of Allen's first resurrection—this waking of expressive soul from those grave-mound contours. And it was a demon-soul the doctor saw awaken: the smile was barbed with fine, sharp hooks of cruelty at the corners of the mouth, while the barbed eyes beamed fond, languorous anticipation of his pain. Remotely, Dr. Winters heard the flat sound of his own voice asking:

"And Eddie Sykes?"

"Oh, yes, doctor. He is with us now, has been throughout. I grieve to abandon so rare a host! He is a true hermit-philosopher, well-read in four languages. He is writing a translation of Marcus Aurelius—he was, I mean, in his free time. . . ."

Long minutes succeeded of the voice accompanying the surreal self-autopsy, but the doctor lay stilled, emptied of reactive power. Still, the full understanding of his fate reverberated in his mind—an empty room through which the voice, not heard exactly but somehow implanted directly as in the subterranean torture it had just described, sent aftershocks of realization, amplifications of the Unspeakable.

The parasite had traced and tapped the complex interface between cortical integration of input and the consequent neural output shaping response. It had interposed its brain between, sharing consciousness while solely commanding the pathways of reaction. The host, the bottled personality, was mute and limbless for any least expression of its own will, while hellishly articulate and agile in the service of the parasite's. It was the host's own hands that bound and wrenched the life half out of his prey, his own loins that experienced the repeated orgasms crowning his other despoliations of their bodies. And when they lay, bound and shrieking still, ready for the consummation, it was his own strength that hauled the smoking entrails from them, and his own intimate tongue and guzzling mouth he plunged into the rank, palpitating feast.

And the doctor had glimpses of the history behind this predation, that of a race so far advanced in the essentializing, the inexorable abstraction of their own mental fabric that through scientific commitment and genetic self-cultivation they had come to embody their own model of perfected consciousness, streamlined to permit the entry of other beings and the direct acquisition of their experiential worlds. All strictest scholarship at first, until there matured in the disembodied scholars their long-germinal and now blazing, jealous hatred for all "lesser" minds rooted and clothed in the soil and sunlight of solid, particular worlds. The parasite spoke of the "cerebral music," the "symphonies of agonized paradox" that were its invasion's chief plunder. The doctor felt the truth behind this grandiloquence: its actual harvest from the systematic violation of encoffined personalities was the experience of a barren supremacy of means over lives more primitive, perhaps, but vastly wealthier in the vividness and passionate concern with which life for them was imbued.

Joe Allen's hands had scooped up the bunched skeins of alien nerve, with the wrinkled brain-node couched amidst them, and for some time had waited the slow retraction of a last major trunkline which seemingly had followed the spine's axis. At last, when only a slender subfiber of this remained implanted, the corpse, smiling once more, held up for him to view its reconcatenated master. The doctor looked into its eyes then and spoke—not to their controller, but to the captive who shared them with it, and who now, the doctor knew, neared his final death.

"Goodbye, Joe Allen. Eddie Sykes. You are guiltless. Peace be with you at last."

The demon smile remained fixed, the right hand reached its viscid cargo across the gap and over the doctor's groin. He watched the hand set the glittering medusa's head—his new self—upon his flesh, return to the table, take up the scalpel, and reach back to cut in his groin a four-inch incision—all in eerie absence of tactile stimulus. The line that had remained plunged into the corpse suddenly whipped free of the mediastinal crevice, retracted across the gap and shortened to a taut stub on the seething organism atop the doctor.

Joe Allen's body collapsed, emptied, all slack. He was a corpse again entirely, but with one anomalous feature to his posture. His right arm had not dropped to the nearly vertical hang that would have been natural. At the instant of the alien's unplugging, the shoulder had given a fierce shrug and wrenching of its angle, flinging the arm upward as it died so that it now lay in the orientation of an arm that reaches up for a ladder's next rung. The slightest tremor would unfix the joints and dump the arm back into the gravitational bias; it would also serve to dump the scalpel from the proferred, upturned palm that implement still precariously occupied.

The man had repossessed himself one microsecond before his end. The doctor's heart stirred, woke, and sang within him, for he saw that the scalpel was just in reach of his fingers at his forearm's fullest stretch from the bound elbow. The horror crouched on him and, even now slowly feeding its trunkline into his groin incision, at first stopped the doctor's hand with a pang of terror. Then he reminded himself that, until implanted, the enemy was a senseless mass, bristling with plugs, with input jacks for senses, but, until installed in the physical amplifiers of eyes and ears, an utterly deaf, blind monad that waited in a perfect solipsism between two captive sensory envelopes.

He saw his straining fingers above the bright tool of freedom, thought with an insane smile of God and Adam on the Sistine ceiling, and then, with a lifespan of surgeon's fine control, plucked up the scalpel. The arm fell and hung.

"Sleep," the doctor said. "Sleep revenged."

But he found his retaliation harshly reined-in by the alien's careful provisions. His elbow had been fixed with his upper arm almost at right angles to his body's long axis; his forearm could reach his hand inward and present it closely to the face, suiting the parasite's need of an eye-hand coordinative check, but could not, even with the scalpel's added reach, bring its point within four inches of his groin. Steadily the parasite fed in its tapline. It would usurp motor control in three of four minutes at most, to judge by the time its extrication from Allen had taken.

Frantically the doctor bent his wrist inwards to its limit, trying to pick through the strap where it crossed his inner elbow. Sufficient pressure was impossible, and the hold so awkward that even feeble attempts threatened the loss of the scalpel. Smoothly the root of alien control sank into him. It was a defenseless thing of jelly against which he lay lethally armed, and he was still doomed—a preview of all his thrall's impotence-to-be.

But of course there was a way. Not to survive. But to escape, and to have vengeance. For a moment he stared at his captor, hardening his mettle in the blaze of hate it lit in him. Then, swiftly, he determined the order of his moves, and began.

He reached the scalpel to his neck and opened his superior thyroid vein—his inkwell. He laid the scalpel by his ear, dipped his finger in his blood, and began to write on the metal surface of the gurney, beginning by his thigh and moving towards his armpit. Oddly, the incision of his neck, though this was muscularly awake, had been painless, which gave him hopes that raised his courage for what remained to do. His neat, sparing strokes scribed with ghastly legibility.

When he had done the message read:

> MIND PARASITE
> FM ALLEN IN ME
> CUT *all* TILL FIND
> 1500 GM MASS
> NERVE FIBRE

He wanted to write goodbye to his friend, but the alien had begun to pay out smaller, auxiliary filaments collaterally with the main one, and all now lay in speed.

He took up the scalpel, rolled his head to the left, and plunged the blade deep in his ear.

Miracle! Last, accidental mercy! It was painless. Some procedural, highly specific anesthetic was in effect. With careful plunges, he obliterated the right inner ear and then thrust silence, with equal thoroughness, into the left. The slashing of the vocal cords followed, then the tendons in the back of the neck that hold it erect. He wished he were free to unstring knees and elbows too, but it could not be. But blinded, with centers of balance lost, with only rough motor control—all these conditions should fetter the alien's escape, should it in the first place manage the reanimation of a bloodless corpse in which it had not yet achieved a fine-tuned interweave. Before he extinguished his eyes, he paused, the scalpel poised above his face, and blinked them to clear his aim of tears. The right, then the left, both retinas meticulously carved away, the yolk of vision quite scooped out of them. The scalpel's last task, once it had tilted the head sideways to guide the bloodflow absolutely clear of possible effacement of the message, was to slash the external carotid artery.

When this was done the old man sighed with relief and laid his scalpel down. Even as he did so, he felt the deep, inward prickle of an alien energy—something that flared, crackled, flared, *groped for* but did not quite find its purchase. And inwardly, as the doctor sank towards sleep—cerebrally, as a voiceless man must speak—he spoke to the parasite these carefully chosen words:

"Welcome to your new house. I'm afraid there's been some vandalism—the lights don't work, and the plumbing has a very bad leak. There are some other things wrong as well—the neighborhood is perhaps a little *too* quiet, and you may find it hard to get around very easily. But it's been a lovely home to me for fifty-seven years, and somehow I think you'll stay. . . ."

The face, turned toward the body of Joe Allen, seemed to weep scarlet tears, but its last movement before death was to smile.

OR ALL THE SEAS WITH OYSTERS

Avram Davidson

There are two SF stories whose plots everyone seems to know, stories that have become part of our shared cultural heritage to a sufficient degree, passed on by word of mouth from one person to another, like an Urban Legend. If you mention the details of their plotlines, most people will say, "Oh, yeah! That one!" even if they have no idea who wrote them or have in fact never actually read them in the first place. One of them is Damon Knight's "To Serve Man" ("It's a cookbook!" Remember now?). The other one is the mad little classic that follows, detailing the sex cycles of coat hangers and paper clips, which demonstrates that aliens among us might find it expedient to hide in the very plainest of plain sight . . .

For many years, the late Avram Davidson was one of the most eloquent and individual voices in science fiction and fantasy, and there were few writers in any literary field who could match his wit, his erudition, or the stylish elegance of his prose. During his long career, Davidson won the Hugo, the Edgar, and the World Fantasy Award, and his short work was assembled in landmark collections such as The Best of Avram Davidson, Or All the Seas With Oysters, The Redward Edward Papers, Collected Fantasies, *and* The Adventures of Doctor Esterhazy. *His novels include the renowned* The Phoenix and the Mirror, Masters of the Maze, Rogue Dragon, Peregrine: Primus, Rork!, Clash of Star Kings, *and* Vergil in Averno, *and a novel in collaboration with Grania Davis,* Marco Polo and the Sleeping Beauty. *His most recent books are a posthumously released collection of his erudite and witty essays,* Adventures in Unhistory, *and a mammoth retrospective collection,* The Avram Davidson Treasury, *which appeared on just about every critic's list as one of the best collections of 1998.*

When the man came in to the F & O Bike Shop, Oscar greeted him with a hearty "Hi, there!" Then, as he looked closer at the middle-aged visitor with the eyeglasses and business suit, his forehead creased and he began to snap his thick fingers.

"Oh, say, I know you," he muttered. "Mr.—um—name's on the tip of my tongue, doggone it . . ." Oscar was a barrel-chested fellow. He had orange hair.

"Why, sure you do," the man said. There was a Lion's emblem in his lapel. "Remember, you sold me a girl's bicycle with gears, for my daughter? We got to talking about that red French racing bike your partner was working on—"

Oscar slapped his big hand down on the cash register. He raised his head and rolled his eyes up. "Mr. Whatney!"

Mr. Whatney beamed. "Oh, *sure.* Gee, how could I forget? And we went across the street afterward and had a couple a beers. Well, how you *been,* Mr. Whatney? I guess the bike—it was an English model, wasn't it? Yeah. It must of given satisfaction or you would of been back, huh?"

Mr. Whatney said the bicycle was fine, just fine. Then he said, "I understand there's been a change, though. You're all by yourself now. Your partner . . ."

Oscar looked down, pushed his lower lip out, nodded. "You heard, huh? Ee-up. I'm all by myself now. Over three months now."

The partnership had come to an end three months ago, but it had been faltering long before then. Ferd liked books, long-playing records and high-level conversation, Oscar liked beer, bowling and women. Any women. Any time.

The shop was located near the park; it did a big trade in renting bicycles to picnickers. If a woman was barely old enough to be *called* a woman, and not quite old enough to be called an *old* woman, or if she was anywhere in between, and if she was alone, Oscar would ask, "How does that machine feel to you? All right?"

"Why . . . I guess so."

Taking another bicycle, Oscar would say, "Well, I'll just ride along a little bit with you, to make sure. Be right back, Ferd." Ferd always nodded gloomily. He knew that Oscar would not be right back. Later, Oscar would say, "Hope you made out in the shop as good as I did in the park."

"Leaving me all alone here all that time," Ferd grumbled.

And Oscar usually flared up. "Okay, then, next time *you* go, and leave *me* to stay here. See if I begrudge you a little fun." But he knew, of course, that Ferd—tall, thin, pop-eyed Ferd—would never go. "Do you good," Oscar said, slapping his sternum. "Put hair on your chest."

Ferd muttered that he had all the hair on his chest that he needed. He would glance down covertly at his lower arms; they were thick with long black hair, though his upper arms were slick and white. It was already like that when he was in high school, and some of the others would laugh at him—call him "Ferdie the Birdie." They knew it bothered him, but they did it anyway. How was it possible— he wondered then; he still did now—for people deliberately to hurt someone else who hadn't hurt them? How was it possible?

He worried over other things. All the time.

"The Communists—" He shook his head over the newspaper. Oscar offered an advice about the Communists in two short words. Or it might be capital punishment. "Oh, what a terrible thing if an innocent man was to be executed," Ferd moaned. Oscar said that was the guy's tough luck.

"Hand me that tire-iron," Oscar said.

And Ferd worried even about other people's minor concerns. Like the time the couple came in with the tandem and the baby-basket on it. Free air was all they took; then the woman decided to change the diaper and one of the safety pins broke.

"Why are there never any safety pins?" the woman fretted, rummaging here and rummaging there. "There are *never* any safety pins."

Ferd made sympathetic noises, went to see if he had any; but, though he was sure there'd been some in the office, he couldn't find them. So they drove off with one side of the diaper tied in a clumsy knot.

At lunch, Ferd said it was too bad about the safety pins. Oscar dug his teeth into a sandwich, tugged, tore, chewed, swallowed. Ferd liked to experiment with sandwich spreads—the one he liked most was cream cheese, olives, anchovy and avocado, mashed up with a little mayonnaise—but Oscar always had the same pink luncheon-meat.

"It must be difficult with a baby," Ferd nibbled. "Not just traveling, but raising it."

Oscar said, "Jeez, there's drugstores in every block, and if you can't read, you can at least reckernize them."

"Drugstores? Oh, to buy safety pins, you mean."

"Yeah. Safety pins."

"But . . . you know . . . it's true . . . there's never any safety pins when you look."

Oscar uncapped his beer, rinsed the first mouthful around. "Aha! Always plenty of clothes hangers, though. Throw 'em out every month, next month same closet's full of 'm again. Now whatcha wanna do in your spare time, you invent a device which it'll make safety pins outa clothes hangers."

Ferd nodded abstractedly. "But in my spare time I'm working on the French racer . . ." It was a beautiful machine, light, low-slung, swift, red and shining. You felt like a bird when you rode it. But, good as it was, Ferd knew he could make it better. He showed it to everybody who came in the place until his interest slackened.

Nature was his latest hobby, or, rather, reading about Nature. Some kids had wandered by from the park one day with tin cans in which they had put salamanders and toads, and they proudly showed them to Ferd. After that, the work on the red racer slowed down and he spent his spare time on natural history books.

"Mimicry!" he cried to Oscar. "A wonderful thing!"

Oscar looked up interestedly from the bowling scores

in the paper. "I seen Edie Adams on TV the other night, doing her imitation of Marilyn Monroe. Boy, oh, boy."

Ferd was irritated, shook his head. "Not that kind of mimicry. I mean how insects and arachnids will mimic the shapes of leaves and twigs and so on, to escape being eaten by birds or other insects and arachnids."

A scowl of disbelief passed over Oscar's heavy face. "You mean they change their *shapes?* What you giving me?"

"Oh, it's true. Sometimes the mimicry is for aggressive purposes, though—like a South African turtle that looks like a rock and so the fish swim up to it and then it catches them. Or that spider in Sumatra. When it lies on its back, it looks like a bird dropping. Catches butterflies that way."

Oscar laughed, a disgusted and incredulous noise. It died away as he turned back to the bowling scores. One hand groped at his pocket, came away, scratched absently at the orange thicket under the shirt, then went patting his hip pocket.

"Where's that pencil?" he muttered, got up, stomped into the office, pulled open drawers. His loud cry of "Hey!" brought Ferd into the tiny room.

"What's the matter?" Ferd asked.

Oscar pointed to a drawer. "Remember that time you claimed there were no safety pins here? Look—whole gah-damn drawer is full of 'em."

Ferd stared, scratched his head, said feebly that he was certain he'd looked there before . . .

A contralto voice from outside asked, "Anybody here?"

Oscar at once forgot the desk and its contents, called, "Be right with you," and was gone. Ferd followed him slowly.

There was a young woman in the shop, a rather mas-sively built young woman, with muscular calves and a deep chest. She was pointing out the seat of her bicycle to Oscar, who was saying "Uh-huh" and looking more at her than at anything else. "It's just a little too far forward ("Uh-huh"), as you can see. A wrench is all I need ("Uh-huh"). It was silly of me to forget my tools."

Oscar repeated, "Uh-huh" automatically, then snapped to. "Fix it in a jiffy," he said, and—despite her insistence that she could do it herself—he did fix it. Though not quite in a jiffy. He refused money. He prolonged the conversation as long as he could.

"Well, thank *you*," the young woman said. "And now I've got to go."

"That machine feel all right to you now?"

"Perfectly. Thanks—"

"Tell you what, I'll just ride along with you a little bit, just—"

Pear-shaped notes of laughter lifted the young woman's bosom. "Oh, you couldn't keep up with me! My machine is a *racer!*"

The moment he saw Oscar's eye flit to the corner, Ferd knew what he had in mind. He stepped forward. His cry of "No" was drowned out by his partner's loud, "Well, I guess this racer here can keep up with yours!"

The young woman giggled richly, said, well, they would see about that, and was off. Oscar, ignoring Ferd's outstretched hand, jumped on the French bike and was gone. Ferd stood in the doorway, watching the two figures, hunched over their handlebars, vanish down the road into the park. He went slowly back inside.

It was almost evening before Oscar returned, sweaty but smiling. Smiling broadly. "Hey, what a babe!" he cried. He wagged his head, he whistled, he made gestures, noises like escaping steam. "Boy, oh, boy what an afternoon!"

"Give me the bike," Ferd demanded.

Oscar said, yeah, sure; turned it over to him and went to wash. Ferd looked at the machine. The red enamel was covered with dust; there was mud spattered and dirt and bits of dried grass. It seemed soiled—degraded. He had felt like a swift bird when he rode it . . .

Oscar came out wet and beaming. He gave a cry of dismay, ran over.

"Stand away," said Ferd, gesturing with the knife. He slashed the tires, the seat and seat cover, again and again.

"You crazy?" Oscar yelled. "You outa your mind? Ferd, no, don't, Ferd—"

Ferd cut the spokes, bent them, twisted them. He took the heaviest hammer and pounded the frame into shapelessness, and then he kept on pounding till his breath was gasping.

"You're not only crazy," Oscar said bitterly, "you're rotten jealous. You can go to hell." He stomped away.

Ferd, feeling sick and stiff, locked up, went slowly home. He had no taste for reading, turned out the light and fell into bed, where he lay awake for hours, listening to the rustling noises of the night and thinking hot, twisted thoughts.

They didn't speak to each other for days after that, except for the necessities of the work. The wreckage of the French racer lay behind the shop. For about two weeks, neither wanted to go out back where he'd have to see it.

One morning Ferd arrived to be greeted by his partner, who began to shake his head in astonishment even before he started speaking. "How did you *do* it, how did you *do* it, Ferd? Jeez, what a beautiful job—I gotta hand it to you—no more hard feelings, huh, Ferd?"

Ferd took his hand. "Sure, sure. But what are you talking about?"

Oscar led him out back. There was the red racer, all in one piece, not a mark or scratch on it, its enamel bright as ever. Ferd gaped. He squatted down and examined it. It *was* his machine. Every change, every improvement he had made, was there.

He straightened up slowly. "Regeneration . . ."

"Huh? What say?" Oscar asked. Then, "Hey, kiddo, you're all white. Whad you do, stay up all night and didn't get no sleep? Come on in and siddown. But I still don't see how you done it."

Inside, Ferd sat down. He wet his lips. He said, "Oscar—listen—"

"Yeah?"

"Oscar. You know what regeneration is? No? Listen. Some kinds of lizards, you grab them by the tail, the tail breaks off and they grow a new one. If a lobster loses a claw, it regenerates another one. Some kinds of worms— and hydras and starfish—you cut them into pieces, each piece will grow back the missing parts. Salamanders can regenerate lost hands, and frogs can grow legs back."

"No kidding, Ferd. But, uh, I mean: Nature. Very interesting. But to get back to the bike now—how'd you manage to fix it so good?"

"I never touched it. It regenerated. Like a newt. Or a lobster."

Oscar considered this. He lowered his head, looked up at Ferd from under his eyebrows. "Well, now, Ferd . . . Look . . . How come all broke bikes don't do that?"

"This isn't an ordinary bike. I mean it isn't a real bike." Catching Oscar's look, he shouted, "Well, it's *true!*"

The shout changed Oscar's attitude from bafflement to incredulity. He got up. "So for the sake of argument, let's say all that stuff about the bugs and the eels or whatever the hell you were talking about is true. But they're alive. A bike ain't." He looked down triumphantly.

Ferd shook his leg from side to side, looked at it. "A crystal isn't, either, but a broken crystal can regenerate itself if the conditions are right. Oscar, go see if the safety pins are still in the desk. Please, Oscar?"

He listened as Oscar, muttering, pulled the desk drawers out, rummaged in them, slammed them shut, tramped back.

"Naa," he said. "All gone. Like that lady said that time, and you said, there never are any safety pins when you want 'em. They disap—Ferd? What're—"

Ferd jerked open the closet door, jumped back as a shoal of clothes hangers clattered out.

"And like *you* say," Ferd said with a twist of his mouth, "on the other hand, there are always plenty of clothes hangers. There weren't any here before."

Oscar shrugged. "I don't see what you're getting at. But anybody could of got in here and took the pins and left the hangers. *I* could of—but I didn't. Or *you* could of. Maybe—" He narrowed his eyes. "Maybe you walked in your sleep and done it. You better see a doctor. Jeez, you look rotten."

Ferd went back and sat down, put his head in his hands. "I feel rotten. I'm scared, Oscar. Scared of what?" He breathed noisily. "I'll tell you. Like I explained before, about how things that live in the wild places, they mimic other things there. Twigs, leaves . . . toads that look like rocks. Well, suppose there are . . . things . . . that live in people places. Cities. Houses. These things could imitate— well, other kinds of things you find in people places—"

"*People* places, for crise sake!"

"Maybe they're a different kind of life-form. Maybe they get their nourishment out of the elements in the air. You know what safety pins *are*—these other kinds of them? Oscar, the safety pins are the pupa-forms and then they, like, *hatch.* Into the larval-forms. Which look just like coat hangers. They feel like them, even, but they're not. Oscar, they're not, not really, not really, not . . ."

He began to cry into his hands. Oscar looked at him. He shook his head.

After a minute, Ferd controlled himself somewhat. He snuffled. "All these bicycles the cops find, and they hold them waiting for owners to show up, and then we buy them at the sale because no owners show up because there aren't any, and the same with the ones the kids are always trying to sell us, and they say they just found them, and they really did because they were never made in a factory. They grew. They grow. You smash them and throw them away, they regenerate."

Oscar turned to someone who wasn't there and waggled his head. "Hoo, boy," he said. Then, to Ferd: "You mean one day there's a safety pin and the next day instead there's a coat hanger?"

Ferd said, "One day there's a cocoon; the next day there's a moth. One day there's an egg; the next day there's a chicken. But with . . . these it doesn't happen in the open daytime where you can see it. But at night, Oscar—at night you can *hear* it happening. All the little noises in the night-time, Oscar—"

Oscar said, "Then how come we ain't up to our belly-button in bikes? If I had a bike for every coat hanger—"

But Ferd had considered that, too. If every codfish egg, he explained, or every oyster spawn grew to maturity, a man could walk across the ocean on the backs of all the codfish or oysters there'd be. So many died, so many were eaten by predatory creatures, that Nature had to produce a maximum in order to allow a minimum to arrive at maturity. And Oscar's question was: then who, uh, eats the, uh, coat hangers?

Ferd's eyes focused through wall, buildings, park, more buildings, to the horizon. "You got to get the picture. I'm not talking about real pins or hangers. I got a name for the others—'false friends,' I call them. In high school French, we had to watch out for French words that looked like English words, but really were different. '*Faux amis*,' they call them. False friends. Pseudo-pins. Pseudo-hangers . . . Who eats them? I don't know for sure. Pseudo-vacuum cleaners, maybe?"

His partner, with a loud groan, slapped his hands against his thighs. He said, "Ferd, Ferd, for crise sake. You know what's the trouble with you? You talk about oysters, but you forgot what they're good for. You forgot there's two kinds of people in the world. Close up them books, them bug books and French books. Get out, mingle, meet people. Soak up some brew. You know what? The next time Norma—that's this broad's name with the racing bike—the next time she comes here, *you* take the red racer and *you* go out in the woods with her. I won't mind. And I don't think she will, either. Not *too* much."

But Ferd said no. "I never want to touch the red racer again. I'm afraid of it."

At this, Oscar pulled him to his feet, dragged him protest-ingly out to the back and forced him to get on the French machine. "Only way to conquer your fear of it!"

Ferd started off, white-faced, wobbling. And in a mo-ment was on the ground, rolling and thrashing, screaming.

Oscar pulled him away from the machine.

"It threw me!" Ferd yelled. "It tried to kill me! Look—blood!"

His partner said it was a bump that threw him—it was his own fear. The blood? A broken spoke. Grazed his cheek. And he insisted Ferd get on the bicycle again, to conquer his fear.

But Ferd had grown hysterical. He shouted that no man was safe—that mankind had to be warned. It took Oscar a long time to pacify him and to get him to go home and into bed.

He didn't tell all this to Mr. Whatney, of course. He merely said that his partner had gotten fed up with the bicycle business.

"It don't pay to worry and try to change the world," he pointed out. "I always say take things the way they are. If you can't lick 'em, join 'em."

Mr. Whatney said that was his philosophy, exactly. He asked how things were, since.

"Well . . . not *too* bad. I'm engaged, you know. Name's Norma. Crazy about bicycles. Everything considered, things aren't bad at all. More work, yes, but I can do things all my own way, so . . ."

Mr. Whatney nodded. He glanced around the shop. "I see they're still making drop-frame bikes," he said, "Though, with so many women wearing slacks, I wonder they bother."

Oscar said, "Well, I dunno. I kinda like it that way. Ever stop to think that bicycles are like people? I mean, of all the machines in the world, only bikes come male and female."

Mr. Whatney gave a little giggle, said that was *right,* he had never thought of it like that before. Then Oscar asked if Mr. Whatney had anything in particular in mind—not that he wasn't always welcome.

"Well, I wanted to look over what you've got. My boy's birthday is coming up—"

Oscar nodded sagely. "Now here's a job," he said,

"Which you can't get it any other place but here. Specialty of the house. Combines the best features of the French racer and the American standard, but it's made right here, and it comes in three models—Junior, Intermediate and Regular. Beautiful, ain't it?"

Mr. Whatney observed that, say, that might be just the ticket. "By the way," he asked, "what's become of the French racer, the red one, used to be here?"

Oscar's face twitched. Then it grew bland and innocent and he leaned over and nudged his customer. "Oh, *that* one. Old Frenchy? Why, I put *him* out to stud!"

And they laughed and they laughed, and after they told a few more stories they concluded the sale, and they had a few beers and they laughed some more. And then they said what a shame it was about poor Ferd, poor old Ferd, who had been found in his own closet with an unraveled coat hanger coiled tightly around his neck.

ANGEL

Pat Cadigan

*Pat Cadigan was born in Schenectady, New York, and now
lives in London, England. She made her first professional
sale in 1980, and has subsequently come to be regarded as
one of the best new writers in SF. She was the co-editor of*
Shayol, *perhaps the best of the semiprozines of the late '70s;
it was honored with a World Fantasy Award in the "Special
Achievement, Non-Professional" category in 1981. She has
also served as Chairman of the Nebula Award Jury and as
a World Fantasy Award Judge. Her story "Pretty Boy
Crossover" has recently appeared on several critic's lists as
among the best science fiction stories of the 1980's; her short
work has been assembled in two landmark collections,* Patterns *and* Dirty Work. *Her first novel,* Mindplayers, *was released in 1987 to excellent critical response, and her second
novel,* Synners, *released in 1991, won the prestigious Arthur
C. Clarke Award as the year's best science-fiction novel, as
did her third novel,* Fools, *making her the only writer ever
to win the Clarke Award twice. Her most recent book is a
major new novel,* Tea from an Empty Cup.*

*The story that follows, "Angel," was a finalist for the
Hugo Award, the Nebula Award, and the World Fantasy
Award, one of the few stories ever to earn that rather unusual distinction. In it, she gives us an elegant and bittersweet lesson in the consequences of trust . . .*

S*tand with me* awhile, Angel, I said, and Angel said he'd
do that. Angel was good to me that way, good to have with
you on a cold night and nowhere to go. We stood on the

street corner together and watched the cars going by and the people and all. The streets were lit up like Christmas, streetlights, store lights, marquees over the all-night movie houses and bookstores blinking and flashing; shank of the evening in east midtown. Angel was getting used to things here and getting used to how I did nights. Standing outside, because what else are you going to do. He was *my* Angel now, had been since that other cold night when I'd been going home, because where are you going to go, and I'd found him and took him with me. It's good to have someone to take with you, someone to look after. Angel knew that. He started looking after me, too.

Like now. We were standing there awhile and I was looking around at nothing and everything, the cars cruising past, some of them stopping now and again for the hookers posing by the curb, and then I saw it, out of the corner of my eye. Stuff coming out of the Angel, shiny like sparks but flowing like liquid. Silver fireworks. I turned and looked all the way at him and it was gone. And he turned and gave a little grin like he was embarrassed I'd seen. Nobody else saw it, though; not the short guy who paused next to the Angel before crossing the street against the light, not the skinny hype looking to sell the boom-box he was carrying on his shoulder, not the homeboy strutting past us with both his girlfriends on his arms, nobody but me.

The Angel said, Hungry?

Sure, I said. I'm hungry.

Angel looked past me. Okay, he said. I looked, too, and here they came, three leather boys, visor caps, belts, boots, keyrings. On the cruise together. Scary stuff, even though you know it's not looking for you.

I said, them? *Them?*

Angel didn't answer. One went by, then the second, and the Angel stopped the third by taking hold of his arm.

Hi.

The guy nodded. His head was shaved. I could see a little grey-black stubble under his cap. No eyebrows, disinterested eyes. The eyes were because of the Angel.

I could use a little money, the Angel said. My friend and I are hungry.

The guy put his hand in his pocket and wiggled out some bills, offering them to the Angel. The Angel selected a twenty and closed the guy's hand around the rest.

This will be enough, thank you.

The guy put his money away and waited.

I hope you have a good night, said the Angel.

The guy nodded and walked on, going across the street to where his two friends were waiting on the next corner. Nobody found anything weird about it.

Angel was grinning at me. Sometimes he was *the* Angel, when he was doing something, sometimes he was Angel, when he was just with me. Now he was Angel again. We went up the street to the luncheonette and got a seat by the front window so we could still watch the street while we ate.

Cheeseburger and fries, I said without bothering to look at the plastic-covered menus lying on top of the napkin holder. The Angel nodded.

Thought so, he said. I'll have the same, then.

The waitress came over with a little tiny pad to take our order. I cleared my throat. It seemed like I hadn't used my voice in a hundred years. "Two cheeseburgers and two fries," I said, "and two cups of—" I looked up at her and froze. She had no face. Like, *nothing*, blank from hairline to chin, soft little dents where the eyes and nose and mouth would have been. Under the table, the Angel kicked me, but gentle.

"And two cups of coffee," I said.

She didn't say anything—how could she?—as she wrote down the order and then walked away again. All shaken up, I looked at the Angel, but he was calm like always.

She's a new arrival, Angel told me and leaned back in his chair. Not enough time to grow a face.

But how can she breathe? I said.

Through her pores. She doesn't need much air yet.

Yah, but what about—like, I mean, don't other people *notice* that she's got nothing there?

No. It's not such an extraordinary condition. The only reason you notice is because you're with me. Certain things have rubbed off on you. But no one else notices. When they look at her, they see whatever face they expect someone like to her have. And eventually, she'll have it.

But you have a face, I said. You've always had a face.

I'm different, said the Angel.

You sure are, I thought, looking at him. Angel had a beautiful face. That wasn't why I took him home that night, just because he had a beautiful face—I left all that behind a long time ago—but it was there, his beauty. The way you think of a man being beautiful, good clean lines, deep-set eyes, ageless. About the only way you could describe him— look away and you'd forget everything except that he was beautiful. But he did have a face. He *did*.

Angel shifted in the chair—these were like somebody's old kitchen chairs, you couldn't get too comfortable in them—and shook his head, because he knew I was thinking troubled thoughts. Sometimes you could think something and it wouldn't be troubled and later you'd think the same thing and it would be troubled. The Angel didn't like me to be troubled about him.

Do you have a cigarette? he asked.

I think so.

I patted my jacket and came up with most of a pack that I handed over to him. The Angel lit up and amused us both by having the smoke come out his ears and trickle out his eyes like ghostly tears. I felt my own eyes watering for his; I wiped them and there was that *stuff* again, but from me now. I was crying silver fireworks. I flicked them on the table and watched them puff out and vanish.

Does this mean I'm getting to *be* you, now? I asked.

Angel shook his head. Smoke wafted out of his hair. Just things rubbing off on you. Because we've been together and you're—susceptible. But they're different for you.

Then the waitress brought our food and we went on to another sequence, as the Angel would say. She still had no face but I guess she could see well enough because she

put all the plates down just where you'd think they were
supposed to go and left the tiny little check in the middle
of the table.

Is she—I mean, did you know her, from where you—

Angel gave his head a brief little shake. No. She's from
somewhere else. Not one of my—people. He pushed the
cheeseburger and fries in front of him over to my side of
the table. That was the way it was done; I did all the eating and somehow it worked out.

I picked up my cheeseburger and I was bringing it up
to my mouth when my eyes got all funny and I saw it coming up like a whole *series* of cheeseburgers, whoom-
whoom-whoom, trick photography, only for real. I closed
my eyes and jammed the cheeseburger into my mouth,
holding it there, waiting for all the other cheeseburgers to
catch up with it.

You'll be okay, said the Angel. Steady, now.

I said with my mouth full, That was—that was *weird*.
Will I ever get used to this?

I doubt it. But I'll do what I can to help you.

Yah, well, the Angel *would* know. Stuff rubbing off on
me, he could feel it better than I could. He was the one it
was rubbing off *from*.

I had put away my cheeseburger and half of Angel's
and was working on the french fries for both of us when
I noticed he was looking out the window with this hard,
tight expression on his face.

Something? I asked him.

Keep eating, he said.

I kept eating, but I kept watching, too. The Angel was
staring at a big blue car parked at the curb right outside
the diner. It was silvery blue, one of those lots-of-money
models and there was a woman kind of leaning across from
the driver's side to look out the passenger window. She
was beautiful in that lots-of-money way, tawny hair swept
back from her face, and even from here I could see she
had turquoise eyes. Really beautiful woman. I almost felt
like crying. I mean, jeez, how did people get that way and
me too harmless to live.

But the Angel wasn't one bit glad to see her. I knew he didn't want me to say anything, but I couldn't help it.

Who is she?

Keep eating, Angel said. We need the protein, what little there is.

I ate and watched the woman and the Angel watch each other and it was getting very—I don't know, very *something* between them, even through the glass. Then a cop car pulled up next to her and I knew they were telling her to move it along. She moved it along.

Angel sagged against the back of his chair and lit another cigarette, smoking it in the regular, unremarkable way.

What are we going to do tonight? I asked the Angel as we left the restaurant.

Keep out of harm's way, Angel said, which was a new answer. Most nights we spent just kind of going around soaking everything up. The Angel soaked it up, mostly. I got some of it along with him, but not the same way he did. It was different for him. Sometimes he would use me like a kind of filter. Other times he took it direct. There'd been the big car accident one night, right at my usual corner, a big old Buick running a red light smack into somebody's nice Lincoln. The Angel had had to take it direct because I couldn't handle that kind of stuff. I didn't know how the Angel could take it, but he could. It carried him for days afterwards, too. I only had to eat for myself.

It's the intensity, little friend, he'd told me, as though that were supposed to explain it.

It's the intensity, not whether it's good or bad. The universe doesn't know good or bad, only less or more. Most of you have a bad time reconciling this. *You* have a bad time with it, little friend, but you get through better than other people. Maybe because of the way you are. You got squeezed out of a lot, you haven't had much of a chance at life. You're as much an exile as I am, only in your own land.

That may have been true, but at least I *belonged* here, so that part was easier for me. But I didn't say that to the

Angel. I think he liked to think he could do as well or better than me at living—I mean, I couldn't just look at some
leather boy and get him to cough up a twenty dollar bill.
Cough up a fist in the face or worse, was more like it.

Tonight, though, he wasn't doing so good, and it was
that woman in the car. She'd thrown him out of step, kind
of.

Don't think about her, the Angel said, just out of
nowhere. Don't think about her any more.

Okay, I said, feeling creepy because it was creepy when
the Angel got a glimpse of my head. And then, of course,
I couldn't think about anything else hardly.

Do you want to go home? I asked him.

No. I can't stay in now. We'll do the best we can tonight,
but I'll have to be very careful about the tricks. They take
so much out of me, and if we're keeping out of harm's
way, I might not be able to make up for a lot of it.

It's okay, I said. I ate. I don't need anything else tonight,
you don't have to do any more.

Angel got that look on his face, the one where I knew
he wanted to give me things, like feelings I couldn't have
any more. Generous, the Angel was. But I didn't need those
feelings, not like other people seem to. For awhile, it was
like the Angel didn't understand that, but he let me be.

Little friend, he said, and almost touched me. The Angel
didn't touch a lot. I could touch him and that would be
okay, but if *he* touched somebody, he couldn't help *doing*
something to them, like the trade that had given us the
money. That had been deliberate. If the trade had touched
the Angel first, it would have been different, nothing would
have happened unless the Angel touched him back. All
touch meant something to the Angel that I didn't understand. There was touching without touching, too. Like
things rubbing off on me. And sometimes, when I did touch
the Angel, I'd get the feeling that it was maybe more his
idea than mine, but I didn't mind that. How many people
are going their whole lives never being able to touch an
Angel?

We walked together and all around us the street was

really coming to life. It was getting colder, too. I tried to make my jacket cover more. The Angel wasn't feeling it. Most of the time hot and cold didn't mean much to him. We saw the three rough trade guys again. The one Angel had gotten the money from was getting into a car. The other two watched it drive away and then walked on. I looked over at the Angel.

Because we took his twenty, I said.

Even if we hadn't, Angel said.

So we went along, the Angel and me, and I could feel how different it was tonight than it was all the other nights we'd walked or stood together. The Angel was kind of pulled back into himself and seemed to be keeping a check on me, pushing us closer together. I was getting more of those fireworks out of the corners of my eyes, but when I'd turn my head to look, they'd vanish. It reminded me of the night I'd found the Angel standing on my corner all by himself in pain. The Angel told me later that was real talent, knowing he was in pain. I never thought of myself as any too talented, but the way everyone else had been just ignoring him, I guess I must have had something to see him after all.

The Angel stopped us several feet down from an all-night bookstore. Don't look, he said. Watch the traffic or stare at your feet, but don't look or it won't happen.

There wasn't anything to see right then, but I didn't look anyway. That was the way it was sometimes, the Angel telling me it made a difference whether I was watching something or not, something about the other people being conscious of me being conscious of them. I didn't understand, but I knew Angel was usually right. So I was watching traffic when the guy came out of the bookstore and got his head punched.

I could almost see it out of the corner of my eye. A lot of movement, arms and legs flying and grunty noises. Other people stopped to look but I kept my eyes on the traffic, some of which was slowing up so they could check out the fight. Next to me, the Angel was stiff all over. Taking it in, what he called the expenditure of emotional kinetic energy. No right, no wrong, little friend, he'd told me. Just energy, like the rest of the universe.

So he took it in and I *felt* him taking it in, and while I was feeling it, a kind of silver fog started creeping around my eyeballs and I was in two places at once. I was watching the traffic and I was in the Angel watching the fight and feeling him charge up like a big battery.

It felt like nothing I'd ever felt before. These two guys slugging it out—well, one guy doing all the slugging and the other skittering around trying to get out from under the fists and having his head punched but good, and the Angel drinking it like he was sipping at an empty cup and somehow getting it to have something in it after all. Deep inside him, whatever made the Angel go was getting a little stronger.

I kind of swung back and forth between him and me, or swayed might be more like it was. I wondered about it, because the Angel wasn't touching me. I really was getting to *be* him, I thought; Angel picked that up and put the thought away to answer later. It was like I was traveling by the fog, being one of us and then the other, for a long time, it seemed, and then after awhile I was more me than him again, and some of the fog cleared away.

And there was that car, pointed the other way this time, and the woman was climbing out of it with this big weird smile on her face, as though she'd won something. She waved at the Angel to come to her.

Bang went the connection between us dead and the Angel shot past me, running away from the car. I went after him. I caught a glimpse of her jumping back into the car and yanking at the gear shift.

Angel wasn't much of a runner. Something funny about his knees. We'd gone maybe a hundred feet when he started wobbling and I could hear him pant. He cut across a Park & Lock that was dark and mostly empty. It was back-to-back with some kind of private parking lot and the fences for each one tried to mark off the same narrow strip of lumpy pavement. They were easy to climb but Angel was too panicked. He just *went* through them before he even

thought about it; I knew that because if he'd been thinking, he'd have wanted to save what he'd just charged up
with for when he really needed it bad enough.

I had to haul myself over the fences in the usual way,
and when he heard me rattling on the saggy chainlink, he
stopped and looked back.

Go, I told him. Don't wait on me!

He shook his head sadly. Little friend, I'm a fool. I could
stand to learn from you a little more.

Don't stand, run! I got over the fences and caught up
with him. Let's go! I yanked his sleeve as I slogged past
and he followed at a clumsy trot.

Have to hide somewhere, he said, camouflage ourselves
with people.

I shook my head, thinking we could just run maybe four
more blocks and we'd be at the freeway overpass. Below
it were the butt-ends of old roads closed off when the freeway had been built. You could hide there the rest of your
life and no one would find you. But Angel made me turn
right and go down a block to this rundown crack-in-the-
wall called Stan's Jigger. I'd never been in there—I'd never
made it a practice to go into bars—but the Angel was pushing too hard to argue.

Inside it was smelly and dark and not too happy. The
Angel and I went down to the end of the bar and stood
under a blood-red light while he searched his pockets for
money.

Enough for one drink apiece, he said.

I don't want anything.

You can have soda or something.

The Angel ordered from the bartender, who was suspicious. This was a place for regulars and nobody else, and
certainly nobody else like me or the Angel. The Angel knew
that even stronger than I did but he just stood and pretended to sip his drink without looking at me. He was all
pulled into himself and I was hovering around the edges.
I knew he was still pretty panicked and trying to figure out
what he could do next. As close as I was, if he had to get
real far away, he was going to have a problem and so was

I. He'd have to tow me along with him and that wasn't the most practical thing to do.

Maybe he was sorry now he'd let me take him home. But he'd been so weak then, and now with all the filtering and stuff I'd done for him, he couldn't just cut me off without a lot of pain.

I was trying to figure out what I could do for him now when the bartender came back and gave us a look that meant order or get out, and he'd have liked it better if we got out. So would everyone else there. The few other people standing at the bar weren't looking at us, but they knew right where we were, like a sore spot. It wasn't hard to figure out what they thought about us, either, maybe because of me or because of the Angel's beautiful face.

We got to leave, I said to the Angel but he had it in his head this was good camouflage. There wasn't enough money for two more drinks so he smiled at the bartender and slid his hand across the bar and put it on top of the bartender's. It was tricky doing it this way; bartenders and waitresses took more persuading because it wasn't normal for them just to give you something.

The bartender looked at the Angel with his eyes half closed. He seemed to be thinking it over. But the Angel had just blown a lot going through the fence instead of climbing over it and the fear was scuttling his concentration and I just knew that it wouldn't work. And maybe my knowing that didn't help, either.

The bartender's free hand dipped down below the bar and came up with a small club. "Faggot!" he roared and caught Angel just over the ear. Angel slammed into me and we both crashed to the floor. Plenty of emotional kinetic energy in here, I thought dimly as the guys standing at the bar fell on us, and then I didn't think anything more as I curled up into a ball under their fists and boots.

We were lucky they didn't much feel like killing anyone. Angel went out the door first and they tossed me out on top of him. As soon as I landed on him, I knew we were both in trouble; something was broken inside him. So much for keeping out of harm's way. I rolled off him and lay on the pavement, staring at the sky and trying to catch my breath. There was blood in my mouth and my nose, and my back was on fire.

Angel? I said, after a bit.

He didn't answer. I felt my mind get kind of all loose and runny, like my brains were leaking out my ears. I thought about the trade we'd taken the money from and how I'd been scared of him and his friends and how silly that had been. But then, I was too harmless to live.

The stars were raining silver fireworks down on me. It didn't help.

Angel? I said again.

I rolled over onto my side to reach for him, and there she was. The car was parked at the curb and she had Angel under the armpits, dragging him toward the open passenger door. I couldn't tell if he was conscious or not and that scared me. I sat up.

She paused, still holding the Angel. We looked into each other's eyes, and I started to understand.

"Help me get him into the car," she said at last. Her voice sounded hard and flat and unnatural. "Then you can get in, too. In the *back* seat."

I was in no shape to take her out. It couldn't have been better for her if she'd set it up herself. I got up, the pain flaring in me so bad that I almost fell down again, and took the Angel's ankles. His ankles were so delicate, almost like a woman's, like *hers*. I didn't really help much, except to guide his feet in as she sat him on the seat and strapped him in with the shoulder harness. I got in the back as she ran around to the other side of the car, her steps all real light and peppy, like she'd found a million dollars lying there on the sidewalk.

We were out on the freeway before the Angel stirred in the shoulder harness. His head lolled from side to side on the back of the seat. I reached up and touched his hair lightly, hoping she couldn't see me do it.

Where are you taking me, the Angel said.

"For a ride," said the woman. "For the moment."

Why does she talk out loud like that? I asked the Angel.
Because she knows it bothers me.

"You know I can focus my thoughts better if I say things
out loud," she said. "I'm not like one of your little
pushovers." She glanced at me in the rear view mirror.
"Just *what* have you gotten yourself into since you left,
darling? Is that a boy or a girl?"

I pretended I didn't care about what she said or that I
was too harmless to live or any of that stuff, but the way
she said it, she meant it to sting.

Friends can be either, Angel said. It doesn't matter which.
Where are you taking us?

Now it was *us*. In spite of everything, I almost could
have smiled.

"Us? You mean, you and me? Or are you really referring to your little pet back there?"

My friend and I are together. You and I are *not*.

The way the Angel said it made me think he meant more
than not together; like he'd been with her once the way he
was with me now. The Angel let me know I was right. Silver fireworks started flowing slowly off his head down the
back of the seat and I knew there was something wrong
about it. There was too much all at once.

"Why can't you talk out loud to me, darling?" the woman
said with fakey-sounding petulance. "Just say a few words
and make me happy. You have a lovely voice when you
use it."

That was true, but the Angel never spoke out loud unless he couldn't get out of it, like when he'd ordered from
the bartender. Which had probably helped the bartender decide about what he thought we were, but it was useless to
think about that.

"All right," said Angel, and I knew the strain was awful
for him. "I've said a few words. Are you happy?" He sagged
in the shoulder harness.

"Ecstatic. But it won't make me let you go. I'll drop
your pet at the nearest hospital and then we'll go home."
She glanced at the Angel as she drove. "I've missed you
so much. I can't *stand* it without you, without you mak-

ing things happen. Doing your little miracles. You knew
I'd get addicted to it, all the things you could do to people. And then you just took off, I didn't know what had
happened to you. And it *hurt*." Her voice turned kind of
pitiful, like a little kid's. "I was in real *pain*. You must
have been, too. Weren't you? Well, *weren't you*?"

Yes, the Angel said. I was in pain, too.

I remembered him standing on my corner, where I'd
hung out all that time by myself until he came. Standing
there in pain. I didn't know why or from what then, I just
took him home, and after a little while, the pain went away.
When he decided we were together, I guess.

The silvery flow over the back of the car seat thickened. I cupped my hands under it and it was like my brain
was lighting up with pictures. I saw the Angel before he
was my Angel, in this really nice house, the woman's house,
and how she'd take him places, restaurants or stores or parties, thinking at him real hard so that he was all filled up
with her and had to do what she wanted him to. Steal sometimes; other times, weird stuff, making people do silly things
like suddenly start singing or taking their clothes off. That
was mostly at the parties, though she made a waiter she
didn't like burn himself with a pot of coffee. She'd get
men, too, through the Angel, and they'd think it was the
greatest idea in the world to go to bed with her. Then she'd
make the Angel show her the others, the ones that had been
sent here the way he had for crimes nobody could have
understood, like the waitress with no face. She'd look at
them, sometimes try to do things to them to make them
uncomfortable or unhappy. But mostly she'd just stare.

It wasn't like that in the very beginning, the Angel said
weakly and I knew he was ashamed.

It's okay, I told him. People can be nice at first, I know
that. Then they find out about you.

The woman laughed. "You two are *so* sweet and pa-
thetic. Like a couple of little children. I guess that's what
you were looking for, wasn't it, darling? Except children
can be cruel, too, can't they? So you got this—*creature* for
yourself." She looked at me in the rear view mirror again

as she slowed down a little, and for a moment I was afraid
she'd seen what I was doing with the silvery stuff that was
still pouring out of the Angel. It was starting to slow now.
There wasn't much time left. I wanted to scream, but the
Angel was calming me for what was coming next. "What
happened to you, anyway?"

Tell her, said the Angel. To stall for time, I knew, keep
her occupied.

I was born funny, I said. I had both sexes.

"A hermaphrodite!" she exclaimed with real delight.

She loves freaks, the Angel said, but she didn't pay any
attention.

There was an operation, but things went wrong. They
kept trying to fix it as I got older but my body didn't have
the right kind of chemistry or something. My parents were
ashamed. I left after awhile.

"You poor thing," she said, not meaning anything like
that. "You were *just* what darling, here, needed, weren't
you? Just a little nothing, no demands, no desires. For anything." Her voice got all hard. "They could probably fix
you up now, you know."

I don't want it. I left all that behind a long time ago, I
don't need it.

"*Just* the sort of little pet that would be perfect for you,"
she said to the Angel. "Sorry I have to tear you away. But
I can't get along without you now. Life is so boring. And
empty. And—" She sounded puzzled. "And like there's
nothing more to live for since you left me."

That's not me, said the Angel. That's you.

"No, it's a lot of you, and you know it. You know you're
addictive to human beings, you knew that when you came
here—when they *sent* you here. Hey, you, *pet,* do you know
what his crime was, why they sent him to this little back-
water penal colony of a planet?"

Yeah, I know, I said. I really didn't, but I wasn't going
to tell her that.

"What do you think about *that,* little pet neuter?" she
said gleefully, hitting the accelerator pedal and speeding
up. "What do you think of the crime of refusing to mate?"

The Angel made a sort of an out-loud groan and lunged at the steering wheel. The car swerved wildly and I fell backwards, the silver stuff from the Angel going all over me. I tried to keep scooping it into my mouth the way I'd been doing, but it was flying all over the place now. I heard the crunch as the tires left the road and went onto the shoulder. Something struck the side of the car, probably the guard rail, and made it fishtail, throwing me down on the floor. Up front the woman was screaming and cursing and the Angel wasn't making a sound, but, in my head, I could hear him sort of keening. Whatever happened, this would be it. The Angel had told me all that time ago, after I'd taken him home, that they didn't last long after they got here, the exiles from his world and other worlds. Things tended to *happen* to them, even if they latched on to someone like me or the woman. They'd be in accidents or the people here would kill them. Like antibodies in a human body rejecting something or fighting a disease. At least I belonged here, but it looked like I was going to die in a car accident with the Angel and the woman both. I didn't care.

The car swerved back onto the highway for a few seconds and then pitched to the right again. Suddenly there was nothing under us and then we thumped down on something, not road but dirt or grass or something, bombing madly up and down. I pulled myself up on the back of the seat just in time to see the sign coming at us at an angle. The corner of it started to go through the windshield on the woman's side and then all I saw for a long time was the biggest display of silver fireworks ever.

•   •   •

It was hard to be gentle with him. Every move hurt but I didn't want to leave him sitting in the car next to her, even if she was dead. Being in the back seat had kept most of the glass from flying into me but I was still shaking some out of my hair and the impact hadn't done much for my back.

I laid the Angel out on the lumpy grass a little ways

from the car and looked around. We were maybe a hundred yards from the highway, near a road that ran parallel to it. It was dark but I could still read the sign that had come through the windshield and split the woman's head in half. It said, *Construction Ahead, Reduce Speed.* Far off on the other road, I could see a flashing yellow light and at first I was afraid it was the police or something but it stayed where it was and I realized that must be the construction.

"Friend," whispered the Angel, startling me. He'd never spoken aloud to me, not directly.

Don't talk, I said, bending over him, trying to figure out some way I could touch him, just for comfort. There wasn't anything else I could do now.

"I have to," he said, still whispering. "It's almost gone. Did you get it?"

Mostly, I said. Not all.

"I meant for you to have it."

I know.

"I don't know that it will really do you any good." His breath kind of bubbled in his throat. I could see something wet and shiny on his mouth but it wasn't silver fireworks. "But it's yours. You can do as you like with it. Live on it the way I did. Get what you need when you need it. But you can live as a human, too. Eat. Work. However, whatever."

I'm not human, I said. I'm not any more human than you, even if I do belong here.

"Yes, you are, little friend. I haven't made you any less human," he said, and coughed more. "I'm not sorry I wouldn't mate. I couldn't mate with my own. It was too . . . I don't know, too little of me, too much of them, something. I couldn't bond, it would have been nothing but emptiness. The Great Sin, to be unable to give, because the universe knows only less or more and I insisted that it would be good or bad. So they sent me here. But in the end, you know, they got their way, little friend." I felt his hand on me for a moment before it fell away. "I did it after all. Even if it wasn't with my own."

The bubbling in his throat stopped. I sat next to him for awhile in the dark. Finally I felt it, the Angel stuff. It was kind of fluttery-churny, like too much coffee on an empty stomach. I closed my eyes and lay down on the grass, shivering. Maybe some of it was shock but I don't think so. The silver fireworks started, in my head this time, and with them came a lot of pictures I couldn't understand. Stuff about the Angel and where he'd come from and the way they mated. It was a lot like how we'd been together, the Angel and me. They looked a lot like us but there were a lot of differences, too, things I couldn't make out. I couldn't make out how they'd sent him here, either—by *light,* in, like, little bundles or something. It didn't make any sense to me, but I guessed an Angel could be light. Silver fireworks.

I must have passed out, because when I opened my eyes, it felt like I'd been laying there a long time. It was still dark, though. I sat up and reached for the Angel, thinking I ought to hide his body.

He was gone. There was just a sort of wet sandy stuff where he'd been.

I looked at the car and her. All that was still there. Somebody was going to see it soon. I didn't want to be around for that.

Everything still hurt but I managed to get to the other road and start walking back toward the city. It was like I could *feel* it now, the way the Angel must have, as though it were vibrating like a drum or ringing like a bell with all kinds of stuff, people laughing and crying and loving and hating and being afraid and everything else that happens to people. The stuff that the Angel took in, energy, that I could take in now if I wanted.

And I knew that taking it in that way, it would be bigger than anything all those people had, bigger than anything I could have had if things hadn't gone wrong with me all those years ago.

I wasn't so sure I wanted it. Like the Angel, refusing to mate back where he'd come from. He wouldn't, there, and I couldn't, here. Except now I could do something else.

I wasn't so sure I wanted it. But I didn't think I'd be able to stop it, either, any more than I could stop my heart from beating. Maybe it wasn't really such a good thing or a right thing. But it was like the Angel said: the universe doesn't know good or bad, only less or more.

Yeah. I heard *that*.

I thought about the waitress with no face. I could find them all now, all the ones from the other places, other worlds that sent them away for some kind of alien crimes nobody would have understood. I could find them all. They threw away their outcasts, I'd tell them, but here, we *kept* ours. And here's how. Here's how you live in a universe that only knows less or more.

I kept walking toward the city.

AMONG THE
HAIRY EARTHMEN

R. A. Lafferty

Ever since Chariots of the Gods *galloped to the top of the bestseller list a few decades ago, we have been deluged by books and television shows purporting to reveal evidence that Earth at the dawn of history was visited by a race of highly advanced aliens, hailed as "gods" by our ignorant and credulous ancestors. Supposedly, these godlike aliens were then obliging enough to act as mentors to the infant civilizations of Earth—if indeed they weren't the founders of those civilizations in the first place—and the saucerfolk have subsequently been credited with every major human accomplishment from Stonehenge to Chichen Itza, not forgetting the Easter Island statues, and, of course, the Great Pyramid of Cheops.*

But there's more to civilization than earthworks and monuments and giant statues, and there are more types of cultural influence than just the ham-handed obvious kind. Here R. A. Lafferty—a writer possessed of one of SF's wildest and most quirky imaginations—depicts a variety of alien meddlings with human civilization more bizarre, more droll, more far-reaching, and, frighteningly, more plausible than anything in Von Daniken.

R. A. Lafferty started writing in 1960, at the relatively advanced age (for a New Writer, anyway) of 48, and in the years before his retirement in 1987, he published some of the freshest and funniest short stories ever written in the genre, as well as a string of vivid and unforgettable books such as the novels Past Master, The Devil Is Dead, The Reefs of Earth, Okla Hannali, The Fall of Rome, Arrive At Easterwine, *and* The Flame is Green, *and landmark collections such as* Nine Hundred Grandmothers, Strange Doings, Does Anyone Else Have Something Further to Add?, Golden Gate and Other Stories, *and* Ringing the Changes. *Lafferty won the Hugo Award in 1973 for his story "Eurema's Dam," and in 1990 received the World Fantasy Award, the prestigious Life Achievement Award. His most recent books are the collections* Lafferty in Orbit *and* Iron Star. *He lives in Oklahoma.*

There is one period of our World History that has aspects so different from anything that went before and after that we can only gaze back on those several hundred years and ask:

"Was that *ourselves* who behaved so?"

Well, no, as a matter of fact, it wasn't. It was beings of another sort who visited us briefly and who acted so gloriously and abominably.

This is the way it was:

The Children had a Long Afternoon free. They could go to any of a dozen wonderful places, but they were already in one.

Seven of them—full to the craw of wonderful places—decided to go to Eretz.

"Children are attracted to the oddest and most shambling things," said the Mothers. "Why should they want to go to Eretz?"

"Let them go," said the Fathers. "Let them see—before they be gone—one of the few simple peoples left. We ourselves have become a contrived and compromised people. Let the Children be children for half a day."

Eretz was the Planet of the Offense, and therefore it was to be (perhaps it recently had been) the Planet of the Restitution also. But in no other way was it distinguished. The Children had received the tradition of Eretz as children receive all traditions—like lightning.

Hobble, Michael Goodgrind, Ralpha, Lonnie, Laurie, Bea and Joan they called themselves as they came down on Eretz—for these were their idea of Eretz names. But they could have as many names as they wished in their games.

An anomalous intrusion of great heat and force! The rocks ran like water where they came down, and there was formed a scarp-pebble enclave.

It was all shanty country and shanty towns on Eretz—clumsy hills, badly done plains and piedmonts, ragged fields, uncleansed rivers, whole weedpatches of provinces—not at all like Home. And the Towns! Firenze, Praha, Venezia, Londra, Colonia, Gant, Roma—why, they were nothing but towns made out of stone and wood! And these were the greatest of the towns of Eretz, not the meanest.

The Children exploded into action. Like children of the less transcendent races running wild on an ocean beach for an afternoon, they ran wild over continents. They scattered. And they took whatever forms first came into their minds.

Hobble—dark and smoldering like crippled Vulcan.

Michael Goodgrind—a broken-nosed bull of a man. How they all howled when he invented that first form!

Ralpha—like young Mercury.

And Lonnie—a tall giant with a golden beard.

Laurie was fire, Bea was light, Joan was moon-darkness.

But in these, or in any other forms they took, you'd always know that they were cousins or brethren.

Lonnie went pure Gothic. He had come onto it at the tail end of the thing and he fell in love with it.

"I am the Emperor!" he told the people like giant thunder. He pushed the Emperor Wenceslas off the throne and became Emperor.

"I am the true son of Charles, and you had thought me dead," he told the people. "I am Sigismund." Sigismund was really dead, but Lonnie became Sigismund and reigned, taking the wife and all the castles of Wenceslas. He grabbed off gangling old forts and mountain-rooks and raised howling Eretzi armies to make war. He made new castles. He loved the tall sweeping things and raised them to a new height. Have you never wondered that the last of those castles—in the late afternoon of the Gothic—were the tallest and oddest?

One day the deposed Wenceslas came back, and he was possessed of a new power.

"Now we will see who is the real Emperor!" the new Wenceslas cried like a rising storm.

They clashed their two forces and broke down each other's bridges and towns and stole the high ladies from each other's strongholds. They wrestled like boys. But they wrestled with a continent.

Lonnie (who was Sigismund) learned that the Wenceslas he battled was Michael Goodgrind wearing a contrived Emperor body. So they fought harder.

There came a new man out of an old royal line.

"I am Jobst," the new man cried. "I will show you two princelings who is the real Emperor!"

He fought the two of them with overwhelming verve. He raised fast-striking Eretzi armies, and used tricks that only a young Mercury would know. He was Ralpha, entering the game as the third Emperor. But the two combined against him and broke him at Constance.

They smashed Germany and France and Italy like a clutch of eggs. Never had there been such spirited conflict. The Eretzi were amazed by it all, but they were swept into it; it was the Eretzi who made up the armies.

Even today the Eretzi or Earthers haven't the details of it right in their histories. When the King of Aragon, for an example, mixed into it, they treated him as a separate person. They did not know that Michael Goodgrind was often the King of Aragon, just as Lonnie was often the Duke of Flanders. But, played for itself, the Emperor game would be quite a limited one. Too limited for the children.

The girls played their own roles. Laurie claimed to be thirteen different queens. She was consort of all three Emperors in every one of their guises, and she also dabbled with the Eretzi. She was the wanton of the group.

Bea like the Grande Dame part and the Lady Bountiful bit. She was very good on Great Renunciations. In her dif-

ferent characters she beat paths from thrones to nunneries
and back again; and she is now known as five different
saints. Every time you turn to the Common of the Mass
of Holy Women who are Neither Virgins nor Martyrs, you
are likely to meet her.

And Joan was the dreamer who may have enjoyed the
Afternoon more than any of them.

Laurie made up a melodrama—Lucrezia Borgia and the
Poison Ring. There is an advantage in doing these little
melodramas on Eretz. You can have as many characters as
you wish—they come free. You can have them as extrav-
agantly as you desire—who is there to object to it? Lucrezia was very well done, as children's burlesques go, and
the bodies were strewn from Napoli to Vienne. The Eretzi
play with great eagerness any convincing part offered them,
and they go to their deaths quite willingly if the part calls
for it.

Lonnie made one up called The Pawnbroker and the
Pope. It was in the grand manner, all about the Medici
family, and had some very funny episodes in the fourth
act. Lonnie, who was vain of his acting ability, played
Medici parts in five succeeding generations. The drama left
more corpses than did the Lucrezia piece, but the killings
weren't so sudden or showy; the girls had a better touch
at the bloody stuff.

Ralpha did a Think Piece called One, Two, Three—Infinity. In its presentation he put all the rest of the Children
to roast grandly in Hell; he filled up Purgatory with Eretzi-
type people—the dullards; and for the Paradise he did a
burlesque of Home. The Eretzi use a cropped version of
Ralpha's piece and call it the Divine Comedy, leaving out
a lot of fun.

Bea did a poetic one named the Witches' Bonfire. All
the Children spent many a happy evening with that one,
and they burnt twenty thousand witches. There was something satisfying about those Eretzi autumnal twilights with
the scarlet sky and the frosty fields and the kine lowing in
the meadows and the evening smell of witches burning.
Bea's was really a pastoral piece.

• • •

All the Children ranged far except Hobble. Hobble (who
was Vulcan) played with his sick toys. He played at Ate-
liers and Smithies, at Furnaces and Carousels. And often
the other Children came and watched his work, and joined
in for a while.

They played with the glass from the furnaces. They made
gold-toned goblets, iridescent glass poems, figured spheres,
goblin pitchers, glass music boxes, gargoyle heads, dragon
chargers, princess salieras, figurines of lovers. So many
things to make of glass! To make, and to smash when
made!

But some of the things they exchanged as gifts instead
of smashing them—glass birds and horses, fortune-telling
globes that showed changing people and scenes within,
tuned chiming balls that rang like bells, glass cats that
sparked when stroked, wolves and bears, witches that flew.

The Eretzi found some of these things that the Children
discarded. They studied them and imitated them.

And again, in the interludes of their other games, the
Children came back to Hobble's shops where he sometimes
worked with looms. They made costumes of wool and linen
and silk. They made trains and cloaks and mantles, all the
things for their grand masquerades. They fabricated tapes-
tries and rugs and wove in all sorts of scenes: vistas of
Home and of Eretz, people and peacocks, fish and cranes,
dingles and dromedaries, larks and lovers. They set their
creations in the strange ragged scenery of Eretz and in the
rich contrived gardens of Home. A spark went from the
Children to their weaving so that none could tell where
they left off and their creations began.

Then they left poor Hobble and went on to their more
vital games.

There were seven of them (six, not counting the backward Hobble), but they seemed a thousand. They built themselves Castles in Spain and Gardes in Languedoc. The girls
played always at Intrigue, for the high pleasure of it, and
to give a cause for the wars. And the wars were the things

that the boys seldom tired of. It is fun to play at armies with live warriors; and the Eretzi were live . . . in a sense.

The Eretzi had had wars and armies and sieges long before this, but they had been aimless things. Oh, this was one field where the Eretzi needed the Children. Consider the battles that the Children engineered that afternoon:

Gallipoli—how they managed the ships in that one! The Fathers could not have maneuvered more intricately in their four-dimension chess at Home.

Adrianople, Kunovitza, Dibra, Varna, Hexamilion! It's fun just to call out the bloody names of battles.

Constantinople! That was the one where they first used the big cannon. But who cast the big cannon for the Turks there? In their histories the Eretzi say that it was a man named Orban or Urban, and that he was Dacian, or he was Hungarian, or he was Danish. How many places did you tell them that you came from, Michael Goodgrind?

Belgrad, Trebizond, Morat, Blackheath, Napoli, Dornach!

Cupua and Taranto—Ralpha's armies beat Michael's at both of those.

Carignola—Lonnie foxed both Michael and Ralpha there, and nearly foxed himself. (You didn't intend it all that way, Lonnie. It was seven-cornered luck and you know it!)

Garigliano where the sea was red with blood and the ships were like broken twigs on the water!

Brescia! Ravenna! Who would have believed that such things could be done with a device known as Spanish infantry?

Villalar, Milan, Pavia! Best of all, the sack of Rome! There were a dozen different games blended into that one. The Eretzi discovered new emotions in themselves there—a deeper depravity and a higher heroism.

Siege of Florence! That one called out the Children's every trick. A wonderfully well-played game!

Turin, San Quentin, Moncontour, Mookerhide!

Lepanto! The great sea siege where the castled ships broke asunder and the tall Turk Ochiali Pasha perished with all his fleet and was drowned forever. But it wasn't so forever as you might suppose, for he was Michael Goodgrind, who had more bodies than one. The fish still remember Lepanto. Never had there been such feastings.

Alcazar-Quivar! That was the last of the excellent ones—the end of the litany. The Children left off the game. They remembered (but conveniently, and after they had worn out the fun of it) that they were forbidden to play Warfare with live soldiers. The Eretzi, left to themselves again, once more conducted their battles as dull and uninspired affairs.

You can put it to a test, now, tonight. Study the conflicts of the earlier times, of this high period, and of the time that followed. You will see the difference. For a short two or three centuries you will find really well-contrived battles. And before and after there is only ineptitude.

Often the Children played at Jealousies and raised up all the black passions in themselves. They played at Immoralities, for there is an abiding evil in all children.

Masking and water-carnivals and balls, and forever the emotional intrigue!

Ralpha walked down a valley, playing a lute and wearing the body of somebody else. He luted the birds out of the trees and worked a charm on the whole countryside.

An old crone followed him and called, "Love me when I'm old."

"*Sempremai, tuttavia,*" sang Ralpha in Eretzi or Earthian. "For Ever, For Always."

A small girl followed and called, "Love me when I'm young."

"Forever, for always," sang Ralpha.

The weirdest witch in the world followed him and called, "Love me when I'm ugly."

"For always, forever," sang Ralpha, and pulled her down on the grass. He knew that all the creatures had been Laurie playing Bodies.

But a peculiar thing happened: the prelude became more important than the play. Ralpha fell in love with his own song, and forgot Laurie who had inspired it. He made all manner of music and poem—aubade, madrigal, chanson; and he topped it off with one hundred sonnets. He made them in Eretzi words, Italian words, Languedoc words, and they were excellent. And the Eretzi still copy them.

Ralpha discovered there that poetry and song are Passion Deferred. But Laurie would rather have deferred the song. She was long gone away and taking up with others before Ralpha had finished singing his love for her, but he never noticed that she had left him. After Hobble, Ralpha was the most peculiar of them all.

In the meanwhile, Michael Goodgrind invented another game of Bodies. He made them of marble—an Eretzi limestone that cuts easily without faulting. And he painted them on canvas. He made the People of Home, and the Eretzi. He said that he would make angels.

"But you cannot make angels," said Joan.

"We know that," said Michael, "but do the Eretzi know that I cannot? I will make angels for the Eretzi."

He made them grotesque, like chicken men, like bird men, with an impossible duplication of humeral function. And the Children laughed at the carven jokes.

But Michael had sudden inspiration. He touched his creations up and added an element of nobility. So an iconography was born.

All the Children did it then, and they carried it into other mediums. They made the Eretzi, and they made themselves. You can still see their deep features on some of those statues, that family look that was on them no matter what faces they wore or copied.

Bronze is fun! Bronze horses are the best. Big bronze doors can be an orgy of delight, or bronze bells whose shape is their tone.

The Children went to larger things. They played at Realms and Constitutions, and Banks and Ships and Provinces. Then they came down to smaller things again and played at Books, for Hobble had just invented the printing thing.

Of them all, Hobble had the least imagination. He didn't

range wide like the others. He didn't outrage the Eretzi.
He spent all his time with his sick toys as though he were
a child of much younger years.

The only new body he acquired was another one just
like his own. Even this he didn't acquire as did the other
Children theirs. He made it laboriously in his shop, and
animated it. Hobble and the Hobble Creature worked together thereafter, and you could not tell them apart. One
was as dull and laboring as the other.

The Eretzi had no effect whatsoever on the Children, but
the Children had great effect on the Eretzi. The Children
had the faculty of making whatever little things they needed
or wanted, and the Eretzi began to copy them. In this manner the Eretzi came onto many tools, processes, devices
and arts that they had never known before. Out of ten thousand, there were these:

The Astrolabe, Equatorium, Quadrant, Lathes and Tra-
versing Tools, Ball Bearings, Gudgeons, Gig Mills, Barom-
eters, Range Finders, Cantilever Construction, Machine
Saws, Screw Jacks, Hammer Forges and Drop Forges, Print-
ing, Steel that was more than puddled Iron, Logarithms,
Hydraulic Rams, Screw Dies, Spanner Wrenches, Flux Sol-
der, Telescopes, Microscopes, Mortising Machines, Wire
Drawing, Stanches (Navigation Locks), Gear Trains, Paper-
Making, Magnetic Compass and Wind-Rhumb, Portulan
Charts and Projection Maps, Pinnule-Sights, Spirit-Levels,
Fine Micrometers, Porcelain, Firelock Guns, Music Nota-
tion and Music Printing, Complex Pulleys and Snatch-
Blocks, the Seed-Drill, Playing Cards (the Children's
masquerade faces may still be seen on them), Tobacco, the
Violin, Whiskey, the Mechanical Clock.

They were forbidden, of course, to display any second-
aspect powers or machines, as these would disrupt things.
But they disrupted accidentally in building, in tooling, in
armies and navies, in harbors and canals, in towns and
bridges, in ways of thinking and recording. They started a
thing that couldn't be reversed. It was only the One Afternoon they were here, only two or three Eretzi Centuries,

but they set a trend. They overwhelmed by the very number of their new devices, and it could never be simple on Eretz again.

There were many thousands of Eretz days and nights in that Long Afternoon. The Children had begun to tire of it, and the hour was growing late. For the last time they wandered off, this time all Seven of them together.

In the bodies of Kings and their Ladies, they strode down a High Road in the Levant. They were wondering what last thing they could contrive, when they found their way blocked by a Pilgrim with a staff.

"Let's tumble the hairy Eretzi," shouted Ralpha. "Let him not stand in the way of Kings!" For Ralpha was King of Bulgaria that day.

But they did *not* tumble the Pilgrim. That man knew how to handle his staff, and he laid the bunch of them low. It was nothing to him that they were the high people of the World who ordered Nations. He flogged them flat.

"Bleak Children!" the Pilgrim cried out as he beat them into the ground. "Unfledged little oafs! Is it so that you waste your Afternoon on Earth? I'll give you what your Fathers forgot."

Seven-colored thunder, how he could use that staff! He smashed the gaudy bodies of the Children and broke many of their damnable bones. Did he know that it didn't matter? Did he understand that the bodies they wore were only for an antic?

"Lay off, old Father!" begged Michael Goodgrind, bleeding and half beaten into the earth. "Stay your bloody bludgeon. You do not know who we are."

"I know you," maintained the Pilgrim mountainously. "You are ignorant Children who have abused the Afternoon given you on Earth. You have marred and ruined and warped everything you have touched."

"No, no," Ralpha protested—as he set in new bones for his old damaged ones—"you do not understand. We have advanced you a thousand of your years in one of our afternoons. Consider the Centuries we have saved you! It's as though we had increased your life by that thousand years."

"We have all the time there is," said the Pilgrim solidly. "We were well and seriously along our road, and it was not so crooked as the one you have brought us over. You have broken our sequence with your meddling. You've set us back more ways than you've advanced us. You've shattered our Unity."

"Pigs have unity!" Joan shouted. "We've brought you diversity. Think deep. Consider all the machines we have showed you, the building and the technique. I can name you a thousand things we've given you. You will never be the same again."

"True. We will never be the same," said the Pilgrim. "You may not be an unmixed curse. I'm a plain man and I don't know. Surety is one of the things you've lost us. But you befouled us. You played the game of Immoralities and taught it to us Earthlings."

"You had it already," Laurie insisted. "We only brought elegance instead of piggishness to its practice." Immoralities was Laurie's own game, and she didn't like to hear it slighted.

"You have killed many thousands of us in your battles," said the Pilgrim. "You're a bitter fruit—sweet at the first taste only."

"You would yourselves have killed the same numbers in battles, and the battles wouldn't have been so good," said Michael. "Do you not realize that we are the higher race? We have roots of great antiquity."

"We have roots older than antiquity," averred the Pilgrim. "You are wicked Children without compassion."

"Compassion? For the Eretzi?" shouted Lonnie in disbelief.

"Do you have compassion for mice?" demanded Ralpha.

"Yes. I have compassion for mice," the Pilgrim said softly.

"I make a guess," Ralpha shot in shrewdly after they had all repaired their damaged bodies. "You travel as a Pilgrim, and Pilgrims sometimes come from very far away. You are not Eretzi. You are one of the Fathers from Home going in the guise of an Eretzi Pilgrim. You have this routine so that sometimes one of you comes to this world—and to every world—to see how it goes. You may have come to investigate an event said to have happened on Eretz a day ago."

Ralpha did not mean an Eretzi day ago, but a day ago at Home. The High Road they were on was in Coele-Syria, not far from where the Event was thought to have happened, and Ralpha pursued his point:

"You are no Eretzi, or you would not dare to confront us, knowing what we are."

"You guess wrong in this and in everything," said the Pilgrim. "I am of this Earth, earthy. And I will not be intimidated by a gangle of children of whatever species! You're a weaker flesh than ourselves. You hide in other bodies, and you get Earthlings to do your slaughter. And you cannot stand up to my staff!

"Go home, you witless weanlings!" and he raised his terrible staff again.

"Our time is nearly up. We will be gone soon," said Joan softly.

The last game they played? They played Saints—for the Evil they had done in playing Bodies wrongly, and in playing Warfare with live soldiers. But they repented of the things only after they had enjoyed them for the Long Afternoon. They played Saints in hairshirt and ashes, and revived that affair among the Eretzi.

And finally they all assembled and took off from the high hill between Prato and Firenze in Italy. The rocks flowed like water where they left, and now there would be a double scarp formation.

They were gone, and that was the end of them here.

There is a theory, however, that one of the Hobbles remained and is with us yet. Hobble and his creature could not be told apart and could not finally tell themselves apart. They flipped an Eretzi coin, Emperors or Shields, to see which one would go and which one would stay. One went and one stayed. One is still here.

But, after all, Hobble was only concerned with the sick toys, the mechanical things, the material inventions. Would it have been better if Ralpha or Joan stayed with us? They'd have burned us crisp by now! They were damnable and irresponsible children.

This short Historical Monograph was not assembled for a distraction or an amusement. We consider the evidence that Children have spent their short vacations here more than once and in both hemispheres. We set out the theses in ordered parallels and we discover that we have begun to tremble unaccountably.

When last came such visitors here? What thing has beset us during the last long Eretzi lifetime?

We consider a new period—and it impinges on the Present—with aspects so different from anything that went before that we can only gasp aghast and gasp in sick wonder:

"Is it *ourselves* who behave so?"

"Is it beings of another sort, or have we become those beings?"

"Are we ourselves? Are these our deeds?"

There are great deep faces looking over our shoulder, there are cold voices of ancient Children jeering "Compassion? For Earthlings?" there is frozen vasty laughter that does not belong to our species.

I'M TOO BIG BUT I LOVE TO PLAY

James Tiptree Jr.

As most of you probably know by now, multiple Hugo and Nebula Award-winning author James Tiptree, Jr. was actually the pseudonym of the late Dr. Alice Sheldon, a semi-retired experimental psychologist and former member of the American intelligence community who also wrote occasionally under the name of Raccoona Sheldon. Dr. Sheldon's tragic death in 1987 put an end to "both" careers, but not before she had won two Nebula and two Hugo Awards as Tiptree, won another Nebula Award as Raccoona Sheldon, and established herself, under whatever name, as one of the very best science fiction writers of our times. As Tiptree, Dr. Sheldon published two novels, Up the Walls of the World *and* Brightness Falls From the Air, *and nine short-story collections:* Ten Thousand Light Years From Home, Warm Worlds and Otherwise, Starsongs of an Old Primate, Out of the Everywhere, Tales of the Quintana Roo, Byte Beautiful, The Starry Rift, *the posthumously published* Crown of Stars, *and the recent posthumous retrospective collection,* Her Smoke Rose Up Forever.*

Here she tells us the bittersweet story of an alien who tries his best to fit into human society, tries hard to be just one of the boys—but who, in the final analysis, is just too damn big.

S*orry, Jack. You're right. Yes, I'm upset. No, it's not the campaign, for God's sake the campaign is perfect. It's not the crowds, either, I love them, Jack, you know that. Strain? sure it's a strain, but—*

Jack. Listen. Frightened. That's what happened to Man-ahasset. Scared out of my mind. Because of, because of this feeling I get, this sensation. Too big! Every time now when things are going well, when I'm getting to them—the rapport, it's working—all of a sudden this awful buildup starts, this sensation I'm swelling up too big. Terribly, ghastly too big! Listen, Jack: brain tumor.

Brain tumor.

I can't go to a goddamn doctor now, there's no way, they'd find out. I can't tell Ellen. I can't— Started? Oh, Christ, I know exactly when it started, it started after the Tobago weekend. At Tobago. That night. I know, you told me. But all I did was swim out and loaf around. Unwind. By myself. I had to, Jack. That's when it started. The Monday after, at the Biloxi airport. You remember, I cut it off fast?

That was the first. The mayor, and that clot from Memphis, Dick Thing, you know, they were shouting questions, and the crowd started singing, and all of a sudden, Jack, I looked over at the mayor and you. And you were about two feet high, both of you. And the plane. Tiny! I couldn't get into it! And this feeling, this churning—

Jack. Don't. I know about infantile omnipotence. You don't suddenly get delusions of infantile omnipotence at eleven-fifty on a Monday in Biloxi airport. Not unless there's something physical. It's physical, Jack. The bigness, the swelling, the—vortex—like I'm starting to explode, Jack. It's got to be brain—

Alone of his kind, perhaps, he did not outgrow joy. Play-joy in the crowded galaxies, the nursery of his race. Others matured soon away from the pleasures of time and space and were to be found immensely solitary, sailing the dimensionless meadows beyond return. They did not know each other, nor he them. How could they? For him, still the star-tangles. To ride—how rich-riding the swirling currents between the stars! How various, the wild-swarm photons upon his sensors! And games could be invented:

For example—delicious!—to find some solitary little siz-
zler and breast close against its radiance, now tacking art-
fully, now close-hauled in the shadow of its planet, now
out again to strive closer and closer to the furious little
body, to gain the corona itself, to poise, gather—and then
let go! Let all go! All sailing nucleus over ganglia out and
out in a glory-rush—until that sun's energy met another's,
and he was swept whirling down the star-streams to floun-
der roiled in some sidereal Sargasso.

Here he would preen and sort his nearly immaterial vastness, amusing himself with bizarre energic restructurings,
waiting for a new photon-eddy to catch his vectors and bil-
low him off again.

Sometimes what served him for perception gave him
news that a young one of his kind was—or had been—following him. This lasted but briefly. They could not match
his skill and would soon veer off. Of his equals he saw
none. Was he alone of his age in his preoccupations? It
did not occur to him to wonder. No member of his race
had ever exchanged information. That he might be alone
in his games of exostructure he did not know nor care, but
played.

New games: resting behind a ball of matter on his approach to a red sun, his temporary nucleus snug in the
shadow, his perimeter feathering out past the system turbulence—it occurred to him to invest his receptors more
closely round the little ball's surface. What he sensed there
diverted him. Energy distributions—but tiny! And how
complex!

He curled more closely around it, concentrating himself
to the density of a noisy vacuum. Here was an oddity indeed: pockets of negative entropy!

To him, as to all his race, the elaboration and permuta-
tion of field-energies was life. But he had never before
conceived of energy-interaction of this density. And to *con-
ceive*, with him, was not a passivity but a *modeling*. A re-
structurement into knowing. He hauled in a half-parsec of
immaterial relatedness and began ineptly to experiment.
Scarcely had he begun to concentrate when an incautious

unbalancement exposed him to the red sun's wind and sent him sweeping out of the system with his ganglia in disarray.

But what passed for memory among his kind persisted, and now and again he would hover to inspect a likely lump. And he found, oh, attractive, the patterns! A vast gamesomeness grew in him; he played Maxwell's demon with himself, concentrating, differentiating, substreaming complex energy interchanges. Skill mounted, fed back to structure. He tackled subtle challenges. And on planetary surfaces where scaled, skinned or furry creatures focused dim sense-organs on the skies, one and another across the galaxy would be shaken by the sight of incorporealities vastwavering among the stars.

Shaken more especially, when they could recognize monstrous auroral versions of themselves. For technique was coming to obsess him. What had been play was becoming art. This phase culminated in the moment when he was fashioning—without in the least knowing it—a Sirian monitor shrimp family. His tension was great, and at its peak a resonance somehow ignited and *held* through the glorious backlash of release!

Greater feats! Were they possible? A new era of experimentation opened and claimed him.

High on the dunes of Lake Balkhash Natalia Brezhnovna Suitlov surveyed the beach, which was unfortunately deserted. Natalia cocked her white-blonde Baltic head. From the far side of the dune, faint but throbbing: music. Not the most advanced, but promising.

Natalia strolled a bit higher, studying the lake. She paused. Face sun-rapt, she stretched prolongedly. Then one hand dropped absently to the knot of her diaper. With fluent ease, first the diaper and then Natalia slowly sank from sight into a hollow.

Here she disposed her bronze body for maximum sun. The music ceased. Natalia hummed a few beats, husky but true.

From the far side of the dune came a scrabbling. Natalia's eyelids drooped. A bullet-shaped shadow appeared in the grass at the top of the dune. Natalia's expression became very severe.

For a long moment the tension-system held beautifully. The receptors in the bullet-head belonging to Timofaev Gagarin Ponamorenko focused upon Natalia. Natalia radiated strongly back. The system grew, recruited.

Action became imperative. Timofaev gave a perfunctory glance around—and inhaled yelpingly.

A hundred meters up the little ridge something huge was happening. Part of it was a gassy figure resting on the ground in Natalia's same posture. It was Natalia—but fifty meters long and obscenely distorted. Giant-Natalia solidified, took on color. But it was not alone! On the ridge above it, a great head—Timofaev's head—and his hands—and—

Natalia herself was up in a crouch and staring too. The giant head of Timofaev lacked hair, the hands lacked arms, they were floating in the air. And floating behind them were other portions of Timofaev, partly unrecognizable, part plain as a pikestaff—those portions of his being which had been energetically and reciprocally resonant with Natalia.

The youngsters screamed together and the monstrous images began to boil. Sand, air and grass rose whirling, and the dune imploded round them in thunder.

SOMETHING WRONG! WITHDRAW! REDEFINE SYSTEM!

Guerero Galvan swung his legs against his burro and gazed sourly down into the great barranca beside the trail. He was hot and dry and dusty. When he was rich he would ride to Xochimilicho in a private *avion*. But when he was rich he would not live in Xochimilicho. Very surely, he would live in a concrete palace full of girls at Mazatlan, by the sea. The sea? Guerero considered the sea. He had never seen it. But all ricos loved the sea. The sea was full of girls.

The burro hobbled on. Guerero kicked it reflexively, squinting at the trail ahead.

Coming toward him was another rider.

Guerero prodded his mount. The trail was narrow here, and the stranger was large. He too was prodding his mount, Guerero saw. But where had he come from? The trail had been clear to the pass a few moments before. He must have dozed.

As they came abreast Guerero raised three fingers in a studiedly casual greeting. The stranger did likewise. Guerero came fully awake, began to stare. There was something odd here. A diligent student of the mirror, Guerero saw that the stranger, though larger, looked very much like himself.

"*Bueno,*" he muttered, tracing his own dark, slightly adenoidal features, his own proud gold glitter of bicuspid. And the burro—the same! The same tattered blanket! He crossed himself.

"*Bueno,*" said the stranger, and crossed himself.

Guerero took one long look and began to scream prayers, hauling, wrestling his animal, flailing his legs. Next moment hc had leaped free and was racing down the trail.

The voice had been his own voice, but *it had come from the burro.*

Careening, Guerero risked a look behind and redoubled his speed. The false Guerero-devil was trying to dismount too—but the flesh of its legs seemed to be joined to the sides of the devil-burro. Behind the devils the mountain was convulsing. Guerero flung himself into a gully and cowered while trail, pass and devils vomited themselves into the sky.

MISTAKE! WITHDRAW! SUBCIRCUITS IMPRECISE!

Through the noise of his party Ches Mencken was keeping one ear on the moonlit terrace. Majorca moonlight could get chilly. The three couples who'd gone skinny-dipping with Elfa had come dripping and giggling back and were applying themselves to the juice. Where was Elfa?

He mixed rock-vodkas, peeking at the electroquartz time-piece in the wide reptilian band around his wide mammalian wrist. Thirty-five minutes. He jerked his jaw clear of the turtleneck and pressed a glass into La Jones' steamy paw. She breathed at him. Sorry, Jones-baby, Elfa is my score . . . Where the hell is she?

Jones-baby gurgled through her hair. Those earrings are real. But Elfa's got all that glue. Pity Jones doesn't fall on his head and leave you with the basic Xerox, things might be different for you and me, know that?

Automatically his eyes gave her the message: *You—me—different—*

Only it wouldn't be, he thought. It'd be the same old ratass. Christ but he was tired! Whacked out. . . . Young cunt, old cunt, soft, sinewy, bouncy, bony, wriggly, lumpy, slimy, lathery, leathery cunt squeaking shrieking growling—all of them after him, his furry arms, his golden masculinity, his poor old never-failing poker—Oh Ches I've never oh Ches it's so it's oh Ches oh Darling darling darlingdar-lingdarling—

Wonder what it'd be like to go gay? Restful, maybe, he brooded, checking bottles. Better yet, go off the juice onto pot. They say you don't, with pot. After he landed Elfa that's what he'd do: go on pot and retire. Surprise for Elfa. Only, where was Elfa?

Oh God no.

A pale form was wavering about the moonlit terrace. Not a stitch on and slugged. She must have had a bottle down there.

He disengaged fast and raced around through the bedroom, snatching up a rebozo.

"Darling you'll get chilled!" Capturing her in the wool lace, leading her into the bedroom. She was slugged all right but not out.

"Don't know . . . clothes? What this?"

"Warm you, baby. What a doll, num-num—"

Automatically moving in, his expert hands. Really a damn good stack for her age, she's kept herself up. Care-

ful, now. Mustn't upset her. With Elfa it's got to be love.
Elfa is special. Elfa is the retirement plan.

"Ches!"

"Sorry baby, I'll be good."

"No, I mean, I feel so—Ches!"

"Little girl, you're—"

"Ches, so intimate, I never—I mean, I loved Maxwell
terribly, you know I did, Ches?"

"Yes, little heart?"

"But he never, I never! Oh, Ches—"

Oh God it was the pitch, he saw, and that damn crowd
outside. They'd have to go. Life or death.

"—Drink this down for Ches, Ches wants you to drink
it so you won't get chilled, see? My little girl sit down
right here just one minute, Ches is coming right back—"

"Ches—"

As he closed the door she was saying plaintively, "Ches,
why am I so big? So terribly, terribly—"

Somehow he got them out. She was sipping and croon-
ing to herself where he'd put her.

"Li'l bitsy!"

"Ches loves you."

"Ches! Li'l bitsy moon!"

"Li'l bitsy you, m'm m'm." Taking the glass, carrying
her to the bed, she saying again, "Ches, I'm so big! Li'l
you!"

He didn't hear her. This was serious, this was make or
break. She'd remember tomorrow, all right. It had to be
the big thing. Was she too drunk? Her head lolled. O Jesus.
But his technique was good. Presently he knew he needn't
have worried. She was coming into it beautifully, puffing
and panting. The nose knows. Mellow relief; I *am* good.
Maybe I should be some kind of guru, give lessons.

She was gabbling incoherently, then suddenly plain. "Oh
Ches I'm getting bigger!" *Real panic?*

"It's good, honey," he panted. "It's what you want, let
it happen, let it happen to you—"

He didn't register the white figure wavering on the terrace outside until it stumbled into the glass and began to

mouth. He glanced up, blurry—it was Elfa out there! *How Elfa? No! ELFA?*

The thrashing in his arms went rigid, arched.

"Ches I'm go-oo-ing explo-OO-OOO—"

Under intolerable stress the nebulous extension which had been compressed into a mimic of the woman by the water reverted to its original state. A monstrous local discontinuity comprising—among other things—the subatomic residuals of an alligator watchband, bloomed into the thermosphere from the Majorca cliffs.

NEW ERROR! ONE-TO-ONE INTERMIX? OOH HOW MORE?

Standing on the wet rocks, helit laughed. Laughing helit laughed more. To feel! To know feeling! To know knowing! A past flooded in—voices—speech-patterns—events—concepts—MEANING! Laughter roared.

The little subsystem was right! It worked. It lived!

But the little system was not right. The system was under strain, it demanded closure. It demanded to be itself, be whole. Something was outside, disequilibrating it, intruding alien circuits. The little system had integrity, it would not be a subsystem. It fought the disequilibrium, hauled and pulled on the incongruent gap.

He fought back, idly at first, then strenuously—fighting to keep his nucleus outside, to retain the system subsystem hierarchy. It was too late, no good.

Soundless as a soap-film snapping, the great field reorganized. The system inverted, closed and came to equilibrium with everything crammed in.

But it was not the same equilibrium.

. . . The moonlit surf creamed and hissed quietly around the rocks at his feet. Something he did not examine floated further out. After a moment he lifted his head to watch the little moon slicing cirrus cloud. The breeze dried his skin. He felt an extraordinary . . . Pleasure? Pride?

Perhaps that he was still young enough to break a business trip with an impromptu swim?

He began to climb up the rocks. Beneath the pleasure was something else. Pain? Why was he so confused? Why had he come here? Surely not just for an idle swim. Not *now*. But yet he was happy. He let himself slide into pleasure as he found his clothes, dressed.

Dressing himself was actively enjoyable; he'd never noticed. A moment of panic seized him as he climbed back to Overlook 92 where he had left his car. But it was there, safe. With his briefcase.

Images of the spinning surf, the streaming clouds, wheeled in his mind as he drove, merged with the swirl of the car as the huge coastal cloverleaf carried him up and around over and dip down through the mercury lights flashing—sweeping—

Ooee-ooee-ooee! went his signaler. As his power cut the cop rolled in beside him. He answered automatically, produced his papers. The interchange excited him. It seemed delicious to see the cop's thick lips murmuring into his 'corder. From ID card through the eyes through the brain through the sound-waves through the 'corder tape pulse—

"Who reads the tape?" he asked.

The officer stared at him, tight-lipped.

"Does a human being listen to it? Or does it go to another machine?"

"Where did you say you're going, Doctor, uh, Mitchell?"

"I told you. San Berdoo Research. My meeting up north ended early, I decided to drive back. Fine night."

In fact, he remembered now, he had been unspeakably depressed.

"Doing one fifty in a ninety kay-em zone. Keep it down." The cop turned away.

Mitchell—he was Mitchell—drove on frowning. His dashboard needles fanned, dial lights blinked. Giving him information. The car communicated with him, one way. Whether it wanted to or not.

I was like the car, he thought. He made me communicate with him one-way. There was a roiling inside him. Where is the circuit, he wondered.

He raced on through the night, communications springing at him. Right lane must turn right, he read. Food gas lodging next exit. His black mood lifted. Green-to-red, green-to-amber, flashing-amber, All Night Funeral Home. He laughed aloud.

He was still grinning when the garage opened to his beeper and the house door opened to his thumb. The house was dark, silent. He expected that, he realized. His wife was visiting her mother. *Eleanor.*

But his wife's name was not Eleanor, his wife was Audrey.

Depression descended. Suddenly he saw he had been evading reality. Swimming and playing games with the cops instead of doing the serious thinking he had planned to do. Before tomorrow's meeting.

He turned out the lights and lay on the bed, trying to concentrate. There were paragraphs in his mind. Other things. He must concentrate. The moon set. It grew darker, and presently, very slowly, lighter. He failed to notice that he did not sleep. When the little sun rose he got up and redressed.

The San Bernardino lot was still quite empty when he pulled in; the guards seemed surprised to see him. His office, though, was sunny. Did not need light. He found the files.

His secretary came in at eight-thirty tip-toeing.

"Miss Mulm," he said brightly. He pushed the files away.

"Yes sir?" She was instantly wary, a small, dark, soft-lipped girl.

"Sir?" he echoed. "Indicating deference, subordination . . . are you afraid of me, Miss Mulm?"

"Why, no, Dr. Mitchell." Staring gravely, shaking her dark head.

"Good. There's too much of that sort of thing. Too much one-way communication. No true interaction. Entropic. Don't you feel it?"

"Well, I guess . . . uh—"

"Miss Mulm. You've been with me five years now. Since before I was Director. You came over from the department with me."

She nodded, watching him intently: yes.

"Have you any feelings about the sort of work we do here?"

"I'm not sure what you mean, Doctor Mitchell."

"Do you—well, do you approve of it?"

She was silent. Wary. But somehow brimming.

"I—of course I don't understand all of it, not really. But it—it seems more military than I expected. I mean, Colonel Morelake, I guess—"

"And you don't feel quite right about military-type research?"

"Doctor Mitchell," she said desperately, "if you think it's all right—"

Her eyes, face brimmed, communicating information.

"My God," he said slowly, studying her. "Do you think I think—does everybody here think I—No. You can't answer that, of course. I guess I, since Hal's been away I've been doing some—" He broke off.

"Miss Mulm! Does it strike you that we are engaged in a most peculiar interaction process?"

She made a helpless confused noise.

"On the one hand we're discussing, verbally, the work of this institution. And at the same time there is another quite different communication taking place between us. Without words. Are you aware of that? I feel it has been going on for some time, too. Don't you think so? By the way, my name is Colin."

"I know," she said, suddenly not confused at all.

He came closer and slowly, experimentally, reached his hands and arms out along the force-lines of the emergent system. The system of two.

"*Eleanor*," he said. The system tightened, connected body to body, changing both. His body began to move along the field stresses. It felt wonderful. It felt resonant. Resonances tuned, building to oscillation. Feedback began to drive—swelled stress—

"Eleanor!" He was galvanized with delicious danger. "Eleanor—I—"

"Yes Colin!" Brimming at him, five years of small, dark very intense—

"I—I—I—" Bracing against the forcefield's bulge, *"What?"*

"The intercom! They—they—it's time, Doctor Mitchell!"

"Oh." It was flashing, buzzing, down there very small and far away. The . . . the meeting. Yes. What the hell had hit him. Damp. Damp the circuits. The room came back. And the paragraphs.

He was quite himself when the staff meeting opened. The project leaders, as usual, led off with their reports. There were eighteen bodies and an empty chair: the fourteen project directors, Admin, Security, Colonel Morelake, himself and the empty chair for his deputy Hal, on leave at Aspen. The reports were officially being made to him as Director, but most of the speakers seemed to be talking directly to Colonel Morelake. Again as usual.

Jim Morelake bore a disarming resemblance to a robin. A slim, neat robin with a perfectly good PhD and lots of charm. He bobbed his head in obviously genuine interest at each report. When old Pfaffman got into a tangled complaint—this time to Mitchell—Morelake spoke up.

"Colin, I believe I know where we can get some computer time to help Max."

Pfaffman grunted without looking at him and subsided.

That wound up the routine. They looked at Mitchell.

"About Cal Tech North," Colin Mitchell said. "I spent over six hours with Will Tenneman yesterday, before and after the general meeting. Essentially he was very ready to deal, provided we can work out the details of the grant allocations, and I feel they'll be reasonable. In fact, there was so little to talk over until we get down to specifics that I came back early. I think the main thing that was worrying him was parking space."

That brought the ritual chuckle.

"However," Mitchell went on. "There's something bothering me. This business brings it to a head. The Cal Tech North link-up is completely logical and desirable, *provided* we continue as we have been going. I'd like to do a little review. As you all know, especially those of you who have been here from the start—" He paused, momentarily aware of how many new faces were around him.

"This group was set up as an independent research facility annex to the university proper. It was our role to service a wide spectrum of basic research projects which could attract special funding arrangements. We started with eight projects. Two were medical, one was a short-term data analysis on traffic fatalities, another was historical, two were interdepartment teams in the anthro-sociology area, one was concerned with human developmental and learning processes, and one was an applied project in education. Of these, four were funded by N.I.H., one by private industry, one by the Department of Commerce, one by N.S.F., and one by the Department of Defense. Right?"

A few heads nodded, old Pfaffman's the hardest. Two of the younger men were staring oddly.

"At the present time," Mitchell went on, "we have increased to fourteen projects in hand. There has been a three-fold increase in personnel, and a commensurate growth in support facilities. Of these fourteen projects, one is funded by N.I.H., three by private industry, and Commerce is still continuing the traffic study. The rest, that is nine, are funded by the Department of Defense."

He paused. The empty chair beside him seemed to be significant. Things were different without Hal. He had chosen Hal, relied on him as an energizer. And yet—was it since Hal's time that the D.O.D. connections had tightened?

"Everyone is, of course, very pleased," he said heavily. "But I wonder how many of us have taken time to analyze these projects, which we live with daily. If you stand back, as I have been doing over this past week, and classify them very naively from the standpoint of their ultimate product, I think it is fair to say that five of them have no conceivable application except as means to injure or destroy human life. Three more probably have no other application, although they may yield a small return in basic knowledge. That's eight. Number nine is devoted to the remote electrical control of human behavior. Ten and eleven are exploring means for the sterilization of plants. Twelve and thirteen are limited engineering problems in metallic structure. The last is one of the original—I might say, surviving—projects concerned with human cognitive development."

That was Pfaffman. He was looking at his hands.

"When we link up with Cal Tech North," Mitchell went on, "*when and if* we link up with Cal Tech North, this imbalance will be intensified. I am not familiar with their entire panel, since so much of it is classified. But they are *entirely* funded by D.O.D."

The silence was absolute. Colonel Morelake's eyes were on the table, his expression attentive. Even sympathetic.

Mitchell took a breath. Up to now his voice had been light and controlled, as if reciting a long-prepared speech. He went on, still quietly.

"I would like to have your comments."

One or two heads moved. Feet shifted. One of the younger men—the neural impulse broadcaster—let his teeth click audibly. No one said a word.

The pulse under Mitchell's ear began to pound. The wrangles—the free-for-alls that had gone on around this table! How had he let things drift so far? He leaned back, his elbow on the empty chair.

"I'm surprised," he said, still mildly. "Let me remind you of the way we set up. Perhaps some of you haven't read the charter. It calls for periodic reviews of our program—our *whole* program—giving each of you as project head a voice, a vote if you like, in evaluating what it regrettably refers to as the *thrust* or the *social impact* of our work. As Director, I have two votes—three, with Hal away. Gentlemen, I am calling for your evaluation."

Three men cleared their throats simultaneously. Mitchell looked toward Bill Enders, one of the phytocide biologists.

"Well, Colin," Enders said awkwardly. "Each of these projects *was* discussed, at the time of initiation. I . . . I frankly don't quite see—"

There were several nods, a shuffling release of tension.

Morelake, as a non-voting consultant, kept his eye on his papers throughout.

Mitchell drew a breath.

"I confess I am surprised that no one sees anything to discuss here." His voice sounded oddly thick in his own ears.

"Colin." A crisp voice; Chan Boden, biochemist was the oldest man present bar Pfaffman, with a lush, long-term grant.

"One sees what you mean, of course, Colin. These problems in values, social responsibility. It's always been a difficult aspect. I'm sure all of us maintain awareness of, for example, the triple-A. S. ventilations of the problem. In our private lives," he smiled warmly, "we all undoubtedly do a bit of soul-searching from time to time. But the point is that here, in our professional personae, we are scientists."

The magic word; there was audible relaxation.

"That is exactly the point." Mitchell's voice was dead level. "*We are scientists.*" This too was in the paragraphs, this had been expected. But why were the paragraphs fading? Something about the way they refused to respond. He shook his head, heard himself plow on.

"Are we doing *science,* here? Let's get down to basics. Are we adding to man's sum total knowledge? Is knowledge merely a collection of recipes for killing and subjugating men, for eliminating other species? A computerized stone axe? I'm not talking about the horrors of gore and bloodshed, mind you. The hell with that—some bloodshed may be a fine thing, I don't know. What I mean—"

He leaned forward, the paragraphs all gone now, the pound in his neck building.

"Entropy! The development of reliable knowledge is anti-entropic. Science's task in a social system is comparable to the function of intelligence in the individual. It holds against disorganization, oscillation, noise, entropy. But we, here—we've allied ourselves with an entropic subsystem. We're not generating structure, we're helping to degrade the system!"

They were staring, rigid.

"Are you accusing me of being a virus particle, Colin?" Jim Morelake asked gently.

Mitchell turned on him, eager for connection. The room seemed momentarily clearer.

"All right, Jim, if you're their spokesman now. You must see it. The military argument. Biotic agents—because the other side has. Mutagenesis—because they may get it first. But they know we do it, and so they—Christ! This is at the ten-year-old level. Runaway forward oscillation!"

He was fighting himself now, peering down at the dwindling table.

"You're a scientist, Jim. You're too good a man to be used that way."

Morelake regarded him gravely. Beside him Jan Evans, an engineer, cleared his throat.

"If I understand you, Colin, and I'm not sure that I do, perhaps it might help if you gave us an example of the kind of project you feel is, ah, anti-entropic?"

Mitchell saw Pfaffman freeze. Was the old man afraid he would cite his work? *Afraid?* The awful churning rose in his gut.

"Right," he said clumsily. "Of course, one can't, at a moment's notice but here—communication! Two-way communication. Interlocking flow." He felt suddenly better. "You can understand why a system would seek information—but why in hell does it *offer* information? Why do we strive to be understood? Why is a refusal to accept communication so painful? Look at it—a process that ties the whole damn human system together, and *we don't know fact one about it!*"

This was good! Panting with relief, shining-eyed, Mitchell searched from face to face for what must be coming. At the edge of his mind he noticed the Admin man was by the door. He didn't count.

"Fascinating idea, Colin," Morelake said pleasantly. "I mean, it truly is seminal. But let's go back one moment. What exactly are you suggesting that we do?"

Annoyance tugged at him. Why didn't the others speak?

Something wrong. The swelling feeling came back, rose hard.

"That we stop all this," he said thickly. "Close out the damned projects and kiss off D.O.D. Forget Cal Tech North. Get out and hustle some real research."

Someone gave a snort of amusement. Mitchell looked round slowly in the silence. They seemed to be down there below him, the little faces—hard and blank as that cop's. Only old Pfaffman and the lad whose teeth clicked—they looked scared. The swirling grew inside him, the pound of seeking resonance. Why would they not respond? Mesh, relieve the charge that was hunting wildly in him, straining the system?

"You won't even discuss it," he said with terrible urgency. Dimly he saw that two little guards had come into the shrinking room.

"Colin, this is very painful," said Morelake's voice from the pulsing roil.

"You're going to pretend I'm sick," his own voice chattered. Pygmy guards were closing on him, reaching out. Faces were in the doorway now. One small dark head. Incongruous newspaper in her hand: Eleanor Mulm had been reading that the nude body of a man identified as Dr. Colin Mitchell had been found on the rocks below coastal lookout 92.

"Believe me, Colin, this is very painful," Morelake was saying to the choking thing that looked like Mitchell.

"Entropy!" it gasped, fighting hard. "We must not!"

The guards touched him. The human circuits—the marvelously dense gestalt he had modeled from the man-system floating in the sea—retained its human integrity long enough to make him yell:

"ELEANOR! RUN! RU—UU—UU—"

—And the strained equilibrium ruptured.

The huge energy which had been stressed into the atomic lattice of a human body reverted back to immaterial relatedness and blossomed toward Vega from a point in Lower California. The resulting implosion degraded much of San

Bernardino County, including Colonel Morelake, Pfaffman, the S.B.R. Institute, and Eleanor Mulm.

—and he came finally to equilibrium among the stars.

But it was not the same equilibrium . . .

What served him for memory had learned the circuitry of self-consciousness. What served him as emotion had sampled the wonder of communication between systems, the sharing of structure.

Alone of his lonely race, he had touched and been touched, essayed to speak and been heard.

Reforming himself, he perceived that the nuclear portions of his being were still caught against the little planet by the solar wind—naturally, since the eversion had occurred at noon. It was no trouble to balance there on the standing wave.

He considered for a time, as his distributions stabilized. Then zestfully, for he was a joyful being, he let the radiance take him, swerved out and around to the haven of the planet's shadow. Here he hung idle his immense periphery feathered out to the nearby stars. He preened new structural resonances, tickled by wandering wavicles.

Then he began to scan the planetary surface, tasting, savoring the play of tiny structurances. But it was different now. Somewhere in his field gradients, impalpable residuals of the systems he had copied lingered on. An astronomer in the Andes found something like a burro on his plates of Beta Carinae and chewed out his darkroom aid. A Greek farmer saw the letters *E L E A* glimmering in Scorpio, and carried corn and laurel to a certain cave.

The planet turned, the continents passed into the shadow where he hung, a lonely vastness slightly other than a vacuum. Playing his random scan, relishing energic intricacies. Feeling in what was not a heart a huge and capricious yearning which built and faded erratically, now so faint that he let himself diffuse almost to where the currents would whirl him eternities away, now so strong that he focused to a point on one human creature alone for a moment in the open night.

Temptation grew, faded, grew in him again. Would he? Again?... He would. Which?... Water; they were often by water, he had found. But which? This one, who played ... was it *music?* ... on the shore? He was seeking, he recalled now, a *communicator.* The world turned, carried the music-maker away. One who ... spoke?... and was received, respoken. A linker. One-one? Or why not one-many? Was it possible? Restlessly, he drew a few parsecs of himself into the system, spelled *D.O.D.* in colliding photons, and began more intently to search for something to become.

—tumor. *That's what scares me, Jack. Everything gets small. It's so real—Headaches? No, no headaches, why? No colored haloes on things, either. Personality change? I wouldn't know, would I? You be the judge, I don't think so. Except for the fear, Jack, I tell you, it's physical! The interaction starts, the rapport—that terrific feeling that we're really communicating—all those people, I'm with them. Agh, we don't have words for it. Do we? And then this other thing starts, this swelling—the bigness, I mean BIG, Jack. Big like bigger than houses, bigger than the sun maybe! Like the interaction feeds it, it's going to burst, it's going to kill everybody—*

All right, Jack. All right.

If you think so. I know it sounds crazy, that's why—Do you honestly? Do you think so? That's true, I don't have headaches. I've heard that too. Maybe I— Yes, I know I can't quit now. You're so right. But I have to take a day off, Jack. Cancel something. Cancel that Dartmouth thing, it's entropic anyway. Useless, I mean. We've got to take a day and hole up somewhere and rest. You're right, Jack. You fix it. Before we tackle Dallas.

THE HERO AS WERWOLF

Gene Wolfe

Gene Wolfe is perceived by many critics to be one of the best—perhaps the best—SF and fantasy writers working today. His most acclaimed work is the tetralogy The Book of the New Sun, *individual volumes of which have won the Nebula Award, the World Fantasy Award, and the John W. Campbell Memorial Award. His other books include the classic novels* Peace *and* The Devil in a Forest, *both recently re-released, as well as* Soldier in the Mist, Free Live Free, Soldier of Arete, There Are Doors, Castleview, Pandora by Holly Hollander, *and* The Urth of the New Sun. *His short fiction has been collected in* The Island of Doctor Death and Other Stories, Gene Wolfe's Book of Days, The Wolfe Archipelago, *the recent World Fantasy Award-winning collection* Storeys From the Old Hotel, *and* Endangered Species. *His most recent books are part of a popular new series, including* Nightside the Long Sun, The Lake of the Long Sun, Calde of the Long Sun, *and* Exodus from the Long Sun.

In the brilliant and evocative story that follows, the aliens hiding in the shadows are us, ordinary, everyday people, in a strange high-tech future where that is no longer good enough . . .

> *Feet in the jungle that leave no mark!*
> *Eyes that can see in the dark—the dark!*
> *Tongue—give tongue to it! Hark! O Hark!*
> *Once, twice and again!*
> —RUDYARD KIPLING
> *"Hunting Song of the Seeonee Pack"*

A*n owl shrieked,* and Paul flinched. Fear, pavement, flesh, death, stone, dark, loneliness and blood made up Paul's world; the blood was all much the same, but the fear took several forms, and he had hardly seen another human being in the four years since his mother's death. At a night meeting in the park he was the red-cheeked young man at the end of the last row, with his knees together and his scrupulously clean hands (Paul was particularly careful about his nails) in his lap.

The speaker was fluent and amusing; he was clearly conversant with his subject—whatever it was—and he pleased his audience. Paul, the listener and watcher, knew many of the words he used; yet he had understood nothing in the past hour and a half, and sat wrapped in his stolen cloak and his own thoughts, seeming to listen, watching the crowd and the park—this, at least, was no ghosthouse, no trap; the moon was up, nightblooming flowers scented the park air, and the trees lining the paths glowed with self-generated blue light; in the city, beyond the last hedge, the great buildings new and old were mountains lit from within.

Neither human nor master, a policeman strolled about the fringes of the audience, his eyes bright with stupidity. Paul could have killed him in less than a second, and was enjoying a dream of the policeman's death in some remote corner of his mind even while he concentrated on seeming to be one of *them.* A passenger rocket passed just under the stars, trailing luminous banners.

The meeting was over and he wondered if the rocket had in some way been the signal to end it. The masters did not use time, at least not as he did, as he had been taught by the thin woman who had been his mother in the little home she had made for them in the turret of a house that was once (she said) the Gorous'—now only a house too old to be destroyed. Neither did they use money, of which he like other old-style *Homo sapiens* still retained some racial memory, as of a forgotten god—a magic once potent that had lost all force.

The masters were rising, and there were tears and laughter and that third emotional tone that was neither amusement nor sorrow—the silken sound humans did not possess, but that Paul thought might express content, as the purring of a cat does, or community, like the cooing of doves. The policeman bobbed his hairy head, grinning, basking in the recognition, the approval, of those who had raised him from animality. *See* (said the motions of his hands, the writhings of his body) *the clothing you have given me. How nice! I take good care of my things because they are yours. See my weapon. I perform a useful function—if you did not have me, you would have to do it yourselves.*

If the policeman saw Paul, it would be over. He was too stupid, too silly, to be deceived by appearances as his masters were. He would never dare, thinking him a master, to meet Paul's eye, but he would look into his face seeking approval, and would see not what he was supposed to see but what was there. Paul ducked into the crowd, avoiding a beautiful woman with eyes the color of pearls, preferring to walk in the shadow of her fat escort where the policeman would not see him. The fat man took dust from a box shaped like the moon and rubbed it between his hands, releasing the smell of raspberries. It froze, and he sifted the tiny crystals of crimson ice over his shirt-front, grunting with satisfaction; then offered the box to the woman, who refused at first, only (three steps later) to accept when he pressed it on her.

They were past the policeman now. Paul dropped a few paces behind the couple, wondering if they were the ones tonight—if there would be meat tonight at all. For some, vehicles would be waiting. If the pair he had selected were among these, he would have to find others quickly.

They were not. They had entered the canyons between the buildings; he dropped farther behind, then turned aside.

Three minutes later he was in an alley a hundred meters ahead of them, waiting for them to pass the mouth. (The old trick was to cry like an infant, and he could do it well; but he had a new trick—a better trick, because too many had learned not to come down an alley when an infant cried. The new trick was a silver bell he had found in the house, small and very old. He took it from his pocket and removed the rag he had packed around the clapper. His dark cloak concealed him now, its hood pulled up to hide the pale gleam of his skin. He stood in a narrow doorway only a few meters away from the alley's mouth.)

They came. He heard the man's thick laughter, the woman's silken sound. She was a trifle silly from the dust the man had given her, and would be holding his arm as they walked, rubbing his thigh with hers. The man's black-shod foot and big belly thrust past the stonework of the building—there was a muffled moan.

The fat man turned, looking down the alley. Paul could see fear growing in the woman's face, cutting, too slowly, through the odor of raspberries. Another moan, and the man strode forward, fumbling in his pocket for an illuminator. The woman followed hesitantly (her skirt was of flowering vines the color of love, and white skin flashed in the interstices; a serpent of gold supported her breasts).

Someone was behind him. Pressed back against the metal door, he watched the couple as they passed. The fat man had gotten his illuminator out and held it over his head as he walked, looking into corners and doorways.

They came at them from both sides, a girl and an old, gray-bearded man. The fat man, the master, his genetic heritage revised for intellection and peace, had hardly time to turn before his mouth gushed blood. The woman whirled and ran, the vines of her skirt withering at her thought to give her leg-room, the serpent dropping from her breasts to strike with fangless jaws at the flying-haired girl who pursued her, then winding itself about the girl's ankles. The girl fell; but as the pearl-eyed woman passed, Paul broke her neck. For a moment he was too startled at the sight of other human beings to speak. Then he said, "These are mine."

The old man, still bent over the fat man's body, snapped: "Ours. We've been here an hour and more." His voice was the creaking of steel hinges, and Paul thought of ghost-houses again.

"I followed them from the park." The girl, black-haired, gray-eyed when the light from the alley-mouth struck her face, was taking the serpent from around her legs—it was once more a lifeless thing of soft metal mesh. Paul picked up the woman's corpse and wrapped it in his cloak. "You gave me no warning," he said. "You must have seen me when I passed you."

The girl looked toward the old man. Her eyes said she would back him if he fought, and Paul decided he would throw the woman's body at her.

"Somebody'll come soon," the old man said. "And I'll need Janie's help to carry this one. We each take what we got ourselves—that's fair. Or we whip you. My girl's worth a man in a fight, and you'll find I'm still worth a man myself, old as I be."

"Give me the picking of his body. This one has nothing."

The girl's bright lips drew back from strong white teeth. From somewhere under the tattered shirt she wore, she had produced a long knife, and sudden light from a window high above the alley ran along the edge of the stained blade; the girl might be a dangerous opponent, as the old man claimed, but Paul could sense the femaleness, the woman-rut from where he stood. "No," her father said. "You got good clothes. I need these." He looked up at the window fearfully, fumbling with buttons.

"His cloak will hang on you like a blanket."

"We'll fight. Take the woman and go away, or we'll fight."

He could not carry both, and the fat man's meat would be tainted by the testicles. When Paul was young and there had been no one but his mother to do the killing, they had sometimes eaten old males; he never did so now. He slung the pearl-eyed woman across his shoulders and trotted away.

Outside the alley the streets were well lit, and a few passers-by stared at him and the dark burden he carried. Fewer still, he knew, would suspect him of being what he was—he had learned the trick of dressing as the masters did, even of wearing their expressions. He wondered how the black-haired girl and the old man would fare in their ragged clothes. *They must live very near.*

His own place was that in which his mother had borne him, a place high in a house built when humans were the masters. Every door was nailed tight and boarded up; but on one side a small garden lay between two wings, and in a corner of this garden, behind a bush where the shadows were thick even at noon, the bricks had fallen away. The lower floors were full of rotting furniture and the smell of rats and mold, but high in his wooden turret the walls were still dry and the sun came in by day at eight windows. He carried his burden there and dropped her in a corner. It was important that his clothes be kept as clean as the masters kept theirs, though he lacked their facilities. He pulled his cloak from the body and brushed it vigorously.

"What are you going to do with me?" the dead woman said behind him.

"Eat," he told her. "What did you think I was going to do?"

"I didn't know." And then: "I've read of you creatures, but I didn't think you really existed."

"We were the masters once," he said. He was not sure he still believed it, but it was what his mother had taught him. "This house was built in those days—that's why you won't wreck it: you're afraid." He had finished with the cloak; he hung it up and turned to face her, sitting on the bed. "You're afraid of waking the old times," he said. She lay slumped in the corner, and though her mouth moved, her eyes were only half open, looking at nothing.

"We tore a lot of them down," she said.

"If you're going to talk, you might as well sit up straight." He lifted her by the shoulders and propped her in the corner. A nail protruded from the wall there; he twisted a lock of her hair on it so her head would not loll; her hair was the rose shade of a little girl's dress, and soft but slightly sticky.

"I'm dead, you know."

"No, you're not." They always said this (except, sometimes, for the children) and his mother had always denied
it. He felt that he was keeping up a family tradition.

"Dead," the pearl-eyed woman said. "Never, never,
never. Another year, and everything would have been all
right. I want to cry, but I can't breathe to."

"Your kind lives a long time with a broken neck," he
told her. "But you'll die eventually."

"I am dead now."

He was not listening. There were other humans in the
city; he had always known that, but only now, with the
sight of the old man and the girl, had their existence seemed
real to him.

"I thought you were all gone," the pearl-eyed dead
woman said thinly. "All gone long ago, like a bad dream."

Happy with his new discovery, he said: "Why do you
set traps for us, then? Maybe there are more of us than
you think."

"There can't be many of you. How many people do you
kill in a year?" Her mind was lifting the sheet from his
bed, hoping to smother him with it; but he had seen that
trick many times.

"Twenty or thirty." (He was boasting.)

"So many."

"When you don't get much besides meat, you need a
lot of it. And then I only eat the best parts—why not? I
kill twice a month or more except when it's cold, and I
could kill enough for two or three if I had to." (*The girl
had had a knife.* Knives were bad, except for cutting up
afterward. But knives left blood behind. He would kill for
her—she could stay here and take care of his clothes, pre-
pare their food. He thought of himself walking home under
a new moon, and seeing her face in the window of the turret.) To the dead woman he said: "You saw that girl? With
the black hair? She and the old man killed your husband,
and I'm going to bring her here to live." He stood and
began to walk up and down the small room, soothing himself with the sound of his own footsteps.

"He wasn't my husband." The sheet dropped limply now

that he was no longer on the bed. "Why didn't you change? When the rest changed their genes?"

"I wasn't alive then."

"You must have received some tradition."

"We didn't want to. We are the human beings."

"Everyone wanted to. Your old breed had worn out the planet; even with much better technology we're still starved for energy and raw materials because of what you did."

"There hadn't been enough to eat before," he said, "but when so many changed there was a lot. So why should more change?"

It was a long time before she answered, and he knew the body was stiffening. That was bad, because as long as she lived in it the flesh would stay sweet; when the life was gone, he would have to cut it up quickly before the stuff in her lower intestine tainted the rest.

"Strange evolution," she said at last. "Man become food for men."

"I don't understand the second word. Talk so I know what you're saying." He kicked her in the chest to emphasize his point, and knocked her over; he heard a rib snap. . . . She did not reply, and he lay down on the bed. His mother had told him there was a meeting place in the city where men gathered on certain special nights—but he had forgotten (if he had ever known) what those nights were.

"That isn't even metalanguage," the dead woman said, "only children's talk."

"Shut up."

After a moment he said: "I'm going out. If you can make your body stand, and get out of here, and get down to the ground floor, and find the way out, then you may be able to tell someone about me and have the police waiting when I come back." He went out and closed the door, then stood patiently outside for five minutes.

When he opened it again, the corpse stood erect with her hands on his table, her tremors upsetting the painted metal circus-figures he had had since he was a child—the girl acrobat, the clown with his hoop and trained pig. One of her legs would not straighten. "Listen," he said, "you're not going to do it. I told you all that because I knew you'd think of it yourself. They always do, and they never make it. The farthest I've ever had anyone get was out the door and to the top of the steps. She fell down them, and I found her at the bottom when I came back. You're dead. Go to sleep."

The blind eyes had turned toward him when he began to speak, but they no longer watched him now. The face, which had been beautiful, was now entirely the face of a corpse. The cramped leg crept toward the floor as he watched, halted, began to creep downward again. Sighing, he lifted the dead woman off her feet, replaced her in the corner, and went down the creaking stairs to find the black-haired girl.

"There has been quite a few to come after her," her father said, "since we come into town. Quite a few." He sat in the back of the bus, on the rearmost seat that went completely across the back like a sofa. "But you're the first ever to find us here. The others, they hear about her, and leave a sign at the meetin'."

Paul wanted to ask where it was such signs were left, but held his peace.

"You know there ain't many folks at *all* anymore," her father went on. "And not many of *them* is women. And *damn few* is young girls like my Janie. I had a fella here that wanted her two weeks back—he said he hadn't had no real woman in two years; well, I didn't like the way he said *real,* so I said what did he do, and he said he fooled around with what he killed, sometimes, before they got cold. You never did like that, did you?"

Paul said he had not.

"How'd you find this dump here?"

"Just looked around." He had searched the area in ever-widening circles, starting at the alley in which he had seen the girl and her father. They had one of the masters' cold boxes to keep their ripe kills in (as he did himself), but there was the stink of clotted blood about the dump nonetheless. It was behind a high fence, closer to the park than he would have thought possible.

"When we come, there was a fella living here. Nice fella, a German. Name was Curtain—something like that. He went sweet on my Janie right off. Well, I wasn't too taken with having a foreigner in the family, but he took us in and let us settle in the big station wagon. Told me he wanted to wed Janie, but I said no, she's too young. Wait a year, I says, and take her with my blessing. She wasn't but fourteen then. Well, one night the German fella went out and I guess they got him, because he never come back. We moved into this here bus then for the extra room."

His daughter was sitting at his feet, and he reached a crooked-fingered hand down and buried it in her midnight hair. She looked up at him and smiled. "Got a pretty face, ain't she?" he said.

Paul nodded.

"She's a mite thin, you was going to say. Well, that's true. I do my best to provide, but I'm feared, and not shamed to admit to it."

"The ghost-houses," Paul said.

"What's that?"

"That's what I've always called them. I don't get to talk to many other people."

"Where the doors shut on you—lock you in."

"Yes."

"That ain't ghosts—now don't you think I'm one of them fools don't believe in them. I know better. But that ain't ghosts. They're always looking, don't you see, for people they think ain't right. That's us. It's electricity does it. You ever been caught like that?"

Paul nodded. He was watching the delicate swelling Janie's breasts made in the fabric of her filthy shirt, and only half listening to her father; but the memory penetrated the young desire that half embarrassed him, bringing back fear. The windows of the bus had been set to black, and the light inside was dim—still it was possible some glimmer showed outside. *There should be no lights in the dump.* He listened, but heard only katydids singing in the rubbish.

"They thought I was a master—I dress like one," he said. "That's something you should do. They were going to test me. I turned the machine over and broke it, and jumped through a window." He had been on the sixth floor, and had been saved by landing in the branches of a tree whose bruised twigs and torn leaves exuded an acrid incense that to him was the very breath of panic still; but it had not been the masters, or the instrument-filled examination room, or the jump from the window that had terrified him, but waiting in the ghost-room while the walls talked to one another in words he could sometimes, for a few seconds, nearly understand.

"It wouldn't work for me—got too many things wrong with me. Lines in my face; even got a wart—they never do."

"Janie could."

The old man cleared his throat; it was a thick sound, like water in a downspout in a hard rain. "I been meaning to talk to you about her; about why those other fellas I told you about never took her—not that I'd of let some of them: Janie's the only family I got left. But I ain't so particular I don't want to see her married at all—not a bit of it. Why, we wouldn't of come here if it weren't for Janie. When her monthly come, I said to myself, she'll be wantin' a man, and what're you goin' to do way out here? Though the country was gettin' bad anyway, I must say. If they'd of had real dogs, I believe they would have got us several times."

He paused, perhaps thinking of those times, the lights in the woods at night and the running, perhaps only trying to order his thoughts. Paul waited, scratching an ankle, and after a few seconds the old man said: "We didn't want to do this, you know, us Pendeltons. That's mine and Janie's name—Pendelton. Janie's Augusta Jane, and I'm Emmitt J."

"Paul Gorou," Paul said.

"Pleased to meet you, Mr. Gorou. When the time come, they took one whole side of the family. They was the Worthmore Pendeltons; that's what we always called them, because most of them lived thereabouts. Cousins of mine they was, and second cousins. We was the Evershaw Pendeltons, and they didn't take none of us. Bad blood, they said—too much wrong to be worth fixing, or too much that mightn't get fixed right, and then show up again. My ma— she's alive then—she always swore it was her sister Lillian's boy that did it to us. The whole side of his head was pushed in. You know what I mean? They used to say a cow'd kicked him when he was small, but it wasn't so— he's just born like that. He could talk some—there's those that set a high value on that—but the slobber'd run out of his mouth. My ma said if it wasn't for him we'd have got in sure. The only other thing was my sister Clara that was born with a bad eye—blind, you know, and something wrong with the lid of it, too. But she was just as sensible as anybody. Smart as a whip. So I would say it's likely Ma was right. Same thing with your family, I suppose?"

"I think so. I don't really know."

"A lot of it was die-beetees. They could fix it, but if there was other things too they just kept them out. Of course when it was over there wasn't no medicine for them no more, and they died off pretty quick. When I was young, I used to think that was what it meant: diebeetees—you died away. It's really sweetening of the blood. You heard of it?"

Paul nodded.

"I'd like to taste some sometime, but I never come to think of that while there was still some of them around."

"If they weren't masters—"

"Didn't mean I'd of killed them," the old man said quickly. "Just got one to gash his arm a trifle so I could taste of it. Back then—that would be twenty aught nine, close to fifty years gone it is now—there was several I knowed that was just my age. . . . What I was meaning to say at the beginning was that us Pendeltons never figured on anythin' like this. We'd farmed, and we meant to keep on, grow our own truck and breed our own stock. Well, that did for a time, but it wouldn't keep."

Paul, who had never considered living off the land, or

even realized that it was possible to do so, could only stare
at him.

"You take chickens, now. Everybody always said there
wasn't nothing easier than chickens, but that was when
there was medicine you could put in the water to keep off
the sickness. Well, the time come when you couldn't get
it no more than you could get a can of beans in those stores
of theirs that don't use money or cards or anything a man
can understand. My dad had two hundred in the flock when
the sickness struck, and it took every hen inside of four
days. You wasn't supposed to eat them that had died sick,
but we did it. Plucked 'em and canned 'em—by that time
our old locker that plugged in the wall wouldn't work.
When the chickens was all canned, Dad saddled a horse
we had then and rode twenty-five miles to a place where
the new folks grew chickens to eat themselves. I guess you
know what happened to him, though—they wouldn't sell,
and they wouldn't trade. Finally he begged them. He was
a Pendelton, and used to cry when he told of it. He said
the harder he begged them the scareder they got. Well, finally he reached out and grabbed one by the leg—he was
on his knees to them—and he hit him alongside the face
with a book he was carryin'.""

The old man rocked backward and forward in his seat
as he spoke, his eyes half closed. "There wasn't no more
seed but what was saved from last year then, and the corn
went so bad the ears wasn't no longer than a soft dick. No
bullets for Dad's old gun, nowhere to buy new traps when
what we had was lost. Then one day just afore Christmas
these here machines just started tearing up our fields. They
had forgot about us, you see. We threw rocks but it didn't
do no good, and about midnight one come right through
the house. There wasn't no one living then but Ma and
Dad and brother Tom and me and Janie. Janie wasn't but
just a little bit of a thing. The machine got Tom in the leg
with a piece of two-by-four—rammed the splintery end
into him, you see. The rot got to the wound and he died
a week after; it was winter then, and we was living in a

place me and Dad built up on the hill out of branches and saplings."

"About Janie," Paul said. "I can understand how you might not want to let her go—"

"Are you sayin' you don't want her?" The old man shifted in his seat, and Paul saw that his right hand had moved close to the crevice where the horizontal surface joined the vertical. The crevice was a trifle too wide, and he thought he knew what was hidden there. He was not afraid of the old man, and it had crossed his mind more than once that if he killed him there would be nothing to prevent his taking Janie.

"I want her," he said. "I'm not going away without her." He stood up without knowing why.

"There's been others said the same thing. I would go, you know, to the meetin' in the regular way; come back next month, and the fella'd be waitin'."

The old man was drawing himself to his feet, his jaw outthrust belligerently. "They'd see her," he said, "and they'd talk a lot, just like you, about how good they'd take care of her, though there wasn't a one brought a lick to eat when he come to call. Me and Janie, sometimes we ain't et for three, four days—they never take account of that. Now here, you look at her."

Bending swiftly, he took his daughter by the arm; she rose gracefully, and he spun her around. "Her ma was a pretty woman," he said, "but not as pretty as what she is, even if she is so thin. And she's got sense too—I don't keer what they say."

Janie looked at Paul with frightened, animal eyes. He gestured, he hoped gently, for her to come to him, but she only pressed herself against her father.

"You can talk to her. She understands."

Paul started to speak, then had to stop to clear his throat. At last he said: "Come here, Janie. You're going to live with me. We'll come back and see your father sometimes."

Her hand slipped into her shirt; came out holding a knife. She looked at the old man, who caught her wrist and took the knife from her and dropped it on the seat behind him,

saying, "You're going to have to be a mite careful around
her for a bit, but if you don't hurt her none she'll take to
you pretty quick. She wants to take to you now—I can see
it in the way she looks."

Paul nodded, accepting the girl from him almost as he
might have accepted a package, holding her by her narrow
waist.

"And when you get a mess of grub she likes to cut them
up, sometimes, while they're still movin' around. Mostly I
don't allow it, but if you do—anyway, once in a while—
she'll like you better for it."

Paul nodded again. His hand, as if of its own volition,
had strayed to the girl's smoothly rounded hip, and he felt
such desire as he had never known before.

"Wait," the old man said. His breath was foul in the
close air. "You listen to me now. You're just a young fella
and I know how you feel, but you don't know how I do.
I want you to understand before you go. I love my girl.
You take good care of her or I'll see to you. And if you
change your mind about wanting her, don't you just turn
her out. I'll take her back, you hear?"

Paul said, "All right."

"Even a bad man can love his child. You remember that,
because it's true."

Her husband took Janie by the hand and led her out of
the wrecked bus. She was looking over her shoulder, and
he knew that she expected her father to drive a knife into
his back.

They had seen the boy—a brown-haired, slightly freckled boy of nine or ten with an armload of books—on a
corner where a small, columniated building concealed the
entrance to the monorail, and the streets were wide and
empty. The children of the masters were seldom out so
late. Paul waved to him, not daring to speak, but attempting to convey by his posture that he wanted to ask directions; he wore the black cloak and scarlet-slashed shirt, the
gold sandals and wide-legged black film trousers proper to
an evening of pleasure. On his arm Janie was all in red,
her face covered by a veil dotted with tiny synthetic blood-

stones. Gem-studded veils were a fashion now nearly ex-
tinct among the women of the masters, but one that served
to conceal the blankness of eye that betrayed Janie, as Paul
had discovered, almost instantly. She gave a soft moan of
hunger as she saw the boy, and clasped Paul's arm more
tightly. Paul waved again.

The boy halted as though waiting for them, but when
they were within five meters he turned and dashed away.
Janie was after him before Paul could stop her. The boy
dodged between two buildings and raced through to the
next street; Paul was just in time to see Janie follow him
into a doorway in the center of the block.

He found her clear-soled platform shoes in the vestibule,
under a four-dimensional picture of Hugo de Vries. De
Vries was in the closing years of his life, and in the few
seconds it took Paul to pick up the shoes and conceal them
behind an aquarium of phosphorescent cephalopods, had
died, rotted to dust, and undergone rebirth as a fissioning
cell in his mother's womb with all the labyrinth of genetics still before him.

The lower floors, Paul knew, were apartments. He had
entered them sometimes when he could find no prey on
the streets. There would be a school at the top.

A confused, frightened-looking woman stood in an otherwise empty corridor, a disheveled library book lying open
at her feet. As Paul pushed past her, he could imagine Janie
knocking her out of the way, and the woman's horror at
the savage, exultant face glimpsed beneath her veil.

There were elevators, a liftshaft, and a downshaft, all
clustered in an alcove. *The boy would not have waited for
an elevator with Janie close behind him. . . .*

The liftshaft floated Paul as spring water floats a cork.
Thickened by conditioning agents, the air remained a gas;
enriched with added oxygen; it stimulated his whole being,
though it was as viscous as corn syrup when he drew it
into his lungs. Far above, suspended (as it seemed) in crystal and surrounded by the books the boy had thrown down
at her, he saw Janie with her red gown billowing around
her and her white legs flashing. She was going to the top,

apparently to the uppermost floor, and he reasoned that the boy, having led her there, would jump into the downshaft to escape her. He got off at the eighty-fifth floor, opened the hatch to the downshaft, and was rewarded by seeing the boy only a hundred meters above him. It was a simple matter then to wait on the landing and pluck him out of the sighing column of thickened air.

The boy's pointed, narrow face, white with fear under a tan, turned up toward him. "Don't," the boy said. "Please sir, good master—" but, Paul clamped him under his left arm, and with a quick wrench of his right broke his neck.

Janie was swimming head down with the downshaft current, her mouth open and full of eagerness, and her black hair like a cloud about her head. She had lost her veil. Paul showed her the boy and stepped into the shaft with her. The hatch slammed behind him, and the motion of the air ceased.

He looked at Janie. She had stopped swimming and was staring hungrily into the dead boy's face. He said, "Something's wrong," and she seemed to understand, though it was possible that she only caught the fear in his voice. The hatch would not open, and slowly the current in the shaft was reversing, lifting them; he tried to swim against it but the effort was hopeless. When they were at the top, the dead boy began to talk; Janie put her hand over his mouth to muffle the sound. The hatch at the landing opened, and they stepped out onto the hundred-and-first floor. A voice from a loudspeaker in the wall said: "*I am sorry to detain you, but there is reason to think you have undergone a recent deviation from the optimal development pattern. In a few minutes I will arrive in person to provide counseling; while you are waiting it may be useful for us to review what is meant by 'optimal development.' Look at the projection.*

"*In infancy the child first feels affection for its mother, the provider of warmth and food. . . .*" There was a door at the other end of the room, and Paul swung a heavy chair against it, making a din that almost drowned out the droning speaker.

"Later one's peer group becomes, for a time, all-important—or nearly so. The boys and girls you see are attending a model school in Armstrong. Notice that no tint is used to mask the black of space above their air-tent."

The lock burst from the doorframe, but a remotely actuated hydraulic cylinder snapped it shut each time a blow from the chair drove it open. Paul slammed his shoulder against it, and before it could close again put his knee where the shattered bolt-socket had been. A chrome-plated steel rod as thick as a finger had dropped from the chair when his blows had smashed the wood and plastic holding it; after a moment of incomprehension, Janie dropped the dead boy, wedged the rod between the door and the jamb, and slipped through. He was following her when the rod lifted, and the door swung shut on his foot.

He screamed and screamed again, and then, in the echoing silence that followed, heard the loudspeaker mumbling about education, and Janie's sobbing, indrawn breath. Through the crack between the door and the frame, the two-centimeter space held in existence by what remained of his right foot, he could see the livid face and blind, malevolent eyes of the dead boy, whose will still held the steel rod suspended in air. "Die," Paul shouted at him. "Die! You're dead!" The rod came crashing down.

"This young woman," the loudspeaker said, *"has chosen the profession of medicine. She will be a physician, and she says now that she was born for that. She will spend the remainder of her life in relieving the agonies of disease."*

Several minutes passed before he could make Janie understand what it was she had to do.

"After her five years' training in basic medical techniques, she will specialize in surgery for another three years before—"

It took Janie a long time to bite through his Achilles tendon; when it was over, she began to tear at the ligaments that held the bones of the tarsus to the leg. Over the pain he could feel the hot tears washing the blood from his foot.

MOTHERHOOD, ETC.

L. Timmel Duchamp

Here's a sly and fascinating story that suggests an ingenious new reason why you shouldn't hang around with an alien in hiding if you should happen to meet one: something might rub off...

New writer L. Timmel Duchamp has become a frequent contributor to Asimov's Science Fiction *and* The Magazine of Fantasy and Science Fiction, *and has also made sales to* Full Spectrum, Pulphouse, Starshore, Memories and Visions, The Woman Who Walked Through Fire, *and elsewhere. She lives in Seattle, Washington.*

The room has a long, glass-topped conference table, the room's windows look out on the ocean, but the chair to which they direct her puts her back to the view. The man wearing a black-and-white polka-dotted tie identifies himself as Wagner. He introduces the bald man facing her across the table as Dr. Johns. Wagner asks most of the questions. The other man stares moodily over her shoulder, at the ocean.

"He called himself Joshua," she answers the first question. And: "I liked him because he was different," she answers the second.

The man across from her jerks his eyes off the ocean to stare at her. She blushes. Already she has made a mistake.

"Different, I mean, from all the other guys I'd ever gone out with," she amends. "He liked to talk about real things. And he listened, too. A lot. He had a cute laugh." She looks down at her hands, folded tightly and whitely together. "And the most wonderful brown eyes."

She gets stuck there, does not want to go on. Her eyes skim the walls, looking for the video camera. They are clever about these things, but she thinks she has found it, embedded in a metal sculpture. The bead of red light gives it away.

An "interview," is how they'd billed this ordeal. No one used the word *interrogation*. And no, they said, she was not under arrest. Though she cannot of course go home. If she were reasonable, she would understand why.

They kept telling her to be reasonable. To consider "the implications." They said that the interview . . . would help. Would help them, the "authorities." Who would know best what to do, much better than she. Who was only an inexperienced, nineteen-year-old . . . female. Who was in no position to judge the danger, to understand the stakes. She must trust them.

Right.

Wagner prompts her. He has moved to her side of the table. He perches on it, uncomfortably close to her. One of his feet rests on the chair to her right. The cuff of his somber black pant leg is rucked up. The black sock underneath looks as though it could be silk. Probably, she guesses, it goes all the way up to his knee. Certainly it covers his calf. She's sure that the skin of his leg is dead white. And crawling with coarse red hair. The hair on the backs of his hands and knuckles, certainly, is coarse red. And plentiful. Probably it covers his body.

"We saw one another just about every other night for a month before I first stayed over with him," she replies to the next question. She swallows, and looks away from Wagner's looming bulk, and wishes she could get away from him. He wants all the details, "Everything," he says. Like the prurient evangelist con artist who corners the timid into confessing all sin, all filth, all wickedness in their hearts. So she elaborates, "Yes, we slept together when I stayed over. In pajamas. Both of us. And wearing underpants."

God, Ulrike, he's so weird. I mean, he said I couldn't sleep with him unless I'd keep my underpants on and wear at least the bottoms of the pajamas. He says he doesn't

*want to spoil our emotional relationship, which is what he
says will happen if we rush ahead with the sexual side of
things. He says he knows from past experience. And that I
have to trust him.*

Telling it to Ulrike had (at the beginning, at least) made
it seem all quite wonderful, an exemplar for what "normal" *should* be. But it hadn't *felt* "normal." It would be
middle-of-the-night dark when Joshua's lips and fingers
woke her. She'd hear his breathing, and her own, and other
noises she knew involved her (or his?) genitals—*sexual*
noises she couldn't identify. And little sounds coming from
her own throat, that she couldn't mute, because of the explosive sensations rippling in wild, lingering streams of
movement through her body. All the while a small observing part of her tried to visualize—as though to watch—
what was happening, tried to fit it all into the fictional and
theoretical ragbag that constituted her "knowledge" of Sex.
His hands are now *there,* doing *this,* the detached observer
would note. His right thigh is *there.* And his genitals are . . .

But little of it fit. And his genitals . . .

"Are you saying," the bald man grates, impatiently tapping the closed manila folder on the table before him, "that
you ever saw his genitals? Even once? That you never felt
them with your hands? And that you didn't think it ab-
normal that after five months' sleeping together you still
had not had intercourse with him?"

He sounds incredulous.

There is no way she's going to tell these men that only
now and then had she managed to cop a feel, a vague fleet-
ing touch to his genitals before Joshua had maneuvered
them out of her reach. Joshua had claimed that her touching him there would turn him on too much. Timidly, she
had suggested that since he used his fingers (et cetera) to
bring her to orgasm, that she should do the same for him.
How can she explain? In the night, she did think it weird.
But she couldn't know for sure, because she'd never slept
with a man before. And besides, Joshua always made her
feel, well, *weird* for wanting more. Isn't it enough? he'd

ask her. How can you miss what you've never known? Don't you enjoy what we do?

Sometimes they spent half the night coming. She recalls that one night he got up three times to change his underpants. (It is unreal remembering, with Wagner looming over her and Dr. Johns looking cold and dissatisfied and writing in a small thin script on the yellow pad to one side of the manila folder. They keep saying they want her to tell them everything. Imagine having them write *that* down. *Three pairs of underpants.* They'd probably ask her what his come smelled like. And whether it left stains.)

He had made her feel that wanting to touch his genitals was . . . immodest. Or at the least premature. Which was totally weird, considering all their discussions about Freedom and Being and the need to find Meaning in the face of an utterly random Universe. . . .

These men, she thinks, would feel comfortable with the archaic terminology she and Ulrike had used to discuss it. "Virginity," "hymen," and an "unnaturally prolonged state of innocence." And "clitoral versus vaginal orgasm . . ." They giggled when they used such language. But it was the only way she had known how to talk about it to Ulrike.

Now Wagner presses Dr. John's incredulity. She knows he must have figured out he's found one of her most vulnerable spots.

"Look," she says, "I'm nineteen. I'd never been with a man before. Sure, maybe I thought something might be a little strange. But hey, when you're new at it, *all* sex is weird."

Wagner lays his freckled hairy paw on her neatly (but tensely) folded hands. The touch of it, even the *sight* of it, makes her want to throw up. Talking about sex in general and about her and Joshua in particular with these creeps is obscene. "You're making me feel like an old goat, young lady," he says with one of those man-style chuckles (utterly unlike Joshua's frank crackups).

"But intercourse, you must have known that vaginal intercourse is the normal point of sexual relations," Dr. Johns lectures her. He raps his knuckles on the manila folder. "It says on your transcript that you've had three psychology courses. You can't expect us to believe you didn't know something was wrong!"

She is blushing again. And not only can she not stand a second longer of Wagner's touch, but her hands have started trembling. Chagrined, she snatches them away and buries them in her lap. Then she scoots her chair back from the table and glares up at him, though he's definitely too close for comfortable eye contact. (But what distance would be comfortable? A thousand yards?)

"What are you accusing me of?" she demands. "I've never heard that people have a legal obligation to report men who don't take every available opportunity to fuck a willing woman! I have a right to know what you think I've done wrong," she adds, though without faith that they're going to be willing to grant her any "rights" whatsoever, however de rigueur they were supposed to be.

"Now, Patty," Wagner remonstrates. "You know we're not accusing you of anything. We're talking public health, public safety here. We're talking *viruses.* Patty, *communicable* viruses. We're talking a virus that this guy whose name you won't tell us passed to you." He leans forward, so that his thickly freckled face is right up in hers. "Now I thought your doctor explained all that to you. Am I right?"

Patty. On top of everything else, their calling her that just about made her want to scream. But no way was she going to tell *them.* They'd probably just go on calling her that to bug her. And besides, as she'd long ago figured out, if adults you didn't know called you something you didn't ordinarily answer to, a name that was basically alien to you, it meant you were just that much more private from them, and that every time they used the hated name it reminded you of what jerks they were to call you something without first finding out what it is you wanted to be called.

Now the bald man in the navy silk suit opens the manila folder he's been persistently fingering. *Dr. Johns,* she sneers to herself. *Wagner.* Prurient jerks extraordinaire. Much, much worse than the doctor at the hospital. Whether they are as bad as the federal official who'd coerced her into submitting to the exam and photography remains to be seen. The vibes she is getting off Wagner, though, make her feel, in her gut, that they might be worse.

"I told you," she insists. "He said to call him Joshua. If he mentioned his last name to me, I don't remember."

Wagner shakes his head and sighs. "I can't believe a bright young lady like you could be so careless. You know you can't tell these days what you might be getting into, don't you? There's some pretty nasty STDs out there, raging out of control. Besides AIDS. You do know that, Patty, don't you?"

The doctor, now standing, leans over the table and arranges half a dozen or so photos—all 8½ by 11 inches—down the center of the table. Pat stares at the little tuft of gray, like feathers, gracing the top of his shiny pink dome. He sits down and glares at her. "You've got a problem with denial," he announces. "But you can't deny *these*." He takes a stapled sheaf of pages from the folder and waves them at her. "Your DNA has mutated. Your blood doesn't match any known type, even though your medical records say you are type O. And your sex chromosomes now have three Xs and one Y. Which is to say, strictly speaking you're not a woman." He points at the photo nearest her. "And take a look at the eruptions of tissue, there." His words are coming through his teeth, as though he's almost too furious to talk.

Face aflame, she jumps out of her chair and grabs wildly at the photos. "How *dare* you," she seethes as she gets a look at her own pubic hair in larger-than-lifesize glossy black and white. "How dare you *slimeballs* turn my body into sleaze!" She wants to rip the photos to shreds and burn them. *Her* genitals, on public display. For creeps like these!

The doctor goes for the photos, to protect them, and Wagner for her—to slam her back into her chair and keep her pinned there by the shoulders. "Now Patty, I want you to calm yourself," he says.

"Take your filthy hands off me!" she spits, struggling to twist out of his hold.

"You're not going to get hysterical on us, are you?" he says.

The cold spot of fear inside her—that first appeared yesterday—spreads. When she refused to let them examine her, the federal guy also warned her against "getting hysterical," saying that if she did they'd have to give her something to calm her down. Totally cowed, she went along with everything, the crowd of masked witnesses, the cameras, *everything*.

"These photographs are the property of the federal government, young lady," the doctor scolds. "Perhaps you weren't aware of it, but intentional destruction of government property is a very, very serious offense. One you could go to prison for."

She folds her arms across her chest. "Government property," she sneers. "Of sleaze. I can just imagine."

"Important scientific evidence," the doctor snaps.

"Sleaze," she repeats. "Made and distributed without my permission, and definitely against my will."

The doctor looks over her head at Wagner. "People used to say that about Sigmund Freud, you know. But then there have always been people with minds too small and narrow to accept Science."

"And maybe Freud really was just a dirty old man," Pat mutters. She glares at the doctor, who looks as though he'd like to slap her—and ignores (as best she can) the increase of pressure on her shoulders. "Consider, after all, whose side he took in rape and incest cases."

The doctor's eyes lift, presumably to exchange knowing looks with Wagner. "This is intolerable," he says. "We have about two dozen important questions it is essential she answer. And she hasn't answered even one of them yet."

The room is suddenly so quiet that Pat can hear the surf of the ocean through the double panes of glass behind her. The doctor's eyes are still focused over her head, so she guesses the men are involved in some sort of silent communication.

"It's really, you know, that Patty here doesn't yet understand just how serious this situation is," Wagner finally says. His hands lift from her shoulders. For a few seconds she hears him moving around behind her. "And, you know, girls her age are sometimes painfully embarrassed about anything to do with sex." His manly chuckle rumbles briefly. "Especially with men our age." His face is suddenly right next to Pat's. "Am I right, Patty?"

Embarrassed, right. You stupid boob.

But fear is gaining on anger. She feels too exhausted to shove his face away, or scratch it, or do any of the other things popping into her head every second he's bent over her. "Yeah," she says, "that must be it." She coughs delicately and scoots her chair to the right. "No offense, but I think I must be allergic to your cologne." And she puts her hand to her mouth and hacks loudly, to disguise the giggles suddenly shaking her.

Wagner's breathing gets considerably heavier, but he moves out of her face. She wonders how he's going to get back at her. (There's no doubt in her mind that he will: he's just that kind of guy.) A scenario involving drugs starts playing through her mind. Is there, she wonders, really something called *truth serum*? Can they shoot her up with a drug that will make her babble indiscriminately?

She just can't stand the idea of reviewing her sexual relations with Joshua for creeps like these. And she doesn't believe they have valid reasons for prying inside her head. What she does with another person is none of their business. It's her body. Which is sacred ground. Off limits. And no one's concern but her own.

The walls and windows resonate with a fast rapping on the door.

"The CDC has arrived," Wagner mutters, presumably to Dr. Johns.

The door swings open and a blond giant fills the threshold. The thought flicks through Pat's head that the blond has been imbibing a Wonderland cocktail labeled DRINK ME. "Elliott Hardwick, CDC," he booms. "Apologies. My plane was late."

Though blonds are not Pat's type, she has to admit the

man is a knockout. "A pretty boy," Ulrike would call him. He exudes energy and good health. You can see it rippling beneath his soft loose Pima cotton shirt, shining out of his purest of thick-lashed blue eyes, bursting out from his smile. She watches him shake hands, first with Baldie, then— leaning across the table—Wagner. She loves his salmon pink suspenders, she thinks they're perfect for the black jeans and pearl gray shirt. She only wishes he wore at least one gold ring in his ears.

"And *this*," the knockout says, crinkling his eyes in a major heat storm of a smile, "must be Patricia Morrow." He thrusts his hand at her. "How do you do. I'm Elliott Hardwick. Everyone calls me Sam, I hope you will, too."

He's overwhelming her. On purpose, she thinks. But she gives him her hand to shake.

"And what do you go by?" he wonders. "Patricia, Pat, Patty, or something entirely different?"

The blue eyes are like something out of a book, of the trashy romance sort. *Amused, knowing, powerful* . . . Also, he's still holding her hand after shaking it. She blushes, and clears her throat. "Pat," she says. "I go by the name Pat."

He nods, squeezes her hand and lets it go. It's almost a relief when he takes his eyes off her to swing his attache case onto the table and open it.

Wagner walks to the end of the table, rounds it and walks back up the other side to the center. "If I could have a word with you outside, Sam," he says, jerking his head towards the door.

Elliott "Sam" Hardwick flashes his smile all around. "Sure, Bill," he says in such an easy way that Pat wonders if he has a West Coast background. "But you know, before we settle down to the hard work of eking out the story, what say we take a little break. My working style is just a little bit different." He *winks* at Pat. "I'd like, for one thing, if it's okay by her, to stretch my legs for a bit on the beach." He beams at Pat. "I bet *you're* up for a walk, Pat, am I right?"

Baldie makes a nasty sound in his throat. Pat shoots a

quick glance at him. He looks as though he's swallowed something disagreeable, but though he tamps together the sheaf of photos with undue violence, he says nothing.

Pat shoves back her chair, grabs her bag and stands up. "Damned straight I'm up for it," she tells Sam.

He nods at her bag. "You don't need *that*."

Pat looks at Wagner, then back at Sam. She slings the strap of the bag over her shoulder and quickly rounds the table. Somebody ransacked her house last week. Her doctor was indignant when she suggested he might know who had done it. They're all sleaze, even Gorgeous Sam. And she knows she'd be a fool to forget it.

While Sam "snatches a quick briefing" from the Dynamic Duo, Pat waits outside. Scanning the beach, she wonders if there's any point in trying to run. Her guess is that most of the homes (if that's what they are) overlooking this beach are encased in heavy-duty security fences. But supposing she did get up to the street. She doesn't know the terrain in this La Jolla neighborhood. Buses aren't frequent. And taxis simply don't cruise residential areas looking for fares at ten A.M.

A sudden gust of wind makes her full skirt balloon up. *Surely you must have noticed,* her doctor had chided her for not having come in "at once." And now she's afraid to wear pants or any close-fitting skirts, except with a long loose shirt or sweater that could be counted on to keep the line of her crotch well disguised. As for what is *there* . . . it makes her queasy every morning when she wakes and finds all of it there, between her legs, crowding and sweat-making, scary because if you move or touch yourself the wrong way it can hurt, and making it so damned involved to pee, every morning its presence inexorable, something to be gotten used to all over again, like a bad dream about losing a body part that on waking turns out to be true. . . .

It can all be removed, quite easily, they say. Only they want to wait, to see just how far "it" develops. . . .

Every morning she's nauseated with revulsion, yes . . . but sometimes, especially in the evening, after a day of having accepted it, a perverse excitement breaks out of her, and she knows that though she wants it removed so that she can at least *look* normal (even if her blood and DNA will never again be), there's something powerful about the experience, too. And sometimes a secret voice in her head says there's something neat about being a freak. (If only she hadn't gone to the doctor in the first place.) And sometimes that voice whispers to her that there's a reason, there's a *meaning* in it all, that it's not just an accident of nature but a special event, fated to her in particular. . . .

And of course Joshua hadn't thought the changes in her genitals in the least bit odd. (Though of course he'd only seen the early stages.) And so she had in turn thought that maybe so much stimulation and excitement just naturally caused certain (small) changes, which she thought of as swellings. (But that was before everything had gotten out of hand.) It had made a weird kind of sense to her when she thought of all that blood suffusing those tissues for hours and hours and hours.

Such matters had always been mysterious to her. And so she had told herself that just because people didn't talk about the enlargement of the urethra and swelling just below it didn't mean such things weren't commonplace. It's not as though she had ever read any sex manuals or descriptive pornography that could be counted on to reveal such mature-audience side effects. And ever since she had been a little girl, she had been discovering that where sex and reproduction are concerned, the weirdest most unthinkable things often turn out to be true.

There still lurks in the back of Pat's mind the weird superstitious thought that the cause of the virus is to be found in the hours and hours of "messing around." A book that Ulrike had shown her, warning about such perversity, claimed that sexually stimulated women suffer "congestion" when they fail to achieve "deep vaginal orgasm," which (it claimed) can come only from "proper heterosexual intercourse." Ulrike's concern had been so embarrassing. It had gotten so that Pat hated to come home mornings and face the question *Well, did you finally do it? Have you lost the Big Vee?* And so she had mostly let Ulrike think they didn't do much besides, well, cuddle and *sleep.*

After about fifteen minutes Sam opens the door above and comes out onto the top deck. He waves at her, then starts down the stairs, past the middle deck and the hot tub, to the deck set on stilts into the sand. There he stops to remove his Birkenstocks and the beautiful salmon socks that match his suspenders. When he straightens up he gestures her to join him. Pat sighs, but heaves the bag back onto her shoulder and trudges over the bit of beach between them and up the bottom flight of stairs to the deck.

"Gotta say that after twenty days of Atlanta's temperature inversion, this is purely fantastic," he says, tossing a tube of sun block at her.

She catches it, looks at the label, then up at the sky. "The sun isn't hitting the water yet," she points out. "I really think this is overkill."

"If you knew the stats that I know," he remarks, "you'd never be caught out in UV rays without it."

She nods at his golden-tanned face. "But you go in for *tanning salons?*"

His eyebrows shoot up, and then he laughs. "Oh, you're referring to my face. Believe me, it only goes down as far as my neck. From the slopes. Got this great package deal, for weekend skiing this winter."

Pat sighs and rubs some of the #12 cream into her face. She will humor him. But she wishes she weren't so attracted to him. On top of Joshua, it makes her feel like a nymphomaniac. Sam may be a dish, but pretty boys aren't ordinarily her type.

They walk for a while along the water line, then pause to look out at the lusciously turquoise water. They may not have as long a stretch to walk as they would at Torrey Pines, but this beach is certainly a lot more private. "I gather," Sam begins, "you've gotten into a pretty adversarial relation, shall we say, with my colleagues." When Pat snorts, Sam grins at her. "Right. You don't have to say anything. But what *I* want to say about that is that all that's just a problem of communication. We're basically on the same side, Pat. Now I'm not saying it's *all* their fault, but my guess is that your, well, negative reactions are probably due to their not leveling with you, not explaining what we do and don't know, and what you know and can tell us that we need to know—and, maybe most important, *why* we need to know."

Pat's heart starts racing. "Look, I just don't think any of this is anybody's business but my own!" she exclaims. "Okay, my body's fucking up. I understand that. But I'm not a danger to anyone. I haven't done anything wrong. Whatever my relationship with Joshua is is my own damned business!"

Sam puts his back to the surf. The sun that pours onto his face makes his eyes sparkle the same lush blue of the water. "Pat, can I ask you to do something for me?"

He gazes intensely down into her eyes, and Pat has to swallow several times. Even in the throes of so much magnetism, she's practically squirming at her own reaction. She's convinced she's so transparent he's deliberately manipulating her. She wishes she could say *Fuck you!* and stomp off down the beach. But she can't. She's too interested in milking every second out of him she can. Instead, she says, "Will I be allowed to go back to classes when the new quarter starts next week?"

It makes her mad to hear the childish pleading anxiety in her voice. How could her voice so betray her, when she was feeling snarlingly surly at the very second the words came out? And it doesn't help when Sam lightly touches her shoulder and says: "I wish I knew the answer to that, because if I did I would tell you. But for one thing, I've just been brought in on this, so I can't begin to guess how things are going to go. Certainly we'll do everything we can to keep from disrupting your life any more than necessary. But I also have to add, Pat, that the answer depends a great deal on you. On how quickly we can get the most important questions answered. . . ."

Blackmail, Pat thinks. Covert, but intended. The bastard.

Pat drops her bag to the sand and shoves her hands into

her skirt pockets. She wonders if all this would have been avoided if she'd gone home over break. But she and Joshua had planned to have an entire week together, and she hadn't been able to bring herself to tell her parents he'd (apparently) canceled. . . .

Better yet if she hadn't gone to the doctor to get an IUD in the first place. Then it would be just her—and Joshua's—little secret.

"No, Pat, please," Sam says quickly, seemingly reading her face if not her mind. "It's not going to help if you get pissed at me for telling you the truth. As I said before, what we have here is a mystery. A very frustrating and serious mystery. And though some of the answers will be hard to find, others of them, of almost equal consequence, are there, inside your head, if only you would give them to us."

Pat's hands, still in her pockets, ball into fists. "You *say* they're important. But what I *know* is that everybody wants me to surrender my privacy, just like that." Her face burns as she remembers the photos and Wagner's questions and sly innuendo. "Because to you people, it's nothing. Like I have no rights. Like I'm this pornographic *object* you're all screwing over!"

Her outburst both embarrasses her and further fuels her rage. She can't remember ever talking to an adult this way before, except of course her parents and their co-members in the collective. Close to tears, she picks up her bag and taking big rapid strides resumes her progress up the beach. If the water weren't so cold she'd walk straight out into the surf, to hide.

"Pat, wait, please!" The wind whips Sam's words at her. "Please, if you would just stop for a minute and let me tell you what we need to know and why." He's caught up with her, and has her by the arm. "I know it would put a whole different spin on what you've been perceiving as a reckless invasion of your privacy."

Pat stops. Her breath is coming fast. She stares down at the sand. The man talks like the baby-boomer he is. "Right," she gasps. "I've heard it all already, from those goons up there." She jerks her head back up the beach. "They're grossed out. And they *think* I might be contagious!"

"Listen, I've seen your transcript. There's not a doubt in my mind that you can understand the specifics."

She looks at him, and twists her mouth into a derisory smile. *He* probably thinks he's being flattering. All her A's, and Advanced Placement and a double major in biology and English. Adults are always pretending that sort of thing is "impressive." Right. But she's still just a nineteen-year-old *female*. Which is to say, she's somebody to be browbeaten and manipulated and sidetracked from everything important.

His eyes scan the beach fronts, and he lifts his hand to his brow to shield his eyes from the sun. Pat wonders whether he sacrificed wearing shades on the walk—protection from the wicked UV rays bombarding them—so as to seem more accessible. He points to a concrete bench at the foot of some stairs not far from them. "Shall we sit for a bit?" he proposes.

Pat is glad for the chance to get the bag off her shoulder, so she shrugs and follows him into dry, loose sand. When they are settled, well above the high-tide mark (toward which the dirty-foamed water line is inexorably creeping), Sam, staring out at the water, begins: "I'm not sure how much you've been told. So what I'm going to do is tell you the story as it unfolded in the file they faxed me last night." Pat thinks of the photos, and her throat closes painfully. The very existence of such a file, and its being faxed who knows how many times to who knows how many people. . . .

Sam draws a deep breath. "That there was a problem first became apparent during your office visit to your gynecologist, to be fitted with an IUD." He looks at her. "It occurs to me from the things you've been saying that you might feel more comfortable talking with a woman, Pat. But I have to say that I assumed you wouldn't mind my being a man for the simple reason that you chose a male gynecologist."

Pat snorts. "Do you have any idea how hard it is to get a woman? Everybody wants them. And there aren't that many of them. So if you're in a hurry you don't have much choice. You know?"

Sam nods. "I see. Well, the problem is, we're in something of a hurry here, too, and all the principal investigators in this case are men. And like women gynecologists, women epidemiologists are hard to come by in a hurry, too."

Pat crosses her arms over her chest. She has to bite her lip to keep from flinging at him her own intention to become a medical researcher.

"But to continue." Again Sam gazes out at the water; and Pat does the same. "It seems your doctor initially diagnosed you as having a case of what is known as androgen-dihydrostestosterone deficiency. Which, in plain English, is a genetic condition that often does not become apparent until adolescence, in which the male sex organs make a late appearance in an individual that had previously been mistaken for female."

"That's interesting," Pat remarks. Some of the waves are coming in crooked. It amuses her to see them crash into one another from odd angles. "And I have to say it's the first time I've heard of it." She smiles bitterly. "You see, my doctor never bothered to *share* his diagnosis with me."

"Well there were tests he was having done," Sam says quickly. "I'm sure he was just waiting for confirmation. But then when both the chromosomal analysis and blood chemistry reports came in, everything got much more complicated. Because, you see, the first startling thing was the discovery that your sex chromosome was polyploid." Sam looks at her. "To be specific, instead of having an ordinary diploid chromosomal pair, you've somehow got a quadriploid, a double pair. Given all the biology you've had, I assume you understand what I mean by *that*."

Pat frowns. "Except that it sounds like gibberish. I mean, how could I possibly have four sex chromosomes?"

"That's one of our mystery questions," Sam says drily.

"Of course polyploidism is not completely unknown—in nonhuman species. Mostly in plants. Often engineered. And in such cases the mechanisms of reproduction are asexual. But that's neither here nor there."

"So I can think of myself as becoming like a plant?" Pat retorts.

Sam clears his throat. "I'm going to assume you mean that as a joke." His folded hands tug isometrically against his right black jean-clad knee, which he's raised a little above his left. "To continue. Your doctor had good reason to doubt his diagnosis, even before seeing the first batch of lab reports. For one thing, he knew from his examination that your female sexual and reproductive organs were all fully developed and morphologically normal. For another, because you were being fitted with an IUD, you were menstruating at the time of the examination. So right from the start there were reasons to doubt the diagnosis." Sam glances at her. "But one can hardly blame him for the mistake. Intersexes are usually discovered at birth, and forced into one sex or the other. An ob/gyn would be understandably fuzzy about the possibilities. So. Your test results start trickling in. The tissue sampled is indeed discovered to be male genital cells. Which seems to confirm the diagnosis. But your blood chemistry shows something else. First, that your sex chromosomal pair is not a pair, but one pair of each sex. Second, that your blood is no longer type O, as it had been when you donated blood in a drive at UCSD last fall. So, given all these mysteries, your doctor takes more blood from you, orders more tests, and seeks consults from colleagues in three different fields of specialization. And the new tests show estrogen in your blood." Sam grins at her. "And you know what that means, don't you?"

Pat snatches a quick look at him, then concentrates again on the water. "Sure. It means that my ovaries are working. Because estrogen is produced primarily in the ovaries, just as testosterone is produced in the testes."

"Right. So your doctor sees there's a problem, but a rather intriguing one. He—and one of the three specialists he's consulting—decides that you have two separate problems, unrelated. His idea is that you're an odd, hitherto unobserved case of intersex, a *true* hermaphrodite, manifesting organs of both sexes that are not only morphologically correct, but—as we now think will be the case—*functionally* correct. Which would be quite an interesting phenomenon, since intersexes on the whole tend to be sterile."

"But there's the problem of other cellular changes," Pat says when he pauses.

"A coincidence, your doctor believes," Sam chuckles. He has a pleasant, not unduly "manly" chuckle. Pat decides, though it doesn't compare with any of Joshua's so-infectious giggles, chortles and belly laughs. "But, needless to say, not what the hematologist thinks."

Pat crosses her legs, and catches herself mentally bracing for the squashing of her balls. She has half a dozen times in the last two weeks, on moving incautiously, been afflicted with horrible abdominal cramps. This time, though, the shift goes off safely, and the sensation of that extra bit of flesh pressing against sexually sensitive places is strictly pleasurable.

"The endocrinologist is also not so certain. And the oncologist is positive it's not."

"Oncologist!" Pat exclaims. "Are you saying this growth is cancerous?" The thought has not before occurred to her, for no one has said anything about changes other than in her blood type, her chromosomes and her genitals. But she sees now that she should have been worried about such a possibility all along.

Sam lays his hand over hers. "The indications are good that this is a controlled, directed growth, Pat. We can't be sure, of course. But the theory everyone's going with now is that the new genetic material is directing the growth." He sighs. "But that leaves open the question as to whether there have been other chromosomal changes. And, most important, what caused the change in your DNA to start with."

Pat snatches her hand away. "Well, it just burns me up that that damned bastard never mentioned any specialists, any doubts, any problems. Until yesterday I thought it was some kind of freak endocrine problem. That's what he led me to believe! And that once the so-called 'new tissue' had 'fully developed' it would be removed, and everything would be hunky-dory!" Her hands clench into fists. She'd like to pummel him. He's one of *them,* even if he is finally telling her *some* of the truth. (To manipulate her!) And it only makes matters worse that she's feeling *excessively* attracted to him—and in spite of the resentment. (And so what that he knows how to dress? That proves nothing. Her parents' generation's mania about judging people by hair and dress attest to that!)

Sam raises his legs, and staring at his bare toes, wriggles them. Even his feet are strong and shapely (though white white). "He's older, isn't he," Sam says. "Well, his generation was taught that women especially want doctors to be God. That you don't tell patients more than you have to, especially when you're not a hundred percent certain of what you think you know." He sighs, and lowers his legs. "You want to get your blood pressure up sometime, you should read through the ob/gyn journals of the nineteen fifties and sixties." He sweeps the air with his hand. "But to continue. Ongoing, intensive work is being done on your blood. The leading theory currently is that there's a virus at work." He shrugs. "The big breakthrough, though, came last week. When it was confirmed that your blood is infectious." Frowning, he looks her in the eye. "Did they tell you this part? That every blood sample put into contact with yours showed the same signs of alteration? Namely, the blood type altered, and an extra chromosomal pair was added. An XY pair for female blood, and an XX pair for male blood."

Pat gasps. "That's *incredible!*"

Sam snorts. "You could say that."

Which explains why they hauled her off to the hospital yesterday and wouldn't let her out of their sight.

"But of course the next mystery—beyond etiology and the like," Sam resumes, "is how the thing was transmitted to you. According to your file, when questioned yesterday you swore up and down that the only needles ever stuck into your body were of legitimate medical provenance. And we know from visual examinations that your hymen is still intact, that you have no vaginal or anal tearing. . . ." Sam clears his throat. "Don't you see, Pat. We need to know if this thing was transmitted sexually. Or if not, just how it *was* transmitted." He presses his lips together. "Your roommate's blood test has come up negative, so we know it can't be entirely casual, say through aerobic or dermal contact."

Pat thinks of how he put his hand on hers a few minutes ago—he's obviously confident he couldn't catch "it" from her in that way. "I don't understand what you're asking me." Her voice comes out small. And her cheeks, damn them, are burning again.

Sam executes a long elaborate ritual of cracking all the joints on his knuckles one at a time. "You were being fitted for an IUD, presumably because you intended to have sexual intercourse." He frowns fiercely as he finishes the knuckles on the right hand and starts on the left. "You know, Pat, I feel compelled to interject here that if you're going to be having sexual intercourse you should be using a condom. Since there's more than simply contraception at stake."

"I told them all already," Pat snaps (wanting to ask him whether *he* uses condoms every time he has sex). "I was only seeing one man, Joshua. And I decided to get fitted just in case we did decide to . . . have sex. It wasn't that we were necessarily going to. But that I wanted to be prepared in case we did."

"Your roommate says you were out most nights over the last five months."

Pat swallows. It drives her nuts that Ulrike has been dragged in. Testing her. Asking her questions. And telling her what? That she, Pat, is carrying some new plague virus no one has ever seen before? The thought enrages her. "Yes," she seethes, "yes I slept with him. As I already told the others, with pajama bottoms." She glares at him. "Pretty damned funny, isn't it. That a man and woman who aren't married would sleep with one another without screwing. A real pair of freaks, right?"

Sam rises and plants his bare foot on the concrete bench, just at the edge of her skirt. "Why do you say that?" he wonders. Pat stares out at the ocean. The waves, it seems to her, are getting smaller. "What I'm really asking is, was there anything sexual? Did you, for instance, *kiss*?"

Pat's eyes fill with tears. "Yes," she answers. "Yes, we kissed. A lot."

"And petted?"

Her throat chokes with emotion. "Yes, if that's what you want to call it." Even though she's so furious she wants to destroy something, tears overflow her eyes.

"Genital petting?"

She stands up and crosses her arms over her chest. "I don't want to talk about it anymore," she announces.

"Pat. You know how sexually transmitted diseases are passed. You have to know what I'm asking and why. Don't you?"

She turns her back on him and the ocean. For a few seconds she listens to the surf beating on the sand and distant rocks. When she closes her eyes she can almost imagine she is on Torrey Pines Beach. She can almost imagine Joshua is nearby, his fingers ready to touch hers, his arms ready to enfold her when she presses herself close.

But Joshua is gone. And she is here, on this private beach, with an "investigator" wanting to know the details of her sex life with him. She hates them, all of them, for picking at her, for prying into her private self, for frightening Joshua away. A month ago everything was beautiful and life was a constant high.

She opens her eyes to the glare and turns and faces him. "His semen never touched my lips," she spits out. "I never even *saw* his penis. Okay? But he . . . we had . . . cunnilingus." Her tongue trips over the word, so technical, so nothing to do with the real thing. She stares out at the water. "And I had no cuts or sores in the pubic area at any time. Is that what you wanted to know?"

The world is silent, except for the surf and the cry of

a gull circling overhead. Then, "Yes, Pat. And I thank you. You can be sure now that no one's going to ask you any more questions about sex."

Pat hefts her bag to her shoulder and they head back for the institute. Sam tells her about how backwards he was, compared to her, doing his required premed courses as an undergraduate (Princeton, '72). As they walk Pat watches the waves rip crookedly to shore. Never has she missed Joshua as much as she does now.

The four of them pile into the shiny gray Mercedes parked in the circle drive just outside the front entrance. Pat and Sam sit in the back. Wagner drives. And Shelley, introduced as "support" (the designation given on the institute photo-badge pinned to her dress), rides shotgun with a laptop in her lap and a radio clipped to one shoulder. (Overkill, Pat thinks, noting the cellular phone in the dash.) It is Sam's idea that Pat would feel more "comfortable" with a woman present during meetings that are not "one on one." At lunch he told the story of how he had had his "consciousness raised" a couple of years back, when, dining out, he had overheard a group of women talking at a nearby table. One of them had told how she had been in an elevator that morning with six men, the lone woman for a twenty-floor ascent, and of how creeped-out she had been. The others had then chimed in with similar tales. The conversation, Sam, said, had "struck" him. He said that before then he had always assumed women felt unsafe with single men rather than a crowd, since by his logic a woman could always count on at least one man to come to her rescue against the depredations of another. . . . Wagner and Johns had rolled their eyes, but agreed to assign Shelly to "chaperon duty" (as they keep calling it). Shelley looks and acts so Vanna White, though, that Pat has so far taken little "comfort" in her presence.

The car is comfortable and she knows she should be glad for the chance to get out, but Pat is in such an aftermath of confusion that all she can think is that a) it is weird to be going out driving when she is really basically a prisoner, and b) her parents would not approve of the car. As they pass through the outer set of gates she fantasizes flinging open the door and running, and yelling that she's been held prisoner against her will. But at once the idea strikes her as crazy. She imagines that anyone who happened to be around to hear (and there are only cars in this neighborhood, certainly no pedestrians that she's yet spotted) would assume her to be a paranoid schizophrenic and simply ignore her claims. She thinks that is how she herself would likely react were she in their shoes.

They drive south down La Jolla Boulevard. Pat snatches glimpses of the water as it repeatedly enters and leaves their line of vision. They are going to Hillcrest, they told her. Supposedly to look for Joshua.

She has the feeling that what just happened on the top deck was important. Certainly it upset Wagner. If only she could have some time to herself to *think*. But the wine at lunch and all these *people* constantly surrounding her make it just about impossible.

Lying on the chaise lounge, headphones feeding her a much-needed hit of Sinéad's power passion, she fell asleep. Stuck in that hospital isolation unit, she hadn't slept much during the night. And she wasn't used to drinking wine at lunch. The Big Boys were all inside, having a meeting. (She could just guess about what.) Shelley, nearby, sat at a white metal table, under an umbrella, tapping a keyboard—presumably keeping her under surveillance. Still, closing her eyes and listening to Sinéad, she could almost believe she was lying in the sun at Torrey Pines Beach. The wind felt the same on her skin, and the air smelled of the same salt sea. It was, therefore, *natural* that she fall asleep and dream . . . about Joshua.

In the dream they were on Torrey Pines Beach after dark, lying on Joshua's old chenille bedspread. The remains of a wood fire smoldered nearby. The pounding rhythm of the surf engulfed them, the way it sometimes did. And Joshua's hands were caressing her balls and penis, and his tongue was sliding between her labia, making her close to crazy with sensation. She pressed her hands against the sides of his head, tight. And then slipped her index fingers into his ears. She thought she might be making a lot of noise, but Sinéad kept belting out *Nothing compares, nothing compares to you,* again and again and again.

"Pat!" a voice—not Joshua's—dragged her out of the dream.

"Jesus God it's gross! It makes me sick to my stomach, kind of like that creepy feeling I got in sophomore English class, having to look at Mrs. Anderson's flat-as-a-washboard no-titness from two to three o'clock every fucking afternoon. Only this, man, this is really, really *sick!*"

That was Wagner talking, Pat discovered when she opened her eyes. He was staring at her, shaking his head, staring staring staring as if she were the Gorgon and he couldn't take his eyes away though the sight of her was killing him. Really foul stuff kept coming out of his mouth, Major Misogyny—until Sam, after telling him to "Cool it, man," went over to him, grabbed him by the lapels, and warned that if he didn't "chill out" he'd be "yanked from the case."

Pat had no idea what had set Wagner off. But then Dr. Johns said: "Don't you believe in wearing underwear, young lady?" Pat gaped at him, and first wondered how he knew, and then grew suspicious that they had somehow peeked under her skirt while she was sleeping. "If modesty doesn't concern you, perhaps you might be interested to know you're just asking for a bladder infection," he went on. "And if there's one thing women are always getting besides yeast infections, it's bladder infections." And he *tsk*ed-*tsk*ed at her in that you're-so-disgusting way all adults, no matter their ideological persuasion, have.

"How do you know I'm not wearing underwear?" Pat demanded of him.

Sam came over to her and bent to whisper in her ear. "Your erection is showing."

Astonished, she looked down at her lap and saw her skirt flare up into a point, then as suddenly drop flat. The movement, she noticed, coincided with one of those delicious new genital sensations that had been introduced in the dream. Preoccupied with this revelation, she said (somewhat absently), "It's just that none of my underwear fits right, and larger sizes don't work because then they're too big everywhere else and just slide off."

Pat understands what happened up to this point. Gazing out the window, observing that they were accessing the San Diego Freeway, she can't help but smile at the memory of her having created such a humorous sight, *viz.,* her penis popping up and down, basically out of control. (How much easier, she thinks, not having to worry about the signs of one's sexual arousal showing. This new experience is a little like the kind of practical and psychological hassle you go through when you first start menstruating, or when your breasts are growing and you have to worry about bras, cupsizes, straps, and the embarrassment of bouncing and all that. . . .)

No, it's what happened next that she doesn't understand. Actually, it was perfectly *natural* for her to put her hand over it—to hide it from view (and to keep it under control). Maybe it was the greasy white look on Wagner's face, or the pursed lips on Baldie's and the echo of Sinéad's voice endlessly repeating *Nothing compares, nothing compares to you* . . . (*not* from her tape player, which had long since shut off). But when she put her hand on it, it reminded her of putting her hand on Joshua's—maybe because it was through cloth, as she'd always felt his? But also, the pressure of her hand had caused a wonderful, shimmering sensation that ran through her entire body. . . . And so, smiling (she remembers that she was, because her whole being had in that moment been illuminated with joy), not thinking, she just started rubbing it, gently, with one finger. . . .

Except, of course, that Wagner had then gone *berserk.* And Sam said, "Pat, hey, *cool* that—if you'll just think for a second how you'd feel if *we* did that in front of *you!*"

Which had made her *giggle* (she still doesn't know why)—and say to Baldie off the top of her head, "I guess Freud was wrong, hunh? When he said that little boys feel threatened with castration when they discover that a woman or a girl doesn't have a penis. Because if that were true, wouldn't men feel less threatened when they saw that a woman did have a penis?" At which Wagner, cursing, screaming at her to "shut your mouth," charged her. And then suddenly Sam and Shelly were pulling her out of the chaise lounge and hustling her off to the bathroom, Sam all the while lecturing her about "behaving" herself and threatening her with "fifty-seven different kinds of hell to pay" if she didn't.

What stymies her is that the whole thing makes her want to laugh—and masturbate (both sets of genitals). Never has she in front of another person touched herself in a sexual way. Previously the idea would have horrified her. So why isn't she mortified at having been caught in the act by four people?

When they pass the exit to Interstate 8, Pat speaks for the first time since getting into the car. "Hey, I thought we were going to Hillcrest?"

"We are," Sam says, "but we're going to stop at your place first." He stretches his arm along the back of the seat. "So, tell me something, Pat."

Pat makes a face and turns almost sideways to stare out the window, to put her back to him. She hates it when men use their arms and legs to mark territory in that fake-casual way.

"I've been wondering, given what you said earlier about your reasons for not going to Berkeley or Santa Cruz," Sam plows on anyway, "whether you've told your parents about what's happening to you."

Pat freezes. Most of the time she lay awake in the hospital bed last night had been spent debating whether or not to tell them. Her first thought had been that they would make a big deal about it, would get lawyers, possibly the ACLU, maybe even involve the press. Which would turn her into a freak. And her parents and their collective would probably get hassled, her father's record dragged out. (SEX FREAK'S FATHER SHOT OFF TWO TOES OUTSIDE ARMY INDUCTION CENTER DURING VIETNAM WAR! HISTORY OF FAMILY INSANITY! WAS IT IN THE GENES ALL ALONG?) The winery could get blacklisted, or people might come to associate it with a mysterious virus, thereby washing twenty years of hard work down the tubes. . . .

"Did you even tell them you were seeing Joshua?" Sam presses. "or are you so estranged from them that—"

Pat rockets back in her seat. "My relationship with my parents is none of your fucking business!" she blazes at him. All that seemingly *casual* conversation on the beach, about college choices, about how *weird* it was that someone who'd taken UC summer courses at Santa Cruz during her last two years in high school, someone with test scores as exceptional as hers, would go to a place like UCSD when Berkeley would obviously be glad to have her: all that was simply a fishing expedition.

Sam leans slightly forward and puts his hand on Shelley's headrest. "Could you take down a note for me, Shelley?"

Shelley flicks on the laptop (which Pat hadn't thought could be used literally in one's lap), flips the screen upright and makes several keystrokes. "All right, Dr. Hardwick, I'm all ready to go. Shoot."

Sam checks his Casio. "Two-twelve P.M. Subject continues to display signs of escalating aggression. Take blood sample immediately on return to institute to have testosterone levels checked. Speculation that t-production has surged since lunch. End note, Shelley." Sam settles back. "And thanks."

"Hah, hah, hah, that's really really cute," Pat jeers, just barely holding onto her temper. But that scene in the bathroom . . . She supposes that's what he means by aggression. Well if he thinks he can bamboozle her into believing such raging-hormone shit . . .

"I'm serious," Sam says.

Wagner swings the car off the freeway onto Fifth Avenue. "The sooner she has her operation, the better," he rumbles—then hits the horn in irritation at another driver's braking before giving a turn signal.

A lump rises in Pat's throat. Without thinking, she touches her hand to her lap. Though she was eager enough to get rid of it all only a few hours ago, the thought of losing these new sensations stuns her. They can't *make* her. have it all removed, can they?

Whether they can or not, she vows that they won't. And it comes to her, for the first time, that it is all she has left of Joshua.

Ulrike had left a letter in the usual place. Acutely aware of Sam's gaze, Pat pounces on it. The entire crew has swarmed into the cottage, like locusts ready for a good chomp. "What are you doing?" Pat shouts at Wagner when she sees that he's seated himself at her desk and is going through the drawers. Hadn't they seen there was nothing to find when they searched the place last week?

"You let us in yourself, honey," Wagner says, unperturbed. "But don't worry. We won't *take* anything."

Pat rounds on Sam, who's still watching her (probably with designs on the letter). "You tricked me," she accuses.

"Go pack your bag," is all he says.

Shelley follows her into the bedroom, like a shadow. Thinking of how easy it would be to "lose" the letter, Pat stuffs it down the front of her shirt.

When they'd pulled up alongside the "court" of cottages, Sam had told her they were there so that she could pack "a few things" that would make her "stay at the institute more comfortable." Always thinking of her comfort, that man. What a guy! "For how long are you people holding me?" she nevertheless demanded. "I told you what you wanted to know. *I* kept *my* side of the bargain."

"Bargain?" he repeated, as though incredulous. But then he sidled close and half-whispered, "It'll just be for a couple of days, Pat. So that we can run a few more tests. And make sure the virus doesn't kick anything else up at you. The institute's more comfortable than the hospital, isn't it? Anyway, I've no doubt you'll be returning to classes on Monday. So if I were you I'd just relax, and enjoy the beach and the food and whatever else we can do for you." And then he leaned past her and opened the door.

Instead of getting out, she said, as though the idea had

just occurred to her, "This is crazy, Sam. You know? It's not like this virus is *deadly*. You don't even treat people infected with HIV like this!"

"We don't *know* that it's not deadly," he said very gently. "And more importantly," he went on, his eyes agleam with sudden excitement, "you're the only one known to have it. Imagine if we'd gotten hold of the first case of HIV before it had been trans—" But there he stopped, as though realizing he was giving away more than he'd intended.

Pat throws a few things into a suitcase and heads for the bathroom. The door's got a bolt, and this she at once slides home. Relieved to be alone at last, she settles on the floor against the door and pulls out the letter.

Monday evening

Pat—

There's so much I have to tell you. (Though I don't know if you'll even get this—that's how little idea I have of what the eff is going on.) First, regret to say I'm off to L.A. as planned. Feel bad about leaving town, even for three days when god knows what your situation really is. But I don't think there's anything here I can do straight off, and then of course my parents have paid a lot for the workshop. . . . Suspect I'll be too worried to get much out of it. If so, I'll exit prematurely.

Hope you won't be pissed at me when I say I did a stupid thing, namely blabbed out some stuff about Joshua before I realized I shouldn't. (Me and my big mouth.) I said, for one thing, that you'd been staying over with him regularly. I also told how you met him at the Quel. (It was their GREAT interest in that that made me wake up, sorry to say.)

I really feel rotten about this. I mean, I don't even know what it is you have. THEY seemed to think it was ultra-dangerous. Why didn't you tell me, Pat O'Pat? Don't you know I care too much to be scared off? If you had AIDS I'd be sad, sure, but not PHOBIC for christsake. ('Course, I suppose I could still turn out to have this thing—otherwise why would they have taken a blood sample. And then we'd be in the same boat together, right?)

Never mind, as you-know-who always said . . .

Now. The second Big Thing. God, Pat, I agonized like mad over this one. But I finally decided to do it. I called your parents, and told them about the men who questioned me and took my blood. I mean, it sounds like SOMEBODY should know where you are. Since they wouldn't tell me, or let me talk to you on the phone much less visit, how the hell do I know if you're all right? To my nose, the whole thing stinks like rotten fish. And anyway, if you're seriously ill, they need to know. I mean hell, Pat, you may not like them being so political and all, but you're close, still, in spite of the differences. Considering how my folks are—busy in their respective remarried lives, not all that interested in the detritus of divorce. . . . Anyway. The bad thing is, I knew only your gynecologist's name. Couldn't tell them anything else. But they're flying down here tomorrow. Probably they'll find you before you find this letter.

Anyway. If I don't hear from you by the time I'm back, I'll join forces with your parents and tear this damned county apart looking for you. (And that's a PROMISE.) If only, though, I had your address. . . . (But then I might as well wish we were both telepathic, right?)

Hang in there kid—
U.

Knuckles hit the door, making it rattle against Pat's back. "Pat?" Shelley calls. "Are you all right? You've been in there a long time."

Feeling sick to lose this small scrap of not-aloneness, Pat rips the letter into shreds, drops the shreds into the bowl and flushes. Ulrike hadn't known when she wrote the letter that she tested out negative. What the hell could she be thinking and feeling? And if she knew? What would she think *then*? Sharing a cottage with *that*?

Pat opens the medicine chest and pulls out the toiletries she wants to pack. Seeing the tube of Chap Stick makes her think of lipstick and the old trick of writing messages on mirrors. But neither she nor Ulrike wears lipstick. Or uses eyebrow pencil or mascara. Her eyes rove the shelves. . . .

This time a fist lays into the door. "Pat?" Sam shouts. "I want some voice contact, woman. And now! Or we'll come in through the window!"

Pat unscrews the cap on the tube of toothpaste. "You wouldn't fit!" she yells back. And then she quite carefully dabs GLEASON INST. OFF LA JOL BLVD, BEACHFRNT on the plain metal surface lining the inside of the cabinet door.

"What the hell are you doing in there, taking a bath?"

"No, of course not. I'm too horny for that!" Pat shouts back—but then spoils it by dissolving into giggles.

"Shit, man, she's *masturbating*!" It's Wagner's voice, right beside the door. Pat imagines the three of them crowded against it, competing for a place to lay their ears.

Very very gently Pat clicks the cabinet door shut. Then she checks the bowl to make sure the paper all flushed, gathers up the toiletries, slides the bolt back, and flings open the door. She's disappointed when only Wagner falls into the room.

Sam hustles her out to the car. "Surely you must have some memory of how you got from your house to his?" he says when Wagner asks for instructions.

Pat sighs; she studies her nails; she puts her hand to her throat. "Really, I don't. It was always dark. And we were on a motorcycle. From a motorcycle everything looks the same, nothing looks familiar. As I said before, it was one of those residential sections, somewhere in the vicinity of the zoo."

Sam leans his head back against the seat. "Liar," he mutters. But instead of trying to strike another bargain with her, he simply tells Wagner to drive to the other side of the park, near the zoo. They will "pick up the trail there," he says.

All the time he's watching, waiting, for something to show in her face. A facial twitch or a verbal slip are their only chances of finding Joshua. Which is why she's going to keep her nose glued to the window, out of sight, and her mouth shut whenever Joshua is mentioned.

Joshua's kisses on her neck, and the soft stroking of his hand on her belly, wake her, and his special smell fills her with recognition and joy. For a few seconds, in the dark, she's confused. Her senses tell her she's in Joshua's bed, and that Joshua himself is lying beside her, his hands and lips caressing and kissing her. But as she comes fully awake she knows that cannot be. She has a very clear and distinct memory of going to sleep in the room they'd given her in the Gleason Institute, of lying in a proper bed made with starched hospital sheets. Yet the sheet now covering her body is soft, unstarched cotton, and reaching out over the edge of the bed she can knock the wood floor with her knuckles. And when she strains to hear the ocean, she hears instead a car passing, as she had not done either while sitting up in bed reading or lying flat with the lights out, trying to go to sleep.

But she's so happy to have Joshua back she gives herself over to the delight of feeling, smelling, tasting and touching him, without trying to decide whether she's dreaming, hallucinating, or somehow really with him. She murmurs his name between kisses, and it becomes an incantation she chants again and again and again in honor of the dream, hallucination or miracle she wants the incantation to preserve.

It's when he's pulling the nightgown over her head that she realizes he's completely naked. No underwear, no pajama bottoms, no sweat pants keep her now from touching him. And how strange and delicious it is, taking in through her fingers such riches, warm and mysterious and slippery to the touch, folds and bulges and odd textures to stroke and penetrate. "Do you like it? Are you glad?" Joshua whispers, bringing the first words (other than names) into the night.

"It's beautiful," Pat whispers back. "But will you let me see?"

Joshua switches on the reading lamp he keeps on the floor next to his mattress and focuses on the light on the wall. They stare for a long time into one another's eyes. "I'm sorry I had to leave for a while," he says finally. And then he lies back and spreads his legs wide.

Pat examines him with amazement. (Is this what *she* looks like?) She's aware that she has no live experience of male genitalia with which to compare it, but she knows this is the way it's *supposed* to be. At last, she thinks, she knows what is wrong with human beings. Sexual dimorphism, it is obvious, has been nothing but a disaster!

"I just couldn't stand it any longer, being around you while I was waiting," Joshua says. The smooth full lips under his mustache are curved into a smile, in amusement at the intentness of her examination, she thinks. "I guess I should have told you in advance, so that you wouldn't have exposed yourself to that doctor. But I was afraid you'd be horrified if you knew. And so I just couldn't." Joshua takes her hand. "I hope you're not mad at me for not asking you first?"

Pat imagines herself drowning in his dark liquid eyes. "I'm so happy to see you," she says. She ignores the hard knot forming in her stomach, she keeps herself from thinking much about his admission that it is he who's caused her to change. "And I love it, the way I am now. Though at first I hated it and felt like a freak, now I wouldn't give it up for anything." She frowns. "Except, maybe my freedom."

Joshua gestures at the room around her. "You don't need to worry about that," he says. "Haven't you noticed, I've sprung you?"

She glances around at the dimly lit walls, at the window exactly where it is supposed to be, at the dust bunnies dancing in the slight draft coming in through the window, at the cracks in the ceiling and even the cobweb in the corner where it has been allowed to remain for months undisturbed (since Joshua does not believe in killing spiders that aren't poisonous). She *knows* she's not at the Gleason Institute, she *knows* she's not dreaming. She peers at Joshua speculatively. If he could induce her body to grow a second set of genitals, perhaps "springing" her while she's asleep isn't such an impossible feat to have pulled off. He does look beautiful lying there, staring up at her. And his body is so . . . *there*.

She takes his hand and brings it to her mouth. "They're just dying to remove everything they think doesn't belong there," she remarks between kisses to his palm. "But I won't let them, Joshua. Just as I wouldn't let them find you." Almost breathless, she turns his hand over and kisses the back of it knuckle by knuckle, and then licks and sucks his index finger.

For the next couple of hours they don't stop to talk. It's all so fantastic Pat wants to do it again and again in every combination she can think of. Later, though, when they are lying quietly, drifting almost into sleep, her mind resumes work. "What a shame we can't both screw one another simultaneously," she says, sighing. "Don't you think that would be *neat*?"

"In most things human, precise complementarity is disastrous," Joshua observes, as though stating a universally acknowledged truth. "Hadn't you noticed? Also, though in theory it would be nice, geometrically it would be a little like trisecting the angle." Pat giggles at the image, and Joshua joins her. "But we call *this* symmetrical equivalence. Given this sexual arrangement, we can all get pregnant, can all impregnate, can all even do it solo, through artificial insemination. Though of course since it wouldn't be too good for the collective gene pool, self-impregnation is virtually taboo."

"Like incest," Pat says, then thinks that "doing it solo" would really mean that the same genes would be reproduced, rather than a possible slew of recessives. So the analogy doesn't quite hold up. But this *we* that Joshua refers to, as though a whole community of persons are as he is himself and has made her to be . . . It is time, she thinks, to pin him down. "Who *is* this 'we' you're referring to?" she asks him. "Are you saying there are others like you?" She has, since he admitted he had changed her, been thinking that his chromosomes must have mutated, and have mysteriously developed the power to cause hers to mutate, too. But then there's the mystery of how he got her from the institute to his room (and without waking her, yet). . . .

Joshua props himself on an elbow and gazes down into her face. "If I told you any of it, you'd think I was handing you a *National Enquirer* special."

That cracks Pat up. And so she has to tell him the conversation she overheard, in which Sam said that when he started reading the file Lewis had faxed him, he'd thought it was a hoax, *National Enquirer* style. "So," she concludes, "I don't think you have to worry about my dismissing it out of hand, considering how improbable *this*—" she gestures at his and her own genitals—"is."

"First, there aren't many of us left here." Joshua's face grows sober. "Which is why I broke the rules and got involved with you. I was born here—on this planet, I mean—but this is not where my people come from. Before I was born, a subset of our constellation—this is hard to explain, I'm not sure what the best English equivalences are. By constellation I mean something remotely like a guild, or association—but no. The thing is, it's more like a tribe, to which a certain kind of work had been allotted. . . ." Joshua frowns. "But 'tribe' must sound primitive to your ears, and it's not that. . . ." He fidgets with the top hem of the sheet. "Well, a number of us, from the group that is meant to do comparative sorts of studies—sort of a combination of your disciplines of anthropology, sociology, psychology, history and philosophy with quite a lot of the sciences thrown in— anyway, a group of us arrived here about one hundred years ago. Humans are especially interesting to us because they're physiologically very similar—except that they're sexually dimorphic." He smiles, almost shyly, and blinks his so- sweet brown eyes slowly at her. "You can't imagine how weird my people find it that most of the large animals on your planet are sexually dimorphic. Though actually, I probably can't imagine how weird it is to them, either, since I was raised here, and so have been used to it all my life."

It's all coming so fast. It's fantastic, but one part of her, the part coldly watching, doesn't feel all that surprised. Still, she knows she should be astounded and disbelieving (even after all that has happened to her). "You're saying you—your family or whatever—are from *another planet*!" she exclaims. And the watcher inside her thinks of how he told her nothing about this before, of how he did not warn her that her body would be changing (much less ask her permission to change it). . . .

He half laughs; his eyes meeting hers get even shyer. "You see, I told you. Anyway, the problem is that most of us have died. Which we weren't supposed to do. I mean, ordinarily our lifespan is several of your centuries. But disease and all sorts of accidents have been a problem." He shrugs. "I suppose if my constellation had realized that before the window-for-transit next opened humans would develop the capacity for destroying the planet any number of ways, we probably wouldn't have come. Anyway, we're stuck here. And those few of us born here who have survived are in need of mates. But of those available to my age-cohort all are forbidden me, because they are too closely affinial. And so I knew that if I wanted to have a child I'd have to mate with a human to do so. And though it's forbidden to mate with humans . . ."

It wildly elates her to think that not only did he choose *her*, but that he went against his own people in doing so. She grabs his free wrist. "You're saying you broke your people's laws when you got involved with me?"

His smile is so warm it touches even the watcher. She wonders how he rates with his own people, and whether they will accept what he has done. "Well, yes. But I think it will be all right. Because, you see, there are so few of us left here. And the travel window won't open until after I've passed the age at which I can bear children."

Pat flops onto her back and stares up at the dimly lit

ceiling. "I can't handle this. You're saying *you* want to get pregnant by *me*?"

Joshua nods. "I suppose that sounds strange to you—because you think of me as a male. But remember, I'm no more a male than you are."

She turns her head and gestures. "But your mustache and beard. And you don't have developed breasts."

"All secondary characteristics, Pat. I chose them when I elected to present myself as a male. Since one must choose one or another on this world. And we've learned the hard way it's too risky to present as females. Too many times those of us presenting as females have been sexually attacked—and discovered. In addition to being less vulnerable to rape, men have greater mobility and access than women. It's simply safer for us to look like men."

"Does that mean I'm going to be growing out a beard, too?"

Joshua laughs. "Only if you want to."

She shakes her head. "I don't see how. Controlling hormones and all that . . ."

"It's easy. I'll show you." He leans over and kisses her lips very lightly. "Well, what do you think? Am I a liar or a lunatic?"

Pat throws her arms around him. "A charmer," she retorts. "I'm completely taken in." Or almost, the watcher murmurs. Because how can you really trust someone who has lied so massively, who chooses manipulation over honest discussion and decision-making? Half smiling, she strokes his flat furry stomach and tries to imagine it swelling under her hands with the persistent fullness of pregnancy. (With *her* child.) She kisses his shoulder. "There's just one thing. . . ."

He withdraws a little to look into her face. "What's that?"

"Will you please just say the words, 'I want to have your baby'?"

Joshua's eyes gleam. "Pat, darling, I want to have your baby," he repeats with utter gravity.

Pat laughs hysterically. Now *that,* she thinks, is true *Na-*

tional Enquirer. But when she finishes laughing, she sits up so as to be more serious. "Another thing," she says, "that I absolutely have to know. How can we be here in your room? When I first woke I thought I must be dreaming, or maybe hallucinating. How *could* we be *here*?"

Joshua sits up, too. "I can't tell you. The strictures against showing our technology to humans are even more serious than those forbidding me to mate with you." He frowns. "Which reminds me, Pat, you must not ever have sexual intercourse with another human, or give others your blood." He gestures at her genitals. "It would spread, you know."

"I know." She bites her lip. More decisions he's making for her, about what to do with *her* body? "I'm not sure I like your deciding for me that I'm going to be permanently monogamous." She frowns. "But wait a minute, that's not how you changed me, is it. Because we never did have intercourse. So how *did* you do it?"

Joshua hesitates a few seconds before answering. "You remember that time you cut yourself chopping onions?"

Pat shakes her head. "No, not really . . ."

"Well, you did. It was, I think, in January. And I kissed and licked the cut." His lips pressed tightly together. "Because I forgot. It completely slipped my mind that I could change you that way—though all the while I was being so excruciatingly careful in our sexual relations. . . ."

Pat's stomach drops. After maybe half a minute she asks in a very small voice: "You mean you didn't *mean* to?" So he *didn't* specially choose her?

Joshua sighs. "I'm afraid not." His eyes meet hers. "But I'm glad I did. My people are scattered all over the world—mostly in Asia. A person gets lonely. And, as I said, now I'll be able to bear a child."

Pat nods slowly. So it was an accident. But he came back for her anyway, didn't he. And surely that counts for a lot. . . .

Dawn is breaking when they finally settle down with the intention to sleep. In the morning, she thinks (even as she's watching the walls lighten), she'll call the collective, and they'll tell her where her parents are staying. They'll raise hell for her, and the bastards won't be able to touch her. All of her genitals will be left intact, of that she is determined. And they will not reincarcerate her. Next Monday she'll start classes, right on schedule. They don't *know* it's a virus. And whether it should be considered harmful or not is in any case a social, not a medical, issue.

Lying with her head on Joshua's chest, drifting off to sleep, she thinks how easy it would be to spread the virus. His people are here to study humans' innate perversity. It seems only fair to take advantage of her privilege, to spread the wealth around to others. She would be a traitor to her own kind if she didn't. So what if she spoils Joshua's and his people's research project? Humans did not ask to be studied. And what could be a more massive violation of privacy than to treat an entire sentient species as research subjects without their knowing consent?

Drifting to the edge of sleep, Pat imagines Wagner pregnant. Would it change even his kind? But how could it not?

A little fear scrapes up that cold pit in her stomach again. Joshua won't approve when he finds out. And Sam will know who's responsible. But she struck no "bargains" with either of them. And Joshua did not even ask her first. And besides, the privilege Joshua's bestowed on her confers its obligations. She may not choose to bear a child in her womb like Joshua, but she can be another kind of mother, mother to an age, mother to the Age of the Hermaphrodite. . . .

At nineteen, yet.

When Pat drops off to sleep she's smiling. It's a big job, changing the world. But she's ready for it.